THE DEVIL'S REVOLVER

OTHER TITLES BY V. S. MCGRATH

Writing as Vicki Essex

Her Son's Hero
Back to the Good Fortune Diner
In Her Corner
A Recipe for Reunion
Red Carpet Arrangement
Matinees with Miriam

THE DEVIL'S REVOLVER

V. S. MCGRATH

THE DEVIL'S REVOLVER BOOK 1

BRAIN MILL PRESS
GREEN BAY, WISCONSIN

The Devil's Revolver is a work of fiction. Names, places, and incidents either are products of the author's imagination or are used fictitiously. Any resemblance to actual persons, living or dead, or locales is entirely coincidental.

Published in the United States by Brain Mill Press.
Print ISBN 978-1-942083-54-2
EPUB ISBN 978-1-942083-57-3
MOBI ISBN 978-1-942083-55-9
PDF ISBN 978-1-942083-56-6

Cover illustration by Cassandre Bolan.
Cover design by Ranita Haanen.
Print spread by Ampersand Book Design.
Interior illustrations by Ann O'Connell.

www.devilsrevolver.com

CONTENTS

LAND ACKNOWLEDGMENT STATEMENT

The place I call home and on which I produced this work is the traditional territories of the Haudenosaunee and the Mississaugas of New Credit, and is subject to the Dish with One Spoon wampum. I acknowledge the Indigenous people who have lived and worked this land for over 15,000 years and continue to seek justice today.

THE DEVIL'S REVOLVER

CHAPTER ONE

NEWHAVEN, MONTANA
JUNE 1895

Hettie couldn't say what had woken her; her eyes had simply snapped open and she'd known something was amiss.

Sure enough, she found the rope had been chewed through, the frayed ends still wet. *Dammit, Abby.* This was the third time in two weeks. She yanked her coat over her thin nightgown, grabbed her boots and Winchester, and padded quickly down the stairs. Outside, she pushed her bare feet into the cold, hard leather and checked her rifle's action, loading it quickly. Coyotes were often seen roaming the ranch, and there'd been rumors of a pack of wolves roving the hills. But out here, it was men Hettie feared most.

Silvery-blue light fringed the horizon like a cataract. She scrubbed the crust from her eyes and scanned the fields for any sign of her sister. Though she was nearly ten, Abby was small for her age and barely left footprints. Ma sometimes said she tread the world like a ghost. The long, dry grass bowed with a sigh beneath a sudden gust of wind, revealing a freshly trampled break in the fronds. Hettie headed in that direction.

She found Abby standing knee-high in the creek, her nightgown soaking up to her hips. Her glazed, unblinking violet eyes stared into the middle distance, mouth gaping open. She didn't even register Hettie's arrival.

Hettie slung the rifle across her back and sloshed into the icy-cold water. She gave her a gentle shake. "Abby, what are you doing?"

"Oh." The little girl blinked sleepily up at her and smiled. "I was just talking to my friends."

"What have we told you? You shouldn't be wandering away from the house." Hettie led her onto the creek bed, where she did her best to wring out her sopping nightgown.

"The water helps me hear them better," Abby said simply.

Hettie reined in her annoyance. Abby's "friends" always wanted to talk at the most inconvenient times. "Well, you're going to have to say good-bye to them for now."

She tilted her chin to the side, and her gaze clouded. "Okay. They say that's fine." She shivered. Hettie put her coat around her sister's shoulders, rubbing her arms vigorously, then led her back toward the house.

Over the edge of the embankment, she heard the crunch of grass as a lean figure trudged along the path. Hettie unslung the Winchester in a flash and pointed it at the man's heart.

He halted, staggering back. "Man alive, Hettie. What're you doing out here?"

"Uncle." The thumping of her heart eased as she lowered the rifle. "Abby got out of her harness again."

The old man scratched his gray-white stubble, frowning. "You need to lock her in her room at night. Keep her from leaving."

Hettie swept past him without responding, urging Abby on with one hand protectively at her back.

"It's for her own safety," he insisted, trailing them back to the house. "There're protection spells all over the place she might accidentally stumble over and ruin. Magic ain't cheap anymore, you know. And I ain't responsible if she goes stepping into a fox trap."

"That why you're up so early, *Uncle*?" It was hardly a term of endearment, since they weren't related, but Pa had insisted she call the old man that. She noted his rumpled clothes and bloodshot eyes. His breath reeked of whiskey.

He glared. "I'm up 'cuz your pa expects me to keep watch over things while you're both in town. I'll be makin' sure this one doesn't wander off, that's for sure."

Hettie kept her mouth shut. If he watched Abby as well as he watched the cattle, her sister would be halfway to China by the time he noticed.

The three of them clomped into the house. Her father was already awake and brewing coffee. "Mornin', Jeremiah," he greeted Uncle, then raised one dark eyebrow at his damp, half-dressed daughters. "This something we need to tell your mother about?" he asked as they warmed up by the stove.

"We need stronger rope," Hettie mumbled.

"And a latch on the door," Uncle added.

John Alabama's thick black mustache twitched. He smoothed Abby's fine, white-blond hair off her wide brow and gave her a kiss. She didn't react, engrossed by the fire licking up the wood in the stove. He sighed. Abby had been born like this—*touched*, Ma sometimes said—and while they all loved her, it pained Hettie to see how much effort it took Pa not to show his sadness and frustration. Her father poured coffee for himself and Uncle just as Grace Alabama swept into the kitchen, swathed in her heavy dressing gown.

"Why didn't you wake me, John? I could've made you breakfast."

"We've got biscuits and cheese for the road. We'll be fine. Besides, I wanted to let you sleep." He pecked his wife on the cheek and cut Hettie a look. She understood his directive. Ma's health was delicate, so they kept as much out of her hands as possible. She quickly took her sister back to her room and got her changed out of her wet clothes before getting dressed herself.

"There are wolves in the fire," Abby murmured, blinking slowly as she returned to her senses.

Hettie chucked her under the chin. "You don't have to worry about them. Long as I've got my gun, you're safe." She brandished her Winchester rifle. "I'll get those wolves for you. Bang, bang!"

Abby silently followed her back to the kitchen.

"The Robson boys' shooting contest is today, isn't it? You could go and watch with your friends. Wouldn't you rather wear your church dress to town?" Grace asked hopefully.

Hettie looked down at her shirt and trousers—old, stained hand-me-downs from her brother, Paul. "It'll just get dirty on the drive. Besides, I don't want Pa looking like he has to protect a young miss on the road by himself."

Her mother heaved a resigned sigh as Uncle slurped his coffee. "Yer seventeen now, girlie. If you don't start worrying about your looks, you'll never catch a husband."

She ignored him. "Ma, can't you convince Pa to enter the contest?"

Grace's lips curved. "You say that as if I have any sway over your father's wishes."

"But it's only a dollar to enter."

"Money hardly worth gambling away," John said. "We don't have it to spare, you know that."

"But you wouldn't be gambling it away," Hettie argued. "You'd win it back, and then some."

"And the Robson boys would chisel themselves a handsome profit for doing nothing." He shook his head. "Besides, where's the fun for everyone else if I enter?"

"But Pa—"

"Not another word on it, Hettie. We earn our living honestly— with hard work."

Hettie didn't get why Pa was being so stubborn when they desperately needed the money—the talismans on the northern ridge had weakened, and the safety barrier surrounding the herd was at risk of collapsing. But when John Alabama said no, he meant no.

"Don't mind your father, girlie." Uncle Jeremiah leaned back in his chair. "He's just got an overdeveloped sense of fairness."

The wagon bounced along the rutted road, kicking up clouds of dust that whipped back into their faces. Hettie tipped the brim of her hat down, but Pa only squinted and drove on, ignoring the blast of grit. They kept their mouths shut and their eyes open, watching the distant rolling hills. They didn't have anything worth taking— even Pa's old mare, Jezebel, wasn't worth rustling, despite being magicked—but outlaws were always a threat.

They clattered into town, and John dropped her off in front of the mercantile. "Meet me at the blacksmith's when you're done with your errands."

"Yes, Pa." She shouldered her Winchester and took off.

Newhaven was one of the few mining towns that had survived after the gold rush, mainly thanks to the pocket of magic in the region. Some places were just stronger than others, Pa had explained, though that seemed to be changing, too, if the surging price of spells and talismans was anything to go by. Uncle grumbled constantly how magic wasn't "sticking" anymore, and complained whenever Pa asked him to shore up some of the spells around the farm. Hettie didn't know much about magic, but she suspected Uncle was just being lazy.

A knot of children playing Blackthorn Rogues crowded the dusty thoroughfare. Hettie paused to watch as the boys and girls walked in a circle around a stick on the ground, chanting the rhyme:

> *Round and round the circle whirls*
> *Red blood flows through boys and girls*
> *Who so e'er the black thorn pricks*
> *Is the one Diablo picks.*

Young Jake Finney rushed to the stick and snatched it up. The other children scattered, shrieking. He wielded the stick like a wand of old, chasing the others around, tapping each in turn to make them a part of his "gang" until the group cornered the lone survivor, long-limbed Liam West. They tackled him viciously, and he cried out. Jake brought the switch down again and again. The beating didn't let up. Lanky Liam had always been an easy target.

Hettie waded into the fray. "Break it up, young 'uns. Let 'im up."

"But he's the last of the Blackthorns!" Jake Finney cried. "He's gotta be punished for betraying the gang!"

She snatched the stick from Jake's hands. "Don't make me break this over your thick skull, Jake. Let him up, I say."

They helped their playmate up and shot off in all directions. Liam sent her a rueful look, clearly ungrateful for the interference.

See if I help you next time, she thought, tossing the stick away. She got a splinter for her troubles and sucked the bead of blood welling up on her thumb.

Farther up the main street, Hettie gave a wide berth to a knot of Mundane Movement followers handing out antisorcery flyers. Their leader, a clean-shaven man, held the pamphlet aloft, spittle flying from his mouth as he proselytized about the evils of magic. "Hell and darkness and fiery damnation await those who'd suffer a witch to live!" he screamed. His gimlet eyes connected with Hettie's, and he glowered. "Sorcery is nothing but the devil's work. Repent! When magic gives the negro power over the white man, it is an abomination against God and nature, and He will smite the vile demons who perform such wickedness!"

Shock and anger surged through Hettie. She struggled to respond, wanting to yell at him and tell him to keep his hate to himself. Pa was gifted, after all, and he was the kindest and most forgiving man on the good green earth.

"Bunch of zealots," Henry Bale growled from the porch of the sorcerer's salon. She glanced up at the young sorcerer who worked in the town's magic workshop. Rumor was he was one of only a few Academy-trained gifted negroes in the whole county. The charms dangling from Henry's neck caught the light as he spat in the dirt. "Don't pay them any mind. They've conveniently forgotten magic's in everything, from the meat they eat to the coffins they'll be buried in. Might as well be trying to ban metal tools and air."

"Don't suppose you've got a mind to put a silence spell on them or something?" she said.

He grinned. "And waste good magic? They ain't worth the effort."

A *fwoosh* sound from within the magic workshop had Henry pushing off the banister. "God's knees, Julius, I told you not to mess with that potion!" He hurried inside as a cloud of blue smoke wafted out the door. Hettie moved on.

A newspaper seller shouted out the day's headlines, and she paused to listen. The Division of Sorcery was calling for able-bodied laborers and sorcerers to shore up the Wall on the Mexican border. The Duryea brothers were working with Mechaniks from England to make their new horseless carriage automobiles three times faster. A joint task force was being set up to hunt down members of the notorious Crowe gang. And four more children were reported missing in Wyoming and North Dakota.

The growing number of kidnappings disturbed Hettie, considering Abby's habit for wandering. Locking her up was not an option, though; and while her rope and harness helped keep track of her, they needed a more permanent solution.

At the general store, Hettie handed Ma's grocery list to the shopkeeper and browsed through the shop's selection of sweets, ribbons, and talismans, none of which she could afford. It was fun to imagine having a charm for extra wakefulness, or an amulet to alert her of encroaching coyotes, but Pa had warned her that she couldn't trust any talisman that hadn't been made by him or someone else she knew. A pretty bauble wasn't worth risking a geis, and too many mundanes had been taken in by rogue sorcerers.

She lingered over a catalog of exotic potions, magicked medicines guaranteed to cure all kinds of ailments. She turned to the page under Clarity of Mind she'd often pored over and traced her finger over a ribbon floating around the picture of the seductively curvy phial. The words *Sound Mind, Memory, Spirit, Body and Faculty* advertised its promises across its length.

"Thinking about ordering it this time?" Mr. Hooper asked cheerfully.

"I will if I win the contest today." She glanced up. "Don't tell Pa."

He smiled. "Wouldn't dream of it. I know you mean well for Abby."

Abby and Ma, she thought. There was enough in that dose to bring her mother back to full health; and maybe Abby would finally stop having fits and trances. That would be fully worth disobeying Pa.

When the hour of the shooting contest arrived, Hettie headed for the tannery at the edge of town. More than half of Newhaven had gathered to watch. Men made their way into the fenced-off contest area where the Robson brothers collected entry fees. Groups of boys pooled their nickels and dimes to enter their best shot. Older men with scarred hands and lined faces scrutinized their opponents from the sidelines before throwing in their dollars.

That entry fee was Hettie's only obstacle now. She spotted Will Samson hanging on the fringe of the crowd, long limbs dangling over the split-rail fence. She sidled up next to him and leaned against the fence post. "Rumor has it the prize is half the pot," she said by way of greeting, giving him her most winsome smile.

He pushed his bangs out of his eyes. "Hello, Hettie. You in town with your pa?"

"He's at your father's now, getting a wheel repaired. You thinking of entering?" she asked casually.

He gave a bark of laughter. "You know I'm a terrible shot."

"Thought maybe you'd enter just for fun. Maybe show off to a certain young lady?" She nodded toward golden-haired Sophie Favreau, a beacon of beauty and sophistication among the folks of Newhaven. Resting in the shade of a tree, she held court with a group of well-dressed young men and ladies from town. Sophie's grandmother, Patrice Favreau, the Soothsayer of the South, had made the family wealthy with her ability to see the future. Sophie was only in Newhaven because of her father's business interests in Montana—her status set her head and shoulders above everyone here.

Will jammed his hands in his pockets, and his cheeks bloomed with color. "I'm not making a fool of myself with them watching."

"You know, if you front me the dollar for the entry fee, I could double your investment."

"No way. They'd never let you in."

"Why not?"

"'Cuz." He shuffled his feet. "You're a girl."

"All the more reason to let me try. They'll take my money and think they'll get a few laughs. But you and I both know I can tag a fox's tail at two hundred yards." She gave her most confident smile. "Spare me a dollar and I'll make it worth your while."

"Only *if* you win."

"You forgetting who my pa is?"

"You're not your father," he huffed.

Someone in the crowd shouted, "Last call! All entrants, last call!"

Hettie clasped her hands together. If she had to resort to waterworks, she would. "Will, *please*. You know I can do it." She waved toward Sophie and her entourage. "I bet you could buy Sophie a bunch of ribbons with the prize money. She *loves* ribbons."

Will licked his lips, and Hettie sensed his imminent capitulation. "Fifty-fifty split."

"Ten-ninety," she countered.

"Forty-sixty."

"Thirty-seventy, and not a cent more. I'm doing all the hard work, after all."

"Done."

Yes! They shook on it, and she grabbed his money and hurried into the contestants' arena.

"Ladies and gentlemen, thank you all for coming,"Tate, the elder of the Robson brothers, bellowed. "We're going to start shortly, but I want to make the rules clear. First: magical charms, spells, talismans, potions, lotions, creams, unguents, or any other non-mundane aids are prohibited. We'll ask that you strip off all jewelry and empty your pockets before entering the range."

"Might as well ask us to strip down to our skivvies!" someone shouted, and the crowd laughed. It was only a half joke, though; some people actually sewed talismans into their clothes.

"All we ask for are your charms, though I'd suggest you remove any more…er…private items before you step up. Winston Bluefeather will ensure you're being honest, and will safekeep your belongings." He gestured to the man at his right, a sorcerer in a charcoal-gray Western suit. Eagle feathers and bright blue beads were woven into his hair. Hettie could almost feel the magic shimmering around him.

"This is a contest of pure human skill, ladies and gentlemen." Tate pointed to seven cans balanced on the far fence that bordered the tannery. "Over yonder are the targets. Each contestant will be given three guns, each with four bullets. You must knock down as many as possible with the ammunition and weapons provided. More than five qualifies to win. In the event of a tie, the contestants will have a quick-draw sudden death shootout. The prize money is a tidy twenty-five dollars."

Hettie inhaled sharply. Minus Will's cut, that would be almost enough to get the potion for Abby. She could work off the rest for Mr. Hooper, or maybe pay him in game. He did love quail.

Tate's brother, James, opened three gun cases with a flourish. The crowd murmured.

Hettie frowned.

"What's wrong?" Will asked at her side.

"I'm no good with a Colt," she whispered harshly.

Will's gaze bounced between the revolver and her. "How's that possible? Your pa has one just like it. What kind of rancher are you that you don't use a six-shooter?"

"I said I'm no good with it, not that I can't use it." She wondered if the Robsons would let her use her own weapon. Not likely, since the wood stock of the Winchester had been magicked so it'd never warp. "I don't get a lot of practice with Pa's gun."

Will wrung his hands, then patted her shoulder gingerly. "You can do it, Hettie. I believe in you." It wasn't a ringing endorsement, but Hettie was in too deep now to back out.

She joined the contestants. James asked, "You got your entry fee, son?"

She toyed with the idea of playing the charade through. She was forever being mistaken for a boy in Paul's clothes. Instead, she pulled off her hat, letting the long, dark, thick braid tucked beneath slide past her shoulders like a heavy coil of rope. James flinched as if it were a dead snake.

"Don't you know who that is?" Tate chuckled, joining them. "That's John Alabama's little girl."

"Hettie?" James peered at her, sobering. "Good heavens, you look just like your brother, God rest his soul."

"If she's as good a shot as her pa, then we've got ourselves a real competition." Tate ushered her into the lineup. "Pardon me, gentlemen, but as the expression goes, ladies first."

"That's all right, Tate. Give the fellas a sporting chance. I insist." She wanted to see how everyone else handled the weapons.

He shrugged and let her take her place in the lineup next to Ling Tsang, who smiled down at her. He occasionally worked odd jobs on the ranch and tended the herd with Uncle. Pa couldn't afford to have him around full-time, but whenever he needed help he'd hire Ling and even let him sleep in the barn when he didn't have anywhere else to go. "Hello, Ling. Haven't seen you around much."

"Miss Hettie," he greeted, tugging on the brim of his hat. Tall and lean, with high cheekbones and hair cut short and neat without the braided queue most of his countrymen wore, Ling was quite handsome, in Hettie's opinion. "I've been busy on a couple of other ranches, but if your father ever needs me, I'll come. I hope you don't find it impertinent that I compete against you."

Ling's English and manners were better than most folks'. She wondered if that was the reason the other Chinese in town avoided him. She'd always thought he could do better in a big city, but he'd told her he "preferred the air and scenery" in Montana.

"Not at all. I look forward to whomping you and every other man here."

"I don't doubt it."

She got a good look at the weapons as she passed the table. In the first case lay a double-barreled shotgun. It was the kind of thing a man would use to take down a bear, and complete overkill for this contest. Maybe that was the point, throwing the contestants off by thinking that power meant accuracy. Pa had made sure she'd learned that lesson second. The first was never to point a gun at a man unless you meant to kill him.

The second case held a Winchester repeater, a finely crafted rifle with gold inlay on the stock and a filigreed brass receiver. A less-seasoned marksman might have mistaken the dazzling showpiece for a well-used, well-cared-for weapon.

The Colt revolver in the last case was battered and dull. James loaded the .45 bullets efficiently, spun the wheel, and handed it to the first contestant, Francis Fawker from the livery. He walked to a spot marked by two sticks and spent a long time steadying his aim. He cocked the gun and pulled the trigger. The sound was more of a pop than a bang. He fired off all four shots but didn't hit a thing.

He went for the fancy Winchester next. It looked out of place against Francis's stained and patched shirt, but he held it snug against his shoulder and let loose four booming shots. He knocked down one can to some mild applause.

He hit nothing with the shotgun. Hettie could see it was going to be a struggle for her to use it—the kickback rocked the man on his heels.

The targets were reset while the next contestant stripped off his talismans. He knocked down two cans with the Winchester, but nothing else. Six contestants later, only one man had managed to knock down five of the seven cans.

Then Ling went up. He picked up the Winchester, weighed it, put it back. He picked up the revolver, spun the wheel, put it back.

He grabbed the shotgun. His smile broadened as he leveled it at the fence. A few people clucked and whistled to spook him—they hadn't done so for any of the other contestants. When that shotgun roared, two cans fell at once, silencing everyone. He aimed half an inch to the right and fired again. Another two cans fell. He did it twice more, leaving only one can standing.

"He's a dirty cheater!" the large man with dark hair and beady eyes who'd knocked down five cans shouted. "I didn't even hear those shots hit!"

Tate turned to Winston. "Bluefeather, do you concur?"

"No magic here," the sorcerer said.

"What about all that mystic Eastern junk, huh? He could be using ether magic on us!"

Ling spun around, shotgun pointed at the ground. "I don't need magic to win this contest. But if you think I'm cheating, I'll bow out right now and we can settle this like real men."

"Whoa, partner, there's no need for that." Tate steered him back toward the targets. "This is just a friendly competition. C'mon. Why don't you finish this? Show them what you're made of."

Ling gazed around, absorbing the suspicion cast his way. "The sparkle of the challenge has dulled." He stalked out, leaving awkward silence in his wake.

Hettie watched him go, feeling sore for Ling. He would've won—it was hardly fair that a bunch of jealous blowhards could drive him off. She glared at the knot of accusers, whose narrowed eyes followed Ling out.

"You're up next, Miss Alabama," James said. "Your talismans?"

She removed the protective necklace her parents had paid quite a lot for, feeling naked without it. She'd been gifted the charm when her menses had come and had been warned never to remove it, especially around men, but rules were rules, and she didn't want to be caught out and humiliated in front of the crowd by refusing to take it off. Chin high, she dropped it into Winston's bowl, along with the meager contents of her pockets, and handed her own rifle over.

The sorcerer muttered a spell and waved his hand over the vessel, then gave her a probing look, as if he were seeking something at the bottom of a pond. A strange feeling rippled through her. He nodded silently at Tate, who gestured for her to proceed.

"You think that tomboy'll hit anything?" She heard someone snicker.

"With that face, she's more likely to scare the cans off the fence." The laughter from the sidelines wormed its way between Hettie's ears. She'd heard it all before. She'd inherited none of her mother's delicate looks. She had her father's broad, strong nose, though it seemed to be permanently upturned like a bat's. Her cheeks were freckled and puffy, and her dull brown eyes were too close together. Not that looks mattered when it came to breaking horses or herding cattle. Part of her wished she could show those townies just how good a shot she was and take off the tips of their ears, but that dandified lot wasn't worth wasting bullets on.

She inspected each gun as Ling had. "Do I have to use all the shots in each gun at once?"

"No rules about that. You fire these guns however you want."

She picked up the shotgun first. "What's this loaded with?"

"Buckshot."

She squinted at the targets. "Those cans filled with something?"

Tate's lips twisted into a grim smile. "You've been the only one to ask. Yes, in fact, they're each half full of sand. It's just to keep them from blowing off the fence, you understand. You've seen them fall, so you know it's still a fair contest."

Perhaps *he* thought it was fair, but it changed the game significantly.

Hettie judged the distance to the fence at about fifty yards and sucked in a lip. Shotguns weren't great at distance, since the pellets scattered. But at the line, she could see how Ling had knocked down two sand-filled cans at once three times in a row: the graying split rail had fresh gouges in the wood. Ling had aimed for the railing to shake those cans off.

Hettie tucked the butt of the gun snugly into her shoulder. Ignoring the catcalls from the sidelines, she focused on the same spot Ling had.

She exhaled as she squeezed the trigger and let her body absorb the recoil, rocking back on her wide stance. The first two cans jumped off the rail.

She handed the shotgun back, noting the silence that had fallen. "Winchester, please."

A befuddled look on his face, James passed her the rifle. She had a feel for the shotgun now; she needed to know what the others were like so she wouldn't waste her bullets. She aimed for the can at the far right end. The first shot missed. The second made the can hop but not fall. Sand poured from the bullet hole, glinting gold in the sunlight.

She put the rifle down. "Revolver."

James handed it to her. The thing was heavy and felt alien in her hands. A rifle was an extension of her body—she could put her weight behind it. But the Colt .45 handgun with its overlong barrel felt awkward in her small-seeming hands. She knew the recoil would strain her wrists.

She wrapped both hands around the grip and sighted down the barrel. She aimed for one of the middle of the five remaining cans.

Sending up a prayer, she squeezed the trigger.

Blam! The revolver threw her locked hands up so high she nearly punched herself. The crowd hooted in laughter. "Give up, girlie!" someone shouted.

"Winchester," she gritted, handing the revolver back. This contest wasn't done yet.

She knocked down the far left can with the Winchester's remaining two bullets. But even with three shells in the shotgun, she only knocked down one more can. That left three cans and three bullets in the revolver.

She picked up the revolver again. The grip felt too big, the balance all wrong.

"You gonna shoot or what?" someone yelled. "Hurry up already!"

She breathed deep, squaring her shoulders and hips, letting the jeers fade. The rustle of the leaves shushed. The air stilled.

She squeezed the trigger. Down came the first can. She shifted her aim, squeezed again. Down went the second.

One bullet. One can.

She narrowed her eyes until the space around the can was fuzzy and pulled the trigger.

The can remained stubbornly on the fence.

A roar of disappointment spilled into her head.

"That was fantastic!" Will exclaimed. "No one'll beat that score."

She glowered at the lone can on the rail. The thing must be nailed to the fence.

Two men remained in the lineup. Old George Sanders didn't hit a single target, but the stranger who stepped up last made the short hairs on the back of her neck stand on end.

He was tall and broad and dressed almost entirely in black, his white shirt a sharp contrast against his funereal garb. Seeing all those heavy layers of black—including a heavy black duster— glistening in the June heat made Hettie sweat.

He glanced at her from beneath the shadowed brim of his hat. His startling blue gaze sent a stinging dart of cold fire through her.

"Your charms," Tate prompted, breaking his unblinking stare.

The stranger slowly extracted a number of stones and bits of rope and hair from various pockets and turned. "There's still more," Winston prompted, and the man in black stopped.

"Not sure if you want to hold what I've got," he murmured, his lips hitching up at one corner.

"Rules are rules." Tate grinned toothily.

The stranger looked around him slowly, his gaze almost palpable as it swept the crowd. Hettie felt it brush over her, and her skin broke out in goose pimples.

"Think you'll be able to handle this, Chief?" The stranger shucked his duster and slung it over the sorcerer's shoulders. Winston stumbled as if the coat weighed half a ton. Maybe it did, in magical terms.

The stranger rolled his shoulders. The stained white cuffs of his shirt peeked from beneath the well-worn black suit. He strolled up to the table and dragged his blunt fingertips across the three gun cases, his expression thoughtful.

"What do you think his deal is?" Will whispered in awe. "You think he's a Kukulos warlock?"

Hettie doubted it. Kukulos warlocks used blood magic—they didn't need to wear heavy mantle coats with all kinds of charms and talismans sewn into them. Their conduit was blood, which meant the smallest open wound was enough to deploy a spell. If the stranger were using magic, though, Winston would catch him.

She was about to explain her theory when the man snatched up all three weapons, tucking the Colt in the front of his pants. He slung the shotgun across his back and started toward the markers, but long before he reached them he brought the Winchester up and started firing, still walking.

He emptied the rifle in rapid succession and knocked down three cans, tossed the weapon carelessly aside, and brought up the shotgun. Down went two more cans. He was still walking toward the markers when he lifted the Colt and squeezed the trigger. The sixth can dove off the rail as if it had been scared away. He narrowed his eyes as his next two shots missed and his feet halted at the marker.

Hettie chewed her lip. The stranger tilted his head, and his eye caught hers.

He raised the gun and fired his last bullet straight into the sky.

The stunned silence erupted in a confused babble, but Hettie hardly heard it. The stranger was smiling at her.

CHAPTER TWO

Sudden death!" James hollered.

Tate ushered Hettie toward the marker where the stranger waited. She dragged her feet. She didn't want to get any closer to the man in black.

"Fine shooting there," Tate said to the stranger, sounding a touch suspicious. "You seem like a good man to have in a spat."

"I've been told otherwise." His eyes remained fixed on Hettie. She tried to meet his blue-eyed gaze but ended up staring at his scuffed leather belt and then lower to the dusty tips of his boots. Heat crawled up her neck, and her shirt stuck to her sweating skin.

James handed a loaded Colt to Hettie grip-first. "You know how to quick draw?" Tate asked worriedly. "I don't want your pa coming at me if you shoot yourself in the foot."

"I can draw and shoot fine," she said, though obviously not as well as this stranger. She glanced at him once more. He was still giving her that long, probing look.

"Ain't polite to stare at a lady," she snapped.

His grin broadened. "I beg your pardon, miss." He tipped his hat. "I don't come across many pretty girls like you in my line of work."

Hettie's cheeks flamed. The nerve! He didn't need to mock her any more than he already had. She snapped her attention toward Tate.

"Rules are simple," he said. "You've got six bullets each. Draw when we say go, and knock down your respective cans." He indicated the fence, which now sported two cans. "First one to knock theirs down wins."

Hettie grimaced as she checked the Colt. She gave the wheel a spin and snapped it back into place. "I don't have a holster," she said.

The Robson boys scrambled for a belt and holster for Hettie. Since she preferred her rifle, she'd never needed to wear one. Tate brought her one straight off the hips of scrawny old Solomon McKay. Hettie strapped it on and holstered the weapon.

"You might want to loosen that," the stranger drawled. "Let it hang lower, closer to your thigh." His gaze dragged down the length of her body. The way he said it made it sound indecent, and her face heated further.

"I can adjust my own clothing, thank you."

"Wouldn't dream of putting you at a disadvantage is all." He flashed even, white teeth.

Hettie squared herself off, palms damp. The crowd shifted as the sun beat down on them, the heat stirring tremulous little waves across the tufty grass between her and the fence. Her mouth went dry.

"On go," Tate shouted.

"Ready!"

Hettie planted her feet.

"Set!"

Her fingers twitched.

"Go!"

She slapped her hand on the grip and tugged, but the long barrel snagged as she drew, wasting a precious moment. She squared herself and took aim.

She heard the *bang bang bang* of her opponent's weapon as she exhaled. Her father's lessons whispered through her. *No sense firing fast unless you aim to miss.*

She squeezed the trigger.

The can jumped, spinning midair.

Will whooped, and a cheer rose from the crowd.

"Hettie Alabama wins!"

Someone slung an arm around her shoulder as she was handed a small, heavy satchel of coins. Big, liberal hands attached to big, grinning faces pounded her back in congratulations.

"I never shoulda doubted you," Will crooned as she counted out a handful of coins.

"Yeah, well... don't spend it all at once." She kept looking back at the rail, judging the distance, checking the wind. She'd missed. She knew she had. So how had that can come down?

Out of the corner of her eye, she caught the stranger watching her. With a tip of his hat and a crooked smile, he turned and walked in the opposite direction.

The crowd dispersed. Will trailed after Sophie and her cabal. It was only with a tinge of bitterness that Hettie turned her back on them. She couldn't have possibly expected him to stick around and celebrate with *her* when he could be with someone like Sophie.

Of course, Hettie didn't need to be popular like Sophie. The weight of her winnings reassured her of that.

Poor, deluded Will, she thought with a wry twist of her lips. There weren't enough ribbons in the world to tie a highfalutin' girl like Sophie Favreau to a lowly blacksmith's son.

Hettie tucked her prize away and slung her Winchester across her back, a skip in her step. She was late meeting Pa, but she wanted to get to Mr. Hooper's to order the potion for Abby and Ma, so she took a shortcut behind the buildings on the main thoroughfare. Pa wasn't going to be happy she'd disobeyed him, but it was better to ask for forgiveness than permission.

As she drew closer to the laundry, she heard gruff voices and cruel laughter.

"Think you can get away with cheatin' us, huh?" She recognized the burly tough's voice and peered around the corner. The man who'd shot down five cans, along with two other men, a blond and a redhead, had Ling backed against the side of the building. "I don't like Eastern magics. My brother died at a Celestial soothsayers'. The old crone stole his soul."

Ling raised his chin. "Unlikely. Your brother probably died of opium use."

The man slugged him across the jaw. Hettie's nails dug into the wood siding as anger and fear collided inside her.

"You think you're better than us, don't you? Where'd you get these fancy clothes?" He fingered the lapel of Ling's Western shirt and vest. "No Chinaman could afford these. Bet you stole them." He slammed him against the wall, pulled out a knife, and held it to Ling's throat. "I say we strip them off and skin him."

Hettie pressed her back against the side of the building, heart thundering. She didn't have time to call the marshal for help. Nerves balling in her gut, she unslung her Winchester and chambered a round all in one smooth motion. "I think y'all should step back now," Hettie announced, voice quavering as she rounded the corner and put the men in her sights.

The burly tough with the dark beard turned. He let go of Ling's collar. "Well, well, if it isn't the chit who stole the prize." He advanced toward her.

She ground her heels into the dirt. The tips of her fingers felt cold. "That's far enough, unless you want a bullet in the gut."

"Look at you, playing a big boy. You're ugly enough to be one, that's for sure." The other men snickered. Hettie tightened her shaking grip around the rifle. The man spread his arms and walked slowly toward her. "Well, go on, then. Shoot me. You want to prove to everyone you're special? Go ahead." He was barely five feet away now. Whiskey wafted from between tobacco-stained teeth. "You think the marshal will have pity on you 'cuz yer a girl? Killing an unarmed man's a hanging offense."

When she hesitated, the man lunged and grabbed the rifle barrel, slamming the butt into her nose with a sickening crunch. Hot blood spurted in her mouth. A fist slammed into the side of her face, and stars burst behind her eyelids. She landed in the dirt, and her Winchester clattered to the ground. He grabbed her collar, and the antimolestation talisman around her neck glowed hot and sparked. He yelped and let go.

"You little whore," he growled, clutching his hand. "I'm going to rip that abomination off your neck right before I tear your tiny tits off."

A clod of earth struck him in the back of the head, raining dirt over them both.

"Run, Miss Hettie!" Ling tackled the blond man who'd drawn his sidearm. He swung him around as he squeezed the trigger. The gun popped, and the redhead collapsed, moaning and gripping his side. Ling kicked the gun out of the blond's grip and smashed an elbow into his face. They fell to the ground in a pile of limbs, wrestling for dominance.

Hettie scrambled for her rifle, but the burly man kicked her shoulder and sent her sprawling. He seized her by the ankle and dragged her several feet across the ground. The talisman fizzed and crackled, and she screamed.

"You keep on just like that," the man said, yanking the charm off her neck. It fizzled in his fist. "I like strugglers." He grabbed her braid and pulled so hard, tears sprang in her eyes. A flash of metal— The tension on her scalp suddenly went slack, and she landed in the dust. Above her, the man dangled her long braid.

"Now you're a real boy." She tried to scramble away from his oily grin, but he caught her ankle once more and dragged her toward him.

Hettie screamed again and kicked, but with all the bustle and noise in town, no one would hear the ruckus behind the laundry. As he bent over her, she stabbed her thumbs into his eyes and raked her short nails across his face. He howled. She dove for the downed redhead and pulled his revolver out of his holster, swinging it around and pointing it at the burly man. She pulled the trigger.

A bullet hole appeared between his eyes. It was an almost comical moment as he stood there, mouth rounded in an O. His massive body toppled into the dust.

Ling drove a fist into the blond man's solar plexus, spun and slammed a heel in a downward kick across his shoulder. He went down face first into the dirt. Ling limped toward her, picking up the blond's revolver. "Are you all right, Miss Hettie?"

"I-I'm fine." She was vaguely aware that Ling had sat her on a crate and pressed a handkerchief to her bloodied nose. His own lip was split and swollen, his scraped cheek puffy. His probing look sent a tingle over her skin. He lifted the stanch gently—the bleeding had stopped. The pain wasn't so bad, either, though that might have been shock.

He heaved a sigh. "You shouldn't have gotten involved." He stooped over the corpse and searched the dead man's pockets.

His words stirred her from her cold funk. "What was I supposed to do? Let them kill you?"

"I can take care of myself." He divested the corpse of a handful of coins and bank notes and his hunting knife.

"What are you doing?"

"Leaving." He nodded toward the hills, where she spotted the injured redhead hobbling across the scrub-covered plain. "He'll be back, either with more men or with the marshal. I don't intend to die today."

"*They* attacked you. You were only trying to defend yourself and me. We just need to talk to the marshal. I'll explain everything—"

"Mobs don't always take the law's side. The fact of the matter is, a white man's dead, and a Chinaman killed him." His jaw firmed. "I'll take my chances out there."

"But you didn't do anything wrong," she exclaimed. "You saved my life."

His expression closed. "If the matter gets resolved in a few weeks, I'll return. Promise me you won't tell anyone. Not even your family. I don't want them involved." He held out his hand. "Promise me, Hettie. Please."

She didn't understand, but she respected his wishes. Reluctantly, she clasped his hand. "I promise."

A prickling sensation skittered up her arm and settled in her chest. Her eyes widened. So it was true. Eastern magic didn't require a talisman or any kind of conduit.

Ling turned to go. "Wait." She fished the prize money out of her pocket, savoring its weight for a precious second. She sighed. "This belongs to you rightfully. I wouldn't have won the contest if you hadn't clued me in to that shaky rail." No sense in keeping what she hadn't really earned. With the winnings went any hope of getting the potion, but she knew deep down it was the right thing to do. Regret cost a great deal more than a sack of silver dollars, and right now, Ling needed the money more.

He wavered for only a second, then took the money. "This is just a loan. I'll pay you back." She watched as Ling and the money and all her hopes for it hurried away, melting into the flow of people on the main strip.

"Well, that seemed unnecessary." The deep voice sent prickles across Hettie's skin, and she shot to her feet. The stranger from the shootout strolled casually over and studied the body lying in the dust.

"You saw what happened," she concluded, her voice shaky. "You saw, and you did nothing?" She glanced at his holstered sidearm.

"I didn't know what I was seeing, and I don't go pulling guns on people and taking sides without figuring out what's going on first. For someone as cautious a shot as you, I figured you'd have used your brain a little more." He gave her a once-over. "You handled yourself all right, though."

All right? She'd been molested, had her nose broken, had her hair—

Her hair! She grabbed at the back of her neck, hoping she'd been mistaken, but her fingers met the stiff, bluntly cropped hairs at her nape. She searched the ground for her braid and scooped it up, careful to gather every last hair. The thing was like a tough, dried root in her hand. Her heart sank, and her throat closed. It was ridiculous to cry over her hair when she'd just nearly escaped death, but...

"It'll grow back," the man said. "It wasn't adding to your looks, anyhow."

Hatred boiled through her. What kind of gentleman mocked a lady in distress? "Who are you?" she demanded as he bent over the blond lying facedown on the ground. He pressed his fingers to the man's neck.

"Still alive. That's good." He pulled a leather thong from his belt and began trussing him up, murmuring an incantation as he did so. "Too bad about Zeke there." He nodded at the corpse. "But he'll still fetch a reward."

Understanding dawned. "You're a bounty hunter."

He flicked her the barest of affirming glances. He wasn't as old as she'd first thought, though his face was weathered. His eyes were a cold, pale blue, his features square and hard.

"But if you saw everything…" Ling's spell clamped down on her hard, cutting off her words. It seemed it would be a secret, no matter who saw what.

"I *didn't* see everything," the stranger returned nonchalantly. "And I can't rightly vouch for a man who robbed the men he attacked and took off."

She wanted to shout, *He didn't attack them!* But the promise spell Ling had put on her made her tongue and throat seize. She blew a breath through her nostrils and carefully rethought what she wanted to say. "I just happened to be by—"

"With a fully loaded Winchester. Does the marshal know you're loaded for bear?" He picked up her rifle and handed it to her.

"He lets me hang on to it for just this kind of thing."

"So the marshal's deputizing little girls now. Must be getting desperate."

She stuck her jaw out. She didn't need to explain herself, or the reasons why Marshal McCowan let her hang on to her weapon.

"Tell me, Miss…?"

"Alabama. Hettie Alabama."

"Walker Woodroffe." He tipped up his hat, revealing a swath of dark hair. "Tell me, Miss Alabama, why is a delicate flower such as yourself slinging a Winchester around like a parasol and entering shooting contests?"

"I think the better question to ask is why you set me up to win."

"Seemed you could've used a little help." His lips hitched up in one corner, showing just the barest hint of white teeth. He couldn't have even salved her ego and denied it.

Her fingers curled. "I would've won if you hadn't showed up."

"But I did show up. Six out of seven ain't bad, but in the real world"—his voice dropped to a husky growl—"six out of seven means one man left to shoot you dead."

Before she could come up with a retort, someone called her name.

"Hettie!" Her father pounded toward her. "I heard shots, and I felt your talisman go off…" His words faded when he saw the blood pooling around the dead man at her feet. John Alabama's gaze went from the stranger poised above him to his daughter's bloodied face, and his features grew dark. "What's going on?" His stance shifted toward the stranger, one hand on his Colt.

"He tried to hurt me…" She gestured vaguely at the corpse. Only then did she realize she was still holding the gun she'd shot him with. A sick feeling swamped her, and the edges of her vision blurred.

"Give that here." He snatched the revolver from her and shoved it into his belt.

"It's true, sir. Your daughter was accosted by this one, and she smartly shot the lout. He cut her hair, see?" He pointed at the braid in Hettie's grip, clutched within Ling's blood-soaked handkerchief. "Best get rid of it quick. Can't have pieces of your girl floating around town for anyone to curse."

"Indeed." Pa took the thick rope of hair from her, along with the bloodied handkerchief, then lit a match and set fire to them. He waited until the whole braid smoked before dropping it on the ground, pointing and uttering a single word that ignited a brilliant flame. Hettie's hair and blood were incinerated instantly. Her father kicked the ashes until they scattered in the wind, and Hettie's desolation deepened.

He picked up the broken antimolestation charm from the ground. Fury stamped hard, tight lines into his face. "I'm gonna kill old Henley for selling me this piece of…" He wiped a hand over his mouth.

"Ain't many who can make talisman magic stick as good as it used to," Walker commented grimly. "I'm surprised it worked at all. Your daughter's mighty brave, that's for sure."

Pa turned his full attention on Hettie and wrapped his arms around her. She leaned into his strength, willing herself not to cry. Her fingers and toes were icy-cold. A tremor began in her stomach, making her whole body quake. "Where else are you hurt?"

"I'm all right. He tried—" She choked on the words. She felt as though a wad of cotton was crawling down her throat. Ling's curse at work. She revised her statement to exclude Ling's presence. "He tried to get fresh. I stopped him."

A storm boiled into John Alabama's features. Pa got to his feet as the blond man stirred and groaned. Walker stood over his bounty. "You chose a bad time to wake up, Frank," he said almost cheerfully.

"Shoulda kept your eyes closed until we reached the marshal's office. Now you gotta face this young lady's papa." He planted his boot against the man's shoulder and rolled him onto his back.

Frank coughed and moaned, then blinked slowly as John Alabama glared down at him. His eyes went huge.

"No—"

In a flash, John drew his gun and shot the blond man twice in the face.

CHAPTER THREE

Hettie didn't have the breath to scream. Blood poured from the red, pulpy cavity into the dust beneath him. Her father's hands trembled. Walker stood perfectly still, gripping his holstered sidearm, staring wide-eyed at John with barely veiled contempt.

It was a long time before Hettie could move. She felt outside of herself, staring at the man who was her father, his black-booted feet planted wide, his wide-brimmed hat casting a broad shadow over his shoulders. She'd never seen that seething anguish and hatred carving his face. "Pa...?"

Her voice seemed to bring him back from whatever hell he'd been visiting in his mind. "I'm sorry...so sorry you had to see that, Hettie. I—" He caught Walker's dark look. "He was a bounty, wasn't he?" He took off his hat. His thick, dark hair was slicked with sweat.

"He'll only be worth half as much now." Walker gave a disgruntled snort. "Of course, if it were my daughter, I might've done the same."

Hettie worried her lower lip. She doubted Marshal McCowan would see it that way. The man had been unarmed, hands tied, on the ground. It hadn't been justice. It'd been an execution.

Pa had just killed a man. And so had she.

"I'm...very sorry." John tugged at his mustache. "I lost my head." He grimaced at his poor choice of words. "I don't have much to offer in compensation, but please, accept my invitation to stay at our ranch. We've got a nice clean stable and plenty of blankets. And my wife is an excellent cook."

Assuming they weren't hauled off to jail. Walker tilted his chin to the side and considered a moment. "I have a little business to attend to first in town, but I'll take you up on your offer. You can expect to see me soon, Mr. Alabama."

He flashed his teeth again, and Hettie couldn't help thinking about wolves.

When the marshal's men arrived, Pa gave them an abbreviated version of the events, and Walker corroborated his story. She was shocked when Marshal McCowan accepted that the shooting had been in self-defense and didn't press any charges. Walker had seen most of what happened, but he hadn't said anything about Ling. And no one asked Hettie any questions—instead, she was led away from the gruesome scene to sit in the shade of the nearby saloon, where the innkeeper brought her a cup of hot coffee and smelling salts in case she fainted. That the marshal had been so lax in his investigation, so accepting of the word of three people...it didn't seem right. But it was what it was.

The bodies were taken away on a flatbed cart, and Walker trailed after the lawmen to collect his bounty. He tipped his hat to John and gave Hettie a discreet wink as he departed.

On the journey home, Hettie worried Pa was cross with her, but if he was, he didn't say anything about it. Their supplies rattled in the cart like bones in a casket. The wheel might be fixed, but the road was as pitted as ever. Her thoughts were almost as restless as she stewed over those men, alive one minute, dead the next.

If a bounty hunter had been after them, that meant they'd been wanted criminals. But it hadn't been just the two of them...That nameless redhead had run into the hills, and now it dawned on her that a wounded man would not have headed in that direction unless he knew there was someone out there to help him.

What if he came back to avenge his friends' deaths…and had more friends to help him?

She chewed on the inside of her cheek. More likely the man was buzzard food. Or maybe Mr. Woodroffe had seen him and was in hot pursuit now.

Something streaked across the hills in her peripheral vision. She grabbed the Winchester, startling Pa.

"Hettie?"

She stared into the distance. Nothing. Her anxiety was starting to play tricks with her mind. She settled back down, and her father sent her a worried sidelong look. "Close your eyes for a while. We'll be all right."

She didn't want to leave him alone, but as her limbs grew heavy, she rested her head against Pa's hard shoulder and fell into a fitful, dreamless doze.

When they got home, Ma was setting the table for dinner. Uncle was already seated across from Abby. He looked up and did a double take. "Tarnation, girl, who'd you lose a fight to?"

"I tripped and smashed my nose on a fence rail." It was a struggle to look embarrassed when inside, she felt sick to her stomach.

"What happened to your hair?" Ma ran her fingers through the raggedy, cropped mess and looked her daughter over fretfully. "Did you trip and fall on that, too?"

"It's all the rage in Europe," Hettie explained quickly. "The French girls make it short and wavy." She tossed her head the way she'd often seen Sophie do it and plastered on a smile. "I got Sarah Bella Thompson to cut it for me."

"With what? A dull ax?" Grace blew out a breath. She glared up at her husband. "Why didn't you take her to see Dr. Wells? Look at her face!"

John was saved from answering when Abby said, "Paul."

Silence fell as everyone turned. The girl sat stirring the contents of her bowl, making strange circular patterns in her stew. Grace's voice was a bare whisper. "What did you say, Abby?"

"Hettie looks just like Paul." She said it as if it were the answer to a simple arithmetic problem.

"You...you remember what he looked like?" Her sister had barely been five when their brother was murdered.

Abby pointed out the window toward Paul's grave on the hill. "We talk sometimes. Over there."

Hettie felt as though someone had poured cold water down her spine. Her mother covered her mouth, and Pa's face grew stony. There was no way... Abby was too young...

Uncle met each of their gazes and slowly asked, "Paul tell you anything else?"

The girl tilted her head. "He misses riding with Hettie."

The smell of cordite lingering on her clothes and the taste of blood in her mouth suddenly made the memory of Paul's death—and the day's horrors—too fresh. Hettie stood abruptly. "Excuse me. I...I'm not hungry."

She hurried out onto the front porch and doubled over, retching, but her stomach was empty, so nothing came up. She breathed deep, pushing back the tears burning her eyes. The last of the sun's rays did little to dispel the chill as the memory of the day her brother was killed surfaced.

Paul had been thirteen, Hettie only eleven. She'd been sitting in the saddle in front of Paul, riding the fence line, when a derelict stranger had jumped out of the grass and seized the horse's reins. He'd dragged Paul off the saddle and stabbed her brother in the side. Then he'd yanked her off, throwing her to the ground. She remembered clearly how his wild eyes were like a starving coyote's. He'd made to silence her with his wicked knife, but Paul had tackled him—

She felt the hot stickiness on her fingers, tasted the salty, bitter tang that seeped into her mouth as she bit her tongue to keep from crying. Hettie's last memories of Paul were of him curled around her, trying to comfort her. He'd never complained once about his injuries, even as his lifeblood soaked her dress.

She clutched herself around the middle. She'd never forget Paul's last words. *You gotta take care of Abby now, Hettie.*

She'd done her best. But he would've been able to take care of Abby better than Hettie ever had. He would've known how to handle her trances and wandering.

He'd know what to do if she said she was talking to the dead.

Cymon trotted up to her and butted his head against her hip, whining. The big, muscly mutt was more jaw than brain, and he smelled terrible, but he always seemed to know when she needed comfort. She smiled a watery smile. "Hey, boy. You haven't been talking to Paul lately, have you?" He stared up at her with unquestioning devotion. "Nah, I guess not." She scratched his ears affectionately. "But then, if you were a necromancer, the elders would come and take you away."

When children reached the age of change, they were brought before the elders, local representatives of the Division of Sorcery, and tested for magical abilities. Those who displayed any talent were sent off to the Division Academy to learn spellcraft and sorcery. Hettie couldn't imagine how Abby would fare without her family. She could barely dress herself. But if they didn't report her abilities, the Division could send truancy agents and drag them all to jail.

It used to be less stringent. Pa had never gone to the Academy. But in the past few years, the government had made attendance mandatory for all gifted, white, negro, Celestial and Indian. All sorcerers had to be reported and registered. The Division said it was to preserve the dwindling number of gifted being born; they said the gifted were destined for better lives. But there were stories about what happened at the Academy. Nightmarish tales of students pushed to their breaking points. Students pitted against each other to test their abilities. Hettie would never allow Abby to end up there.

"If you do see any folks coming for Abby, you'll stop 'em cold, right?" Cy wagged his tail. She picked up a stick and threw it. Cy bolted after it, snatched it up off the ground, and streaked away into the tall, dry grasses. She sighed. He never was any good at fetch.

She was sore all over from the day's events, but she needed to occupy her mind and hands. Pa had hung up his gun belt on the hook on the porch. She took her father's revolver to the back lot, set up a few empty tins on the fence by the edge of the property, and loaded the Colt.

She raised the revolver and steadied herself. The crack of the gun sent a cloud of starlings into the air. They swirled like smoke through a fiery-orange sky. She looked back down to find she hadn't hit a single target.

"You plantin' bullet trees in the hill or something?" Uncle Jeremiah strolled over, hands in his pockets.

"Something like that." The Colt jumped in her grip as she fired, and she clenched her teeth.

Uncle chuckled. "Never seen anyone try to strangle their handgun before. You're locking your elbows too much, and you're pointed too high." He took the Colt from her. "Arms low, elbows slightly bent. You want to be strong here"—he pounded on his chest just in front of his armpits—"and here." He cuffed a wrist with his palm. "Sight along the barrel. Breathe. Squeeze the trigger." He did so in rapid succession and knocked three cans off the rail.

Hettie stared. "Did you learn that from Pa?"

"I learned it from him," John said, walking toward them. "What are you doing out here, Hettie? Your ma's worried about you, and it's getting dark."

"Sorry. Just practicing." She indicated the revolver grimly. His lips firmed, and he nodded.

"You should learn how to do this one-handed." John reloaded the Colt for her. "There'll be times you won't be able to square yourself off all proper." He jammed the Colt into his holster and faced the target casually. In a blink, he'd drawn and fired twice, knocking a tin can off the rail and hitting it midair as it dropped. He held out the gun grip first. "Your turn."

Hettie put the Colt in her holster. She placed her feet apart, her body turned at about sixty degrees to the fence, then drew the too-heavy gun and fired. Her wrist jerked painfully. She hit nothing.

Uncle harrumphed. "You need a smaller gun."

"I need bigger hands." Hettie flexed her fingers.

Pa rubbed his chin. "Maybe we'll look into getting you a Derringer or some smaller caliber pistol. Of course, I'd rather you were chasing boys than learning how to outdraw tin cans."

"I'd rather have a gun than a husband," she muttered, cheeks burning.

Uncle tut-tutted. "Guns won't keep you warm at night, missy."

"I don't need a man," she snapped, furious. "I'm better off on my own."

"Now, Hettie, don't say that. You're going to break some foolish boy's heart with that spinster's attitude."

The two men chuckled, and she clenched her teeth. She yanked off the belt and stomped toward the house.

"Aw, Hettie, don't be mad. We're just kidding!"

She ran up the stairs and flopped onto her bed. Silent tears soaked into her pillow. She'd killed a man today. Pa had killed a second. They'd lied to a lawman, Ling was on the run, and her helpless sister could be snatched away from the family any day by the Division of Sorcery.

How could Pa joke around and pretend as if their world wasn't on the cusp of falling apart?

CHAPTER FOUR

Two days later, Abby wandered off again. Hettie searched the usual places, but when she didn't find Abby, she grew uneasy. She hurried down to the creek and found her sister almost fully submerged, lying on the rocky bed so only her face came above the water, whispering nonsense to the sky.

Hettie screamed for help as she dragged her sister out of the freezing-cold water. Pa came running, and he carried them both to the house in his strong arms. By evening Abby had a high fever. Uncle raced to fetch the doctor. When Dr. Wells arrived, Abby was delirious, muttering gibberish and heaving great, wheezing coughs.

"It could be pneumonia," the doctor said gravely, and Grace gasped. "Whatever you do, don't let her leave the house until this has passed."

Ma stayed with Abby day and night. Hettie took over many of the household duties on top of her own chores. The days fell into a pattern of nonstop cooking, cleaning, washing, and farm work. She got so busy, she'd all but forgotten the horrific events in town.

It was while Hettie was cleaning out the stables and worrying about how the bread she'd left to rise would turn out that she was vividly reminded of that terrible day. "Excuse me, son, can you tell me where to find Mr. John Alabama?"

She froze. She recognized that low drawl.

Walker Woodroffe's tall, broad frame filled the doorway and blocked out the sun. The brim of his hat shaded most of his features, but there was no hiding his clear, ice-blue eyes. He tipped his hat up, grinning slowly. "I do beg your pardon, Miss Alabama. I didn't recognize you." He looked her over and arched an eye. "You make a handsome fella."

Her cheeks flushed. Before she could snap back at him, Uncle appeared at the other end of the barn. "Eh? Who's this now?"

"Walker Woodroffe." The bounty hunter extended a hand. "I'm a...friend of John Alabama's."

"John ain't got many friends I don't know about." He planted his fists on his hips. "State your business."

"Uncle, don't be rude." Hettie didn't want him making the bounty hunter mad or giving him any reason to be less than civil. He could have told the marshal the truth about what happened, and then who knew where she and Pa would be now. "I met Mr. Woodroffe last week in town."

"He's your uncle? Ah, yes. I see where you get your looks from, Miss Alabama."

"We're not blood kin," Uncle snapped. "I'm a friend of John Alabama's, too, and I know his business better than most, so tell me again, stranger, what's a sorcerer of your caliber doing traipsing around our little ranch?"

Hettie's gaze bounced from the bounty hunter to the old man. The barest of smiles curved Walker's lips. "Mr. Alabama invited me to stay awhile to thank me for helping his daughter."

Uncle glanced down at her suspiciously. "What'd he do for you?"

"She was set upon by a gang of thugs," Walker answered for her. "I helped extricate her."

That was stretching the truth, but Ling's curse held firm. She couldn't correct him.

"If you don't mind, I need to speak with your father urgently." Walker directed his comments to Hettie.

Uncle cut in, "You just missed him. He's gone to Hawksville. He'll not be back for a few days."

"I'm afraid my business can't wait. You say he just left?"

"Few hours ago, I guess." Uncle scratched his chin.

"Perhaps I can catch up to him on the road." The man in black nodded. "Thank you, both."

"Safe journey." Uncle watched him make his way out. The tension in the barn didn't ease until the bounty hunter's mount's hoofbeats faded. Hettie unclenched her fingers from around the pitchfork handle.

"Why'd you send him away? Pa's just visiting the Gunnersons. If you think—"

"I think, missy, that you better start telling the truth. Who is that, really?"

Hettie glared back. Uncle glowered and jammed his hands in his pockets. "Who is he?" he asked again.

Hettie felt her lips loosen and her throat squeeze. "Walker Woodroffe. A bounty hunter."

His eyes narrowed. "How did you meet him?"

"He found me after I shot the man who attacked me and—" Ling's spell seized her like an earthquake rumbling through her chest and kept her from speaking. It shook her with such violence that she had to clench her teeth to keep from having her head flap off. Uncle cursed and pulled a leather thong from his pocket. He draped it over her shoulders, held one end, and murmured an incantation. The shaking eased, and as he withdrew the length of leather, she felt the spell slough away like a veil being lifted off her head.

"Mighty strong magics for someone to be using on the likes of you." Uncle stuffed the thong back in his pocket and kept his hands there. "Now tell me who put that spell on you."

"Ling Tsang." Her mouth still had a mind of its own. She fought against the urge to tell him anything—it felt as if she was betraying Ling—but the words wouldn't stop.

"Ling? That hinky Chinaman?" Uncle had always been cool toward the ranch hand. "What does he have to do with this?"

The story tumbled out of her without pause. The words rushed out on a tongue that didn't trip, and she had no idea she was saying them until they reached her own ears.

When her words and breath finally ran out, he took his hands out of his pockets. "So your father was lying to me." Uncle rubbed his bristles. "He told me that Walker fella shot Shadow Frank."

Shadow Frank? She'd seen his name listed on a wanted poster outside of the marshal's office. The blond was a member of the infamous Crowe gang. Was that why Pa had shot him?

"When did you learn to break promise spells? And use truthtelling spells?" she asked. Uncle had never done much more than set up a few protection wards around the ranch.

"It don't concern you." He paced in the aisle between the stalls, jaw grinding. "Finish cleaning the barn. Give the horses extra feed, and make sure all their tack is at hand. If that Walker Woodroffe comes back, don't let him near the house. Keep him out here and away from your ma and Abby. I need to talk to your pa."

Hettie reluctantly did as Uncle said, but only after he'd shut down all her inquiries. An hour later, she was gathering firewood when her father rode in on Jezebel. Uncle intercepted him, talking rapidly as they headed toward his cabin on the edge of the ranch.

Hettie followed, careful to stay out of sight. Something was going on, and she hated being kept in the dark. From a distance, the low log and sod cabin looked like little more than a hummock, almost blending in with the rest of the land. The two men went in the front door, and Hettie tiptoed around to the small window.

"...looking for. But he sure as hell wasn't here on a social call. The man was bristling with so many antifraud charms, I could barely say a word of a lie before I felt them clamping down on me."

"You shouldn't have sent him away. We could've taken care of him."

An ice-cold finger trailed down Hettie's spine. "When he comes back, he'll know something isn't right." A loaded pause dropped into the silence. "You think he's a Pinkerton agent?"

"The Pinks wouldn't beat around the bush if they knew. They'd've come full force. Woodroffe is something else. A man carrying that much magic isn't chasing down criminals for kicks. He's got to be after..." His voice dropped off to an angry whisper. Hettie couldn't hear over the pounding of her heart. She slid closer and heard Uncle say, "We gotta move it."

"Move it where? It's been safe for more than twenty years. If we unearth it now—"

"If we don't, Woodroffe's going to find it. Diablo ain't safe here."

Her skin broke out in goose bumps. She knew *Diablo* meant *devil* in Spanish, but she knew the word better from fireside stories Pa told about Elias Blackthorn, the outlaw gunslinger who couldn't die. Diablo was the demon he'd traded his soul for, a monstrous familiar who did his bidding. A powerful sorcerer had tricked the demon and stolen him from Blackthorn. But because the outlaw no longer had a soul, he was terrified of where he would go if he died. Hell had no place for him, and heaven surely wouldn't. So he refused to die. Through black magic and by eating the souls of naughty children, Elias Blackthorn and his gang continued to roam the land, hunting for the sorcerer and his demon familiar, Diablo.

But it was just a story, a silly game children played to prove they weren't afraid of the boogeyman. Surely Uncle wasn't saying the man and his legend were real?

Hettie heard scuffling, followed by the scrape of something heavy across the floor. "Gimme that crowbar." The crack of wood made Hettie chance a peek. John and Jeremiah were bent over a hole where the old man's bed had been. The boards shone with old markings—dried blood and white paint that, if she put the planks back down, would have made up the lines of a protection spell.

They dug into the dirt below with their bare hands, then pulled out a box about the size of a loaf of bread from the cavity. "Maybe I should open it," John said, a note of resignation and dread heavy in his voice.

"No. Not yet. The box is the last line of defense. I'm taking this out of here." Uncle shoved it into a gunnysack. "Take Grace and your girls somewhere safe. Hide out for a while. I'll come and find you when I know that Walker Woodroffe is out of the picture."

"Dammit, old man, I can't uproot my family. Abby's sick. And besides, Grace'll kill me."

"There are worse things than a woman's scorn, John."

"The girls don't know. How am I supposed to explain it to them?"

"Don't. The less they know, the better. We have to start over."

Go? Start over? What were they talking about? Hettie's heart hammered.

Uncle and Pa were out the door and rounding the cabin before she could get out of sight. "Hettie." Her father's voice slid from anger to concern. "What are you doing out here?"

She squared her shoulders indignantly. "I was listening in, that's what. What's going on, Pa?" She eyed the sack clutched in Uncle's fist. "Is *that* Diablo?" She couldn't imagine a demon being contained within a box in the earth. "Why are you making us move? Why are you afraid of Walker Woodroffe?"

Uncle hitched up his pants, shrugging his shoulders as if hunching against a storm. "We don't have time to explain every little detail to you. Just listen to your father and do as he says."

"Get going, Jeremiah." John looked weary. "Take the gray gelding. He's the fastest."

"But we were going to sell him at auction!"

"Hettie, it's very important you listen to me." He glanced once more over his shoulder. With a definitive nod, Uncle turned and hurried toward the corral. John's big, scarred hands settled over her shoulders heavily. "I'm relying on you to take care of your mother and sister. You watch over them, no matter what happens to me or Uncle."

His grip tightened. He was trembling. "You're scaring me, Pa."

"I'm sorry. Hettie…There are things I've done I'm not proud of. Just know that I love you, and I had to do it for you and Abby and your ma. There isn't time to tell you everything right now." He ushered her toward the house. "We need to get going."

Ma was setting the table when they entered the house. "Dinner's ready," she said, but her smile faded when she caught her husband's bleak expression. The light went out of her eyes, and she gently set down the soup tureen. "It's finally happened, hasn't it?"

John's face was like stone. "Pack your things, Grace. Only the essentials."

"We can't move Abby," she said, voice rising in panic. "Not now. Pneumonia, John. She could die."

He was already moving toward the trunk where he kept his ammunition. "We'll take the wagon. Gather all the blankets you can. We'll make her a bed and shelter her from the wind."

Grace pursed her bloodless lips. "It's that bad?"

John nodded.

Hettie watched her mother speed up the stairs, bewildered. Ma knew. She knew about Pa, about whatever was going on. She stared at her father, wondering who this hard-faced man was.

John opened the trunk, pulling out two heavy blankets and handing them to Hettie. He reached in and extracted the false bottom. From the secret compartment, he drew a battered leather bandolier and a box of shotgun cartridges and bullets. With startling efficiency, he loaded his Colt, then slung the bandolier across his chest with practiced ease. "Hettie, pack light for the road. Bring your gun and all the ammunition you can find, then meet me in the barn. Get leads for the other mustangs in the corral while I harness Jezebel. We don't have time to saddle all of them."

"But where are we going?"

"Away from the ranch." He started loading the shotgun he hunted wolves with. "We can't go to town, though. It'll draw too much attention. We'll need to find someplace where Abby can get better, then work things out."

Her hands shook and she felt weak, but Hettie scrambled to do as she was told, waiting for the moment Pa would turn around and tell her this was all a prank. It felt like some horrible nightmare she couldn't wake from. She found she was holding her breath, but there was a strangely familiar comfort in simply doing as she was told. With no other information to go on, she could only trust Pa's word.

She grabbed her Winchester and loaded a canvas shoulder bag with ammunition and a change of clothes, as well as the few coins she had socked away. She took a last, longing glance around her room, wondering what she was forgetting that she'd regret leaving behind.

She passed her sister's room, where Ma was bundling up Abby. She moaned and gave weak sobs of protest. "Hush, Abby, I know you're tired. Just try to sleep, and we'll be out of here and safe in no time…" The whispers were desperate, but the thread of steel in her mother's voice told Hettie she would not tolerate defiance.

In the corral, the two mustangs sensed Hettie's nervousness and shied when she approached with their leads. Uncle must have really stirred them up when he'd collected the gray gelding. "It's all right, I'm not going to hurt you," Hettie said, reaching out imploringly. She struggled to calm down. Horses were very sensitive to her emotions. "We're all leaving the ranch," she told them evenly, "so you won't be going to market for now, okay?"

The horses stood still, allowing Hettie to tie the leads on and tug them out of the fenced-in area. They followed her to the barn, where Pa was loading blankets and saddles into the wagon. Jezebel chuffed her own anxious confusion, dancing restlessly.

"Sorry, girl, no time to explain." Pa gave her a light smack on the flank, and she glared at him indignantly. "Don't fight me on this. Get to the front of the house."

With a snort, she strained forward. Old she might be, but she was magicked to be smart and strong. In minutes, they were at the porch. Ma hustled out with a basket of provisions.

Hettie spread the blankets out in an effort to make a sheltering nest for Abby.

"No."

She looked up. "Pa?"

He was staring hard into the shadows of the hills. The sun was nearly gone, leaving the barest sliver behind the distant mountains.

"Go back inside," he said quietly.

"Pa—"

"Do it. Lock the doors and windows and barricade them. Stay with your mother and Abby and don't come out, whatever you do." His voice was low and deadly. He hopped down from the wagon seat and unslung the shotgun from his shoulder.

Hettie could see nothing in the dark purples and blues of the land around them, but then something flickered in the gloom. Shapes darting through the scrub, fast as foxes, stealing in like leaves on the wind.

Hettie settled her Winchester in her grip, mustering her courage. "I'm not leaving you out here alone, Pa."

"Just do as I say," he barked, turning his fiercely blazing eyes upon her. "You have to do this for me, Hettie, y'hear? Protect your sister and mother. Don't let anything happen to them."

She snapped her jaw shut. Nodded once.

"John…"

"It'll be okay, Grace," he said softly. "I promise." He hauled her into his arms and kissed her. "I love you." He let go and turned, hastening toward the oncoming figures.

Hettie's heart pounded in her throat as she and Ma rushed around the house, pushing furniture in front of all the points of entry. Her mother was breathing hard, trying to hold back tears, it seemed. Hettie wasn't sure she wanted to know what was happening anymore—she was already so scared, her fingers had gone numb. She focused on Pa's words. They gave her purpose, made sense in this confusing new reality.

Protect your sister and mother. Don't let anything happen to them.

She ushered Ma into Abby's room. Her sister lay half out of bed, the blankets kicked off. Her head lolled as she tried to sit up. "The wolves in the fire. I can hear them coming…"

"It's all right, darling, just go back to sleep." Grace smiled tremulously and smoothed her hair away. She glanced at Hettie, doubt in every line of her suddenly aged face.

Hettie looked at her rifle. It wouldn't do anyone any good trapped in here. "Lock the door and push the dresser in front of it," she ordered her as she checked the load on her weapon.

"Where are you going? Hettie, come back!"

She closed the bedroom door behind her and climbed onto the roof through her own bedroom window. She settled on the cedar-shingled peak and surveyed the ranch's perimeter, searching for any sign of her father.

The moon was a big, low ball on the horizon, casting wan, silvery light upon the land. She let her eyes adjust. Something slid through the shadows within the perimeter of the fences. Her father was nowhere to be seen. A quick glance down and she saw Jezebel had been unhitched, though the mustangs remained tied to the back of the wagon, shifting restlessly.

Hettie shouldered the Winchester and picked her targets. She counted six shadows shambling toward the silo and barn. She stared hard, keeping her rifle at the ready, but she didn't fire in case Pa was one of those shadowy shapes.

The movement stopped. An unearthly hoot broke the tense silence, followed by a shrill bird call. Then a shout.

A blast of heat and light slammed into her. It felt like someone had punched her in the face. She fell flat on her back as a wave of fire and dust sprayed across her. Her ears rang. She dug her nails into the shingles to keep herself from sliding off the roof. Her vision wavered, the world a blur of halos. The night was suddenly brighter, hotter—

She yelped, and her vision snapped into focus. The silo was on fire!

Flames raced up the sides of the tower, casting the world in blinding orange-yellow light. Another shout. It seemed like time slowed when the second blast knocked Hettie off the roof. She tumbled onto the veranda awning and crashed to the hard planks. A sharp, stabbing pain lanced through her left arm, and she cried out breathlessly, trying to find her wits through the fog in her head.

She turned over. Now the barn was on fire, a cacophony of sound and light and heat blasting Hettie. The pigs in the adjacent pen screeched, and the chickens bawled within the henhouse. The mustangs tied to the wagon screamed and reared, yanking on the cart, trying to get away. Hettie pushed to her feet, cradling her left arm, and started toward the barn.

She had to free the livestock. If they were killed, that was the end of—

A broad shadow loomed up in front of her. A monstrously scarred face peered down and grinned like a death's head. "Well, what do we have here?"

The world burst into a whirl of stars as the man slammed his fist into her face. She toppled to the ground, tasting blood and dust.

"Lookee here, boys! Seems Jack had himself a litter!" the man hooted. She heard some shouts in response. Boots pounded against the veranda.

No! Ma! Abby!

She scrabbled for a weapon—anything—and found a fist-sized rock. She lunged to her feet and headed straight for the man, but he grabbed her wrist and socked her again hard, this time in the stomach.

"Mangy little runt," he growled, then kicked her in the knee. Pain splintered through her leg. She collapsed and got another boot to the chest. The blow caved her lungs.

"You wanna fight back?" The man's face glowed demonically in the light of the raging barn fire. The pale starburst scar sprawling from his left temple and down his cheek reminded her of a lake with dozens of little rivers flowing away from it.

He grabbed her ankle and dragged her across the dirt to the woodpile. Pain burned through her whole body, and she struggled to breathe as she rolled to one side. She looked up just in time to see a large wolflike creature bounding toward the rest of the group. As it slowed, its body unfurled, and it staggered onto its hind legs until the wolf had been replaced by a naked man.

Weres. Her blood turned to ice. Shape-shifting was not only against the law, but taboo, and forbidden in nearly every magical tradition. These men weren't just thugs—they were abominations.

A shriek rent the air, tearing at Hettie's senses. Abby! She struggled to sit up but found herself staring into the barrel of a sawed-off shotgun.

"Don't." She stared blearily into the pale green eyes of a young, blond-haired man with a drooping mustache. She heard Abby's scream again, and when she flinched, the blond smashed the butt of his weapon against her temple.

The boom of a shotgun came almost at the same time she saw Cymon streak out of the darkness like a flash of dark brown lightning. The dog lunged for one of the men, who yelped and fell to the ground, writhing and punching wildly as Cy worked his massive jaws around the man's throat. Blood spurted, and he shook him hard once before leaping away, barely dodging the shots that hit the now-still bloody body.

Another boom was followed by the crack of Pa's Colt. A body dropped to the ground beside her, a bullet hole between his eyes, and she instantly recognized the redhead from town. A large black wolf growled and lunged at Cymon, and the two beasts clashed and snarled through the dust. Jezebel's demonic whinny heralded her father's arrival, her thunderous hoofbeats echoing in Hettie's bones.

Someone grabbed her by her shirt collar and yanked her up to her knees. "Hold it right there, Jack." The hot barrel of a gun seared her skin as it ground into her jaw. "I got something that might be yours."

The barn fire clearly outlined Pa's broad silhouette, terror blazing in his eyes despite his cool demeanor. He sat astride the big gray-white mare, shotgun in one hand, his sidearm raised and pointed at her captor's head. Jezebel's nostrils flared, the whites of her eyes showing. Sparks filled the sky as the roof of the barn collapsed with a whoosh and a crackle. The air was thick with smoke and the smell of burning meat.

Hettie heard Cymon yelp and whine.

"Your boy's the spitting image of you," the man holding her said.

John Alabama slipped off Jezebel, and she trotted away quickly. His grip flexed around his weapon. "Let 'im go, Butch."

"So you do remember me." He smiled faintly, though no humor reached his eyes.

"I remember." He said it as if they were discussing the weather. "How'd you find me?"

He shook his head and chuckled lowly. "My, but you've gotten sloppy. You killed Frank and Zeke, but you let Harry get away. Poor son of a bitch." He glanced over at the redhead. "He was so excited when he told me he saw you. Told me you took out Shadow Frank like a pro. Two bullets in the face. That always was your style. By the by, have you met Bill?" He nodded to the blond behind him. Hate filled his eyes. "He's Frank's little brother."

John Alabama didn't acknowledge the man. "What do you want, Butch?"

"You know what I came for."

"Diablo's long gone. Lost it when I hit my head and lost all my memories. Even if I knew where it was, I wouldn't tell you. That thing is a piece of evil."

Butch glowered and twisted Hettie's collar so tight she couldn't breathe. "Tell me where Diablo is or else your boy's brains are gonna be painting the ground." He cocked the gun. "Where is it?"

"Not here."

The blood-curdling scream from the house had everyone turning. A large man with a wide brow and an ill-fitting bowler hat had Abby wrapped in bedsheets and slung over his shoulder. He dumped her on the ground and stepped away as she struggled weakly in the tangle of linen. Butch dropped Hettie and walked toward Abby, gun trained on her head. "How about now, Jack? You remember anything now?"

"Daddy..." Abby sobbed.

"Leave them alone!" John shouted. "They ain't done nothin' to you."

"Everyone done something to me, Jack. That's the thing about life. No matter how well you behave, how good you treat others, you'll still get screwed over in the end. You know that better than anyone, don't you?"

"Pa..." Abby started to get up, and Butch slapped her.

John cocked his gun. "You lay a hand on my child again and I will blow it off, Butch Crowe." He was breathing hard, seething through gritted teeth.

"Hey, Butch! Lookee what I found!" A man with long, greasy dark hair had Grace by the wrists. Her lip was split, her dress torn at the shoulder and collar. Butch grinned, the starburst scar stretching across his cheek.

"Well, well. Mrs. Jack Farham, I presume."

"It's Mrs. John Alabama, you cowardly bastards. Let my children go!"

Butch hummed appreciatively. "Feisty one, aren't you? But then, you always did like fighters, didn't you, Jack?"

"What do you want?" Grace demanded.

"It's simple, really." Butch put a foot up on the woodpile. "I'm looking for a lost treasure, madam. A revolver," he said as if he were explaining his needs to a shopkeeper. "Ivory handle, with a barrel the shade of midnight. Really a fine piece of work. There is nothing like it anywhere else in the world. You couldn't possibly miss it if it were, say, decorating your mantel."

Grace raised her chin. "I've never seen anything like that before."

He cocked his chin to the side and addressed the blond behind him. "Bill?"

The young man closed his eyes, muttering an incantation. "She's lying, Butch," the young blond said after a moment, then let out a long breath.

"Well, of course she is. Otherwise she wouldn't let me do this."

He pointed the gun at Hettie and pulled the trigger. Hettie screeched as fire erupted in her thigh. She clutched the hot, sticky mess, moaning.

"I'll do the little one next if you don't tell me where Diablo is."

"Stop! Just stop! John, please, just give it to them!" Grace cried.

"It ain't here." John's hold on the Colt shook, and his voice broke. "I'm sorry, Grace. It ain't here."

"He's telling the truth," the blond confirmed darkly.

Butch's eyebrows lowered. "If it ain't here," he said slowly, "where has it gone?"

"Far away. Probably where you'll never find it." Pa sounded calm. Resigned.

Butch holstered his weapon and threw his hands into the air. "By all that is unholy— Jack, just tell me where the damned gun is!"

"It went away. I don't know where."

Bill nodded his affirmation. Butch planted his hands on his hips, paced back and forth in two short strides. "Well, well, well, well, well. I suppose that doesn't leave me any other choice, does it?"

In a blink, Butch drew his gun and shot her father in the shoulder. Ma screamed. The greasy-haired man grabbed her to keep her from going to him, roughly groping her breasts and giggling. Her antimolestation charm crackled.

"Hedley." Butch's voice was stern.

"C'mon, Butch, it'll be fun. I'll let y'all watch, and you can have her afterward."

"No, Hedley."

"She's a squealer. I know it, Butch." He buried his nose in her neck. "Squeal for me, pretty-pretty. Squeal!" His hand went down to her crotch, and she screeched, tearing at him like a wildcat.

"Animal!" John snarled, swinging his revolver around.

Another crack. Blood blossomed in the center of Pa's chest. The big man in the ill-fitting bowler hat watched impassively as John Alabama dropped to his knees.

Hettie's cry was lost beneath her mother's scream.

Butch glared furiously over his shoulder at the big man, who sucked in his lip and holstered his smoking gun shamefacedly.

"Hedley," Butch bit out, his words vibrating with barely held patience, "step away from the woman."

The greasy-haired man grumbled, then pushed her away. Grace dove for her husband, sobbing, and pressed her hands to his wounds, clutching him.

Butch sighed and took his hat off, baring a thin pate of dark hair. "Jack, you should know you can never escape the life you lived, never atone for the things you've done, especially to your brothers."

"I'm not your brother," Pa ground out. Bloody spittle bubbled from his mouth. "And your petty revenge against me will never get you Diablo."

"No. I s'pose it won't." Butch shrugged, and a small smile appeared on his lips. "But it feels pretty damned good."

He drew and pulled the trigger. A bullet hole appeared between Grace's eyes.

Hettie's mother fell down dead.

Hettie screamed at the same time Pa howled. The fire raged.

"The little one won't be so lucky, I'm afraid." Butch rubbed the back of his neck, looking almost sympathetically toward Abby, who'd gone quiet and still. Her eyes were glazed and distant. "We've got plans for her."

Pa cradled his wife's body across his lap. His wheezing breaths were slowing, getting more labored.

Hettie pulled herself toward the woodpile. The ax was there. She could stop this. She had to stop this—

"Whoops. Forgot about this one."

Hettie's scalp pulled tight as she was lifted to her knees by her hair. She almost didn't feel the pain as she turned her eyes toward Pa.

He stared back at her, unblinking. Tears flowed down his cheeks. She would always remember that look: perfectly calm, as if this were the right thing to do, despite the pain. He looked so much like Paul.

A hot, hard edge grazed her temple.

She thought about her brother and mother and smiled at the thought of being with them. But then she remembered the man she'd killed, and in that instant knew she was bound elsewhere.

Then Hettie smelled cordite and lilies and then nothing.

CHAPTER FIVE

She's coming 'round."

They were words that Hettie knew, a language she understood, but the meaning wasn't clear.

The pain grew, unfurling like a tightly closed bud until it had fully blossomed into every inch of her being. Fire erupted in her limbs, her bowels. Her head throbbed as an intense rainbow of color flickered behind her eyelids. Blood pushed up through her until it swelled against her skull, threatening to pop the top of her head off.

Something prodded her side, and she flinched from the touch. *Feeling* was such a strange sensation. She opened her mouth and experienced a new agony as her lips cracked and blood welled from the new gaps in her flesh.

Was this the hell she'd earned for killing that man?

"Easy."

Something cool touched her lips, filled her mouth. She swallowed.

She tried to murmur her thanks—Ma had come to soothe her fever. She was sick, wasn't she? Abby must've passed her illness along. That was why she felt like this. It must be past dawn by now—she had to get up to feed the horses. Jezebel was particular about her mealtimes, and Pa would be cross if she didn't get around to it quick...

"You are one lucky son of a bitch."

Her brother's voice was so rough. He must be watching over her, the way Pa always said he would. She tried to smile, but her lips cracked again, and she winced.

"Stop that, now. Ain't nothing for you to be smiling about. You look like a lynched cat."

Sweet liquid trickled into the corner of her mouth, filling her with strength. "Miss Hettie, can you open your eyes?"

She obeyed. Blurry shapes floated around her. Someone brought a lantern close. The world came back into slow, painful focus. Dr. Wells brandished a stethoscope.

But then the doctor's face was no longer his, and a shiny pink starburst of curdled flesh grinned back at her. The bleak, black eye of the gun barrel caressed her head...

She cried out and knocked his hands away. Someone held her down, pressing her against the bed. She was so weak she couldn't fight them. She felt the prick of a needle in her arm, and then blessed oblivion.

She had no idea where she was or what time it was when she woke up next. The pain had dulled to an all-over ache, and though her mind seemed mostly alert, her body felt like lead.

She tested her limbs carefully, eyes still closed. A strange feeling around her ear made her touch the side of her head. It was bandaged heavily, and a rawness at her temple throbbed at the touch.

"The fates smile upon you." Hettie opened her eyes to see Patience Yellowhawk, a Cheyenne healer, smiling at her from the corner. Dr. Wells also stood by her bed, his face more serious. The room contained a couple of chairs, a washbasin, an armoire, and the bed she lay on. In one corner, Uncle sat propped against the wall, seemingly asleep.

"You're very lucky, Miss Alabama. We weren't sure you'd make it," the healer said.

"Where..." Her paper-dry throat sent her into a coughing fit. Dr. Wells brought her a glass of water tinged with herbs and mint.

"Rest. You're in Newhaven, at the Gold Lion Inn. You've been through a lot. It'll take time to regain your strength."

Images of fire and blood swept through her like a gale-force wind, battering her mind. She began to tremble. "Where is my family?"

He darted a pitying look at the healer, who closed her eyes.

"Doc. Miss Yellowhawk." Jeremiah Bassett sat forward, tilting his hat off his face. Dark shadows hung beneath his red-rimmed eyes. "Would you mind giving us some privacy?"

They left. The scrape of a chair across the floorboards was like a scream in Hettie's ears, and she winced. Uncle picked up the chair and set it down next to her. His chapped hands folded over his knee, and he bent his head. "Your ma and pa..." His throat convulsed.

She knew then. Knew it the way you knew the fire in the stove had gone out as cold air seeped into your home. "Where'd you put them?" she asked quietly.

"Next to Paul. Under the cottonwood."

The void that opened up inside her threatened to swallow her whole, but curiously absent was pain. No tears came. Maybe she was hurting too much all over to feel one more hurt. "What about Abby?"

"No sign of her anywhere. They ransacked the house, took the horses. The barn burned to the ground. Silo, too."

The nightmare flashed behind her closed eyes, rang in her ears. "It was a man named Butch Crowe," she said. "He had a scar across his face."

Uncle leaned forward, intent. "You see who else was there?"

"There was a big guy with a bowler hat. Another one with dark hair they called Hedley. And a young blond fella named Bill. Butch said he was Shadow Frank's brother. I think he was a truthteller, or some kind of sorcerer."

"Did you see Walker Woodroffe with them?"

"The bounty hunter?"

"He could've lied to us about that. He doesn't strike me as being totally honest."

She closed her eyes, rifling through her memory, trying to sort out the bandits' faces. "No. I didn't see him."

"Doesn't mean he wasn't there," Uncle murmured.

"They wanted something. A revolver." *Ivory handle, with a barrel the shade of midnight.* She closed her eyes, dizzy, but the memories were pushing through her brain like a line of train cars backing into each other, sending her mind hurtling over a cliff. "The gun is Diablo, isn't it? It was in that box you took with you."

The steady look in his eye gave her his answer.

"But why did they want it? What's it for?"

"Stop asking questions. The less you know, the better."

"They killed my parents for that gun. You owe it to me to tell me."

"No, I owe it to your father to keep you safe." He folded his arms over his chest. "So stop asking me questions, otherwise I'll put a curse on you to keep your mouth permanently shut."

She glowered but refused to let the matter go. "Butch is the head of the Crowe gang, ain't he? He knew Pa. Called him brother. Was Pa in their gang? Were you in that gang, too?"

"No," he snapped, disgusted. Uncle scrubbed his bristled jaw and heaved a sigh. "You should rest. We yanked you back from the brink of death. It cost me a pretty penny, and it cost you even more, so don't go wasting my money by getting sick and dying on me."

Was that all he cared about? "How long have I been asleep?"

"Six days."

"Six days?" Who'd been feeding the chickens? Who was making sure the horses were ready for auction? But then she realized all that was gone. Everything she knew was gone...

Protect your sister and mother. Don't let anything happen to them.

"Abby could still be out there, couldn't she?" she asked, clinging to hope. "They didn't kill her. They said...something about plans for her. They must've taken her somewhere. Where would they take her?"

"Don't work yourself up." He forced her to lie back. "Abby's gone, y'hear? So don't get any ideas in your fool head that you can save her."

"She's gotta be out there somewhere. Has the marshal been looking?"

"Of course he has. But the trail went stone-cold four days ago."

"That's because they're Weres. Some of them, anyhow. I saw at least one of them shift. They didn't come in on horses, either. They must have changed into wolves to escape."

"Shape-shifting?" Uncle's brow scrunched in consternation. "Butch never had that kind of magic before." Hettie was beginning to wonder how Jeremiah Bassett knew the gang so well if he hadn't been a member. He grunted. "If they did shift, they couldn't have taken Abby with them. They would have left her behind—"

"You don't know that. Maybe they took her to a wagon and drove off. Maybe they left their horses somewhere else. Maybe they took a remote Zoom tunnel." Hettie pushed herself into a sitting position, determined. "I want to speak to Marshal McCowan."

"It's the middle of the night, Hettie. The marshal's probably asleep now, and you should be, too, if you know what's good for you."

She locked gazes with him. "I'm not sleeping till I speak with the marshal."

He pinched the flesh between his eyes. "Stubborn little...If I promise to have him come see you tomorrow, will you at least pretend you'll lie there and sleep the night away?"

She reluctantly agreed. When she did drift off, though, Butch Crowe's scarred face leered down at her. She snapped herself awake, jerking and making every muscle groan. For the rest of the night, she couldn't shake off the phantom brush of the gun barrel against her throbbing temple, couldn't stop smelling cordite and lilies.

Marshal McCowan came to see her the next morning. She was still too weak to dress, so she kept the blankets tucked high up beneath her chin and received him in her room. Miss Yellowhawk waited in the hall. She'd been a good nurse, neither forcing conversation on Hettie nor trying to comfort her. But she'd been tight-lipped about what had happened after Hettie had been found shot in the head.

"Miss Alabama," the marshal greeted somberly, sweeping his hat off his head and easing into a chair. "I'm glad to see you awake. I'm very sorry for your loss." She couldn't help but notice how wary he was, how he kept a good arm's length away from her. She wasn't too surprised—not many came back from a gunshot to the head. Perhaps he thought she'd been reanimated as a walking undead.

"It's not all lost yet." She took a deep breath. "I want you to tell me about what you've done to search for my sister and the men who murdered my parents."

He wiped a hand across his mouth. Maybe she was being a little too direct, but every minute she wasted was another minute Abby wasn't home. "We fanned out as far Kilraven's Peak to the north, Faraday's Gorge to the west. I had my best trackers on them, but it seems they just vanished."

Those boundaries didn't sound nearly far enough. She was about to tell him so, but the marshal interrupted her thoughts. "Maybe we should talk about what you saw that night. You're the only eyewitness we have. Whatever you can remember might help us."

She hesitated. If she told him about her father's supposed connection to the gang, the marshal might reconsider helping her find Abby. That meant she couldn't say anything about Diablo, either. Any connection between her father and the Crowe gang could be used against her.

"I know it's hard to relive." McCowan's voice broke through her thoughts. "Just start at the beginning. When did you first see these men?"

She focused her story on Abby's abduction. She described Butch Crowe and the others, told him about their shape-shifting abilities. McCowan frowned deeply. "The Crowes have never had that kind of talent. And it takes a special kind of sorcerer to imbue others with Were powers. Sounds to me like they've got a Kukulos warlock on their side."

It made twisted sense for the Crowe gang to align themselves with a warlock. Blood magic was only used by the most unscrupulous, selfish, greedy, and vain of all sorcerers. The Kukulos believed in the superiority of their form of sorcery over all other magics and worked to convert sorcerers to their cause and eradicate other traditions. They were known for all kinds of atrocities, from transmogrifying people into animals to drinking the blood of children to sustain their power.

If her sister was being taken to this warlock to be used in some evil ritual, they needed to find her fast. "What's it going to take to find Abby?"

Marshal McCowan scrubbed his jaw. "To be frank, Miss Alabama, the trail's gone cold, and we're stretched too thin to continue the search. The sheriff's office simply doesn't have the resources. We've got our hands full just watching Newhaven and the ranches around us."

And where had the patrol been the night of her family's massacre? She tamped down the anger boiling inside her. "Abby's still out there, marshal."

He shook his head. "I'm sorry, Hettie. We're keeping an eye out, but...I just can't spare anyone for a recovery mission."

Recovery. As in, bringing a body home. She squeezed her eyes closed, listening to the throb of her pulse, the air whistling through her clenched teeth.

No. If Abby were dead, she'd know it.

McCowan stood slowly, pushing his hat back on. "I'm sorry again, Miss Alabama."

"*Sorry* won't find Abby," she spat.

If the marshal couldn't help, she'd have to find someone who could.

It was another week before Hettie was strong enough to walk from one end of the room to the other without her legs trembling. She was determined to get better. Every second she delayed carried Abby farther and farther away from her.

Everyone in town had heard about her miraculous recovery. A few people came to visit, bringing small gifts of food and clothing along with their condolences. Hettie couldn't help but think they'd only come to gawk at her. They all said how brave and strong she was, what a tragedy it was to lose her family and livelihood. They cried and said prayers, lit candles and promised her aid if she needed it. But none of their mealy words penetrated. She felt nothing for the life that had been violently taken from her. It was as if that old life were something she'd read in a book. Grief for her parents would not come, so she clung to the one thing she did feel strongly about: the deep-seated need to get out of that room and find her sister.

By the end of the week, she was strong enough to endure the ride to the ranch. The hostler lent them a cart and a strong horse. Marshal McCowan wanted to send a man with her, probably as an olive branch to make up for his paltry efforts in finding Abby. But Uncle told him Hettie needed space to grieve.

The cart jounced her hard as they took to the road at a brisk pace. It was a gray day, the summer heat subdued for the moment. Hettie's right thigh ached horribly. She'd gotten lucky, Dr. Wells had said. The bullet had been easily removed, and the wound had healed cleanly. In some twisted way, she was grateful for the pain. The throbbing, burning, stabbing sensations told her she was alive—told her that she could feel something beyond emptiness.

They crested the hill on the road leading to the ranch. Hettie thought she was seeing a strange twilight land sitting in the middle of a verdant field, but then she realized the smudges of black against gray were what was left of her home. The horse slowed and came to a dead stop at the edge of the property.

Hettie clambered out of the cart, a quiver beginning low in her stomach. Bruise-colored shadows painted everything, and the world was eerily still. No birds sang. The sickly sweet perfume of rotting and overripe fruit drifted to her.

"I had the house boarded up." Jeremiah's gruff voice broke the silence as he got down from the cart. "The Gunnersons' men have been coming by on their patrols, keeping an eye on things…"

His voice faded, drowned out by the rushing in her ears as she took in the destruction all around her. The collapsed, blackened skeleton of the barn creaked in the wind. The silo was nothing but a tall pile of charred timbers, crumbling mortar, and loose stones. Broken glass and singed straw littered the ground.

She turned away from the sight and found herself staring at the woodpile. A dark red-brown stain had soaked into the ground there, and a metallic odor drifted up to her nose.

The starburst scar flashed in her mind, along with Butch's demonic grin. Nausea struck her, and she doubled over, dry heaving.

"You ain't ready for this," Uncle said. "We should take you back."

"I'm fine," she insisted after a few deep breaths. "It's been too long. I need to see Ma and Pa proper."

She crossed the grounds to the cottonwood on the hill. Uncle followed at a distance. She was winded by the time she reached the crest.

Simple wooden crosses adorned with garlands of dried flowers and herbs marked the places where her father and mother rested. The two new graves looked completely out of place next to Paul's. Her father's grave would be the one on the far left, her mother sandwiched between him and her son. There was room for three more to the right of Paul. She could see that someone had started turning up the earth next to his, but it had only been half dug, then hastily filled back in and tamped down.

She knelt to touch the crosses. She thought she'd be racked with sobs by now. Instead, she came up against a hard wall of unfeeling, smooth and numb like a thick callus.

She closed her eyes and tried to squeeze out a tear. She even pinched her arm, but the tears that came were only for the pain she'd inflicted on herself. Her cry of anguish morphed into rage, and she shot to her feet and paced, kicking the tree.

Cry, you idiot. Your parents are dead. Cry!

The wind sighed through the cottonwood's branches.

Hettie...

"Abby?" She looked around frantically. Was her sister hiding somewhere? She took two steps and yelled her sister's name into the wind. "Where are you?"

"Where's who?" Uncle approached, eyes darting around.

Her gaze flew in every direction, searching. What if all this time Abby had been here on the ranch? She looked toward the house.

"I can hear her," she exclaimed. "I can hear Abby." She rushed down the hill and searched through the rubble for signs of life. She called Abby's name over and over as she circled the house, checking all her favorite hiding spots, then finally pried off the boards over the front door with her bare hands and went inside.

Everything within had been torn, smashed, and overturned. She was surprised the Crowe gang hadn't torched the place. When she found no sign of her sister, she closed her eyes, straining.

Hettie...

She bolted out the door and ran to the creek, feet slipping on the wet grass. Abby's voice seemed louder here, and Hettie stared around. "Abby! Where are you?"

She heard whispers, indistinct and breathy. She splashed into the water and they grew even louder, but she still couldn't make out what they were saying. "Abby!" Her breathing came out in ragged gasps. Abby was here. She was alive.

Hettie followed the creek, sloshing through the knee-high water. The bed grew slippery, and she tripped and splashed into the freezing cold, head going under.

It's dark. Help me, Hettie...

A pair of strong hands grabbed her by the shoulders and yanked her up. She sputtered and coughed as the cold walloped her.

Uncle dragged her out of the creek. "What in tarnation are you doing?"

"It's Abby." She wiped water out of her eyes and pushed his hands off. "I can hear her."

"That's it, we need to go back to the inn," Uncle said.

"No, I have to find her..." But her limbs had been sapped of strength, the iciness seeping into her bones. The bandages around her head were soaking wet, and rivulets of pink water ran off her fingertips.

"It's your grief talking," Uncle said. "You were shot in the head, girlie. You're hearing things."

She shook her head, trembling. No. She wasn't crazy. She'd heard Abby. She was certain of it.

The grasses stirred behind her, and they both froze. Uncle whipped out his revolver, but then a streak of dark brown leaped out. Hettie screamed as the mass bowled her over.

"Cymon!" She threw her arms around the dog's thick neck. His body shook with the violence of his wagging tail, and he was caked with mud and covered with scratches. He butted his head against her, whining and howling his joy.

"Good dog." At last, tears brimmed, and she buried her face against his shoulder. A sob broke from her lips as she scratched him behind the ears. He flopped down on the dirt beside her, wriggling and sighing.

Uncle made her go back to the house and ordered her to change out of her wet clothes and pack what she wanted to take with her. Cymon ran in and out of the rooms, sniffing and giving low, questioning woofs. Once Hettie was dry and clean, she packed trousers and shirts, sweaters, boots and undergarments, then got Pa's worn duster and slipped it on. It was too big for her, but it was the best coat for traveling and would keep the elements out. She breathed in the scent of tobacco and grass, rain and horses, and wrapped it more closely around herself.

Uncle looked up as she came out, fully dressed. "Help me find my rifle," she said.

His mouth firmed. "Why? What're you planning?"

She didn't answer as she went room to room, Cymon trailing after her.

They found her Winchester on the roof where she'd dropped it the night of the attack. Veins of orange rust had grown between the joints, and her ammunition had been left out in the elements. It was going to be a mess—it might not even work after she was through cleaning it—but having this vital piece of her old life filled the void, lent her strength.

She'd need strength if she was going to find Abby.

CHAPTER SIX

When they got back to town, Hettie visited Mr. Smitherman, her father's lawyer. He sat down with her and detailed the value of her family's remaining assets. She'd grown up sitting in the chair next to Pa when he went on their regular visits, so the old man didn't condescend.

What she was left with wasn't enough for what she had in mind. "Sell the grazing property. Leave me the house and my family plot."

Mr. Smitherman frowned. "Are you sure about that, Miss Hettie? You've been through an awful shock..."

"I need the money right now, Mr. Smitherman. I appreciate that you're trying to help, but I intend to find my sister, and I'll need the funds. Meanwhile, I'll need the whole of Pa's savings withdrawn in cash."

The lawyer hesitated but didn't argue. He walked with her to the bank and spoke to the manager, who argued that a young woman on her own—and especially one grieving for her family—should keep her money where it could be managed properly.

"I'm not interested in what you have to say about my ability to manage my own funds, Mr. Phipps," Hettie argued, cold steel in her voice. "Unless you're telling me that the bank doesn't have the cash to serve my request."

Mr. Smitherman smiled wryly as the manager sputtered and hurried to make the withdrawal. They watched the manager's lightning-fast fingers count out the bills.

"I've seen that look in the eyes of men before," Mr. Smitherman said to her.

She took the bills and recounted them, then started bundling them into her pockets and her boot. "I intend to hire someone who will bring my sister home." No sense in lying to him.

Mr. Phipps and Mr. Smitherman exchanged looks. "With all due respect, are you sure about this? That's a lot of money to be carrying around. And you without an escort…"

"I trust you and your employees won't be foolish enough to spread rumors about my temporary wealth," she said pointedly.

The manager flinched. "Of course not."

Mr. Smitherman spoke up. "If you need a security escort or a private investigator, the Pinkerton Agency is full of reliable, trustworthy men."

"That's true," Mr. Phipps added. "They helped my second cousin find his wife after she up and left him." He sniffed.

Hettie had heard about the Pinkerton Agency. Some said they employed more sorcerers than the Division did. If that was so, they could probably track down Butch and his men.

At the hotel, she wrote a long letter relating her sad tale and sent it off by express mail to the Pinkerton Agency headquarters in Chicago. While she waited for a response, she settled her affairs with the lawyer. The grazing land was snatched up at a decent price, as were the remaining cattle.

Maybe it was a reckless move financially, but she couldn't run a ranch on her own. Whatever dreams she'd had of taking over for Pa had literally gone up in smoke. She wasn't sure she could ever go back to that place now that it had been desecrated. If she did, it would either be to bury Abby…or join her family in the earth.

Ten long, miserable days went by. She never told Uncle about the letter she'd sent—he was too busy drowning his sorrows in the saloon. She'd nearly given up hearing back until finally, a thick envelop with a bright foil flourish stamped with the letter *P* arrived. She tore the envelope open, and a small, flat stone etched with markings fell out of the pouch. She read the enclosed letter.

Dear Miss Hettie Alabama,

My sincerest condolences regarding your loss. It is always unbearably tragic when we hear about the deaths of good and innocent folk at the hands of uncivilized brutes. We here at the Pinkerton Agency will do whatever we can to track down these bandits and bring them to justice. While we normally charge a finder's fee for missing persons, I am making an exception due to the outrageous nature of this terrible crime. I am giving you my full, personal support, pro bono, in this mission.

We will be dispatching an agent right away via remote Zoom tunnel. Attached, you'll find an amulet beacon that will link the two ends of the tunnel. A drop of your blood pressed into the center will notify us that you are ready to receive us. Time is of the essence: please use the amulet as soon as you receive this letter.

Sincerely,
Detective Thomas Stubbs

Hettie broke into a smile for the first time since she'd awoken from death. She couldn't believe her good fortune. Sending people through remote Zoom tunnels was expensive and dangerous for the sorcerers who controlled the portals. She couldn't believe the Pinkerton Agency's generosity. She quickly found a pin and pricked her finger, then pressed the bead of bright red blood into the center of the amulet. A fizzle went through her veins.

Her heart beat hard. Soon, they'd find Abby and put the Crowe gang behind bars.

The heavy thud of boots clomped up the stairs, and Uncle burst through the door. His eyes were cloudy, his nose red. He muttered, "I need to sleep."

"Uncle, look." She brought him the letter and amulet. "An agent is coming. He's going to help me find Abby."

"A what now?" He blinked down at the letter.

"I wrote the Pinkerton Agency and offered them money to bring Abby home. I know it wasn't a lot, but they're going to do it for free—"

"Pinkerton?" Jeremiah glared down at her. "You wrote to that bunch of amoral black hats?"

"Everyone's vouched for them—" But she didn't get any further as Uncle grabbed his hat off his head and started slapping her with it.

"You stupid, foolish cow!" He chased her to the other end of the room, stumbling and tripping over furniture. "Don't you know what that outfit is?"

"Quit it!" She grabbed his hat and flung it across the room. "They're private investigators and soldiers. We're going to need all the help we can get if we're going to find Abby. What's so wrong about them?"

"What did you tell them? All of it, girl, quickly. What did you write them about?"

"I told them about Pa and Ma and Abby. I told them I survived and that Butch Crowe might have my sister."

"And did you say anything about Diablo?"

"Of course not. I don't want them to think Pa was some kind of outlaw."

"Well, that's something," he muttered.

"I don't see what all the fuss is about, unless *you're* a wanted criminal." She eyed him and waited for him to give away his secret, but even inebriated, his grizzled features revealed nothing. "Anyways, they'll be here soon."

"What do you mean *soon?*"

She held out the amulet. "They're sending the agent by remote Zoom tunnel."

Uncle wheeled around and hauled out her empty bags from under the bed. "Pack. Now."

She shook her head. "I'm not going anywhere." She crossed her arms over her chest. "You're drunk. Go lie down."

"Don't you read the newspaper? The Pinks are nothing but a bunch of thugs for hire. They're no better than the Crowe gang, only they have a license to operate." Jeremiah got right into her face. The whiskey on his breath was strong, but his eyes were focused and lit with menace. "Listen to me. When that agent gets here, he'll suck every last truth out of you, and when he finds out we had Diablo, he'll kill us." He snatched the amulet out of her hand, held it before him, and started muttering in a language she didn't recognize. Slowly, the light gray stone turned dark, and the drying drop of blood reformed into a wet blob that he wiped off with his sleeve. "That's not going to buy us a lot of time."

She stared wide-eyed. "How did you do that?"

He didn't answer as he stuffed clothes into her bag. He drew his revolver and checked it. "Get your money and your gun."

"Why—"

"Will you stop asking questions and just obey me for once?" He snapped the wheel of his revolver back. "Just think for a minute, you half-witted ninny. Why would the Pinkerton Agency send someone all the way out here to investigate a missing child using a remote Zoom tunnel, much less do it for free? You had to have tipped them off somehow. Crowe and his gang are growing larger and more dangerous by the week. The Pinks will wonder why they'd target your family. They'll search the area, and they'll find traces of strong magics. They'll know *I* was there. They'll know your pa was there. And they'll go after you until you can give them Diablo." He holstered his weapon. "I can't let them have it, you hear? And I'd let your ma and pa die a thousand times over to make sure they don't get it."

Her lungs shrank, and her heart turned to lead. She watched, rapt, as he yanked out a long bit of braided twine from around the windowsill, then searched the armoire, removing some smooth river stones and tiny bones. From beneath a loose floorboard under the chamber pot, he pulled out a hank of hair and used it to sweep the top of the door frame off. A bunch of ceramic and glass beads rained down.

"What is all that?" she asked.

"Protection." He collected them hastily and stuffed them into his already bulging pockets.

All the time she'd lain in bed, she hadn't noticed a single one of those talismans. When had Uncle accumulated so many wards? How could he even afford them? Slowly, a hazy picture was forming in her mind, but she still had no idea of what—or who—she was looking at. "You and Pa wanted that box off the ranch after Mr. Woodroffe came." She'd seen how his arrival had scared Uncle sober. "But I thought you told Pa he wasn't a Pinkerton agent."

"Doesn't matter who he was. I knew what he was after." He reached into his pockets. "Put this on." He shoved a braided necklace of hair and small, irregular stones into her hand.

"What is it?"

"A talisman against the Eye."

Heat suffused her. The Eye let a sorcerer watch a subject continuously, even at her most vulnerable and private moments. It was blood magic, too. Gingerly, she pulled the necklace on, feeling a slight tingle along her arms as the magic cloaked her. "How could the Pinkerton Agency Eye me? I didn't send them bits of me they could use..." She glanced around nervously.

"The Pinks have an army of sorcerers working for them. Careful you might be, but you never know what you leave behind—an eyelash, a hair, a bit of skin... And they don't much care if a spell's taboo, so long as it gets the job done. If they want to find you, they will, and they can do a whole bunch of nasty things to you without ever looking you in the face." He picked up her bag and shoved it into her arms. "Out the back. Better if no one knows when we left or where we're going."

She stalled in the doorway, reeling, feeling a sense of déjà vu, same as the night Pa had told them all to pack and flee the ranch. "Why're you just standing there?" Jeremiah barked.

Hettie gestured helplessly. "We haven't paid the bill."

Uncle gripped her arms. "Listen, Hettie." His voice was cold and hard. "The Pinks are out to hurt you. They will find you and make you give them everything. They don't care about anything except getting the job done. The last thing you need to worry about is skipping out on a hotel bill."

Uncle's proclamation clung to her, and suddenly it felt as if the Pinkertons were breathing down her neck. Her heart rate doubled. He gave her a firm push, and she stumbled into the alleyway. Her skin erupted in goose bumps. The air was as cold and crisp as a December morning, even though it was midsummer. Jeremiah sniffed the wind and swore. "C'mon!" He yanked her toward the far end of the street. Hettie stumbled after him, a mixture of bewilderment and terror scraping across her senses like a straight razor on a leather strop.

A shadow blotted out the main thoroughfare as inky clouds gathered directly above. Men shouted, dogs barked, and the people of Newhaven scooped up their children and drew them away from the pinprick of darkness growing in the middle of the road. Crowds gathered in the street to watch.

Uncle swore, "Damnation!" and drew his gun as he crashed against the side of a building. Hettie crouched down next to him, out of breath.

"Uncle, what—"

"You stay here," he said. "Hide and don't make a sound, y'hear? Soon as you get my signal, you take the first horse you find and run. Don't look back. Just *run*." He pushed up from his crouch and streaked away faster than she'd ever seen him move.

Frozen to the spot, Hettie didn't know what to do, and realized too late she had no idea what signal Uncle could possibly mean. The darkness gathering in the thoroughfare had resolved into a small, cloudy vortex about the size of a large dog and was growing bigger. She could see its edges in between the buildings, ribbons of opaque fog swirling around a pancake of blue-black hovering midair. A fistful of light punched through the center and blossomed open. The townsfolk eased back but watched, rapt. For most people in Newhaven, including Hettie, this was their first time seeing a remote Zoom. Everyone stayed far back: getting caught in the path of a Zoom tunnel aperture in the midst of opening or closing could sever a man's limbs like a cigar cutter.

The blinding light grew with the portal. As if someone had opened a door, a harsh, chill wind gusted from the opening, turning the moisture in the damp air into a blanket of mist that rolled out over the dirt. A carpet of delicate crystals formed across the hard-packed earth. The portal was now as big as a horse. And from it stepped a man.

Hettie went cold inside. He was dressed immaculately in black with a spotless bowler hat and a pearly white cravat. A shining silver badge in the shape of an eye was pinned to his breast pocket. He radiated power—even the ungifted could sense it. His gaze slowly swept the thoroughfare but stopped dead when he caught her stare from the narrow alley.

Her heart seized and her limbs turned to jelly as the man turned toward her with the deliberation of a Mechanik's automaton. His unblinking gaze never left hers as he advanced, menace in every step—

His face exploded in a shower of red before she registered the gunshot.

Screams erupted, and the townfolk scattered. Hettie gripped the corner of the building, tasting bile. In the next moment, Uncle was at her side again, sweating and red-faced.

"We gotta go!" he rasped, towing on her stiff form.

"What..." Her mouth worked, but no words came. She finally got past the tight lump in her throat. "What happened?"

"Nothing you need to worry about." The gray mustang awaited them around the corner. Jeremiah mounted and glared down at her, nearly breathless. "Are you going to get on, or are you going to jog behind me?"

She climbed onto the nervous gray's back. Hettie whistled for Cymon.

"We can't take that damn mutt with us," Uncle said as the dog bounded toward them.

"I can't leave Cy alone."

"He's too conspicuous. Anyone who knows you knows that dog. Better he's left here so that people think we're still around town." Cymon trotted happily alongside the horse, tongue hanging out. Jeremiah waved him away, tried to maneuver the mustang into the dog's path, but Cymon was not deterred.

"Tell that dog to scram." Uncle spurred the mustang into a brisk canter. "Or I swear I'll shoot him where he stands."

Hettie glared, then turned in the saddle. "Shoo, Cy. Stay. Go find Will. You're safer with him. I can't take you with me."

Cymon slowed, his happy grin falling. "Stay!" Hettie warned again, hot tears gathering in her throat.

He sat down in the dirt, watching them go, and whined as Uncle whipped the mustang into a full gallop.

Y

Uncle wouldn't tell her anything about what had happened to the Pinkerton agent as they sped away from Newhaven. She suspected he'd been the cause and simply didn't want to scare her, but she was plenty frightened right now.

Twice they'd doubled back and walked the horse in a wide circle, Uncle shaking talismans and muttering spells as he went. Misdirection spells, he'd told her. They seemed to work—she had no idea where she was.

As the sun swept lower over the horizon, she finally recognized the parcel of land they were on.

"Why're we here?" she asked as he hitched the mustang outside the Gunnersons' house. The elderly couple was the closest family within ten miles of the ranch. She couldn't imagine they'd be very helpful with the Pinkerton Agency chasing them.

"We need a horse." He walked up the stoop and knocked, whipping his hat off and smoothing back his hair. A moment later, Mr. Gunnerson came to the door, shouldering a shotgun. He smiled broadly, his moon face creasing with happy lines. "Jeremiah Bassett, so good to see you!" He peered around him, and his smile softened. "And Miss Hettie Alabama. You are a sight for sore eyes. Please, come in. We've got supper on the table and more than enough to share."

Hettie found she was starving. As she wolfed down rabbit stew and good bread, Mr. and Mrs. Gunnerson told her how sorry they were about her parents' deaths, what a tragedy she'd suffered, and how blessed she was that the Lord had spared her life. Hettie endured it as she had all the visitors to her sickbed. She could hear the way they were working up to something, though, and it was only when the childless couple offered to take Hettie in that Uncle interrupted.

"Hettie has an aunt she'll be staying with, and we're aiming to get her there as quick as possible."

Mrs. Gunnerson tilted her chin to one side. "Aunt? I thought Grace and John were both only children."

"Distant aunt," Uncle corrected. Hettie peered at him over her hunk of bread but didn't dispute his claim.

"Well, if it's fast you're aiming for, you could take the train. Cheaper than the Zoom tunnel in any case," Mr. Gunnerson said, and Mrs. Gunnerson nodded in agreement. "Where is this aunt of yours?"

"Boston," Jeremiah replied quickly. "I was hoping you could lend us a horse..."

"Lend—Gracious, I forgot entirely. Your pa's old mare, Jezebel—we found her wandering a few days ago. She's holed up in our stable."

Uncle and Hettie looked at each other and shot to their feet. They followed Mr. Gunnerson to the barn. Sure enough, Jezebel stood in a stall, ears twitching as they approached. Hettie drew closer, and the old mare lowered her head to her shoulder, blowing and snuffling her hair as if checking her for injury. Hettie threaded her fingers through the horse's mane and scratched her behind the ears. Jezebel shuddered.

"I wasn't sure what to do with her when we found her. Wasn't sure she'd even live through the night, she was so...well, I reckon she was heartbroken."

Poor Jezebel, Hettie thought. *She must be grieving for Pa.* She cupped the mare's soft, hairy chin, feeling that peculiar sense of numbness that came over her whenever she tried to think about her parents. How could she feel more for Pa's horse than she could feel for Pa himself?

Uncle murmured some words of gratitude and reached into his pocket for a handful of bills. Mr. Gunnerson started to protest, but Jeremiah forced the money into his hand. Hettie caught a glimpse of something slipped into the man's palm. It looked like a sachet of some kind, possibly a poultice. Instantly, Mr. Gunnerson relaxed.

"We're going to need to borrow a saddle," Uncle said.

"Of course," Mr. Gunnerson replied smilingly.

"And maybe you can convince Mrs. Gunnerson to spare some provisions for the road? Perhaps in exchange for this?" He handed him a second packet, which the farmer took without question.

Hettie watched the old man drift back toward the house without another word.

Uncle sagged, letting out a long breath as he leaned against the stall door. "Get her saddled. We can't stay here."

She did as she was told, feeling a touch queasy. She wasn't sure she wanted to ask what he'd just done to Mr. Gunnerson, but that sachet sure looked like some kind of talisman for a spell. In a few minutes, they were back on the road. The Gunnersons didn't even come to wave good-bye.

"What was that back there?" Hettie asked Uncle warily once they were on their way. Jezebel hesitated beneath Hettie's handling, nickering her own questions and apprehension softly. "What did you do to the Gunnersons?"

"Nothing you need to concern yourself with." Uncle slumped over the saddle horn, pale.

"I wish you'd stop saying that." She kicked the mare a little harder than necessary. Jezebel snorted indignantly and picked up the pace. "I'm not stupid, you know. You put some kind of curse on the Gunnersons, didn't you?"

"It wasn't a curse. I mean, it was. They're just not going to remember much about our visit is all. Perfectly harmless."

Harmless? She didn't think any magic that played with a man's mind was harmless. "Where'd you get all those talismans?" she asked. "Where'd you even learn all these spells?"

"Here and there." His eyes stayed fixed on the sliver of sun sinking below the horizon.

"And that . . . man today in Newhaven? Was that your doing, too?"

He didn't respond. Just kept staring into the distance, even though there was little more to see than the shadows of the mountains melting into the sky. Fed up with his silence, she spurred Jezebel ahead to block the mustang's path. "Answer me, dammit. I want to know what's going on right now, or I swear, I am going straight back to Newhaven and telling everyone you shot that Pinkerton agent."

He clenched the reins tight and snorted. "Shows how much you know. He wasn't shot at all."

Not shot? But... she'd heard the gunshot, hadn't she? "It was you, though, wasn't it?" she asked. "Whatever happened... *you* made it happen somehow."

Uncle glared up at the sky, as if the heavens would send him patience. "If I told you I did, would you get out of my way and keep moving?"

Hettie drew back a little. She'd expected him to deny it. "Tell me how you did... whatever you did to that Pinkerton man."

"Now that you *really* don't need to know." He nudged the gelding around Jezebel, and Hettie followed.

"If you can do magic like that, why are we running? For that matter, why didn't you stick around and help fight off the Crowe gang when they came?"

Jeremiah tucked his chin in. "You wouldn't understand."

"What wouldn't I understand? That you're a yellow-bellied coward? That you ran and left us all to die? That you're running again instead of helping me look for Abby?"

"I ain't no coward." His glare burned like a furnace fire. "Face facts, Hettie. Do you really think Abby's still alive in the hands of those... those..." He bit back his words and cursed. "We have a more important mission now, and that's to get you away from the Pinks."

"Why?"

"I told you why."

She was through with these roundabout non-answers. "If all they want is Diablo, then why not just give it to them? If you'd done that in the first place, Ma and Pa might still be alive."

"No, they wouldn't be," he rasped. His face twisted in pain. "Butch had it out for your pa."

"Why? What'd Pa ever do to him?"

Uncle stared out across the darkening land, past the distant, rolling hills. Wind-blasted rock jutted from the earth like bones on a too-skinny nag. His shoulders straightened, parallel to the set of his lips.

"Your father and Butch ran in the Crowe gang together," he said finally. "Before he was John Alabama, your pa's name was Jack Farham. But most people knew him as Elias Blackthorn."

CHAPTER SEVEN

Hettie's hands went slack around the reins. "You're insane, old man. Pa would never be a part of a gang. And Elias Blackthorn's just a fairy tale."

Jeremiah spat in the dirt. "Elias Blackthorn's a real person. Or persons, I should say. He's an outlaw who never dies because he's always being replaced. The demon in the story is Diablo, the Devil's Revolver, which gets passed down to each successive Blackthorn. So the legend is true to a certain extent."

The pieces of the puzzle were starting to form a larger picture. Pa had shot Shadow Frank on sight...because he'd recognized him. And the night of the massacre, Butch Crowe certainly seemed to be familiar with her pa.

It was almost too fantastic to believe. She pictured Pa's sunny smiles, the way he'd wax his thick mustache on holidays and bow his head in church. The way he'd lean back after eating one of Ma's hearty meals and declare that his wife was the best cook in the county, even if she had burned the bread or overdone the brisket. He'd loved his family, been a strong, patient, and caring father. This was not a man who could have been a murdering outlaw, much less a legendary bandit with a diabolical weapon.

"Why should I believe anything you say?" she asked. Her head throbbed, the wound on her temple feeling as if it might split open.

"You said you wanted to know the truth. I can't be held accountable for what you do or don't believe."

She pinched her lips together. The old man didn't have any reason to lie, unless he was simply being cruel. Part of her hoped that was the case—this was all too fantastical. "How did Pa know Butch Crowe?" she asked slowly.

"John and him were in the Crowe gang since before their voices started to crack. 'Course, it wasn't called the Crowe gang back then—they were the Blackthorn Rogues. Butch's pa was Elias Blackthorn at the time. Just before he died, he gave Diablo to your pa, made him the new Elias. Butch wasn't too happy about that and challenged him for the gun. John—or Jack, as he was known back then—didn't want to fight him, so instead he took off."

Hettie flushed hot with angry disbelief. She refused to believe her father was a coward. Maybe he'd left for other reasons. Maybe he was trying to force the gang to go straight by taking their source of power away. Maybe he'd wanted to escape the outlaw life. She blew out a frustrated breath. "How do you know all this?"

He sighed. "Understand, this is all ancient history. Years ago, I worked as an agent for the Division of Sorcery. I was sent to track down and retrieve the Devil's Revolver. Took me a while, but I eventually caught up with your pa in Alabama. I'd been after him for near on nine months, but he was a slippery fella. I knew if I didn't kill him first, he sure as hell would kill me. Problem was, I was stupid enough to think I could go toe-to-toe with him. But your Pa...he was young. About the age you are now, in fact.

"I had him in my sights, but my shot went wide. I thought I was a goner. But something went wrong with Diablo. I didn't think it could misfire, but it looked like the kickback knocked him out. When he came to, he didn't have a lick of sense in him. Didn't know his name, where he was, what year it was, nothing. I couldn't rightly kill him then. So I took him back to town to see a doctor. He named himself John Alabama, after the state he woke up in."

"And...you stayed with him. You had Diablo, and you still stayed with him."

"Diablo doesn't miss. And normally, neither do I." He rubbed his jaw thoughtfully. "If the Devil's Revolver malfunctioned, it was for a reason. Call it what you will...a sign from the gods, destiny...I've seen too much in my lifetime to ignore fate's intervention. I could just as easily have been the one killed that day, but it didn't happen. Made me think I had some other purpose. So I helped set up your pa with a job riding as security escorts for payrolls. Eventually, we ended up in Montana, where he met your ma. They bought the ranch, and then you bunch came along. You know the rest."

"But what about Diablo? Weren't people still looking for it?"

Uncle scratched his nose. "They were. But Jack—your pa, that is—had disappeared. Butch and his boys were way down South, so I didn't think they'd come all this way looking for him. Didn't think they'd even figure he was still alive. I did what I could to keep John from curious busybodies and stayed off the radar myself. And I made sure Diablo stayed hidden, too." He pulled the brim of his hat lower over his eyes. "Shoulda known it wouldn't last forever."

Hettie struggled to make sense of all this information. She might have chalked it up to an old man's drunken delusions of grandeur if it weren't for the fact that Uncle hadn't had a drink in nearly six hours. "If you were working for the Division, why didn't you take the gun and bring it to them?"

"It's complicated. Let's just say I didn't agree with all their politics. Anyhow, I'd quit the Division long before I found your pa in Alabama. I only kept after him because…" He trailed off, wiped a hand over his mouth. "Well. It's a long story."

"So why is Diablo so important? What makes it so special?"

He pursed his lips. "I've already said too much."

"It's a gun, right? So what does it do? And where is it now?"

"Damned if I tell you," Jeremiah scoffed.

"If Butch's gang has Abby, we could trade it for her."

"By the Almighty, Hettie—" He bit off his words. "Abby's probably maggot food by now. There's no reason to believe otherwise."

Her blood sizzled in her veins, pushing through her hot and thick. She said through clenched teeth, "She's my sister. If she were dead, I'd know it."

He met her eye. "Blood bonds are the strongest, Hettie, but even they can't possibly tell you that."

"I don't care." She had to cling to this if her grip on her old reality was slipping. The world could go to hell; but until she saw

Abby's lifeless body, she would stick to this one truth. She fixed her sight on the horizon. "She's out there somewhere. I won't rest till I find her."

He sighed. "Then I hope you're prepared to never sleep again."

Ⴗ

They made camp when the moon was high and Hettie's chin started to droop. While she started a small fire, Uncle walked in a wide circle around the site, muttering a spell that made her skin feel tight, as though someone had pulled a shroud around her.

"If you can do all these spells, why'd you make Pa buy all those wards? We could've saved that money for other things."

"Didn't they teach you anything in regular school about how magic works? Working long-lasting spells takes strength and willpower. They're like trying to hang on to greased-up boulders. You have too many spells going at once, you're bound to lose your grip on one, and I was juggling ten or fifteen at a time already."

"Why so many?"

"To keep John and me out of sight. The Division never did take my resignation gracefully." He sat heavily, wiping a hand across his brow.

"Are you all right?"

"I've been keeping us under a protection spell all day. I don't have the energy I used to."

She felt a little sorry for the old man. They'd never gotten along much, but he was doing his best to take care of her, she supposed. She was the one who'd gotten them into this mess in the first place. "I'll take the first watch."

He waved her off. "No need. The barrier should keep out all the nasties. Just get some sleep. We've got a long road ahead."

"But where are we going?"

"Georgia. I've got friends there who can protect you."

She bristled. "I don't need protecting. I need to find Abby. And anyhow, aren't we pointed in the wrong direction if we want to go to Georgia?"

"We'll circle back, get a train heading south from Jacobs Springs. The important thing right now is avoiding the Pinks."

She rubbed her temples. "I don't understand. Why are you so worried about them?"

Jeremiah eased himself down onto the dirt, leaning up against his saddle. "Thomas Stubbs, that man who wrote to you—he was a colleague of mine in my government days. He had an unhealthy obsession with finding Diablo and was mad as hell when I was picked for the mission over him. I'll never forget ol' Stubby's face when I rode off." He stirred the fire and then got comfortable, pulling a blanket over him. "I guess he quit and joined up with the Pinks."

He closed his eyes, his breathing evening out. Hettie's mind kept circling back to the object everyone was bent on finding, and she couldn't sleep. "In the stories Pa told me about Elias Blackthorn...his demon—Diablo—could kill five men in one swoop. Does that mean—"

He cracked an eye open. "That the Devil's Revolver can shoot five men dead with one bullet? Far as I know, no. It's an enchanted gun, but it's still a gun. Magic plays by certain rules. No one knows how Diablo's enchanted, though. Your Winchester, for instance"— he nodded toward her rifle—"the wood in the stock was magicked so that it would never warp, never need much in the way of care. It's what keeps it shooting straight." For a moment, he watched the sparks from the fire sail into the sky. "Diablo's made of metal and wood and ivory. It takes bullets, but it doesn't need 'em. Magic takes care of that."

Hettie thought about the other tales she'd heard. "Can it shoot around corners? Like in the story about Elias and the Mad Bull?"

"I wouldn't know about that."

"You mean you had it all this time and you never tested it out?"

His look cut her like the lash of a whip. "You don't need to stick your hand in the fire to know it'll burn."

"I don't get it. What's so dangerous about it?"

He burrowed deeper into his blanket. "Go to sleep, girl. The thing is buried and long gone. No one will ever find it."

Hettie closed her eyes, but she couldn't shake the feeling that wherever Diablo was hiding now, it wouldn't stay hidden forever.

81

Hettie was in a cage. The straw bedding was damp and filthy, and the stench of urine filled the air. Disgusted, she pulled away and drifted up toward the high ceiling. She was in a dark, dank, windowless room. Cages big enough to hold pigs lined the walls. Inside, she saw movement—filthy animals curled in balls... except...

"Abby!" She sat up, the cold night air slapping her to wakefulness. The dream faded, leaving only ghostly impressions of squalor and despair behind.

Jezebel nickered softly from where she was picketed.

"I'm okay," she said, rubbing her eyes. Just a nightmare.

She glanced over to see if she'd awoken Uncle, but he wasn't there. The gray mustang was still picketed, so he couldn't have gone far. Maybe he just had to find some privacy to do his business.

Jezebel chuffed and tugged on her lead line.

"You saw where he went?" The mare tossed her head. Hettie pulled up the stake and climbed onto her bare back. She let the horse take her around the trees and into a hilly area. A lone bat winged across the full moon high above, shrieking.

Jezebel slowed, and Hettie slid off. The hills seemed to pile on top of each other here, fighting for dominance. Fresh clods of moist soil were piled all around the base, almost as if the hummocks had been recently pulled up from the earth. The raised ground formed a crescent-shaped rise. She walked around it to the lower inner curve.

She sucked in a breath when she found Uncle, naked, arms stretched toward the sky. His wrinkled, spotted back was turned to her, and a small fire burned in front of him.

He picked up a raven feather and a hunting knife in each hand, spoke in some alien language loudly. The fire brightened as he put the feather into the flames. Then he plunged the knife into his stomach.

Hettie's throat closed on her scream, and she pressed her palm over her mouth as Uncle dragged the knife across his abdomen with a sickly squelching noise. Blood poured onto the ground.

"What are you doing?" she cried, and leaped forward to stop the old man from this horrific ritual.

She ran straight into a wall and fell back, stunned. She scrambled to her feet and gave him a wide berth as she circled around the invisible barrier spell to face him.

"Uncle—" Her cry was cut off. His pupils had swallowed his eyes so they were fully black. Blood ran down his cheeks. The dagger lay on the dusty ground now, caked with bloody mud. And in his gory hands, Uncle held the box that contained Diablo.

She stared, gorge rising. "Uncle," she whispered, but he didn't answer.

His guttural muttering continued. The wound that should've been spilling his guts onto the ground had closed, though he was still drenched in blood. A foul stench darkened the close air around them.

"Reee...eeee..."

"Uncle Jeremiah?"

The voice was not his. "Re...eeturn...me..." He held the box out to her.

Hettie reached for it, but the barrier slapped her back.

"No!" Uncle thrashed on the ground, arching and spitting like a hissing cat fighting a small snake. Hettie backed away, helpless, until finally, finally, the old man subsided and lay still.

Power shimmered as the barrier collapsed, as if the air blinked, and it was suddenly easier to breathe. She scrambled to Jeremiah's side. He lay half curled in a pool of viscous goo and blood, like some giant stillborn baby. Scratches crisscrossed his face, and a big purple bruise swelled his right cheek. His stomach was bloody, but there was no sign he'd ever cut into himself.

In his arms was the box.

She licked her lips. If Butch Crowe had her sister and he wanted the Devil's Revolver, then she had the ultimate trade for him. Or maybe she could offer it to the Pinkerton Agency in exchange for Abby's safe return...

She reached for the box.

Uncle's eyes snapped open, and Hettie jumped away, startled. He looked down at his naked, bloody body. "Dammit." He pushed into a sitting position. "Don't just sit there, girl, give me some dignity."

She turned around while he pulled his trousers on. "What happened?"

He shoved his arms through the sleeves of his shirt but didn't bother with the buttons. "We have to move. They know where we are."

"Who?"

"The Pinks. Or someone else who wants Diablo. Someone strong. They must have found something of me in Newhaven and opened a channel to my mind. They got into my head while I was asleep and possessed me. Got everything out of me—where we are, where Diablo is. They made me cut it out. We have to move quickly. They'll be on top of us soon."

Mounting Jezebel bareback was difficult, and he winced when the horse started at a brisk pace over the hilly terrain. Uncle gave a low moan.

"Uncle?"

"Just keep moving," he rasped.

They packed up the campsite and saddled the horses quickly. Uncle picked up a handful of dirt, whispering to it, then scattered it across the fire. He coughed harshly. Dark circles ringed his eyes, and the foul, acrid tang of sweat and blood wafted from him.

"Shoulda brought some whiskey," he muttered as he climbed onto his horse. "Change of plans. I'll take you as far as St. Jeffries Landing, but then you're going to ride on to Jacobs Springs alone."

"Why?"

"I've got to get this thing somewhere safe." He patted the box snugged under his arm. The grim lines on his face plainly told her there would be nowhere safe enough.

Hettie had no intention of going anywhere until she found Abby. Diablo might be her only bargaining chip with the Crowe gang. Getting it from Uncle, however, wasn't going to be easy. The way he clutched the thing reminded her of an eagle with a writhing snake in its talons.

"I'm not leaving you," she said staunchly. "Not in your state, and not with Abby still out there somewhere."

"Stubbs's men—"

"To hell with Stubbs's men," she snapped.

And then she realized she wasn't afraid of the Pinkerton Agency. Not nearly as afraid as Uncle insisted she ought to be. She stared. He leaned hard on the pommel, holding his head. Her fear was slowly slipping away, as if someone were drawing a thick blanket off her head and she was remembering what fresh air smelled like.

She patted herself down and found a flat sachet of herbs in the back pocket of her trousers. Her hand trembled as she held out the familiar-looking packet. "You magicked me. You've been manipulating me."

His bleary gaze climbed up to her face. "John always said you were too stubborn for that trick to ever work on you." Jeremiah slouched in his saddle. "You wouldn't listen. I had to make you go. It was the only way."

She threw the sachet to the ground. "How dare you. How dare you violate me like this."

"I'm doing it to protect you."

"From what? You haven't proved a thing to me. All your stories could be lies, for all I know. What if you're just trying to keep Diablo for yourself?"

"You think I *want* this cursed thing on my hands?" He coughed harshly and spat a dark wad on the ground. "Don't ask any more questions. You want to die, then go ahead and stay here, find out what the Pinks'll do to you. If you don't want to throw away everything your parents worked to protect, then the best thing for you to do would be shut up and obey me."

Blood rocketed to her brain. She kicked Jezebel into a sudden gallop, charging at Uncle. As she passed him, she snatched the box from his hold and took off across the field.

Jezebel's rebellious hoofbeats galloped in time with her heart and drowned out Uncle's shouts behind her. As old as the mare was, she was strong and well-rested. She was also ten times smarter than any newly broke mustang, and she chose her path in the dark carefully.

They raced over the hills and across the plain, heading south. Doubt only crept in when Jezebel slowed to a trot. Uncle hadn't followed. Or hadn't been able to.

An hour went by, then two. She kept glancing over her shoulder, expecting to see Uncle waiting for her, his look of stern reprimand skewering her. No one was there. If he was tracking her, he would've caught up to her by now. The old man had been on the verge of collapse. What if he'd fallen off his horse and passed out?

Well, then, he deserved it. He'd kept all these secrets from her about her father, about him, about Diablo—and then putting that influence spell on her to control her! Her fury renewed itself. She wasn't going to let him manipulate her like this, not when Abby's life was at stake.

She inspected the box she'd been clutching. As far as she could tell, it was just a block of solid wood, lacquered on the outside. Uncle's still-wet bloody handprints marred its surface. Nothing rattled within. It was a little heavy, but there was no lid or seam to indicate it could open.

If Diablo was inside, then the box could only be opened by magic.

She stowed it in her bag and dismounted. She lay down on a patch of grass, surrounding herself with a loop of rope to keep the snakes at bay. She hoped Jezebel would warn her of anything worse than that encroaching. Every inch of her was stiff from riding, and her eyes were heavy. If Uncle was going to catch up with her, she might as well be rested enough to take a good thrashing.

She drifted off, but her sleep was not restful. When the birds started singing and the sky turned a pale gray, she groggily sat up. Jezebel pawed the ground nervously.

"Breakfast first," she told the horse. "Then…" Then what? Turn around and find Uncle? Go back to Newhaven?

No, there was no going back. She had to admit Uncle was right—something did seem off about the Pinkerton Agency's interest in her case. She'd been too eager and excited to see that clearly. Working for her pro bono…it was simply too good to be true. Maybe the letter had been spelled to convince her to trust them, the way Uncle's sachet had influenced her.

She wasn't sure she could trust Uncle, either. He'd seemed sincere about protecting her, but what about Abby? He certainly had no intention of looking for her sister.

The only thing she could do was go back to her original plan—find someone to lead her to the Crowe gang and figure out where Abby was.

After a quick breakfast of bread and hard cheese, she set off. She hit the main road, following the signs pointing to Hawksville, which was about a day's ride northwest of Newhaven. By the time she rode into town, the sun was setting, streaking the sky with rusty oranges and pinks as bright as cactus blossoms against a purple backdrop. The city limits were marked by a few skeletal fence rails and a dirt road. No sign to welcome or warn visitors.

Jezebel gave a low neigh. Hettie scanned the streets, keeping the brim of her hat tugged low over her eyes and her Winchester within easy reach. A few rough-looking men smoking cigarettes propped up the walls of the shuttered and abandoned sorcerer's salon, watching her. Pa had said magic didn't stick well here anymore, though no one could say why it'd left Hawksville and not Newhaven. Spells still worked, but they were weak, or else they took a lot more out of the sorcerer to cast. With the sorcerers went a lot of businesses—charm sellers and potion makers and such. The town was pretty thoroughly mundane as a result.

A sand-blasted sign creaked in the breeze above her. The Dove looked about as reputable and hospitable as the rest of the town and was likely the only place she'd get lodgings for the night. She couldn't afford to be picky anyhow.

She hitched Jezebel to the post around the side of the building. The old mare drank greedily from the water trough. At least someone was looking after the animals around these parts. A man across the street eyed the mare steadily, and Hettie gave her a reassuring pat.

"Kick anyone who gets near you," she murmured. Jezebel stomped her hoof in reply.

Inside the saloon, a few patrons as dusty and worn as everything else in this unfriendly town nursed their drinks in silence. Three men in the corner played cards as if they were doing it by rote rather than for entertainment. Hettie went straight to the bartender, a bearded man polishing the bar with little enthusiasm.

"You have a room for the night?" she asked huskily, trying her best to disguise her voice.

The man glanced up. Hettie tugged her hat lower over her bandaged face. With hope, he'd assume she'd been in some kind of scuffle and leave her alone. He scratched his nose. "Who's asking?"

"Paul Dickens."

The barkeep peered at her. "You on your own, son?"

"I've got money. And Pa's meeting me from Bakersfield. He'll be along shortly." Hettie had a feeling it was unwise to advertise that you were traveling alone around these parts.

She paid for a room and a hot meal and to have Jezebel fed and stabled. It was pricey, considering what she was getting, but she didn't haggle. While the barkeeper shouted for food, she took a table with her back to the wall so she could observe everyone coming and going.

Sadly, none of these dirty, wretched-looking men appeared to be the sort who could help her find Abby. They might be desperate enough to accept her meager bounty, but she wasn't about to trust just anyone with her sister's well-being—or her money. Hawksville had once been a thriving mining community, but when the veins of copper and tin had all been dug up and the railway had bypassed the town, good folks up and left, seeking their next employment or a better future for their families elsewhere. Those who'd stayed seemed content to use the town as a place to drown their sorrows. Or maybe they were stuck here—it was hard to tell. Everyone looked about as dried up and worn out as a corn husk doll.

A harried, red-faced woman served her a plate of beans, cold sausages, and bread. Hettie ate slowly, thinking only of her aches and anticipating a good night's sleep. A flea-ridden bed would be better than sleeping alone out in the open.

"Hey there, sugar." Hettie startled as a bawdy girl sidled up to her. She was pretty enough, with strawberry blond hair and thin features. Her complexion was papery, though, as if she'd been in the sun too long, and open sores decorated her mouth. She barely had anything on—just her stays and stockings, and a moth-eaten shawl over that. Hettie couldn't help but grimace. "Aren't you a sweet thang? Awful young to be out here on your own, though."

Hettie pulled her hat lower and averted her eyes. Hopefully, the girl would get the hint and leave.

"You goin' to the fight tonight?" the woman asked. "'Cuz if you ain't, I'm fixin' for a little company."

"Fight?"

"Boss Smythe holds boxing matches down in the warehouse. He's got a prize for whoever knocks out his man, Camden Cobra. Ain't all that interesting if you ask me." She trailed a finger along Hettie's shoulder. "I ain't ever had anyone young and sweet as you. You dipped your wick in the wax yet?"

Hettie jerked away. "My pa'll be here any minute." She tried to force as much warning into her tone, but it came out a squeak.

The woman only smiled more broadly and leaned forward, displaying her ample bosom. "How about a Missy twofer special? I'll do your pa, and you for half price. Hell, I'd give you a free one if it weren't for hard times. I'm awful smitten by you, and I bet you could use a little comfort." She caressed Hettie's cheek, tracing a finger along the edge of the bandage. "Must've been quite a fight you won. I'd like to see what the other guy looks like."

Hettie's face exploded in heat, and she moved out of the woman's reach. "I'm not interested."

She sighed. "Real shame. We coulda had fun." She got up slowly. "You change your mind, you ask for Missy." She sashayed over to the next table, launching into the same sales pitch with the bearded man she'd draped herself across.

Hettie got up. This was a stroke of luck. The warehouse sounded exactly like the kind of place she might find a man skilled enough to track down Abby. She would have to watch carefully, though, for someone with integrity—the last thing she wanted was to be robbed blind in this town.

"If you're headed to the fight, you'll want to leave that behind." The red-faced woman jerked her chin at Hettie's rifle as she passed. "No guns allowed at Boss Smythe's."

Hettie huffed. She hid the Winchester in her room and locked the door.

The large square building at the end of the main thoroughfare sat in a big empty yard and had two levels and giant sliding doors on either side. Oily light spilled out, along with the shouts of men and the smells of stale beer, tobacco, and unwashed bodies.

Past the wall of muscle and bulge crammed tight against a fenced-in ring, two opponents in the center faced off. It was hot and fuggy in the warehouse. A quick glance around at the audience told her none of these hardscrabble men were up to the task of finding her sister. The man Hettie needed would be *in* the fight, not watching it.

Hettie pushed through the crowd and ducked between bodies, seeking out a good vantage point. She climbed the stairs jammed with men and wormed her way into a spot by a post on the upper level.

The two pugilists in the dirt-floor ring were large, muscled men, stripped down to their trousers. One man's bright orange beard was stained with blood. Hettie studied him with the discerning eye of a cattle buyer. He looked plenty tough, and probably full of grit. He moved gracefully, conserving his strength as he faced his opponent.

The other man dripped sweat. A dark wave of damp hair curled around his neck. His back was covered in bruises and scars, and blood flowed freely from a cut above his eye. He swayed slightly, obviously hurt and winded. Hettie frowned. She'd need someone with a lot more staying power than this poor fella.

The dark-haired man circled the ring until she could see his face. With a jolt, she realized it was Walker Woodroffe, the man who'd scared her father and Uncle so thoroughly they'd packed up and left town in the middle of the night. She gripped the post and slid a little lower.

The red-bearded man dove toward Walker. He danced away and raised his fists, wavering where he stood. The crowd booed.

"C'mon, now, lad, you can't run from me all night. Yer sure t'get yer licks sooner or later. I promise t'won't hurt much." Redbeard opened his arms wide. Clumsily, Woodroffe fell for it, sliding in too slowly with a right hook that the other man easily dodged. He feinted, ducked a jab, then slammed a fist into the side of Woodroffe's head.

The crowd cheered as he fell to the ground. He scrambled unsteadily to his feet.

"I know you're better'n that," Redbeard taunted.

Walker rushed him recklessly. Redbeard sidestepped him and landed a blow that flattened him onto his front. Hettie gasped. He lay so still.

The crowd roared as Redbeard soaked in their applause. He stepped over his dark-haired opponent, feet planted either side of his hips, and reached down to grab his hair and yank him up. "Now, then, boyo—"

Walker swept his legs up beneath him, curling, pulling the man down as he grabbed his wrist, kicked the man's feet out from under him, then twisted and threw his weight directly on top of Redbeard. Like a snake, Walker coiled himself around him, pulling his arm up in an unnatural position that seemed to be pulling it out of his shoulder socket.

The crowd cried out as Redbeard screamed. He slapped the ground repeatedly in surrender.

Walker released him. At the edge of the ring, men congratulated him, poured water over his sopping head, and toweled him off. Money flew from hand to hand amid grumbles and whoops. A pair of men led Redbeard limping out of the ring.

A bloated man in a sweat-stained Southern-styled white suit entered the ring. His thin pate of blond hair was slicked back from his pudgy red face. He held a fat unlit cigar in his hand. An onyx stone the size of an egg glittered darkly from his index finger. Looking at him, Hettie couldn't help but think of an overcooked ham hock.

"The winner of this match—Camden Cobra!" He held up Walker's arm. The bounty hunter gave a halfhearted wave, panting. The crowd roared its approval—even the ones who'd lost a substantial bet cheered.

"That makes it Cobra's, what, eleventh fight this week?" the man next to Hettie addressed his companion. She listened surreptitiously. The smaller man with the ten-gallon hat chewed a piece of leathery looking jerky and nodded. "He can't possibly go another round."

"He's got to be using magic or something," the Hat said around his mouthful of jerky. "I'd say the whole thing is rigged, except for Boss Smythe's circle." He nodded at the man in the white suit.

"Don't tell me you trust that snake-oil peddler," the first man spat. "He's got just about enough magic to keep a fly out of the way. Probably borrowed magic, at that. Weak juice, too. No, he's definitely got this whole thing rigged. I'm just waiting for that Cobra to slip up and show his hand. No way a mundane could last all this time. It's gotta be magicked."

"Cobra will be back in fifteen minutes to face his next opponent," Boss Smythe said. "If you're of a mind to face Cobra, see my man. The pot's up to two hundred dollars." He ushered Walker "Cobra" Woodroffe out of the ring and up the stairs.

Walker was headed straight for her. With the landing jammed with men eager to pat Cobra on the back and congratulate him, she had nowhere to hide.

She turned her face to the crowd below. It was too high to jump. She sat paralyzed and prayed he didn't see her.

His big bare feet clomped past. They went to a door at the end of the walkway. She didn't look up until she heard three sharp raps. The door opened.

The blood left her face, and her lungs seized.

She recognized those dull, piggy features. The flaccid lips and thin eyebrows did nothing to help break up the flat expanse of his wide brow. An ill-fitting bowler hat perched upon his head like a sentry, and his belligerent expression suited his babyish countenance about as well as his stained, threadbare waistcoat.

The last time she'd seen this man, he'd shot her father in the chest.

CHAPTER EIGHT

Hettie swallowed tightly. This couldn't be a coincidence. Walker Woodroffe had come to the ranch only hours before the Crowe gang. He and Bowler Hat must know each other somehow.

She breathed deep, trying to still the banging of her heart. She needed more information. Bowler Hat could lead her to Abby and the rest of the Crowe gang.

She sidled up to the door and pressed an ear against it. She couldn't hear a thing with all the noise from the men lingering within the warehouse. She peeked through the dirty office windows.

Walker sat forward in a chair too small for his broad frame, ladling water from a bucket over his head, shoulders, and back. Boss Smythe, the man in the white suit, paced back and forth, gesturing wildly. She still couldn't make out what he said.

Bowler Hat stood at the other end of the room, his puffy face pouting.

Hettie hurried outside. It was a matter of seconds to find a ladder that led up to the corrugated metal roof. Carefully, she tiptoed across the edge, out of sight of the open window and the street, and listened hard.

"...go on." Boss Smythe's voice was harsh and nasal. "One more night, at the very least."

"If you wanted a fighting machine, you'd bring one in from the east."Walker's voice was low and remote. "I can't go another round. Not tonight. Put someone else in."

"They came here to see the Cobra strike! You don't want to disappoint them, do you?"

"That Irishman nearly did him in, Boss."That soft but gruff voice had to be Bowler Hat's. "Cam can fight better if he gets a break. You've already pushed him—"

"I don't pay you to talk or think, Teddy," Smythe snapped.

Teddy remained silent as Boss Smythe went on.

"The next fight'll be easy. Three rounds with a Chinaman. Little fella. Don't think he'll last ten seconds with you." He chuckled softly, but it wasn't a kind laugh.

"And that's supposed to be entertaining?"Walker scoffed.

"So give the fellas a show. Make the suffering last. Pound him till he stops moving and show that slanty-eyed monkey his place. Then you can have the rest of the night off."

Walker responded quietly, "And my cut?"

"You'll get it tomorrow. This is the longest run we've ever had, and the payout's been good. You'll get your share, don't you worry. Now how about we give the fellas a show, huh? Nothing like a good old-fashioned whupping to get them to empty their pockets. Go clean yourself up. I'm going to check on your competition."

The door creaked open and slammed shut. Hettie heard more water splashing. "Boss don't know a thing about fighting, and he sure as hell don't know about Chinamen,"Teddy grumbled. "I hear there are men who can punch through stone walls where they're from. You'll be smart not to underestimate this next one."

"I can take care of myself,"Walker said.

"Just be careful."

The door opened and closed once more. When she looked in, the room was empty.

Hettie dithered. Without her rifle, she had no leverage over Teddy, and she doubted she could offer anyone in the building enough to help her take him down. But she couldn't let Teddy out of her sight either. She slipped back down the ladder and rejoined the throng inside.

Teddy stood by the door to the office, his gaze fixed on the match in progress. She noted the shotgun in his hand and the gun at his hip. She could only hope he wouldn't be carrying both with him when she confronted him. She didn't spot any other Crowe gang members...but she wasn't about to make her presence known before she could say for sure.

She found a spot where she could keep an eye on Teddy close to the door, where the press of people wasn't quite so thick. She couldn't see much of the ring from here, though, only the occasional flash of Woodroffe's dark head.

The audience booed. They were getting bored. They wanted to see blood, and no one was obliging. The man who'd been blocking her view stepped away, and suddenly Hettie could see everything. Her heart shot up into her throat.

Shoeless and shirtless, Ling Tsang stood poised, legs spread, knees bent, arms weaving a slow snakelike pattern in front of him. A look of cool concentration kept his expression neutral, his dark eyes on his opponent, who assessed him with the same calculated calm as they circled. The air around them seemed to vibrate.

"Chicken!" someone yelled, and an apple core bounced off Ling's chest.

Hettie couldn't believe the hand fate was dealing her tonight. If she were more superstitious, she'd say this was a sign. What it was trying to tell her, she had no clue. All she knew was that Ling was in danger, but if she wasn't careful either Woodroffe or Teddy would spot her, and she'd be caught in the open.

She should go back to the Dove and get her gun. Wait Teddy out, see where Walker stood. But then Woodroffe suddenly lunged. Ling twisted at the last minute and in a gravity-defying move kicked up and slammed a heel down on the bounty hunter's shoulder. Walker lurched and crashed against the ropes. The crowd cheered him on, and pushed him back into the fray. Ling met him with renewed caution, prowling. Hettie couldn't tear her eyes away. The air buzzed with something foul and dangerous, and she worried for Ling's health and safety.

He feinted, left and right. Walker had learned his lesson and wasn't so hasty to attack again. He shifted his stance; now he nearly mirrored Ling.

The Celestial became a blur of movement. Walker barely dodged a high kick to his head, blocking a series of lightning-fast punches, but a heel to his abdomen thrust him backward, and he doubled over.

Ling kneed him in the face, smashing his nose, landed two devastating blows to the sides of his head, and then kicked him across the ring.

Walker fell flat on his back. He didn't move.

Hettie covered her mouth to suppress her cheers. The crowd's cries of disbelief and astonishment rose. They grew angry, their shouts and boos boiling to a crescendo.

Smythe and Teddy pushed their way into the ring to check on the Cobra. He was out cold.

Smythe glared down at the leanly muscled Ling and then back at his champion. Hettie got a bad feeling. A really bad feeling.

"Well, well," he gritted, complexion purpling. "Seems you've knocked out Camden Cobra."

"The poster said there was a cash prize for whoever could." Ling's voice was a thread of steel. Acid ate at Hettie's stomach—the crowd didn't look pleased by this turn of events, even if it had won some of them a fat wad of bills.

"They had to knock him out fairly, without the use of magics." Smythe's imperceptible nod summoned two men into the ring. They grabbed Ling by the arms. He struggled as Smythe patted him down. All he had on were pants. There was no way he could hide a talisman on him—

"Aha!" Smythe pulled a string of jade beads seemingly from Ling's pocket, but she saw how he'd slipped them from his own sleeve. The snake! The crowd booed.

Smythe held the beads up in the air like a trophy. "Eastern magic! I knew it! What do we do with cheaters, boys?"

"Run him out of town!"

"Cut off his fingers!"

"String 'im up!"

Ling struggled against his captors. He was yelling something, but then one of the men restraining him cuffed him in the back of the head and he went limp. They dragged him away, and the crowd swallowed him up. Teddy remained behind, still trying to rouse Walker from his daze.

Hettie hesitated. She couldn't let Teddy out of her sight. He was her only lead to the rest of the Crowe gang...

But she couldn't leave Ling to die.

She ran to the saloon, which was emptying out as news of the imminent lynching spread. Even if there was a sheriff or marshal in town, she knew no law could stop a mob this big, bored, and angry. She took the stairs two at a time and crashed into her room. She grabbed her bags and Winchester, and headed down to get Jezebel.

Looked like she wasn't going to get to sleep in that bed after all.

Hettie followed the stragglers up the hill toward the far end of town, where a crudely fenced plot served as a cemetery. Tough scrub sprouted from the sandy dirt at the bases of the worn, cracked headstones and roughly hewn wooden crosses. A gnarled dead tree that'd been stripped of its bark lorded over the graveyard. Someone threw a rope over one of the high branches with practiced ease.

A knot of people hastened toward the tree. Ling hung limply between two men. Hettie's grip tightened on the rifle across her lap.

"Can't string him up yet, boys. Not when he's still asleep." Smythe stepped up and slapped Ling across the face several times. He pulled his pants down and urinated on him. Still, he didn't wake. The crowd laughed and jeered, and Smythe grew even redder in the face.

Hettie prayed Ling stayed asleep until she could come up with a plan.

Jezebel chuffed and trotted toward the side of a building. Hettie had to grab the reins and yank her to a stop. "What are you doing?"

The mare pulled at her lead and kept walking toward a boarded-up store. She stopped by a stack of empty crates and tossed her head.

Hettie looked up. If she could get on the roof, she'd have a perfect vantage of the tree. She climbed the rickety stack and pulled herself over the lip of the roof. It creaked beneath her weight.

It was a good hundred feet to the tree, and the crowd had to number more than fifty men. When that rope tautened, would she be able to shoot it? She sure as hell wouldn't be able to do much else before someone spotted her.

Ling's chin bobbed. Smythe grabbed his cheeks and said something very close to his face.

"It ain't gonna be quick," Smythe declared to the crowd, who cheered raucously.

A sour lump formed in her throat and her stomach. Hettie had seen a lynching when she was very young. It'd happened in Newhaven, and there hadn't been one since. A negro had been accused of raping a girl in town, and the marshal—not McCowan, but the old marshal—had been helpless to stop the girl's father and five brothers from hauling him out of the cell to dispense their own justice. The way the man had kicked and flailed for that long, slow minute had given her nightmares for weeks.

The worst part was that it'd turned out to be a false story, concocted by a jealous suitor. No one had been charged after the fact.

Hettie made sure the rifle was fully loaded, then chambered a round. Assuming she could shoot the rope down, she'd ride Jezebel through the crowd and grab Ling. A few more shots over their heads might scare the mob out of the way before they realized she was just a crazy girl on a horse.

They dragged Ling toward the tree and cinched the noose tight around his neck, then tied his hands behind his back.

Smythe stood on a crumbling tombstone, firelight casting his bulbous white form in a hellish aura. "This is where judgment comes for the weak, the damned. It's time we showed everyone the dangers of foreigners and their demonic magic!" The crowd cheered. "It's time to cleanse our country of these devils and their godless trickery. Real power comes from only one source—the purest blood from the one true Savior!"

At the crowd's roar, the four men hauled on the rope, and Ling was lifted first a few inches, then a foot, then five feet off the ground. He kicked and struggled, his face going red-purple.

Hettie's heart hammered sluggishly. The Winchester had twelve rounds, but she'd only get a few of those shots off before people started noticing. She set her teeth. If she didn't hit the rope and set Ling free, she would make sure he didn't suffer longer than necessary.

She focused on the place where the rope was slung over the worn branch. Ling's face was a dark puce color, but then, by some miracle of strength and contortion, he threaded his legs through the loop of his bound wrists. With his hands in front of him, he twisted and wriggled, prying his finger between the rope and his neck, giving him only momentary reprieve before the crowd shouted and rushed to end him.

Stop moving around so much, she implored silently.

Hettie focused on her target and fired. Chips and sawdust flew from the branch. The mob ducked and scattered, shouts filling the air. She reloaded quickly and fired again. Men drew their pistols as they searched for their assailant.

A shot rang out, then another. A shower of splinters flew up from the shingled roof three feet away. She scrambled back, reloaded her gun, took aim at the rope.

Fire exploded on her right arm as a shot ripped through her shoulder. The rifle tumbled from her grip and clattered to the ground. She gripped the wound, blood oozing between her fingers. A bullet whizzed by her ear, and more pinged off the tin flashing as she scrambled and rolled out of the way.

Jezebel whinnied shrilly as Ling continued to kick at the air. Gritting her teeth, Hettie slid off the roof and tumbled onto the crates, then crashed to the ground. Pain exploded in her shoulder, but she pushed through it, scooped up her rifle, and climbed onto the mare, spurring her toward the tree.

Jezebel gained speed, muscles bunching as her strides lengthened. Hettie took aim, waiting for that breathless instant all of Jezebel's hooves left the ground to squeeze the trigger. She just had to hit the branch where the rope was—

A shock wave slammed into her back, knocking the rifle from her hands. All around her, the world was thrown into a hellish blaze. People screamed as they beat the fire on their clothes. She gripped Jezebel's mane as they charged through the mob. Men leaped out of their path. The mare barreled toward a wall of flame, and Hettie shouted, but they passed through without burning.

Jezebel planted herself between the crowd and Ling, who put his feet on her rump. Hettie used her hunting knife to slice the noose off. She hauled him onto the horse, and he looped his still-tied hands around her waist. "Hang on!" she yelled, and kicked Jezebel hard. The mare reared and let out an unearthly whinny, the inferno raging all around her.

As she wheeled about, Hettie caught Smythe's beet-red face twisted in murderous rage.

They took off. Shots rang out. Hettie stayed low, Ling clutching her waist tight. Another wave of heatless fire washed over them, buffeting her with a blast of air, and men screamed.

Jezebel headed straight out of Hawksville and across the plains. It was a long time before she slowed to a canter, lungs heaving, her flanks damp with sweat.

In the shadow of a slope, Ling slid from the saddle and hacked dryly. Hettie cut the rope on his wrists and passed him her canteen, and he gulped down half its contents. She studied her surroundings. Jezebel had brought them to an area with long, lush grasses. There must be a water source nearby.

"I think we're safe for now," she said once she'd had a drink of water, washing the acrid tang of fear from her mouth. She was shaking, and her arm ached terribly, but the gunshot wound wasn't nearly as bad as she'd thought it would be. She still needed to clean and bandage it, though.

"Thank you for saving me," Ling rasped. "I owe you my life, stranger."

She stared at him perplexed, then remembered her hair and bandage. She took off her hat. "It's me, Mr. Tsang. Hettie Alabama."

"Miss Hettie?" Ling's eyes went huge. "What are you doing here? Where's your father? Is he with you?"

"He...he was killed a few weeks back. Ma, too. And Abby is missing." That peculiar emptiness echoed within her.

"Abby's...missing?" Ling slumped to the ground, arms looped loosely around his knees. "I—I'm very sorry to hear that. Your parents were good people." His grief fled as he noticed the blood soaking her sleeve, and he sat up. "You've been shot."

"Several times, in fact." She couldn't help the dry laughter as she scratched at her bandaged head. "This is just a flesh wound." A giddiness flooded her, and she grinned at the dark stains running down her arm. Some part of her celebrated the wound. She never would have guessed physical pain could be better than emotional numbness.

"I can help you," he said, getting to his bare feet. He was still shirtless, as well, and his chest was streaked with sweat, dirt, and blood. Gently, he took her arm and started muttering a spell, but Hettie drew back sharply.

"It's all right. I'm a healer," Ling said.

Considering all the time he'd spent around her family, she thought it strange she didn't know about his gift. He frowned at her hesitation.

"You don't trust me." He sighed.

"No, it's not that," she hurried to say. "I just thought...Doesn't it take a lot out of you?" Despite all she knew about Ling, she wasn't sure she trusted Eastern magic. Most people plied their spelltrade through conduits like herbs, talismans, potions, and of course blood, giving their spells and power a tether to the real world. But those who practiced ether magic supposedly drew magic directly from the source and channeled it unfiltered through themselves. She couldn't fathom having unearthly, unfettered power going into her body like that.

Ling said, "If you leave this wound as it is, a lot more will be taken out of *you*."

She backed away from him. "Let's just bandage it up for now, okay? It's not that serious. You can do your thing when we've both had some rest and food."

They tore strips from one of Hettie's petticoats for bandages, and Ling attended to the wound. Then they took turns cleaning up in the icy-cold stream Jezebel had sniffed out. By the time Hettie was clean, pain throbbed through her whole body. Just one more ache to add to the collection, she thought, rubbing at her thigh.

"Here." She dug through her pack and found a shirt for Ling. It'd been one of Pa's.

"How did it happen?" Ling asked quietly as he helped Hettie rub Jezebel down. "Your parents' deaths, I mean."

The starburst scar flashed through her mind. She told him briefly, haltingly, about that night, and how Uncle had saved her, but didn't say anything about Diablo. She decided it was safer to keep some things to herself. Ling took it in, expression unreadable.

"Where is Mr. Bassett now?" he asked.

Considering how she'd left him, she decided it would be prudent to keep that part of the story from Ling, too. "Probably at the bottom of a whiskey bottle. He didn't think it was worth looking for Abby."

"You're trying to find her."

She nodded. "I wanted to hire someone in Hawksville to track down the Crowe gang. Then I recognized one of the men who was at the ranch that night at the warehouse—he's one of Boss Smythe's hired muscle, a man named Teddy. And that Camden Cobra fella's really named Walker Woodroffe. At least, I think he is. He came looking for Pa that day, too. I think those two are in cahoots. I was going to follow them, but…" She trailed off. She didn't want to make it sound as though saving Ling's life had kept her from her purpose. "Well, I'm sure they're still in town. I just have to figure out how I can go back to Hawksville…" Her words trailed off and whipped around, searching, hoping she was wrong. She moaned.

"What's the matter?"

"I dropped my rifle back in town." Her immediate worry should have been that someone would find traces of blood or sweat or something on it and use a spell to track her. But she was more devastated by the fact that she'd likely never get her precious rifle back.

Ling's brow furrowed. "This is unfortunate."

"Any chance you know a spell to keep critters away while we sleep?"

"My specialty's in healing."

She paused. "So…that wave of fire back in town wasn't yours?"

"I don't have that kind of skill. It would take a high-level sorcerer to cast an illusion spell that widespread in a magical-drought town like Hawksville. And I was too preoccupied to do that." He pointed at the raw red marks ringing his neck.

She scanned the field for danger. "Well, if anyone from town finds us, we're going to need weapons."

"I doubt we'll need to worry tonight. Everyone will be too tired to pursue us. It's been my experience that mobs generally disperse once their fervor has been spent."

They started a small fire. The night would be too cold without it and only one blanket between them. Hettie asked, "How'd you end up in Hawksville?"

"I'd been on the road for a few days and wanted to see if any bounties had been put on me, and find out if it was safe to go back to Newhaven. I came upon a man in distress on the road, and when I stopped to help him he made off with my horse and most of my belongings. Luckily for me, I had my money on my person. I walked the rest of the way to town and have been stuck here since."

A brisk wind cut through her clothes, and she shivered. Ling couldn't be comfortable in just that shirt, so she scrounged in her bag in search of another layer to add. Her fingers came away wet. Blood. She checked herself but found no wound from which it had come. She emptied the bag onto the ground. The box containing Diablo landed in the dirt with a heavy thud. Uncle's bloody handprint still hadn't dried. Her stomach turned.

"What's that?" Ling asked.

"A...gift from my uncle." Then she remembered. "There's a handgun inside, but I haven't been able to open the box."

"May I see?"

She was strangely reluctant to hand it over. "It's...dirty."

He grimaced at the stains left on his fingers. Holding the box with the corners digging into his palms, he gingerly turned the block. "It's sealed with powerful blood magic."

"Blood magic?" She nearly choked. "But...Uncle's not a Kukulos warlock."

"Blood magic isn't exclusive to the Kukulos. Someone else could have put a spell on this box, too." He inspected it. "I've encountered things like this before. Books and safes that can only be opened with a drop of the owner's blood. Even houses and doors can be locked with blood if the sorcerer is powerful enough." He passed the box back to her. "If this was a gift from your uncle, then it was meant for you alone to open."

She loosened the bandage around her arm and dipped a finger beneath the dressing. Her finger came away sticky. She touched the top of the box. At first, nothing happened, but then a seam formed along the sides. The surface of the wood curdled. The box grew hot, and she dropped it. Ling took a step back, raising a hand as if ready to catch the box should it leap into his face.

With a sigh, the box stopped its transformation. She nudged it with a toe toward the fire to get a better look.

A fine latticework of figures covered the sides—tiny demons dancing around the fires of hell. A ghastly death's skull grinned up at her from the lid.

"Mr. Bassett has…interesting tastes," Ling said slowly.

She picked up the box and slowly lifted the lid. She felt as though she were opening an aeons-old tomb. Quiet awe tinged with dread filled her. Nestled in black velvet was a shiny revolver. The grip was made of buttery white ivory, smooth with a pearly sheen. The barrel and cylinder were shiny black metal, polished to such a gloss it was as if her gaze slipped right off the surface. The trigger was flat and smooth, with the exception of a small, bright red, needle-sharp thorn near the top. She grazed the tip and shivered at the thought of impaling her finger on that little pricker.

"That gun is enchanted with powerful magic," Ling said warily. "Are you sure this was a gift?"

"What can you tell me about it?" She held it out to him. If this was the legendary Diablo, then surely someone would recognize it.

He glanced from her to the revolver and licked his lips. "Miss Hettie, with all due respect, I don't want to touch that thing, and you shouldn't, either."

"It's just a gun." She swallowed thickly. Just a gun…or else it was the Devil's Revolver, a powerful magical weapon that had once been wielded by an immortal outlaw.

She had a sudden memory of the children playing Blackthorn Rogues in the streets of Newhaven. The words from that old rhyme rose in her mind, dripping with new meaning.

> Round and round the circle whirls
> Red blood flows through boys and girls
> Who so e'er the black thorn pricks
> Is the one Diablo picks.

Hettie stared at her bloodied hand. If any of the stories were true, the gun would only allow her to use it if she made a sacrifice of blood.

The stories also said it would make her the next Elias Blackthorn ...

She shook her head. It was just a story, and she was no demonic outlaw. A mob was on their heels, and who knew what else lurked out on these plains? The metal gleamed seductively, winking in the firelight, drawing her in. She could almost feel its weight in her hand and the security it would provide...

Don't be a ninny, she told herself. She was alone in the wilderness and without a weapon. She needed that gun.

She reached down and picked it up off the velvet.

Something zipped through her blood—an arrow of heat that went all the way to her toes. She closed her eyes, feeling lightheaded.

"Miss Hettie?"

She let out a long breath. The sensation dissipated. "I'm all right." She inspected the handgun. Despite the weight of the box, the weapon was much lighter than she'd anticipated. She spun the empty wheel. "I think..." She reached into her bag and brought out a box of cartridges for her Winchester. They loaded easily. She snapped the wheel closed and sighted down its length. "That's handy. I won't even need to buy bullets."

Ling's jaw worked. "Are you intending to use this weapon?"

"Only if I have to." She held the revolver grip out to him, but he didn't take it. "Can you tell me anything else about it?"

"I'm not certain. Magic generally can't enchant metal, but I'm sensing energies coming off all parts of it, the barrel included. That leads me to think it's a Kukulos mage gun. They're the only ones who've had any success at crossing magic and machine. You understand the price of blood magic, don't you?"

Hettie nodded, yet she couldn't find any disgust for the weapon in her hands. It was beautiful—hardly something she would have thought had been forged using the blood of innocents. "So if this is a mage gun..."

"It uses energy from its wielder as its ammunition. Its conduit is blood."

That explained the thorn. She grazed the tip gently—it left a light scratch on the pad of her index finger. "You said there are other weapons like this?"

"I've never seen one before, but yes, there are others. Since blood magic is outlawed just about everywhere, they're not readily available. Besides, it takes a powerful sorcerer to infuse a man-made metal weapon with any amount of magic." He hesitated. "Maybe you should put it away."

She hadn't realized how tightly she was holding the thing. She couldn't deny that she wanted to test it out. But if anyone were looking for them, firing off a gun in the middle of the night was the surest way to be found. She stuffed the revolver into her coat pocket. "We should get some rest." She propped herself up against Jezebel's saddle. "Come morning, I'll drop you off at the nearest friendly farm. Maybe you can find work there until you can earn carriage fare back to Newhaven. No one's looking for you as far as I know."

"And what are your plans?"

"I need to speak with Teddy. Then I'll have to find someone who can help me track Abby down."

Ling rubbed his chin. "The way I see it, you've already found someone." He smiled briefly. "You've saved my life twice now. It's only fair I repay you for at least one of those lives."

She suppressed a frown. "I appreciate the offer, but I can't take you with me."

"My honor requires it. The wilds are no place for a young woman to be traveling alone. If your father knew I let you go on this quest by yourself, he would haunt me to the end of my days."

"My father's dead, and he won't be coming back." Her snapped-out words startled them both. Hettie rubbed the tip of her nose. Ling probably thought she was grieving, but all Hettie felt was anger at that hole in her emotions.

Ling suddenly dropped to one knee and clasped his hands above his bowed head. "Please let me help find Abby, Miss Hettie," he said fervently. "Your father was a decent man who treated me, a lowly Chinaman, with dignity and respect. Please give me the honor of avenging him."

"Don't be bowing and scraping before me like that." Hettie yanked him to his feet. "Pa hated that coming from anybody."

"I take my debts seriously. I owe you and your family. I will help you find Abby. I'll follow you on foot if I have to."

She glanced down at his bootless feet. He must have left his footwear back at Boss Smythe's place, too. And while she appreciated his sentiment, a shoeless Eastern healer wasn't exactly the bounty hunter she was hoping for. Besides, she couldn't waltz back into Hawksville dragging him along.

She knew she'd have a hard time convincing him of that, though. Maybe he'd be useful—he'd knocked out Walker Woodroffe, after all. And he was a healer. Abby might need him.

"All right. At least for now. Until I have other plans…"

He bowed very slightly. "I will serve you loyally."

"Stop with the lowly coolie act. I know just as well as Pa did that you only did that to mock people."

"I wouldn't think to mock you, Miss Hettie." He nodded at her arm. "Let me start by healing that wound. I'd rather do it now and sleep off the night. Now that the bleeding has stopped, it won't take as much out of me."

Hettie hesitated but then slipped her arm out of the shirt sleeve so Ling could look at it. Standing in the open air half naked in front of a man was not how she'd pictured her day going, but nothing about the past few weeks had been particularly normal.

Ling's fingers were cool on her skin as he removed the bandage and delicately probed the cut. He grasped her a little tighter, and she looked away as he began muttering a spell in soft, throaty syllables.

Hettie knew it was stupid to be afraid of Ling's abilities. But the stories she'd heard from the other kids at school came back as heat flooded her. She squeezed her eyes shut when a soft white light flashed up from her shoulder. *Don't look, or you'll lose your soul…*

The throbbing of the wound dulled to an ache. He hissed through his teeth and let go abruptly. "It's done." His face was pale and dotted with sweat. "But there's…something missing. I tried to knit some of the wounds closed, but it's almost as if a piece is missing. Something that can't heal." He inspected her arm, which sported only a faint reddish bruise now. "As far as I can tell, this is fine. You must be a fast healer." He touched her chin and turned her head to look at the scar peeking out from beneath the bandage. With her permission, he unwound it and inspected her temple. She couldn't tell from his expression how bad it was. "You're very lucky infection didn't set in."

"Can you fix it?" she asked hopefully. "I've got this awful headache I haven't been able to shake."

He nodded. "There will still be a scar, though. It's too far along in the natural healing process for it to go away entirely."

She closed her eyes as he murmured the spell. The ache at her temple eased, and she almost felt the flesh knitting together where the itching scabs had been worst. When he let go, sighing, she touched her face, finding smooth, tight skin. The hair hadn't grown back over the scar, though. Nothing she could do about that.

"How do you feel?" Ling asked.

"Clearheaded. Do you think you have any more in you to fix my leg?"

He nodded and healed the bullet wound in her thigh. When he was done, she felt almost normal except for that strange emptiness inside her. Ling curled onto his side then, head on his arm. "I need to rest now."

"Of course. Thank you." She hesitated as she settled in. "I have to go back to Hawksville tomorrow. I have to find Teddy. He's my only lead on Abby."

"It'll be dangerous." Ling's eyes remained closed, his words slurred. "You could be recognized."

Her hand settled over the gun in her pocket. "I may have a plan."

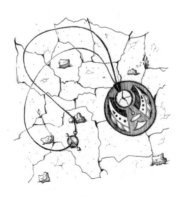

CHAPTER NINE

H ettie smoothed out the wrinkles in the one dress she'd packed as best as she could, but decided a little dishevelment wouldn't hurt her cause. Late in the morning, Ling dropped her about half a mile outside of Hawksville. The healer didn't like her plan one bit, but he couldn't go with her—he'd be recognized for sure. She promised she would rejoin him before nightfall—at least, that was the hope.

She walked into town, gathering plenty of dust on her boots and the hem of her skirt. She'd smeared some of the red mud from the creek bed along her front, as well. It looked like dried blood.

As the buildings came into sight, she focused on her weariness, staggering, trying to bring tears into her eyes. It wasn't hard to look pitiful. She was thirsty and hungry, and her various injuries still ached, though Ling had done a fair job healing the worst of it. As she shuffled into town, she immediately caught the attention of some rough-looking sorts hanging around outside a low building.

"Help me, please," she blubbered, rushing toward them. "My pa's hurt—we were jumped on the road by a savage!"

The men glanced at each other, then pushed off the wall and came toward her. She probably should have had some consideration for her personal safety—she was taking a risk by playing the damsel in distress—but then reminded herself she had a gun. "Here, now, miss, what's the trouble?" one man asked.

"We were headed to Newhaven," she sniffled, "and this wild man jumped from the bushes and bashed my poor pa over the head! He took our horses, our cart—he took everything! Please, help me!"

More men had gathered, anger and shock filling their faces.

"Child, what happened to your hair?" a wizened old man asked.

She'd run Jezebel's spit through it to make sure it stuck up in all directions and matted it over the scar. "The wild man sliced it off. He was using it for some evil spell. I got away when he...he vanished into a puff of smoke!"

"A demon!"

"Maybe a shaman from the territories."

"No, it must be a Kukulos warlock," someone else said. "Sounds like we have a rogue sorcerer on the loose."

The gathering gasped and whispered. Hettie figured that was the perfect moment to swoon. She went limp and dropped.

"Catch her!"

"Someone find some smelling salts!"

"Call Missy Parsons!"

They carried her into the shade of a wood porch. Someone placed a cool cloth across her forehead. She fluttered her eyes open and found herself peering into the face of the bawdy girl from the Dove.

The woman's blue eyes focused on her, but her expression didn't change. She was wearing a simple cotton dress, her hair put up in a loose bun, her face scrubbed clean. "Drink this." She pushed a glass of whiskey at her. Hettie sipped the drink cautiously, coughing as it burned its way down.

"Okay, now, everyone, back off," she snapped. "Give the girl some air."

"My pa," Hettie croaked. "He's still out there..."

"Where at, miss?"

"There was a tree. And a boulder." She made up landmarks as she continued. "And a stream. I think it was north of here. But I got turned around..." She summoned tears and let her hands quake.

The men hesitated at her vague directions. She put in eagerly, "Pa's a rich man. He'll be sure to reward whoever saves him." *If you can't rely on the kindness of strangers, then rely on their greed.* Pa had taught her that.

"We'll bring him back to you, miss, don't you worry. Missy'll take care of you until we do." Several of them tipped their hats and hurried away to search for a man who didn't exist. It would be something of a race, she imagined, as the tale of the lost girl and her rich pa spread through town and people scrambled to find him for an imaginary reward.

If only people were as willing to help find Abby.

"Let's go inside," Missy said. "There's a room you can use to rest."

"Thank you." She made a show of getting up. "I appreciate your hospitality, Miss...?"

"It's just Missy 'round here." The woman's lips curved. "Let it never be said Hawksville is completely full of louts and thugs. The people here are decent enough...for a price. What's your name?"

"Deborah. Debbie. Ashton. My father's George Ashton, the third," she called after the men.

"I doubt they'll need to know his name, Miss Debbie. Ain't many men take the north road to Newhaven. Where you from?"

"Cranston Springs," she replied after a beat. Missy sure did ask a lot of questions.

Hettie followed her into the saloon. As they walked up the stairs, the harried cook popped her head out from behind the bar and peered at Hettie. "Not your usual fare. Who is that?"

"This is Debbie Ashton. She had some trouble on the road. A posse's gone out looking for her pa. She just needs a place to rest awhile."

"She got cash up front?"

"Be a Good Samaritan, Mae. At least till her pa arrives."

The woman muttered something about bills, then disappeared back into her kitchen.

"Don't mind Mae. She just grumbles for the sake of grumbling. Anyhow, your pa'll have some way to pay for a room, right?" Missy unlocked a door and led her in. It was the same room Hettie had paid for yesterday. "Why don't you lie down awhile? If your pa is out there, them boys'll bring him back soon enough."

The last thing Hettie wanted was to get trapped in the inn. "I am awful tired, but I'm not sure I could rest...knowing Pa's still out there with that madman on the loose, I mean."

"You sure about that? You look like you've been...well, running all night." Her eyes gleamed.

Hettie forced herself to remain calm, averting her gaze. "It's been a hard road."

Missy shut the door gently and faced her fully. "All right, it's just us girls now. What kind of scam are you pulling?"

Hettie kept her face somber. "I don't know what you mean."

"Just because I've been making a living on my back doesn't make me stupid. You're the boy from last night. I'm good with faces, you know. Besides, if your pa was a real merchant, he wouldn't move supplies from Cranston Springs to Newhaven by cart. Not on these roads. It'd been cheaper and faster to go by train, and a man doesn't make his fortune by taking stupid risks." She folded her arms over her chest. "Who're you trying to con? 'Cuz there ain't much in this town worth risking neck or nether over."

Hettie darted a look behind her. Should she try to jump out the window? But if Missy knew who she was, she didn't seem too eager to tell anyone else.

"Where's this pa of yours? Is he waiting outside for you?"

"My pa's dead."

Missy blinked. Hettie stiffened her spine and went on. "I'm not trying to con anyone. I'm looking for someone. A man who may know where my missing sister is."

"Is that so?" Missy sat on the lone chair in the room. "And who would that be?"

"Teddy. I don't have a last name. He was at the warehouse fight last night. He works for Boss Smythe."

"You were the one who saved that Chinaman from the hangman's necktie." She nodded. "I thought so. That was some show you put on. Had the whole town in a riot putting out fires that didn't burn. You don't look like much of a sorcerer, though."

She decided not to confirm her suspicions.

Missy assessed her shrewdly. "You telling the truth? About your sister?"

"She was kidnapped by the Crowe gang. They killed my parents, burned my farm, and left me to die."

"So you want revenge."

"I want my sister back."

She leaned forward. "I might know where to find Teddy. I could even lure him out into the open for you."

"For a price," Hettie surmised.

Missy smirked.

"What do you want? I don't have any money."

"Now that's a lie. You had to have money to pay room and board and to stable that magicked white mare of yours. Don't look so surprised—I didn't chat you up just to see if you were interested in a lark. You make a good boy, by the way." She sat back and studied her critically. "I want a new life."

"Excuse me?"

"Look around you. Hawksville is going the way of Louisberg, Wade's Point, Penance...all those towns the railroad bypassed and the Zoom tunnels don't reach. I want to leave this place and start a new life."

"I don't have *that* much money."

"You've got more than you let on, I reckon. If I were meaner, I'd ask you for the lot. Wouldn't take much for me to scream and have the men up here with their guns, after all. Wherever that Celestial's gotten to, he won't get here fast enough to save you if folks decide to string *you* up." She inspected her nails. "But I'm a charitable sort, so I'll make you a bargain. Give me enough for the train heading to New York, and I'll get you Teddy."

Hettie grasped the gun in her pocket, fingers twitching. "I don't have nearly that much. And I need what I do have to hire a bounty hunter."

"No money, no help."

The gun in her pocket felt heavier. She could threaten Missy into helping her. Maybe knock her over the head, tie her up...

What was she even thinking? She was desperate, yes, but not quite enough to assault a fallen woman.

"How about this: I'll give you carriage fare to go to Newhaven. I'll write you a note of introduction. I'm sure someone'll hire you.

If it's a new life you're looking for, that's better than fare to New York."

"Who'd hire a whore in Newhaven?" She snorted derisively. "I don't want to trade one bed for another. Here, at least, I don't have to deal with a pimp."

"I can write that you're a...a washerwoman, or a cook. There'll be plenty of folks who'd take you on if I asked. I'd be the only one who'd know the truth."

"And you're okay with lying about my references?"

"If it gets you to help me, I'll tell them you're the queen of England." Hettie clenched her fists. "Missy, *please*. I can't stall. It's been nearly a month since Abby went missing, and I don't know how much longer..." She bit her lip, stemming the desperate plea. "I need to get to Teddy today," she said quietly.

Missy tilted her chin. "You really mean it, don't you? You'd do anything to find your sister."

Hettie met her gaze. "She's all I have left."

The woman closed her eyes and exhaled. "Dang, I'm getting soft." She opened the door. "All right. It's a deal. I'll get some paper and a pen. You're gonna write that letter first. After that, we can catch Teddy at the warehouse. But what you do with him after I bring him to you is none of my business, understand?"

On their way to the warehouse, Hettie kept her hands tucked in her coat pockets. She fingered the revolver, palms damp, mouth dust-dry. She hadn't even tested the thing. Hopefully the sight of it would be enough to scare Teddy into talking.

"Draw him to the yard in the back of the warehouse," Hettie instructed. "I'll speak to him there alone."

Missy eyed her warily. "You sure this ain't about revenge?"

"If he tells me what I need to know, there won't be any need for trouble."

The hard lines between her eyes and around her mouth softened, and she rubbed her palms over the front of her skirt. "Teddy ain't a bad man, you know. He's downright gentle compared to some of the men who come 'round."

"He shot my pa and let them take my sister."

"Well, I ain't sticking around for this. I'll do my part. After that, you're on your own. If he finds out I helped you—"

"He won't." Hettie walked around the big building and found a spot in the shade to wait. Missy disappeared within.

Hettie's pulse pounded in her temples. It was a long time before she heard any movement, and she spent that time checking and rechecking the bullets loaded in the revolver. She had another six in her pocket but doubted she'd miss at point-blank range.

A door opened, and voices floated through. She gripped the weapon with both hands and pressed her back against the wall. She shivered, her whole body flashing hot and cold. She recognized Missy's lazy come-hither drawl. Hettie leaned against a crate, breathing deep as she regained her balance. The weapon was solid and cool in her death grip.

"Dunno why you came to me now," Teddy's soft, low voice came. "It ain't that I don't appreciate your attentions, Miss Parsons, but…"

He emerged from the back door first, red-faced and wiping his hands on a rag. His bowler hat was perched high on his shiny domed head. He halted at the sight of Hettie, his face a study in puzzlement. Slowly, recognition dawned in his wide green eyes as Hettie pointed Diablo at his chest. Missy melted into the shadows.

Teddy's nostrils flared in his suddenly pale face. "You a ghost?" he asked quietly. "Or did someone bring you back to flesh?"

A sour taste filled her mouth. "Butch missed."

"Butch never misses." His gaze traveled down to the weapon in her hand. "So you had it all along."

"Where's my sister?"

Teddy took a step forward. Hettie pulled the hammer back, and he stopped. "Don't make me do anything rash," she said, hating the tremor in her voice. "Tell me where Abby is and I'll let you live."

"I don't rightly know," he said, hands raised. "We parted ways a night's ride south of your ranch. They took a remote Zoom tunnel back to the hideout."

So that was how they'd eluded the marshal and his men. It told her something else: they had some very powerful sorcerers on their payroll. If the Kukulos were working with them, she shuddered to think what Abby's purpose was. "Is she still alive?"

"Don't know that, either. But I reckon she is if—" He cut himself off ruthlessly, glanced around. "You didn't bring backup, did you?"

"Where'd they take her?"

"Why? You planning on chasing them?" He chuckled and shook his head. "Don't you know who you're dealing with? Butch Crowe is the meanest son of a bitch to ever lead the Crowe gang. He'll eat you alive, especially if he knows you've got Diablo in your hot little hands."

Hettie ground her jaw. *"Where did they take her?"* she repeated.

He lifted his chin. "South, to the Mexican border, a few miles from the Wall. I have no reason to lie. Not if you're going to ride all the way to his front step to deliver that piece of work to him."

Hettie's blood surged, pumping so hard she could feel the pulse in her throat. The gun was getting heavier in her hands. She'd thought it was her imagination, but she had to shift her grip. Teddy's attention was drawn by the motion of her finger stroking the trigger spasmodically.

"You even know anything about that revolver, girl?" He licked his lips. "That thing is cursed. You've no idea what kind of power you're dealing with."

"You're going to take me to my sister," Hettie said. Her shoulders ached, and her arms trembled. "Butch can have Diablo if he gives me my sister, alive and in one piece."

Teddy's face closed. "I'm not going anywhere. I've washed my hands of them. Paid my debts. I want nothing to do with their plans."

"And what would those be?"

"I ain't telling you. Mostly 'cuz I can't."

"Seems we have a disagreement."

His cheeks puffed out as he exhaled in a huff. His hands drifted to his sides. Hettie shouted as he reached for his gun, and she squeezed Diablo's trigger.

A flash of green light, and the gun just barely ticked in her hands. The roar of a train engine rang in her ears, rumbled through her chest. Teddy staggered back, howling. Blood poured from the stump that was his hand, spilling across the dirt.

"You're taking me to Butch Crowe," Hettie declared, her vision clouding at the sight of his gruesome injury. She swallowed her gorge and kept Diablo leveled. "You'll help me find my sister or I swear—"

"Hettie, you blasted idiot!" Out of nowhere, Jeremiah Bassett yanked her wrist above her head. "What are you doing?"

The moment she took her eyes off Teddy, he bolted.

Hettie threw off the shock of seeing Uncle and pounded after Teddy through the warehouse. Shots rang out. She ducked as bullets ricocheted from the metal struts and support columns.

"Coward!" She raced through the building and, momentarily blinded by the darkness, crashed into a barrel. She was still winded when she emerged from the street-side entrance, vision dazzled once more as she streaked into the sunshine.

Her quarry ran up the middle of the street. She had a clear shot. She stopped, squared herself, breathed deep, took aim. All she had to do was wing him—

A force like a locomotive slammed into her side, tackling her to the ground. Hettie shouted and threw wild punches, cracking the grip of her revolver against her assailant's skull.

"Stop that!" Uncle cuffed her so hard her ears rang. "What d'you think you're doing?"

"He's getting away!"

"There's no time. Stubbs has a bead on us now. We have to get out of here." He grabbed her shoulder and started to drag her up.

Hettie pushed him off and rolled to her feet. Teddy heaved his bulk onto a horse, bleeding stump and all. If he got away—

He won't get away.

The thought was crystal clear, superimposed over the image in her mind of his soulless stare, gun smoking, while blood bloomed over Pa's chest.

One-handed, she leveled the gun and pulled the trigger just as Uncle shouted, "No!"

The moment of euphoria became a bubble, expanding, slowing, encompassing all as a ball of searing green energy squeezed out of the barrel seemingly in slow motion. She felt as though her heart was soaring, freed of its mortal confines. She sailed over the hundred yards between her and Teddy, breaching it in a fraction of a heartbeat, and plunged happily through his chest with a satisfying splash.

And suddenly the world was black and red with pain. Hettie tasted the dusty road as she pitched forward. Every muscle in her body pulled like taffy, stretched across her arching skeleton. She felt as though her skin were being dragged inside out and set on fire.

She screamed as her body seized. A thousand needles plunged into her flesh, burning and dissolving like acid through the marrow of her bones. The agony seemed to last forever, but in a too-long blink of an eye, it was over. She lay gasping on the ground. Her eyes burned, and she was soaked in sweat. A ribbon of thin, silvery smoke drifted from the mouth of the gun.

"Hettie. Hettie, you have to get up." Uncle tugged her into a sitting position. "We don't have time."

She staggered to her feet, head spinning, searching for Teddy.

The people who'd taken cover as soon as the shooting started peeked out, gathering around something on the ground. Hettie snatched up her revolver and shoved Jeremiah off in the same motion.

The crowd parted as she approached. Some of the men put their hands on their sidearms, watching her with trepidation. Teddy's bowler hat lay in a wide splatter of blood around the big man's body. His face had locked into a mask of sheer terror, his eyes huge and vacant and staring up at the sky. A meaty hole as big as a cannonball had been blown clean through his chest.

Beneath him, the horse's head was missing.

CHAPTER TEN

Idiot girl, don't just stand there!" Jeremiah barked. He dragged her away from the bloody scene, but her feet barely responded. "Stupid, arrogant, hay-brained, ungrateful whelp you are," he muttered, "leaving an old man to die on the prairie like some mangy coyote. I should turn you over to the Pinks." He snatched the revolver from her, yelped, and dropped it as he clutched his wrist. "Hell's horns!" He grabbed her hands and studied them wide-eyed. "Dammit, Hettie, you bonded?"

She stared at the blood staining her fingers, saw the puncture wound where she'd impaled her trigger finger on the thorn. *Bonded?*

Something at the far end of the thoroughfare caught her attention. The air rippled. A spot about eight feet from the ground darkened, as if a shadow had been cast against an invisible wall there. The circle of darkness widened, and the ripples grew larger, like big waves on a stormy sea.

The townsfolk scattered as the remote Zoom tunnel roared open. Uncle swore and dragged her behind a building.

As the tunnel yawned wide, the wind whipped clouds of dust in the chilled air. The tip of Hettie's nose went numb. The span of darkness flashed, and there, in the middle of the road, was a perfectly circular doorway to another place, as if someone had cut a hole in a theater backdrop, revealing the bare backstage.

Six men in finely tailored suits strode through, guns drawn, rifles at the ready. They appraised the crowd and their surroundings with all the gravitas their shining silver eye-shaped badges afforded them. The air crackled with power, and Hawksville's residents skulked away, blending into the dust and shadows.

"Damn Pinks." Uncle yanked her back. "Take Diablo and get out of here," he whispered. "The mustang is picketed on the east side of town. You take him and ride as fast and far as you can. Get that gun as far away as possible—"

"Jeremiah?" Hettie jumped at the closeness and clarity of that smoke-roughened voice. It sounded as if it was right next to her ear. It must have been some kind of amplification spell. "Jeremiah Bassett, is that your godforsaken magic stinking up the air?"

Uncle closed his eyes and muttered an oath.

Hettie peered around the corner. The remote Zoom tunnel had left a steaming frosted path where it had opened. Mist swirled around the legs of the men, forming a ragged circle around a central figure. One of them restrained a great muzzled beast of a dog. She gasped.

"They've got Cymon!"

Uncle grabbed her collar to keep her from leaping out into the open. Cy's ears perked up, and he looked pitifully in her direction, whining.

The man in the center of the group wore a dark gray suit with a red tie. He took off his bowler hat and wiped his brow. "Damn, it's hot," he said. "How do you stand it, Bassett?"

"Acclimatize," Uncle replied gruffly. To Hettie, he murmured, "Get a move on. They'll kill you if they find you with that." He nodded at the revolver.

When Hettie hesitated, Jeremiah grabbed his hat off his head and smacked her across the shoulder. "Go!"

She shoved Diablo into the inside pocket of her duster as she scurried around the backs of the buildings. She could see the gray mustang two hundred yards away.

"How've you been, Bassett?" the man with the red tie asked casually. Hettie could still hear every word crystal clear.

"Not as well as you, Stubby." Uncle's voice was equally clear. More magic spells the old man knew and hadn't told her about.

"Mighty fine suit you got there. All those talismans you've got sewn in makes a man think you're afraid of something, though."

"Hazards of the business. Plenty of folk would like to see me dead."

"Mighty long way for you to come to pay a social visit."

He snickered, and his voice went cold. "I'm here for Diablo."

"It ain't here. Man who had it slipped outta here after he shot that poor fella and his horse." His words urged Hettie on. She darted from cover to cover, unable to escape the conversation.

"*You* let someone get the slip?" Stubbs's bark of laughter was sharp and humorless. "I don't think so. No one's ever escaped the Hound. Even I'll admit you were good at what you did. Made me wonder why you quit the Division."

"I resigned because I failed my mission."

"But you didn't, did you? Otherwise, why hide yourself all these years? No one believed me when your letter of resignation came. They all thought you were still the honorable, outstanding agent who'd had his heart broke or whatever nonsense you told 'em. They didn't think for a minute you'd lied about losing track of Diablo. But I knew better."

Hettie was only about twenty yards from the horse now. She slid out from cover and hurried toward the mustang.

Something fell across her shoulders, and she jerked back and landed hard on her butt, gasping as the rope closed around her throat and cut off her air. She was dragged backward, kicking and struggling to pry her fingers under the noose.

"Mr. Stubbs, I think we've found the wielder," the man above her said, wrestling her into the street. Cy barked excitedly.

"Well, well, well." The man in the gray suit bent closer. His eyes were a pale blue, making his black pupils stand out like the holes in turquoise beads. "Miss Alabama. We've been searching for you everywhere."

"How do you know who I am?" She cursed herself—she should've denied it.

"There aren't many who would've survived a gunshot to the side of the head." He tapped at his own temple, indicating her scar, and leaned closer. "When the agent I dispatched to help you didn't return from his mission, I thought perhaps he'd been compromised.

Or maybe someone else had absconded with you. We were quite concerned, you know."

She glared. His condescension was irritating and made her fingers itch to reach into her pocket and silence him.

"It's a good thing someone pointed out your canine companion was still hanging around town. He had the stink of magic all around him. It was pretty easy to figure out whose." He smirked. "I take it you haven't found your sister yet?"

Hettie didn't respond, and the man tipped his chin up.

"Forgive my manners, I've failed to introduce myself. I'm Detective Thomas Stubbs of the Pinkerton Detecting Agency." He gave a short, mocking bow.

Cymon pulled at his lead and barked. The man holding his leash yanked hard on the choke chain, and he yelped and sat back.

"Leave him alone," she protested.

"You seem like a smart girl," Stubbs said, "so I'm going to cut to the chase. We're looking for a piece of stolen property. A revolver with a white grip and black barrel. It goes by the name Diablo, or the Devil's Revolver. I have reason to believe you might know of its whereabouts. Tell me where it is, and I'll let you have your dog back safe and sound."

She scowled. "I don't know what you're talking about."

"Why does everyone insist on lying to me?" Stubbs sighed and rubbed the back of his neck, pacing. He faced her. "I can smell the muddy magic on you. Jeremiah Bassett's work is hard to miss. He likes to mix up all the different creeds, you know. He's covered you in a whole shoddy patchwork of protection spells, and there's only one reason for that. He's trying to keep you hidden." Stubbs nodded at his men. "Search her."

Two men groped her roughly. They stripped off the Eyeing ward Uncle had given her and tossed it to Stubbs, who remarked, "Crude, but effective." Then one of the men found the heavy lump in her duster pocket.

"Mr. Stubbs." He reached into her coat and yelped, snatching his hand back as though he'd been bitten.

"That's it." Stubbs yanked Hettie's coat off as if it were on fire. He turned it upside down and flapped it out until Diablo tumbled from the pocket, landing in the dirt with a heavy thud.

"Son of a bitch." He laughed, eyes glinting with triumph. "Finally." He picked it up with a gloved hand, but as he held it, smoke rose between his fingers. He narrowed his eyes, whispering an incantation. The smoke thickened, and he dropped it, swearing. Ashen bits of his glove flaked off. He glared at Hettie. "You bonded with the Devil's Revolver?"

When she didn't answer fast enough, he slapped her across the face. Blood filled her mouth as the sting became a dull ache. "C'mon, speak up."

She spat at his feet. "I don't know what I did."

"Obviously. That's your work there, ain't it?" He pointed at the corpses lying in the street, a thick swarm of flies gathering on them. "Murder's still a crime, far as I know. You'll be swinging before the week's up."

"You're not the law, Stubby," Uncle's voice boomed.

"I can still take this girl into custody for possession of stolen property. My sorcerers on the other side will have the remote Zoom tunnel reopen in a few minutes. We'll take Miss Alabama back with us to Chicago and let the law deal with her there." Triumph and menace tinged his words. He tilted his chin thoughtfully. "I don't have to do any of that, of course." He nodded, and the rope was removed from around her neck. He picked up her duster and flapped it out, then handed it back to her. She stuffed her arms through the sleeves, drawing it closed around her. Diablo still lay on the dirt between her and the lead detective. "In fact, I'm willing to forget any of this ever happened. All I want is to return what's been stolen to its proper owner. I'm sure you can relate. Your sister is very dear to you. Alive or dead, not knowing can be so painful." His smile was brief, grim. "I could ease that pain for you. You've gone through enough with your parents and your ranch. I went out there, you know, had a look for myself. It's a beautiful piece of land. Shame you're giving it up."

Hettie's heart squeezed. Home seemed so far away.

Stubbs went on earnestly, "I can help you find your sister. I'll dispatch my best men to bring little Abby home. We can help you get a good price for your ranch and start you up somewhere new. Or we can buy the farm back for you, and you can run the place yourself. You'd like that, wouldn't you?"

Uncle growled, "He's a lying snake, Hettie. Don't trust him."

She licked her lips. "What do you want from me?"

"Relinquish Diablo. It's bonded to you, and the only way anyone can take it from you is for you to willingly hand it over. That's all you have to do. Then we can start looking for Abby. Why, I bet you'll see her before the end of the week."

Hettie's hands clenched. "If I hand Diablo over right now, you'll just kill me."

"I could have shot you a dozen times over since we started talking. Believe it or not, I'm offering you the easy way out. That gun doesn't belong to you. You owe your sister the best possible chance of being found. Isn't that what your parents would've wanted?"

"I'll shoot the girl myself before I let her hand Diablo over to you. Y'hear me, Stubbs?"

Hettie bristled, could almost feel her head centered in Uncle's cross hairs. What would killing her achieve? Why did everyone want this gun? Too many questions circled her brain, but they were all muddled by the immediate mortal danger she faced.

"He's just trying to make things difficult," Stubbs said dismissively. "It's true. I could just shoot you and take Diablo. But I'd rather not do that. Too many... complications. And I hate it when things don't go smoothly."

Hettie chewed her lip. "So I give it to you, and Uncle shoots me. I don't give it to you, and you shoot me."

He shrugged. "Seems to me you've got a better chance of staying alive if you hand the Devil's Revolver over now. I'm in a charitable mood."

Charitable enough to end her life quickly, she was sure. Her eyes flicked to the gun.

"Don't be stupid. Hand it over. My offer won't stand forever, and I'm losing patience."

She met Stubbs's beady eyes and planted herself firmly. "No."

He sighed and tugged on his cuffs. "That's what I thought." He drew his sidearm and aimed at Cymon.

She didn't have time to cry out. All she thought was, *Stop!* and then time thickened and slowed, as if she'd been dunked in molasses.

Stubbs pulled the trigger. The blast from the muzzle of his gun flared bright and loud but slowly, almost like a flower blooming. She dove for Diablo. The moment the grip was in her hand, she twisted and fired.

The bullets hovering inches from Cymon evaporated in a brilliant beam of light.

Her pulse suddenly sped up, and she gasped as the ground became a solid thing beneath her. She scrambled to her feet, weapon pointed at Stubbs.

"You blasted witch—" His face turned a shade of puce. "That gun doesn't belong to you, y'hear?"

"It doesn't belong to you, either." She pulled the hammer down. The other men's weapons *cha-chacked* in response.

"You don't know what you're dealing with. What that thing can do."

"Blow off a horse's head, punch a hole through a man's chest, and stop bullets midair, from what I've seen so far." Hettie felt as though her insides had turned to liquid, flowing hotly within her. She was calm, but beneath it all, something simmered, making her fingertips tingle. "Wonder what it'll do at point-blank range?"

Stubbs's nostrils flared. "You kill me, and you'll have the full force of the Pinkerton Detecting Agency and the law after you."

In her mind's eye, she'd already pulled that trigger, watching a bloody hole expand in the man's chest. The revolver sagged in her hands as though it had gained ten pounds. She tightened her hold on it with both hands. "Let my dog go."

A beat, and Stubbs gestured to the man behind her. She didn't look away until Cymon bumped up against her thigh, panting happily. He was still wearing a muzzle, but he seemed otherwise unharmed.

"Hettie!" Uncle shouted.

"Barney, take the shot!"

That treacly time lag kicked in at the same moment a familiar wave of power slammed into her. Heatless fire washed across her as she fell to her knees, just as the sniper's bullet bored into the dirt beside her. She rolled away as time sped up once more, bringing Diablo to bear, wrists straining against the weight.

Someone yelled, "Ambush!" just as another wave of fire blew over the group, knocking people to the ground. This time, though, the flames sizzled, heat washing across her cheeks. Hettie smelled singed hair, and dry tinder smoke filled her nostrils.

She scrambled to a half crouch and started running. Cymon bounded at her side.

"Stop her!" Stubbs shouted. Shots rang out, and she ducked and dodged behind a building.

"Go left," a deep, gruff voice uttered in her ear. "There's a chestnut mare there. Take her and ride west."

She didn't question the order. The horse was within sight and watching her expectantly. Hettie leaped onto her back, and the mare took off as soon as she'd seated herself. The big brown dog loped beside them.

Hettie clung to the reins, but it quickly became apparent that she had no control over her mount. The horse headed west, lithe and straight as an arrow, flying across the rugged land away from Uncle and Stubbs, away from Ling who waited for her with Jezebel outside of town. She tried to stop the horse, but the mare wouldn't let up no matter how hard Hettie pulled on the reins.

A flash of light dazzled her eyes as it whizzed past her ear, and she glanced over her shoulder. Two of Stubbs's men were catching up on commandeered horses. She could see from the bloody froth around their mouths and the full whites of their eyes that the poor creatures had been hexed.

Hettie drew Diablo from her pocket. She could barely hold it up.

One of the men had his palms together, speaking some kind of spell. She aimed and pulled the trigger. The syrup feeling came again, and her mind's eye momentarily soared—

The first rider's horse screamed as its legs became bloody mist beneath him. The Pinkerton agent sailed through the air and landed in a crumpled heap in the dust.

Hettie ducked as another ball of energy sizzled through the air, just brushing her right shoulder and sending paralyzing pins and needles through her arm.

Indignation blasted through her. She switched hands, twisted around and fired.

Her shot tore through the air and shredded the man's left arm down to the bone, the greenish light tearing up his shoulder and into his face. His blood-curdling scream was cut off as his horse reared and flung him from the saddle. Hexed and riderless, it streaked away, cursed to run until its heart gave out.

Hettie's momentary relief was shattered as her whole body seized in another bone-racking spasm of agony. The ground rushed up at her.

The world went black.

CHAPTER ELEVEN

The stone floor was cold, the straw even dirtier than before. The cages were fuller, the shadows within whimpering and stirring restlessly. Dirt-crusted fingernails scrabbled at the metal bars. Blood and dark urine ran into a drain in the middle of the floor. The room reeked of fear and desperation.

Hettie...

A wail pierced the air, and Hettie opened her eyes. Slowly, the real world came into focus, the tang of wood smoke replacing the stench of old blood. A coyote's forlorn howl sent chills down her spine.

Her back was hot, her chest cold. She seemed to be staring at a wall of black beyond the ring of tall dry grass. She heard a short whine, then warm, foul wetness bathed her face. She pushed Cymon off and groaned as every muscle in her body screamed with pins and needles.

"She lives." The voice was rough, like the crunch of gravel.

She bolted up to sitting, and her head spun. The orange firelight eventually resolved so she could make out the huge shape looming on the other side.

The man leaned into the light and tipped up his hat. "Miss Alabama."

Her skin prickled. "Mr. Woodroffe." She kept one eye on the bounty hunter while scanning her surroundings, seeking the nearest weapon and exit. For all that he'd done for her, she did not trust him and she did not know him. She summoned all her bravado and added, "Or should I call you Camden Cobra?"

"Walker would be fine."

Cymon's tail wagged, and he butted his head, now free of its muzzle, against the man's thigh. The bounty hunter rubbed his ears affectionately. "That was you who told me to get on the horse," Hettie surmised.

"Lilith would've taken you someplace much safer if you'd held on tighter."

Somewhere in the shadows to their left, the horse nickered her agreement.

Hettie rubbed her hands on her thighs, then suddenly remembered the mage gun. She patted herself down frantically. "Where's my gun?"

"Diablo, you mean." His eyes remained steady on her. "You're bonded with the Devil's Revolver, aren't you?"

Hettie didn't respond at first, but then a pressure began on her tongue and she blurted, "Yes."

He dusted his fingers over his long black coat. "It's safe for now. I didn't want to get shot the minute you woke up."

"Where's my uncle?"

"I don't know."

"You left him in town with the Pinkertons?"

"'Left him' implies we were together to start with." He glanced up at her. "My only aim was getting you and Diablo away from the town and those men."

Her throat tightened. She'd abandoned the old man again. She tried to stand, but her whole body ached. Every muscle was stretched taut, and her joints and tendons pulled like old leather stretched across a too-big frame. "What...what's wrong with me?" She lay back, exhausted.

Walker looked grim. "I suppose no one told you what happens when you use Diablo."

Apart from that euphoric feeling of riding with the bullet? The gold-syrup quality of time and space that she moved through as gracefully as a swan through a pond?

"The reason you're in so much pain is that you've aged, Miss Alabama." He sounded perfectly calm. "That's the price of bonding with Diablo. For every man's life taken by the Devil's Revolver, one year is taken off yours."

Hettie's stomach turned, and her vision grew hazy. She couldn't have heard that right. She ran a shaking hand through her hair and stared at her fingers. "My hair's still short. And my nails, too."

"The curse doesn't change time, just age." Walker stood. "If it had changed time, you'd be dead of starvation."

"How do I reverse it?"

He fixed his hard gaze on her. "You can't take back your life any more than you can bring back the men you killed."

She pressed a fist to her lips, nauseated. She'd killed three men with Diablo. Lost three years of her own life. She touched her face, wondered what three years would have done to her. From seventeen to twenty in days... would she still look the same?

Walker toyed with a talisman on a chain. He spoke a brief incantation and pocketed the charm. "Tell me about your father," he said. "Or should I call him Elias Blackthorn?"

She kept her lips clamped tightly against the building pressure in her mouth.

"You did know your father, the man called John Alabama, was a notorious gang leader named Elias Blackthorn, didn't you?"

Hettie swallowed tightly, trying to stem the words threatening to pour from her mouth. Walker peered at her. "You're putting up quite a fight against my truthtelling spell, Miss Alabama. Bassett must've fixed you up with some serious counterspells." He uttered a single, dismissive word. The pressure on her throat and tongue eased. "Why don't we do this the old-fashioned way," he suggested firmly. "I'll answer your questions if you answer mine."

"What if you don't like my answers?" She was fully aware that she was alone with this man, weakened and unable to fight. And he had very big hands with some very bruised knuckles.

He shrugged his broad shoulders, and the black duster lifted away from his belt. At least three knives, two sidearms, and a set of brass knuckles glinted menacingly from his waist. "I wouldn't be too concerned about whether I like them or not. All I want is the truth. Tell me about how you came to possess Diablo."

If he wanted her dead, he wouldn't be talking to her now, so she took a chance. "You answer a question for me first. You were the one who saved our necks the night I rescued Ling Tsang in Hawksville, weren't you? You used the same fake fire spell on the Pinks back there."

He lifted his chin a fraction. "Wasn't quite so fake this time."

"Why'd you do it?"

"Same reason you stuck your neck out for a Celestial twice now. I don't abide by mob rule, and I'm not a fan of lynchings. Besides"—his lips lifted a fraction—"I can't resist helping a damsel in distress."

She tamped down her irritation and focused. "And that man Teddy—what do you know about him?"

"Theodore Willis's been on and off wanted signs for everything from petty theft to battery and murder. He's been running with the Crowes for nearly a decade. When I ended up in Hawksville looking for your father, I found him working for Boss Smythe."

"Why were you looking for my pa?"

"I'll be frank, Miss Alabama. I'm here for Diablo. I'd been hunting down members of the Crowe gang to see what they knew about it. In all the stories I'd heard, it was the Elias Blackthorn after Jed Crowe who'd absconded with the legendary gun. And he supposedly dropped off the face of the earth. But there was another story. One about a Division agent named Jeremiah Bassett who'd chased him across the country and then gave up somewhere in Alabama. I was tailing Shadow Frank when I heard of a Jeremiah Bassett living around those parts. Common enough name, and I've dead-ended at other doorsteps before. But then I overheard those boys talking to you at the shooting competition. Miss Hettie Alabama, daughter of one John Alabama, a renowned marksman." He gave her a sideways look. "In my business, there's no such thing as coincidence. That's why I joined the shooting competition at the last minute. I wanted to see what you could do, see if you knew about your pa. And then he went and shot Shadow Frank." He rubbed his neck. "I knew then I had the right man. Once I sorted things out with the marshal and collected my reward, I came out to your ranch. All I'd planned to do was ask some questions. I had no idea Bassett would be protecting your father. I underestimated him, too. He had me riding out of Newhaven faster than you could say wild-goose chase. That sneak's probably got an influence spell on the ranch somewhere."

He sat forward. "Now you answer a question for me. What exactly possessed you to bond with Diablo?"

Hettie rubbed her palms over her knees. Her hands were still bloody. "I didn't do it on purpose."

"You sure about that?" He shook his head. "No better way to ensure a magical artifact sticks with you than by bonding. There're a lot of men willing to kill for that gun."

"Including you?"

"You have no idea, do you?" When she didn't answer, he explained, "The reason Stubbs didn't kill you for that gun right away is that if he had, a gate to hell would've opened up. That's why it's called the Devil's Revolver."

She stared. "You're pulling my leg."

"I don't joke when it comes to dark magic, and that piece is as dark as they get. It's best if you hand it over to someone who knows how to deal with it."

"I won't give Diablo up," Hettie said staunchly. "The Crowe gang took my sister and killed my parents, and almost killed me, too. Teddy told me they headed south to the border. I need Diablo to get her back."

One dark eyebrow arched up. "You expect to do that how?"

"Butch Crowe wants Diablo. So I'll offer him a trade."

Walker cast his gaze down. He stirred the fire with a long stick. "You can't do that. That revolver doesn't belong to the Crowe gang. It never even belonged to Elias Blackthorn." He drew the stick out of the fire, studying the orange ember at the tip as it crumbled to ash. "I was hired to bring Diablo back to its true maker. He's a sorcerer in Mexico, goes by the name of Javier Punta."

Hettie was instantly suspicious. "I thought all mage guns were made by the Kukulos using blood magic."

He didn't look impressed by her knowledge. "Blood magic has been a part of many cultures' magical traditions for centuries. The

Kukulos want everyone to believe theirs is the purest and most powerful of the magics, but that's a lie."

"So why does this Javier Punta want Diablo?"

The logs in the fire pit collapsed, sending a flurry of brilliant sparks into the air. They ascended from their fiery crucible to fade to nothing in the sky. "He forged the weapon when he was young and foolish. Unfortunately, the weapon was stolen from him and used to cause much pain and suffering. Now he refuses to die until it is back in his hands and he can take it out of the world with him."

"Why should I believe you?"

He glanced up briefly. "Never said you had to."

"So you want me to just hand it over to you?"

"That would be easiest, yes." He smiled briefly, menacingly. "But that's not going to happen, is it?"

She grew hot beneath the blanket and shivered at the same time. But she refused to be intimidated.

He regarded her thoughtfully with those penetrating blue eyes. "Tell me, what makes you think your sister's still alive? You've...sensed something, haven't you?"

She didn't answer him. She wasn't about to tell a stranger she was having visions of her sister's confinement, or that she'd heard Abby calling her name. He'd dismiss it as the ravings of a grief-stricken female. "In dreams, perhaps, or even visions?" he pressed. "Have you talked to her?"

He was a powerful enough sorcerer that he seemed to know about things she couldn't explain, so she relented. The worst he could do was laugh at her. "Twice now, in my sleep, I saw a stone room with cages. I suppose it could have just been a dream, but I could hear and smell everything as if I was there."

"Was your sister a potential?"

"She was still too young to get tested. But sometimes she'd get all dreamy and tell us she was talking to her friends. Ma was sick when she was pregnant with her, and she was never well after Abby, either. Truth is, Abby's never been altogether right in the head." She felt a little guilty for describing her so perfunctorily. "She also said she can talk to our dead brother."

"So she could be gifted." Walker rubbed his chin. "I won't discount the possibility that your sister's a necromancer, rare as it is. But she could be confusing him with someone else she's talking to. I've heard that some people have the ability to speak to others far, far away with their minds."

"Is it like how you and Uncle and that Thomas Stubbs talked in Hawksville?"

"That was just a voice projection spell. I'm talking about men who can project themselves straight across the country and appear in another person's thoughts, or sometimes show the person they're communicating with their location. It's possible she was trying to tell you where she was." Walker's probing look lingered and made Hettie's skin tingle. She forced herself to meet his eye. "I might be able to help you find Abby if you let me," he said.

Cautious optimism crept into her breast, but she wouldn't let a few promises mislead her again. "How?"

"I can look at your memories of this vision, study the images you've seen. These links leave impressions—like a trail of breadcrumbs. She found you all the way out here somehow, so she'll have left a path. If I can retrace it, we can pinpoint her location."

She recoiled. "I'm not letting you in my head. You want Diablo. What's to say you won't plant some idea to make me hand it over?" She remembered Uncle's manipulation and found herself mad all over again.

Walker's glacial gaze made her wince. "If I were that desperate, we wouldn't be talking right now."

True enough, but she still couldn't trust him. "Don't take it personally, Mr. Woodroffe. I can't afford to trust anyone. Uncle Jeremiah misled me about his intentions, Butch Crowe nearly did me in, the Pinks are out to kill me, and now you come along—"

He moved lightning quick like a striking viper and pinched her chin, forcing her to look directly into his stormy eyes. Her breath hitched, and her heart pounded. "You listen to me, Miss Alabama. I've been nothing but gracious and decent to you. I saved your life back there. Do not compare me to those lowlife sons of—"

His words were cut off as a snarling mass bowled into him. Hettie scrambled back as Walker rolled across the dirt, struggling with a slightly smaller figure. Cymon started barking but didn't join in the fray.

"Miss Hettie, run!"

Walker rose up and slugged his assailant across the jaw, but the slimmer man clung ferociously, long limbs wrapped around his waist and neck.

"Ling?"

Jezebel's familiar whinny confirmed the man's identity. Hettie sat frozen for a heartbeat as the men struggled.

"Ling, stop." She stumbled to her feet just as the two men broke apart. Walker drew his gun. Hettie leaped between them. "Don't shoot." She turned to Ling. "It's okay. Mr. Woodroffe saved me."

Walker grabbed her wrist and yanked her behind him. "You don't know for sure who that is," Walker growled. "Some Pinkerton agents use glamor magic to disguise themselves."

She snatched her hand out of his grip and glared. "Ling, how much money did I give you the day you left Newhaven?"

"You didn't *give* me anything. It was a loan, and one I will repay with blood if I must."

Good enough for her. "Stand down, Mr. Woodroffe. This is Ling Tsang. You've met before."

The bounty hunter's fingers flexed. Then he holstered the gun.

Ling brushed himself off. The soles of his bare feet were cracked and dirty from the treacherous walk across the ground. The two men sized each other up as they had in Boss Smythe's ring. Cymon stayed rooted, tail wagging.

"Miss Hettie, are you...all right?" Ling eyed Walker narrowly, his mouth pinched in the corners. He was probably worried about her honor.

"I'm fine," she hurried to assure him. "This is Walker Woodroffe. He was the one who saved us in Hawksville."

"A fighter and a sorcerer," Ling mused, and addressed Hettie. "When you didn't come back, I went looking for you. Hawksville was left in quite a ruin. Half the town was on fire."

"Wasn't me," Walker said at Hettie's accusing look. "I only cast that spell twice before I hightailed it outta there. Had to be Bassett and that Stubbs fella."

"Did you happen to see my Uncle in town?" Hettie pressed.

Ling blinked. "Mr. Bassett? No. I thought you said he was drinking in a saloon somewhere?"

Hettie's web of lies was starting to tangle. She said quickly, "In Hawksville, yeah."

Ling didn't question her further. She didn't like lying to him, because of the three men she trusted him most. He'd had no idea what Diablo was and hadn't wanted anything to do with it. And he'd expressed his wish to help find Abby, which was more than what either Uncle or Walker had offered. Guilt settled over her like another layer of grime.

The bounty hunter dusted his hands and nodded at Hettie. "She's got some bruised ribs. Think you can do anything for her?"

Ling scowled at his commanding tone, and Walker's dark eyebrow cocked up. "You're a healer, aren't you? I can feel the Qi coming off you, you know."

"I will heal her." The way he said it told them he was doing it for her, not because he'd been ordered to.

"Qi?" she asked.

"It is the source of my power. The energy of the body and spirit." He smoothed a palm over her side, soothing away the aches in her muscles and joints, and she sighed. She was beginning to like his touch a little too much.

While Ling healed her, Walker walked in a wide perimeter around the campsite, weaving his fingers through the air, wrists jangling with talismans as he cast protective spells to shield them. Hettie wondered if he had forgotten to erect them earlier or whether Ling had somehow broken through the barrier and they had to be renewed.

"What does he want?" Ling asked quietly as he probed her ribs.

She considered not telling him about Diablo's history, but she couldn't hide the truth from everyone all at once. Briefly, she explained Woodfroffe's mission and related her past encounters with the bounty hunter, starting with the day of the Robson boys' shooting contest. Then she explained Diablo's curse. Ling remained unperturbed when she told him she'd killed three men since they'd parted early that morning.

"Is there anything you can do to reverse the curse?" Hettie asked hopefully.

"Healing magic can't reverse a geis like this. But I can't claim to know all the secrets of the old masters." Ling lowered his voice further. "Do you trust him?"

"Not even a little. But he hasn't killed me yet, so that's something."

Walker rejoined them, glancing at Ling's bare feet. "Pretty brave to be walking across rattlesnake country with no boots on. You're either lucky or light on your feet." He went to a pile on the ground, where he picked up a pair of boots and tossed them his way. "Don't complain if they don't fit. I got 'em off one of the Pinks Miss Alabama shot."

Without another word, Walker distributed hard biscuits and passed around a canteen of water. She doubted poison was his weapon of choice, and ate ravenously and without complaint. A dank chill had seeped into her bones. She stayed crouched by the fire, soaking up as much of its warmth as she could.

It was a long time before Ling said, "Thank you for saving my life. And Miss Hettie's."

Walker stabbed at the fire. "Not me you need to be thanking. Miss Alabama's the one who got you out of that noose."

"Yes." He bowed his head. "Which is why I've pledged myself to serving and protecting her while she searches for her sister."

"Noble of you." Woodroffe took out a knife from his boot along with a whetstone from his pocket and gave the short, sharp blade a few quick, precise strokes. "But what's in it for you really?"

"Not all of us are out to make a profit." Ling's eyes glinted like two onyx stones. "My honor means more than any bounty ever could."

Walker scoffed. "Honor doesn't put food in your belly or keep a roof over your head. She offer you a reward to help find her sister?"

"I don't need her money," Ling asserted. "Her family provided me with more than I can ever repay."

"Sure." Walker slid the knife back in his boot and rolled out a gun-cleaning kit. He carefully began disassembling his weapons. "So, Miss Alabama, before we were so rudely interrupted by your champion"—he flicked a look toward Ling—"how exactly do you plan to track down your sister?"

The biscuit stuck in her throat. "She went south, so that's where I'll go."

"And what? Storm the Crowe gang's hideout? A girl and a Chinaman with a spark of healing magic and one enchanted six-gun between them hardly stands a chance against that bunch, much less the Pinkertons who're after you."

She crossed her arms. "If you're so concerned about my safety, you should return my gun."

"No, I don't think that's going to happen. Besides, it'd be safer out of your hands. A farm girl like you shouldn't worry her pretty little head about it. Just let me deal with it."

Hettie ground her teeth together. "That gun is *mine*. My father and mother died protecting it. You have no right to keep it from me."

Walker paused, peering over the wheel. "If you fire it again, the Pinkerton Agency will be on you in minutes. Diablo gives off a very powerful signature, like a stone dropping in a still pond. They have a team of remote Zoom tunnel conductors at their disposal, which means they'll find you wherever you are within minutes of pulling that trigger."

"They're already looking for me. They're probably trying to track me down right now." She grew nervous. She hadn't noticed its effects before, but now, without Uncle's anti-Eye charm, she felt exposed. "If I don't have a weapon to protect myself with, I'll be dead for sure."

Walker met her stare coolly. "I'm not giving it back to you."

Hettie clenched her fists. A tremor started in her trigger finger. She curved her hand, picturing Diablo's grip digging into her palm.

The weight became real and solid. She swung her arm up and pointed the gun at Walker.

"You conjured it!" Ling jerked back in surprise.

Hettie's hand trembled. Her finger spasmed over the trigger guard. Heart thumping, she lowered the weapon.

"So it's true." Walker buffed the barrel of his gun, glancing up only briefly. "I had to be certain you were actually bonded," he said. "I put Diablo under a hide spell with a few safety wards. You broke through them like they were nothing."

She stared at the ivory grip, sticky with blood that should have dried by now. It felt as though her hands would never be clean. "I don't know if you realize just how dangerous that is," Walker went on. "With a thought, that weapon is primed and loaded and aimed to kill. It doesn't even need to be in your hand. You get angry or frightened, and it could be there, and you could be shooting someone you loved in the face without realizing you'd done it."

"That won't happen." Hettie shoved it hastily into her pocket and wiped her hands on her soiled skirt. Her one good dress was thoroughly ruined now, she thought, and wondered at the strange trail of her thoughts. Her clothes hardly mattered considering what she faced.

"You don't know that. You don't know anything about that weapon, and your ignorance, more than anything else, is what'll do you the most harm." Walker loaded the freshly cleaned revolver and snapped the wheel back in place. "The way I see it, if you give me the Diablo now, I can take it back to Punta and it'll all be over. No one will chase you, no one will try to kill you. And then I can come back and help you find your sister."

"You say that as though your word means something," Ling said. "What would be in it for *you*? You're just a mercenary for hire."

Hearing his words parroted back to him, Walker sent Ling a dark look. "When I make a promise, I keep my word."

That didn't exactly reassure Hettie, but there was something in his steely demeanor that told her he was a man who wouldn't renege on a deal. "The only time I'll be giving up Diablo is when I get my sister back," she said.

Walker sat back, hands resting on his knees. "Tell me why you think your sister can be found."

"Before he…Before I killed him"—she forced herself to say—"Teddy said something about my sister being taken south to the Mexican border. He said they went by remote Zoom tunnel to a hideout or something."

"The border stretches two thousand miles. You're not exactly narrowing down the search any."

"Why would the Crowe gang take Miss Abby south?" Ling asked.

"The border towns are havens for illegals and cross-border smugglers," Walker said. "I've heard stories of children being sold on both sides of the border as slaves or child brides…or as blood sacrifices."

Hettie thought about her dreams of the stone room with the cages and shuddered. She didn't want to think about what Abby would be used for.

"Whatever it is you saw in your vision, it would help if I could see it, too," Walker insisted.

"You've had visions?" Ling asked.

Hettie told him about her dreams.

"Her sister might be projecting," Walker explained.

Ling considered her a long moment. "If you trust me, I can attempt to rebuild your memory so you can give us clearer details about what you saw. If you can tell us about the surroundings—the vegetation and geography—perhaps Mr. Woodroffe will have a better idea of where to look."

Hettie looked between the two men. She didn't relish the idea of anyone poking through her thoughts, but without something more to go on she would have a hard time finding Abby. She nodded at Ling. "All right. Just promise you won't go messing around with anything in there." She didn't need to look at Walker's face to know he wasn't happy she'd picked Ling over him for this ritual.

Ling sat cross-legged in front of her and placed his palms on either side of her head, lightly brushing her temples. "Think about Abby and the last time you saw her."

She closed her eyes and thought about that night at the ranch, the fire raging through the barn and silo, Abby's piercing scream. Warmth trickled through her, like tepid bathwater running across her skin. The stone room slowly formed in her mind's eye, as if arising from a fog, hazy and dreamlike. All she saw were empty, shadowy cages. She didn't smell the putrid air or feel the cold stone as before. It was a lifeless image, frozen in time.

"I see the room," she said.

"Are there any windows?" Ling prompted.

She looked about. "No."

"What do you see?"

"There are fourteen cages. I can't see what's inside them now, but the last time I saw this place, there were children. There's a wood door on the far wall. And a drain in the floor, with a big grate on top."

"You said there are no windows. How can you see?"

141

She looked up. An oil lamp cast its eerie, unwavering glow around the dungeon. "There's a lantern by the door."

"Pick up the lantern."

She reached out tentatively. The thing wasn't exactly solid, but the fixture moved with her, casting its light now in strange, shifting patterns, like sunlight rippling through little waves in a shallow stream.

"Look at the ground carefully. What do you see?"

"It's damp." She swallowed thickly. "There's blood."

"What else?"

"A bit of straw."

"What about dirt? Sand?"

She squinted. "Sand. Yes, there's a lot of sand in the corners." She looked at the grouting between the roughly hewn stones. "It's on the walls, too."

"What color is it?"

She peered, reached out to the little piles, but they didn't stir at her probing. "Reddish."

"They're in the desert." Walker's voice sent ripples through the vision. The lantern dimmed until she could no longer see the room. "My guess is Arizona."

Hettie opened her eyes, slightly disoriented, blinking away the dazzling firelight. "That narrows it down, doesn't it?"

"Not by much, but it's a start."

Hope flared bright in Hettie, brighter than it had since she'd woken. "Mr. Woodroffe, I'll make you a deal. You're a trained bounty hunter—bring my sister to me alive and I'll give you Diablo."

To her surprise, he shook his head. "It's one thing to go after criminals and men on the run. But facing the Crowe gang in their stronghold while they have some powerful and mysterious sorcerer in their employ?" He gave a dismissive wave. "That's a whole other kettle of fish. Besides, there's no guarantee your sister is alive or will stay alive once I find her."

"She's alive. I'm sure of it." That simple thought kept her sane, kept her going. She caught and held the bounty hunter's blue gaze. "Please, Mr. Woodroffe. She's all I have left. Dead or alive...I need to bring her home. Diablo is yours after that. I promise."

Walker pursed his lips, wiped a hand across his mouth. "I can't be right in the head to even consider this suicide mission." Hesitantly, he spat into his hand and held it out. "All right. We have a deal."

She spat into her own, and they shook. A fizzling sensation streaked up her arm—the bounty hunter had enacted a contract spell to seal the pact.

Walker grimaced. "May God have mercy on us all."

CHAPTER TWELVE

The three travelers set off the following day, pointed south toward Barney's Rock, the closest town with grounded Zoom tunnel access. If they didn't travel by Zoom or train, they'd be on horseback for weeks before they arrived at the Arizona-Mexico border. Hettie kept Jezebel at a brisk trot for much of the journey, spurred on by a lingering sense of urgency. Her mind ran circles around the horrific abuses Abby might be facing. But she refused to allow herself to think it was too late.

The faithful mare was strong, but because she was carrying both Ling and Hettie, she complained loudly after a short while. To keep Jezebel from going lame, Hettie switched off and rode with Walker on Lilith. Hettie had changed back into trousers and a shirt, so at least some of her modesty was preserved. She couldn't settle in the saddle, though, pressed up against the sweltering Walker, who smelled like sour unwashed man and horse.

"You keep fidgeting like that and Lilith is going to throw you," Walker told her sharply. She grumbled an apology and tried to relax. She was tired and sore and hungry, on top of being worried about Abby. Walker sighed. "I know you're anxious. But we can't go much faster than this."

Every night, Walker would erect protective spells around their campsite while she and Ling rubbed the exhausted horses down. They'd eat more of the bounty hunter's hard, flavorless biscuits while massaging saddlesore muscles. Hettie missed hot meals and soft beds, and wondered whether the unnaturally added years were making her feel the lumpy ground more keenly. She refused to complain, though. Her empty stomach did that loudly enough for all three of them.

On their third night, Ling came back from a nearby stream with a pair of fat trout. He cooked them over the fire and insisted Hettie eat the better portion. She tried to resist, but then Ling threatened to give his entire portion to her if she refused. It seemed he was bent on taking care of her the way her parents would, and it both irked and comforted her to know he cared. Walker watched him with suspicion. She was becoming aware of a strange tension between the two men. They didn't speak much, and certainly not to each other. She caught them studying each other through narrowed eyes more than once.

The tall, dry grasses of Montana became greener pastures to the south as they moved into Wyoming. The horses stayed well-fed on the sweet field grass. Cymon was having a grand old time, bounding alongside the riders and scaring game hens out of their nests. He proved a useful companion, bringing her the occasional mangled gopher for supper and providing warmth and comfort when he slept cuddled next to her. The men tolerated him, too, because he seemed to be self-sufficient and never begged for scraps, though he did have the terrible habit of marking his territory too close to the campsite.

Hettie had never ridden so far south. The rolling hills and distant mountains spread beneath the vast blue sky would have been pretty had she not been weighed down with worry for her sister. In her mind's eye, they felt like sentinels keeping vigil, waiting with bated breath for Hettie's first glimpse of Abby since that terrible night on the ranch.

Guilt ate at her for leaving Jeremiah behind, too. Neither Walker nor Ling mentioned him, but it seemed a foregone conclusion that the Pinks had caught the old man. Or possibly killed him. She'd never been terribly attached to the codger, but Pa and Ma had treated him like kin—barely tolerated at times, but a member of their household nonetheless. A space in the family plot had even been saved for him.

One day, in the late afternoon, Hettie spotted movement along the plains—a mottling of color and shadow against the verdant land. She recognized the shapes instantly and grew excited. A herd of wild mustangs grazed in the tall grasses near the bottom of the hill. A big black stallion strolled among them, tossing his head almost haughtily, his jet-black coat rippling over sinewy muscles. Hettie had never seen such a magnificent creature in all her life.

"We need to stop." She pointed. "I want to catch me one of those horses. The big black, there."

"Are you crazy? We don't have time for this. Breaking a horse takes days, if not weeks."

"Then you're doing it wrong. I need a horse. We'll make better time once all three of us are on horseback."

"Except that you don't have a saddle. What are you going to do? Ride bareback all the way to the border?"

She lifted her chin. "If I have to."

"You sure you can catch him without any charms?" Ling asked skeptically. Most people who wanted to rope and break mustangs would use a talisman to lure the beasts and quiet them enough to slip a lasso around their neck. The smarter ones—the ones worth their weight in silver dollars—never fell for the charms. Hettie could already tell the stallion was going to be one of them.

"All I need is some rope and your help." At their hesitation, she glanced up. "Don't worry. I've done this before with Pa."

"You might catch him, but I don't see how you plan to break that monster. He's got to be upwards of fifteen hands."

Hettie gave him a confident smile. "I may not have any magical gifts, but I can break a horse. I broke the last three, in fact."

"In a pen, maybe. Out here, he's more likely to bolt and run until you fall off."

"I know a calming spell," Ling volunteered. "Your father taught it to me to help with the cattle. I'm not sure it'll work on horses, though."

"This is crazy," Walker muttered. "We should be spending this time hunting or resting. Our supplies are running low, and I don't fancy going to bed hungry after chasing a wild stallion all over hell's half acre."

"You're a sorcerer," Hettie said. "You must know a simple barrier spell to pen them in."

Walker pursed his lips. "I can put up a barrier, sure. But you'll never be able to break that mustang without him breaking you first. Why not pick one of the other horses? How about that little filly over there?"

"I want the black," Hettie said firmly. Pa would have picked him, too. She knew she could do it. She didn't have the gift, but she was good with horses. "We need strong horses. If I can't break him..." She trailed off. She'd almost said, *Then how will I face Butch Crowe?*

Walker huffed out a breath. He detached the lariat from his saddle and passed his palms over it, muttering. The air tingled briefly. When he handed the rope to her, it felt heavy, as if it were chains instead of good hemp. "This'll help some, assuming you actually rope him."

She stuck her tongue out. "I lived on a cattle ranch. I learned to rope before I could walk."

He wasn't impressed. "If you do manage to rope him, I can erect a barrier to keep him contained. But if you can't get him to calm down after an hour, I'm taking it down. We shouldn't be wasting daylight on this." He tossed her his leather gloves and spurred Lilith into position.

"Cymon, go with him. Keep the horses together, okay?" The big dog trotted after the bounty hunter. She tugged on Walker's well-worn gloves. They were far too big but would keep her from getting rope burn.

The two men slowly walked their mounts on either side of the herd. The big black watched warily, ears twitching. Hettie prepared her lasso as she walked in a slow half crouch toward the stallion. A few of the animals looked up balefully but continued munching on grass as she crept past. At first the big black didn't pay her any attention, but the scrape of the lasso against the leather gloves made his ears prick toward her.

His nostrils flared, and his ears flattened. He let out a disdainful snort, turned, and trotted away from her.

Jezebel intercepted him, whinnying. The stallion paused, taken aback. The other horses looked up, startled by the intruder among them. Ling sprawled low against the mare's body, almost becoming a part of the saddle he clung to, one hand extended as he muttered an incantation.

The big black let out an angry cry and rushed at Jezebel. She faltered and canted back. Ling fought to stay seated, but the stallion crashed into the horse's side and sent him sprawling into the dirt. He quickly rolled away from the deadly stomp of head-sized hooves.

Hettie worked fast. She could see Walker and Cymon trying to keep the herd contained. If they stampeded, she'd be caught in the rush.

She prepared her lasso hurriedly as the stallion advanced on Jezebel, ears back, head lowered. She danced away when he reared, pawing at the air. Then he turned to glare at the man on the ground.

Ling was once again trying his spell, facing the horse head-on in an attempt to placate the furious beast. The big black stomped the ground and snorted.

Hettie snuck up behind the stallion, staying to the side of his flank just out of reach of a powerful hind kick. He was a lot bigger than she'd first thought, but what a magnificent creature. She twirled the lasso into a good-sized loop, sent up a prayer, and tossed the rope.

The lariat cinched around the beast's head. It took him a moment to realize he was caught, and he let out such a cry of outrage that the herd panicked and bolted.

Hettie danced around to the stallion's side, grabbed his mane, and climbed up, practically scaling the mountain of sleek muscle. The spelled lariat held him in place, keeping the creature from bucking immediately. Walker opened a bag of sand and rode in a wide circle around the mustang as he spoke an incantation. The moment the circle was complete, Hettie felt a tingle, and the air seemed closer.

The stallion must have felt it, too, because his flesh bunched beneath her. In the moment before he started bucking, Hettie thought to herself, *This was a terrible idea.*

She gripped the stallion's mane and squeezed her knees as he burst into motion. He thrashed, head down, hindquarters leaping, jouncing her hard. He caromed into the edge of the invisible barrier, the impact giving the horse a sizzling sting that sent him shying in the opposite direction. He hit the barrier several times more, and when he realized he was trapped, he let out another outraged scream.

The rest of the herd reacted to his cry. They'd been scattered, panicked and directionless, but then, as if roused by their leader's call, they gathered into an arrowlike stream and stampeded as one in a wide crescent that circled back toward the barrier.

Ling remounted and put himself and Jezebel between the magic pen and the column racing toward him. Jezebel stood her ground nervously as he tried to recast the calming spell, but when it became apparent the herd wasn't going to slow, she pivoted and pulled them out of the path of the stampede.

The stallion kept bucking, trying to throw Hettie. She saw the first wild horses crash into the barrier, glancing off its surface like snowballs and continuing on. The wall of the magical pen shimmered, and the stallion gave another unearthly cry.

"Hettie!" Walker shouted. "I can't hold the barrier—"

The magical containing wall collapsed like a window bursting inward, a shower of energy raining in sparks over her. Hettie clung hard as the horse took off. He sped to the front of the column effortlessly, throwing Hettie left and right in spine-jarring zigzags as he gathered speed. If she tried to jump off now, she'd break her neck or get trampled to death.

Cymon raced alongside the herd, barking and gleefully snapping at hooves. Walker and Lilith rode on the left with Ling and Jezebel lagging behind, but they were both outpaced by the brawny stallion. The big black dashed across the plains, the green-gold grasses blurring in Hettie's vision. His gait was smooth even over the pitted terrain, as if he knew every rock, hummock, and divot in the earth. Hettie's fear was momentarily replaced by wild exhilaration. If Pa were here, he'd be whooping—a horse like this, if broken, would have earned them a lot of money. She could only dream of a ride like this, and as much as she loved Jezebel, the old mare would never be able to match the stallion's strength and speed.

Of course, she'd have to gain control of him first.

The air shook with hoofbeats and smelled of grass and musky wet horse hair. The stallion turned a sharp left, circling back, and the herd followed, bending the stream into a U shape.

"You need to slow him down!" Walker yelled as Lilith angled away from the onrush.

As if she didn't know that already? Hettie grabbed hold of the lasso and yanked with all her might. The stallion gave a sharp cry, and he veered right. His gait changed, bouncing Hettie hard. He peeled away from the herd, trapping her companions within the throng of horses as he raced toward a rocky outcropping.

Hettie pulled at the rope as the horse climbed a hill and leaped recklessly into a narrow gully. If she didn't know better, she'd think he knew exactly what he was doing. He skidded and reared, nearly throwing her off. He could've dashed her brains out against the bedrock rising from the soil. Her elbows and shoulder scraped the wall of the chasm several times—thankfully, the leather duster protected her from the worst injuries.

Hettie squeezed her thighs tight and dug in her heels as the horse thrashed, then took off once more. The gully opened into a rocky outcrop. There, the real fight began. The stallion bucked hard, his mane lashing her cheeks with each whiplike jolt. Every muscle in Hettie's body ached as she clung for dear life, but she'd come this far—there was no way she was giving him up. She needed this horse. He bashed his side against a boulder, barely missing Hettie's leg as she drew it up tight.

Angered by his reckless behavior, she yanked on the lasso hard. "Enough!" she shouted. "You stop this right now before you hurt yourself!"

The horse faltered, stepping nervously. He threw his head left and right, trying to escape the enchanted lasso. Steam rose from his massive body, and he snorted hotly.

"I need you," she said staunchly. The horse shied, and she yanked on the rope again. "I need a ride, y'hear? I need to save my sister. She's barely ten and all alone with some very bad people. I promised my parents I'd take good care of her."

The stallion stilled, ears twitching. "You look like a good, strong horse. I promise, I'll turn you loose after I get Abby home. But right now, we gotta head south and find her before the Crowe gang does something terrible to her. Will you help me?"

The stallion sniffed the air and neighed. His eyes had gone huge, the whites showing clearly. Something strange tinged the air here. Goose bumps rose over her neck, and Hettie glanced around.

He reared suddenly, dumping Hettie from her seat. Stars exploded in her eyes as the back of her head hit the ground. The big black jerked away but faltered when he met another rock face. As he wheeled again, the end of the rope whipped through the air and corded tightly around a tree branch. He yanked and thrashed, but it wouldn't come loose.

Hettie sat up slowly. Then she saw the cougar. The big, mangy cat crouched above them, hackles up, teeth bared. It was a monster of a cat with an ugly, battle-scarred face. Hettie scrambled back, automatically reaching for a rifle that wasn't there...

The weight of Devil's Revolver appeared in her hand. Conjured, she realized, and primed and ready to fire. A dozen warnings popped into her head as she trained the muzzle on the creature.

Hettie backed away slowly. The cat's eye stayed on the stallion. Behind her came another low growl, and she spun around. A second cougar stalked her, this one smaller and leaner but no less mean-looking. The stallion shrieked and pulled at the tangled rope. The first cougar crouched, readying to pounce.

"Get outta here! Go away!" She picked up a rock and threw it at the beastly cougar, who only flinched, tail flicking like a question mark. The smaller cat circled to the far left out of her peripheral vision. It was almost as if they were cooperating.

"Get going! Shoo!" She waved Diablo at them, her chest tightening as fear threatened to overtake her. The cougars' ears flattened, and they hissed, lips drawn back to display long, sharp teeth.

The first cougar leaped. With a cry, the horse spun and struck out with his massive hind legs, and the cat slammed against the rock with a sick snap and crumpled to the ground. The second cougar lunged for the horse. Hettie closed her grip around the gun and pulled the trigger.

A flash of green, and the smaller cat's head exploded in a cloud of red mist. Its body hit the ground wetly and slid a few feet before coming to rest.

Despite her racing heart and blurry vision, Hettie knew she didn't have a second to spare. She cut the rope free of the branch. The stallion watched her warily, heaving terrified, labored breaths. "We have to go. Bad men are coming."

The big black slowly bent one knee and lowered his head. He waited expectantly. Hettie knew then this was no ordinary horse. She grabbed his mane and climbed on. "Back to my friends fast as you can."

They took off like a shot, hoofbeats like thunder. She shouldn't have been so surprised—this creature was obviously magicked, as smart if not smarter than Jezebel. But she didn't have time to wonder where he'd come from or who had owned him previously.

Within a minute, they'd rejoined Ling and Walker, who stared wide-eyed as she artfully reined the wild beast in. Her thighs burned from the mad gallop. She was going to have some terrible saddle sores by the end of the day. "I fired Diablo. We have to get moving."

"I told you not to use it," Walker said on a harsh exhale, and kicked Lilith into motion.

They raced across the plain. The stallion's smooth, long strides ate up the ground effortlessly. She relaxed her grip around his middle, found that he was perfectly capable of running on his own and that she could sit him quite comfortably without a saddle. Maybe he'd been spelled to ride bareback. "Where can we go? How do we fight?"

"Fight?" Walker gave her a disdainful look. "We're going to find somewhere to hide. Against the Pinkertons, we're outmanned and outgunned. Best thing we can do is get the hell out of here and hope they don't give chase."

The horses all sensed their urgency, and they raced straight across the green-gold field, pointed roughly northeast. The herd of mustangs rejoined them. Hettie's galloping heart was just one tiny beat mixed in with the earth-trembling stampede. The black stallion gave a triumphant whinny, and he was answered by a piercing cry from the other horses. Exhilarated, Hettie couldn't help but smile. Ling let out a whoop and grinned when some of

the horses replied in kind. Hettie laughed when she noticed he had
Cymon slung across his lap on Jezebel's back. The dog was the only
one who looked unhappy.

She glanced over to find Walker smiling crookedly at her. She
grinned back. Danger, disaster, death—it felt as if they could
outrun it all.

As they neared a hilly area, the stallion let out another loud cry
and peeled away from the group. Jezebel and Lilith followed.

"Lilith, whoa!" The mare didn't obey. Walker pulled on the reins.
"Where's he going? Hettie—"

The stallion chuffed as she patted his neck. "I think he's taking
us somewhere safe."

"Why on earth would you think that?"

"Because Jezebel trusts him." She tilted her head toward her
father's horse. The old mare was too stubborn to take orders from
an upstart wild mustang otherwise.

The valleys between the hills deepened into arroyos, the rock
and earth rising up all around them to form a deep canyon. The
horses slowed, panting. The black stallion took the lead and kept
walking into the close, dark gulch.

"I don't like this," Walker muttered. "This is the perfect place for
an ambush."

"No, I don't think so." Ling stared around hard. "There's
something here. Do you sense it?"

A profusion of vines climbed tenaciously from the shadowed
canyon floor up the jagged walls toward the light. Hettie thought
she saw something move behind the curtain of vegetation. A cold
draft draped itself across her shoulders.

The horses chuffed and plodded on, and they exchanged horsey
noises as if in conversation. Cymon hopped off Jezebel's back and
snuffled around but stayed close, giving a skeptical woof.

The canyon dead-ended in a roughly circular area with steep
walls on all sides. "This can't be good," Walker said as Lilith finally
allowed him to rein her in. "We'll be trapped like animals if the
Pinks track us here."

"All those horses running with us would've stamped out our
tracks," Hettie said. "I think that's what this fella here was telling

them to do." She patted his neck and rubbed his withers. His muscles rippled, and he gave a sigh.

"This place is sacred." Ling dismounted and paced slowly over the ground, inspecting the long, bowed grasses. The sun was low in the sky and cut a wide crescent across the far wall of green. That cool breeze tickled Hettie's nose once more. Ling's gaze panned the area slowly. Then he pointed. "There."

Against the far end of the canyon on the rock face were a bunch of symbols etched across the stone. Hettie wasn't familiar with any of the languages of the local Indian tribes, but the pictographs did look vaguely familiar. Walker dismounted, staring intently at the ground. He knelt and brushed the grass aside.

A long, stained bone jutted up from the ground. Walker flinched but continued pulling the vegetation away until he revealed a complete human skeleton lying in a fetal position on its side, head turned so the skull grinned up at them.

"We're on a damned burial ground." He straightened. "We shouldn't be here."

"No. Not a burial ground." Ling walked back toward them with something in his hands. He held out a rusted old rifle. "A massacre site."

CHAPTER THIRTEEN

Walker grabbed Lilith's reins and pulled, but the chestnut mare wouldn't budge. "We need to get out of here. We have to leave before night falls and the ghosts rise." He looked spooked. "I'd rather face the Pinks than risk a haunting."

The stallion tossed his mane and snorted, then advanced on the bounty hunter with his head lowered menacingly. Walker didn't back down, but he did release Lilith's reins.

"I think he's trying to tell us we're safer here than out there." Hettie couldn't help but smile at the way Walker sized up the stallion.

"Maybe we should stay," Ling said slowly, staring around. "This place is steeped with magic."

"What do you mean?"

"Something about the place is…focusing magical energy here, containing it." He held out a hand and uttered a few words. His palm flashed a brilliant white that banished the shadows briefly before settling down to a warm glow. Ling regarded the light thoughtfully. He lifted his shirt to reveal an ugly yellow-and-black bruise on his side. Hettie gasped—it had to be quite old. Why hadn't he healed himself before? He laid his hand on his side, and the blemish disappeared. "Interesting. Must be why this place was considered sacred to these people." He nodded at the markings on the wall again.

"We're in some kind of…magical funnel?" Walker asked.

"I think so. All the power that would normally leak out of me is staying right here. I'd bet it's enough to hide Diablo's magical signature. Staying here might keep the Pinkerton agents from finding us, at least for a while."

"And if you're wrong, they shoot us like fish in a barrel. Either that, or we have our souls torn apart by angry spirits."

Hettie didn't relish sharing her bed with vengeful ghosts. There'd been all kinds of tales of hauntings in town, some of them real, most of them embellished. The worst spirits had been those of the men wrongly hanged in town, but they'd been exorcised by the elders quickly. Who knew what the dead here would do to a bunch of hapless travelers? But they couldn't hide out on the plain, and they couldn't ride all night. "I vote we stay. Blackie wouldn't lead us here if he didn't think it was safe."

Walker lifted an eyebrow. "That's what you're calling him? Blackie?"

"Unless he tells us his name."

The stallion blew out through his nostrils. She could've sworn he'd just rolled his eyes.

"The magic is strongest in this part of the canyon." Ling walked softly over the long grass. "We should make camp here."

"I am *not* sleeping on the bones of the dead," Walker protested.

Ling scrubbed the bristles on his chin. "Perhaps I can ask for permission."

Hettie glanced at him. "You're a necromancer?"

"Nothing like that. But I can make an appeal—a ritual offering, if you will, to appease the spirits. I need a few things, though. A sacrifice, for one."

"I'm not wasting good food on the dead." Walker pointed to the mouth of the canyon. "I'm setting up camp there. Come midnight, try to keep your screams down. I can't do a thing to protect us against angry spirits." He stomped off.

"I don't know how a man with so much power can have so little faith." Ling sighed. "Will you help me, Miss Hettie? If nothing else, I'd like to perform a ceremony to honor the dead."

They set out a snare, hoping to catch something they could both have for dinner and offer to the spirits. Hettie collected a few flowers and braided some long sweet grass to burn as makeshift incense. Ling set a few large stones in a semicircular shrine and placed the items in the center. By the time they caught a thin raccoon and gutted it, night had fallen. A damp chill settled in the air and clung to her skin.

Over at the far end of the canyon, Walker lay by a small fire, watching them sullenly from beneath the brim of his hat, his sidearm and rifle both at the ready. They wouldn't do a thing against spirits, of course. Blackie, Jezebel, and Lilith munched contentedly on the grass. Cymon sat a few feet from where Hettie and Ling worked, unwilling to come closer. He gave a short whine, then lay down, head between his paws.

"Can I ask you a question?" Hettie ventured. Ling nodded for her to proceed. "It's just that . . . well, you said this place is a magic well. And this tribe must have had some gifted among them." She indicated the pictograms on the walls. "How come they didn't use the magic here to drive their attackers away?"

Ling gathered his thoughts. "I don't know enough about this tribe to know what spells they had at hand, but there's a simple answer to that question: metal is immune to magic. Whoever killed these people had that many more guns. Maybe even a few sorcerers of their own to counter whatever they threw at them." He stared into the bruise-colored shadows as if he could see more than darkness there. "I imagine history would look very different if magic could stop a bullet."

Ling scooped up the raccoon entrails and set them in the shrine. He lit the sweet grass. The smoke wafting from it was white and thick and smelled like honey.

He directed Hettie to kneel beside him and place her palms together. She followed along clumsily as they both kowtowed before the burning grass, flowers, and pile of stinking raccoon guts. She felt a little silly, but really it was no different from saying grace—Ma had always said everyone had their own ways of doing things, and they were all strange to someone. So she didn't laugh.

Besides, laughing might be what angered the ghosts.

Ling's alto chant had a hypnotic, soothing quality about it. He said something in his throaty native tongue and waited in silence. Then he bowed again. "Your turn, Hettie. Ask the spirits if it would be all right to stay the night."

She stared at the far wall of rock and earth, watching the huge, shifting shadows cast by Walker's fire. It'd been a long time since she'd even prayed openly—she'd always attended church with Ma, but it had been out of habit rather than faith. The preacher had been a fire-and-brimstone man, and she'd hated how he'd described hell with its blazing inferno and endless torture. He talked about it as if he'd been there, and seemed convinced Hettie was headed there, too, the way he always met her eye when he screamed, *Damnation!*

Pa had stopped going to church because of him. Hettie only went because she hadn't wanted Ma to be alone.

Talking to ghosts was like talking to God, she supposed. It was likely at least one of them was listening.

"Spirits..." she began tentatively. "My friends and I have been traveling a long time...and we need a place to rest tonight. You see, my sister, Abby, was taken by some terrible men, and I need to find her. My uncle is out there, too, somewhere..." The words stuck in her throat, and she had to clear it before continuing. "There are some men after us. We're not criminals...not really. Blackie over there brought us here, and I ain't ever known a horse smart as him, except maybe Jezebel, so I thought maybe we were okay here, but Ling said a bunch of you were killed in this place, and we don't mean any disrespect. We just really need to stay here awhile, if that's okay." She knew she was babbling, but she supposed it was best to be clear when it came to talking to the dead.

The wind whistled over the top of the canyon, rustling the leaves and grass. Something moved behind the curtain of vines. Hettie stared at the spot, sweat breaking on her upper lip. It was just a trick of the light, she told herself. Nothing was there. Nothing was watching her.

"You didn't have to tell them the whole story," Ling said, a little amused. He paused, closed his eyes. "I think we're going to be fine tonight. If they didn't want us here, they'd have let us know by now."

How they would communicate something like that, Hettie never wanted to find out.

Υ

A heatless bonfire blazed before Hettie. Huge shadows shifted against the canyon walls stretching endlessly above her, but she couldn't see what cast them. The hairs on her neck prickled. Where were Walker and Ling? Where were Cymon and Jezebel and the others?

A figure darted outside of the firelight. "Hello?" Her voice was distant and faint in her own ears. Fighting the urge to curl up into a ball and hide, she followed the shadowy movement into the deep gloom.

Her bare feet went from soft grass to cold stone. She couldn't see her hand in front of her face, but she sensed her quarry fleeing.

"Come back!" Fear climbed into her throat, an utter sense of desolation closing in on her.

Her feet sloshed through a sticky wetness. Dark, crimson blood frothed and swirled around her ankles. She looked for its source but saw nothing.

Something behind her moved, and she nearly jumped out of her skin when a little girl appeared before her. Her long, dark hair fell down past her shoulders. Her eyes were large and empty, like twin caverns, glowing from a dark face. The girl wore a roughly cut smock made of buckskin leather. She was barefoot. She couldn't have been much older than eight.

The girl extended a hand. Hettie wasn't sure why she took it. It just seemed...right. Her fingers were icy-cold and not quite solid. It almost felt as though Hettie were dipping her hand into a fast-flowing stream. The little spirit girl towed her deeper into the gloom. She didn't say anything as the world slowly changed from inky blackness to a land drenched in silvery-blue predawn light.

The earth became solid and uneven beneath her feet, long grasses slippery with dew. The clearing was deserted, yet Hettie felt a suffocating closeness. Then, shouts and cries, the rapport of a gun. More rifle blasts, and then high-pitched screams and heart-wrenching mourning wails. A few rough voices, the rattle of wagons trundling away. The cries of children faded along with everything else...

Hettie glanced down. The little girl was gone. She looked around frantically, not sure how she was supposed to leave this ghost world without her guide.

"Crying Sparrow is long dead," a voice behind her said.

She spun and met the sad eyes of an Indian woman seated on the ground. Hettie had had few dealings with the People, apart from those who lived in town, so she couldn't say for sure what tribe this person was from. Her face was that of a young woman, her body lean and strong, but an air of exhaustion hung about her. She gestured for Hettie to join her by the fire.

"It is rare that anyone journeys along the road in between. Even rarer when they are led here by one of our own."

"So...this isn't a dream?"

"Some might think it such. This is simply the place between life and the spirit realm." She studied her. "You are not dead...but you're not totally alive either. Why are you here?"

Hettie didn't know what to say to that, so she told the truth. "I'm looking for my sister. We didn't mean to disturb your bones, but it was getting late, and my horse..." She snapped her mouth shut as the woman's lips firmed and her dark eyes cast downward.

Get ahold of yourself, you gabbling goose. She marshaled her manners. "Tell me, what happened here?"

"The same thing that happens whenever we try to protect what is ours." The woman's fists closed. "We gave up our land, our livelihood, our heritage and past. But when they told us to give up our children, that's when we had to fight back."

"Someone took the children?"

"They told us they shouldn't be raised among savages. They told us they would take care of them, send them to proper Christian schools. We refused to let them go, so they took them by force." She cupped her fists against the sides of her head as she gave a broken sob. "We were helpless to save them. They were not better off. They were not sent to schools..." She rocked back and forth.

"What happened to them?"

"Crying Sparrow...she was a dream walker. She could travel between places, guide others there. She showed us where they'd

162

taken her, showed us her living nightmare. We saw her last days, saw the cruel, evil things done to her and the other children. Her visions drove some of us mad. Those who were left tried to rescue the children…but we were few, we were weak, and they had strong magics."

Hettie's skin pricked with goose bumps, and her heart pounded in her throat. "Where were they taken?"

"South," she said. "To the land of red sand."

That was too much of a coincidence. Her throat closed as terror took hold. "Can you tell me anything about the people who took your children?"

But before she could answer, the scene jarred, the fire went out, and Hettie found herself flat on her back on the dewy ground, head spinning as she stared up the barrel of a very big gun.

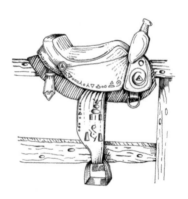

CHAPTER FOURTEEN

Pretty stupid of you two to be sleeping without a guard," Jeremiah Bassett growled. A few feet away, Ling shot out of his bedroll and sprang away from them, crouched and wild-eyed like a cat caught unawares. Uncle sneered. "If I were anyone else, you'd all have your throats slit by now."

A gun cocked behind him. "And you'd have a hole in the back of your head." Walker stepped from the shadow, rifle raised.

"Uncle." Hettie was relieved he was alive, of course, but his arrival stirred all kinds of questions in her. He took his boot off her neck, and she sat up, rubbing at the tender flesh. "You got away from the Pinkertons."

"Yeah." He holstered his weapon, and Walker lowered his Winchester. The old man squatted by the campfire and rubbed his hands. "Been trackin' you awhile now. Didn't get a bead till you fired off that damn gun again. Where is it?"

"Safe with me."

Jeremiah narrowed his eyes. If he noticed her advanced age, he didn't say anything. Cymon pushed his head into Uncle's hands in greeting, tail wagging. Some guard dog he was.

"How'd you escape from Hawksville?" Walker demanded as Uncle stirred the fire to life.

"I may be old, but I still know a few tricks. And Stubby's easier to predict than a deck of twos. I managed to give them the slip, and they went back through the Zoom when it reopened. None of 'em wanted to get stuck walking home."

"I'm surprised they didn't stay to hunt you down," Ling said.

"Bunch of dandies like them wouldn't deign to stick around in this heat and get a little dust on their boots. Besides, they're not smart enough to take maps and compasses out with them. They'll come better prepared next time, though." Uncle cut him a look. "What are you doing out here, Tsang? Or are you just here for a lark?"

"It's a long story," Hettie interrupted. "Did you see any sign of the Pinkertons on the way here?"

"Would I have come straight here if I saw the Pinks?"

Walker slung his rifle over his shoulder. "We should probably leave."

"No need. Not yet. We're safe for a while. Interesting place you chose to pitch your tent." Jeremiah peered around the canyon, and his gaze landed on Walker. "I take it I have you to thank for getting Hettie out of that trouble in Hawksville?"

"Walker Woodroffe, at your service." He gave a mocking tip of his hat.

"Yeah, I know who you are. *What* you are is another matter." He glared at him head to toe. "Borrowed magic, eh?"

A muscle in the bounty hunter's jaw jumped. Stunned, Hettie exchanged glances with Ling. All that magic was borrowed? How was it even possible? Magic could only be passed around in small amounts, and not permanently, either. Siphoning off any magic— or juice, as some folks called it—from a sorcerer weakened the source. When the borrower used power, it only took half of the strength it would normally take, but it meant the lender also assumed half the cost of the spell.

Walker had displayed a full range of power. If he was borrowing magic, the lender must be more powerful than anyone she'd ever known.

Jeremiah poked the fire. "Not that hard to figure out, since you cast some pretty mean spells back there. Most men I know would be flat on their back for a week after raining down a fiery apocalypse like that. You must be pretty juiced up."

"That explains it," Ling murmured. "You're channeling all that power through a lender." He wrinkled his nose disdainfully. "I hope you know your limits. The last thing we want is for you to blow your power source and die."

"It's not something you need to worry about," Walker reassured tightly.

"I suggest we all get some rest, leave at daybreak, and head east," Uncle said, changing topics abruptly. "We'll get you somewhere safe until we figure things out."

Hettie glowered. "Nothing's changed, old man. I'm still going after Abby. Mr. Woodroffe and Mr. Tsang here have both promised to help."

He glared at the three. "It's too dangerous. You've seen what Stubbs is willing to do, and Butch Crowe, for that matter. You really want to face either of them again for your sister who may not even be alive?"

She set her teeth against the tightness in her chest. "She's alive, and she's somewhere near the border in Arizona. And if we find her . . . I think we're going to find a lot of other missing children, too."

The men exchanged glances. "How do you figure that?" Walker asked.

"I had a . . ." *Dream* wasn't quite the word, and it had been so much more than a vision—she wasn't exactly sure what she could call her visit to the in-between. "This Indian woman"—she gestured around her—"while I was sleeping she told me the tribe's children were taken years ago. The same thing is happening now—kids are being taken from the road. Why kids? Why Abby? The Crowe gang has something to do with all of this, and the answers and my sister are somewhere near the border. On top of that, I've seen them, in a dungeon, in cages—"

"Hettie." Uncle reached out to squeeze her shoulder, and she pulled out of his grip. She didn't trust him not to manipulate her again. "You're grieving. It's normal for you to have dreams like this. You feel guilty, so your mind comes up with all kinds of crazy ideas . . ."

She balled her fists, heat suffusing her. "I'm not making this up. It's real." She wanted to stomp her foot.

Uncle spoke to her the way one would coax a frightened calf. "You've been through a lot. What's important now is that we get you and Diablo to safety."

"Safety?" Walker scoffed. "Nowhere's safe from the Pinks."

"Stay out of this, Woodroffe."

"If there's a chance that Miss Abby is alive, we should find her," Ling said. "I've already been through her memories, Mr. Bassett. She's telling the truth. Abby is alive, and we're certain she's in Arizona."

"The woman told me the children were taken to the place of red sand," Hettie added. "That can't be a coincidence."

"All of you, knock it off. I'm the last of Hettie's kin, you hear? She's my responsibility."

"We're not kin," she said. "You used me and lied to me and manipulated me. I'm not going anywhere with you. Not until I find Abby."

Ling stood closer to her and folded his arms. "Where Miss Hettie goes, I follow."

"And seeing as I've been hired and we've got ourselves a little contract spell, I'm inclined to follow the young lady," Walker added primly. "Looks like it's three against one, Bassett."

Cymon barked and sat at Hettie's feet, panting his agreement.

Uncle swore, grabbed his hat, and slapped it across his thigh. "You'll be changing your tune soon enough," he said, pointing at Hettie. "Once you see the desert, you'll know what I know. Abby's gone, and there's nothing you can do about it."

At first light, they set out for Barney's Rock and the Zoom tunnel that would take them south. There was a chance that the Pinkertons would station men in the town to wait for them, but it was a risk they were willing to take. They needed to resupply, and besides, the faster they found Abby, the more likely she'd still be alive.

The prospect of being back in a town worried and excited Hettie. She wanted a bath and meal that didn't consist of hardtack and stringy game. The long days of riding were wearing her down, and while the landscape was beautiful, there was only so much of it and her companions' company she could handle. Being surrounded by smelly, brooding, taciturn men was tiresome.

She looked forward to finding tack for Blackie. Ling had fashioned a rough saddle with ropes and blankets, which Blackie chaffed under. But she was so sore from riding bareback, she didn't care that the blanket slid or that the ropes bit into her hands. In truth, she felt worse for the horse than she did for herself.

It was another week's ride to Barney's Rock, but with Blackie, the journey was much faster. While Jezebel had initially accepted him as the lead horse, it was becoming clear that the old mare was jealous of Hettie's adopted mount. She shied from Hettie's touch and ignored her pampering when they rested. The mare became devoted to Ling instead, nuzzling him affectionately and earning a lot of extra grooming from her rider.

Meanwhile, Blackie was impervious to any attention Hettie lavished upon him. He ignored everyone and accepted only the minimum of care. He had a mind of his own, and even looked as if he resented ever helping them. The others speculated that the enchanted stallion must have escaped a previous owner—he was far too smart and haughty to be a newly broken mustang.

When they made camp, the men would hunt. Scraggly peahens, hares, and raccoons made regular appearances at dinnertime, though there was hardly enough to fill their stomachs. Walker's provisions had to be saved for more desperate times, when game was scarce. Hettie knew she could bring in more game if Walker would lend her his rifle, but the men refused to let her hunt.

"It's not women's work," Uncle told her point-blank, which infuriated her since she'd regularly brought home dinner while hunting with Pa. "We can handle the hunting. You need to stay and tend the fire."

"Let someone else do it for once." She didn't want to whine, but she was out of practice and needed to feel like she was doing something useful. A week was a long time to be worrying over Abby, imagining the worst, and she found herself craving distraction.

Jeremiah gave a long, grumbling sigh. "Hettie, you can't."

"Why not?"

He and Walker exchanged looks. With reluctance, Walker unwrapped his rifle from the oilcloth and held it out to her.

She reached for the butt stock. A million searing needles plunged into her palm as it made contact, and she yelped. When she looked down at her hand, gripping her wrist, she found herself clutching the Devil's Revolver.

"You ever wonder why the stories about Elias Blackthorn never featured him using a different weapon?" Uncle said as the pain slowly subsided. "That there's a jealous piece, almost as petty and vindictive as Jezebel." He nodded. "So long as you're bonded with it, Diablo won't let you use any other gun."

Hettie dropped the revolver back into her pocket, rubbing her still-stinging palm against her hip. It seemed the legendary revolver was causing her more trouble than it was worth. "I could set up snares," she said, focusing on dinner once more.

He shook his head. "It's too risky. I don't want to leave a trail for the Pinks." She thought Uncle was being overly cautious, but the others deferred to him. A tiny part of Hettie wondered if they were all in cahoots, considering the way they camped and traveled and treated her, as if she were the one who needed rescuing instead of Abby.

In the end, she gave up asking to hunt and stuck to her assigned chores. It was too exhausting to fight at the end of a long day of riding. It irked her that she had to rely on Uncle, Walker, and Ling to provide for her. It bothered her more than she cared to admit. But at least she got good at kindling the campfire. She quickly discovered the rate at which certain grasses and bits of wood burned, how much smoke they gave off, what they smelled like. Keeping the flames leaping to a certain height became a game to her.

At night, she would sometimes stare into the hearth, seeing visions of her parents as they'd been in life, smiling and laughing, Ma singing as she weeded the vegetable patch, Pa smoking a pipe. But the memories brought her no comfort, no nostalgia or even sadness. Her parents' lives were like ash to her, and in the morning, when the fire had burned down, she watched the lifeless char float away on the wind as she kicked it out and scattered the remains.

It didn't rain once on their way to Barney's Rock, but that was hardly a blessing. The sun glared mercilessly down on their necks and shoulders. The horizon rippled, teasing them with visions of a cool, deep lake that wasn't there. The grasses went from soft and green to tough gold husks that rustled and crunched as they cut through fields untouched by man or beast. Uncle cautioned them all to be on the lookout—for what, Hettie wasn't sure, but she grew uneasy as the grass thickened, the stalks reaching up toward them like millions of skeletal fingers, brushing their boot tips, then their ankles, and in some places their knees. The horses plowed on, panting with the effort as the grasses swarmed around their legs and grasped at their bodies. Cymon pushed through, his body breaching the field periodically as he leaped through the sea of grass.

"This ain't right, Bassett," Walker said as Lilith huffed and stumbled. They'd been wading through the grass for nearly an hour, and it only seemed to be growing thicker. "Since when does this much grass grow in a drought in Wyoming?"

"It ain't natural, that's for sure." His gray mustang weaved side to side in search of a path.

"It's a grass trap," Ling said suddenly. "It's to slow down buffalo and other game."

"We've been slogging through this for hours. Who can cast a trap spell this big?"

"The Pinkertons could," Uncle muttered. "Don't stop moving, or the grass will take hold."

As hard as they pushed the horses, though, it was clear they were tiring. Blackie plowed ahead of the others. Steam rose off his sleek black hair and matted in damp streaks, but he pressed forward.

"We can't keep on like this," Ling said as Jezebel gave a panicked whinny.

"Get off and pull the horses if you have to, but don't stop. Hettie, stay on Blackie, y'hear? Just keep moving." Uncle slid off his horse. The gray mustang thrashed and complained as Uncle pulled on the lead, drawing his bowie knife and hacking at the grass. "Damn, this stuff is tough."

Walker grimaced. "We need a counterspell."

"I've been trying," Jeremiah called back. "But I can't get this stuff to stop growing."

"What if we make a path?"

"Do I look like Moses to you? I can't part the damn sea." Uncle's mount stopped and wouldn't be pulled any farther. The golden grass twined up its legs like insidious tentacles. Uncle cursed and waded around the horse, slashing and slicing in an effort to keep the mustang from being consumed.

Ling cried out as Jezebel squealed and stumbled to her kneels. The grass reached up for both of them. Ling rolled off and tore at the vegetation climbing up his shoulders.

Blackie's eyes widened until the whites showed. He shied and lifted his legs high, stomping down hard and pulling ahead of the mired travelers. Hettie tried to turn him around, but he stayed focused on moving.

A few feet away, Hettie spotted Cymon chewing at his shoulder where the grass clung. Uncle, Walker, and Ling were all on the ground now, fighting against the field.

"Stop, Blackie, we need to do something!" She drew Diablo. It had put a hole through Teddy's chest and blown a horse's head clean away. It would surely clear a path for them...

"No, Hettie." Ling rolled and pulled grass off Jezebel, who struggled to stand. "That's what they want. If the Pinkertons find us out here, we'll be sitting ducks."

Hettie couldn't let everyone get eaten by the magic weeds. If only they could make a small clearing...

She scrambled for the matches and tinder box in her pocket, then slid off Blackie.

"Damnation, Hettie, I told you to stay on that horse!"

She didn't reply as she waded quick as she could in a wide circle around her companions, snatching handfuls of dry and dead grass as she went. It was like wading through the hayloft at its fullest. The grass caught at her clothes, clung like the toughest spider web, and reached for her hair. She twisted what she'd gathered in her hands into a braid, struck a match, and lit the end. It caught almost immediately. She sent up a prayer and held the makeshift torch toward the gold weeds grasping for her.

A high-pitched hissing sound emitted from the singed grass. It recoiled as it caught fire, writhing as it charred to black ash. Hettie waved the torch around her, and the grass bent away as if a strong breeze were bowing it. Some of the stalks didn't move quickly enough. Shrieking, popping noises filled the air as the fire spread. A breeze picked up the feather-light embers and let them drift farther out. Soon, patches of the land were smoking, then blazing. Hettie made her sluggish way back to her companions, holding the torch in front of her.

"This can't be good." Walker watched the brush fire race across the tinder-dry land. Thick gray smoke filled the air, and the horses thrashed, nostrils flaring.

Hettie waved her torch around the horses and her friends, and the grass let go. Blackie let out a throaty neigh as a flock of birds suddenly rushed up from the ground, darkening the sky. Hettie looked around for Cymon, spotting the dog loping toward her.

"Everyone, mount up!" She raced back toward Blackie and climbed on. "Cymon! Fetch!" She threw him the burning bundle. The dog snatched it midair and streaked ahead, away from Hettie. He never had been good at fetch.

The grasses bent away from him, clearing a path. "Let's go!" Blackie galloped up the narrow, fire-reamed trail her beloved mutt cut for them. The others followed, the grasses closing behind them, still clawing at their legs and clothes.

The field of grass finally thinned out. Cymon dropped the drool-doused torch, tail wagging in victory. A great, sweeping gray-and-black murmuration of starlings whooshed through the sky like living smoke and then evaporated.

"You could've got us all killed, you pyromaniac." Uncle coughed and hacked noisily. Ling offered to ease his breathing, but the old man waved him off as he spat a dark wad.

Hettie planted a fist against her hip. "Better than letting you become plant food."

Walker watched the grass burn. "We need to get out of here," he said tersely. "If this was a Pinkerton trap, they'll know it's been set off, and they'll arrive soon."

Hettie huffed. So much for gratitude.

CHAPTER FIFTEEN

Just past noon two days later, the four riders crested a ridge and halted. Barney's Rock spread below them, a dark stain in the bowl between the hills.

The town was symmetrical, roughly circular around its borders. The Zoom tunnel station resided within a large domed building that sat squarely in the center of a relatively flat field. Wagon-choked roads radiated outward to rings of warehouses and smaller buildings housing customs agencies and delivery businesses.

Hettie had studied Zoom tunnels in school. There were twelve naturally occurring Zoom apertures scattered across the country, located in places that, for reasons no one had figured out, focused magical energies, which could be tapped to open the portals. Several different Indian tribes had mastered the apertures long before settlers had arrived, though few of them used them for travel—they'd been considered sacred. When the white man had spread across the land, a few enterprising companies "purchased" the rights to the apertures with a few beads and casks of whiskey. Those companies eventually consolidated their resources and started the Zoom Union.

The problem with having settlements around Zoom tunnels, however, was that they weren't always conveniently located. In the case of Barney's Rock, the valley was rocky and parched, not an attractive prospect for farmers. A pumping station had been built from the nearest river almost ten miles away to bring water to the town's handful of permanent residents, but the system was hardly adequate to sustain a larger population. With no easy access to water, there were no farms, no green pastures. Most of the trees had been cleared to make way for the town, and what game might have lived off this harsh land had been scared off. It meant all food and supplies were imported. Barney's Rock was simply a transport hub, and neither goods nor people stayed long. People moved swiftly, and with purpose.

Wagons loaded with crates and barrels jammed the roads, headed for the nearest railway station in the next town over. Because they were made of metal, trains and tracks built too close to the apertures destabilized the tunnels. The Zoom and rail unions had learned that quite early on, and several stations had since been shut down due to improper import and export practices. As a result, the Zoom Union also limited the amount of metal passing through the tunnels, so shipments of things like nails and tools, weapons, ammunition, and the like were limited, or were severely taxed. With magic dwindling and no way to know how the tunnels would be affected, those tariffs had started to include things like buttons and jewelry. A traveler would be charged by how many ounces of metal he carried through the portal.

"Keep a sharp eye out," Uncle said as they closed in on the town's outer limits. "Stubbs's men could be waiting for us."

"Something else we're going to have to deal with." Walker nodded at the sign ahead. *No guns. No magic. Surrender all arms and talismans to the border guard.*

"Huh." Jeremiah scratched his chin. "When'd they start being so uppity?"

"Can't have spells or guns influencing legitimate business transactions," Walker said and narrowed his gaze. "There's a null spell suppressing all enchantments over the town, too."

"Well, that's something, at least. If it affects us, it'll affect the Pinks."

"I don't understand," Hettie said. "How can there be a null spell on the town while a Zoom tunnel is functioning inside it? For that matter, how can you make a spell that nullifies other magic?"

"It's complicated," Jeremiah said gruffly. "Basically, the null spell's like putting an empty barrel in a stream. There's nothing inside the barrel, and the water—or magic—is moving outside and around it."

"That's the theory, anyhow," Walker added. "The truth is, no one knows exactly how it works. Some sorcerer put it together a long time ago without knowing what he was doing. He found out by accident that it kept other people from performing spells in his immediate area."

"Much of Western sorcery is like that," Ling commented wryly.

"As if you know the source of *your* powers?" Uncle's eyebrow rose.

The healer lifted his chin. "I know where *my* power comes from. I know how to use it. But I don't pretend all the mysteries of the universe can be easily explained. That's something *your* people seem to be obsessed with." His gaze included Walker.

Hettie could tell the men were about to get into some kind of grand philosophical argument about magic and headed it off. "So how come null spells don't get used in more places?" She could imagine quite a few people who'd like to be unaffected by magic. Her, for one.

Walker scrubbed his chin. "It's a complicated spell. Hard to maintain and expensive to keep up. I'm thinking some business association must be paying a few sorcerers well in Barney's Rock. Anyhow, it doesn't completely nullify magic, it just keeps people inside the bubble from casting spells."

"More like a wet blanket over a pile of tinder, then," Hettie surmised.

"Diablo should still work inside," Uncle said. "But I wouldn't use it if I were you. In fact, it's best to leave it outside of town altogether. Bury it in the sand. Even if someone found it, they won't be able to pick it up."

"What about the Pinks?"

"They won't be looking for a mage gun in the dirt. Long as it doesn't go off, its power can't really be traced unless you're close to it and know what to look for."

Hettie dismounted and walked some ways into the desert. She found some rocks and dug a shallow hole, then wrapped Diablo in a kerchief and laid it in the ground, pushed the sand back over it, and added the stones on top. She memorized a few landmarks, searing the map into her mind. Her duster pocket felt too light as she walked back to the travelers and remounted.

The moment she walked away, a rattler as long as she was tall slithered toward the spot and curled itself around the pile, hugging it tight. It stared back at her, flicking its tongue out. "That's some spell, Uncle," she said, impressed.

He blinked. "I didn't do nothin'. Walker?"

"Wasn't me."

"Nor I," Ling added.

The snake gave a warning shake of its tail. Slowly, they backed away.

At the town limits, a deputy with a bland smile met and escorted them to a small building, took their guns, and stripped them of all their talismans. They gave aliases and informed the bored-looking man behind the counter they were escorting their dear old uncle to visit a sick friend. Jeremiah grumbled about his civil rights as he filled the metal lockbox. They were each given a chip with a number printed on it for when they retrieved their items, which would be transported to the Zoom tunnel station at their departure. But just as they were about to leave the office, another man, broad chested and going to fat around the middle, stepped out of a side door in front of them.

"Hold on." He put out a big palm. "You there. Chinaman. You got any magic?"

"I'm a healer," Ling replied sharply. Walker shot him a warning look.

The man wasn't impressed. "Deputy Givens, did you do a search of this man?"

"He's clean, sir," Givens said nervously.

"Not all Celestials use talismans, Givens. It's right there in the handbook. You bother reading it?"

"Yes, Sergeant Pierce. That is, I've done everything—"

Pierce waved him off and put a thick hand on Ling's shoulder. "You're gonna have to come with me."

"What for?" Walker intervened. "He's done nothing wrong."

"Standard procedure. Ether magic isn't allowed in Barney's Rock. No magic is."

"You've got a null spell on the whole town, though, don't you?"

"We don't know where these people get their magic from, or how it even works." The sergeant cut Ling a nasty look. "The magic ban is in place to protect the people, see? This is a business town, and we have to make sure the wrong element doesn't come in to take advantage."

Ling kept his burning eyes downcast, fists clenched. Hettie flexed her fingers, feeling the shadow of the Devil's Revolver brush her palm as keenly as the edge of her anger. It seemed she could summon the weapon if she needed to, but pointing a gun at the sergeant's fat head wouldn't help their case right now.

"S'cuse me, Sarge?" Jeremiah shuffled up to him, stooping. "I understand your concern—can't trust nobody these days. But this coolie's my manservant. I need him...for all the unspeakables an old man like me needs help with."

Sergeant Pierce's eyebrow arched. "Why can't these two help you?"

"They don't know what they're doing. You ever have a little boy who's scared of a few bullet scars try to wipe your ass, or have a ham-handed grunt like this give me a bath?" He gave Walker and Hettie harsh, reproving glances, then nodded to Ling. "I'd hate to admit it, but Charlie here's my nurse. You wouldn't deprive an old veteran of his loyal servant, would you?" He motioned with his hand, and Hettie caught the glint of silver Uncle passed beneath the man's nose.

Pierce licked his lips and glanced at Ling. "I s'pose I can't. All right, go on, old soldier. But I don't want to see him wandering around on his own." They shook hands. The silver piece disappeared in the sergeant's pocket.

As they left the stuffy office, Uncle gazed around, addressing them under his breath. "Make sure y'all stick to that story. We don't want to arouse any suspicions."

"I'm not wiping your ass, old man," Ling growled.

"Better call me *master* while we're here, just in case."

Ling called him something else entirely, making Hettie's cheeks burn and Walker chuckle.

They arrived at the Zoom tunnel station just in time to see the opening of the aperture and the great swirl of energy that irised open to the New Orleans Zoom station. Hettie watched from the upper gallery as wooden carts were rolled through and waybills were quickly exchanged and signed through the portal. Few people actually traveled with their goods—the Zoom Union charged exorbitant fares for passengers. But with the railways reaching all the major cities now, there'd been speculation that prices would fall to compete with train tickets. That hadn't happened yet, though. The Zoom Union had a tight fist on its business.

Their journey would take them to New Orleans by Zoom and then by train westward to Yuma, but Hettie hadn't anticipated the price of travel. Even with their resources pooled, they didn't have enough for Zoom fare for all four of them plus horses and Cymon.

They could travel to Cheyenne and take the train. It would be cheaper, but Uncle was against it. Being trapped in metal cars on metal tracks would interfere with the spells that were keeping them from being Eyed. On top of that, the train would inevitably pass through numerous checkpoints. A quick getaway would be nearly impossible, since the horses would have to travel in a separate car. Walker agreed with him.

"Maybe we should just ride south," Ling said as they left the Zoom station.

"That'll take weeks." Hettie didn't relish the idea of even more time on the road, and she didn't want this trip to take longer than necessary. God knew what was happening to Abby. "There must be some way to earn enough for the Zoom fare."

Uncle wiped his nose. "Well, we can't stay here. We're wasting our time regardless, and the longer we stay in one place, the better chance the Pinks will have of finding us." He watched Hettie steadily. "Maybe it's time you see some reason—"

"I'm not giving up."

"So what do you propose? That we all get jobs till we can afford Zoom tickets?"

Hettie sat up. "That's it. There must be all kinds of wagons heading to the border with men and supplies. They're shoring up the Wall, aren't they? Surely someone could use an escort or a few extra hands."

Walker rubbed his chin thoughtfully. "It'll still cost whoever takes us through the tunnel a pretty penny, and if we don't cut the right deal we'll be indentured for a couple of years before we pay off that debt."

"Working a security detail would be best," Ling said. "We could bargain our services for the Zoom fare alone."

"We just need to find the right employers." Hettie chewed her lip. This could work.

They split up to trawl the town for work. Ling went with Uncle, while Hettie went with Walker. Cymon trailed after them. It would be easier for her to continue her charade as a boy, playing the role of Walker's younger brother. As long as she didn't say anything and kept her hat pulled low, she could stay in the background.

They went to the train depot, where Walker chatted up some merchants and movers. No one needed help, it seemed. Certainly not from a scruffy, steely-eyed stranger. His smooth talking only seemed to cement their distrust. After all, Walker and his posse could just as easily rob them.

Hettie hung back, her dismay growing with each rejection. While Walker chatted up yet another businessman, a fancy stagecoach pulled in, disgorging a passel of passengers onto the platform. Hettie's eyes widened in surprise as a woman in emerald-green silk and a jaunty hat bobbing with ostrich feathers descended the steps. Men's heads turned as the blond beauty glided past.

What on earth was Sophie Favreau doing here?

The debutante wrinkled her nose and darted out of the way when a large man pushed past her with a laden trolley. A tall, robust maid in a plain gray dress hopped out behind her carrying a thick Bible and a reticule. She shouted at the porters wrestling two large suitcases down off the stagecoach, and the men shrank at her reprimands. Sophie rarely went anywhere without Jemma.

The two women made their way into the street, dodging wagons and carts. Sophie scanned the crowd, her brow furrowed slightly, several steps ahead of the frazzled Jemma. She was so intent in her search, Sophie didn't see the huge Clydesdales barreling toward her.

Hettie darted forward and shouted, "Hey!" Sophie looked her way, disdain turning into horror as Hettie lunged and shoved Sophie out of the horses' path.

The beasts gave a deep cry and pranced, their huge, shaggy hooves stomping the ground with skull-cracking force where Sophie had stood seconds before. Several men jumped in to grab the horses' bridles.

"Miz Sophie, are you all right?" Jemma helped her mistress to her feet. Sophie's hat sat askew, and her neatly coiffed gold ringlets fell in disarray. Her dress was covered in dirt.

"Oaf!" Sophie trembled, bright eyes bulging. "Why don't you—" Her words died on her lips as her eyes flared wide. "You!" The outrage hissed out on her exhaled whisper.

"You're welcome." Hettie was about to turn away when Walker strode up.

"What's going on here?" he demanded, looking from Hettie to Sophie. "Miss...?"

Sophie stared at Walker's lean, dark, towering form, her mouth slightly open, cheeks pinkening. She tucked a wayward curl behind her ear coquettishly. Jemma was slapping the dust off her behind, and Sophie waved her away. "Thank you for coming to my aid, Mister...?"

"Woodroffe. Walker Woodroffe." Walker tipped up his hat in greeting and flashed a grin. Hettie rolled her eyes. It seemed Sophie had entirely forgotten who'd saved her life. "I do recall your face, miss. I believe I saw you in Newhaven a few weeks ago."

"Why, yes! I do recognize you. You were that stranger who almost won the Robsons' shootout." She fluttered like a bird. "I'm Sophie Favreau of the Louisiana Favreaus."

"A pleasure to make your acquaintance, Miss Favreau." He took her hand and bowed over it, kissing the air above her fingers with gentlemanly affection.

Hettie scowled, crossing her arms over her chest. Of course Walker would fall at Sophie's dainty feet. She'd yet to meet a man who hadn't.

"What brings you out to these parts, Mr. Woodroffe?" Sophie batted her lashes, her ordeal all but forgotten.

"We're headed to Arizona." He gestured toward Hettie. "This is...my associate, um..."

Sophie laughed, and it was an unpleasant sound. "I'm not simple, Mr. Woodroffe. I know this country mouse. But what are you doing here, Hettie? And dressed like *that*?"

Hettie balled her fists, but Walker intervened before she could tell Sophie exactly what she was doing. "She's with me." He flashed Sophie a startling smile, broad and white and unlike anything Hettie had seen from the bounty hunter before. "A group of us are hoping to earn our Zoom passage to New Orleans. We're headed to Arizona. You wouldn't happen to know anyone who'd need an escort?"

Sophie's bright eyes stayed locked on Walker's face, as if she was dazzled. Her maid glared between them. "Miz Sophie, I think he's—"

Jemma was cut off with a sharp, reproving look from her mistress. "It just so happens I'm on my way to New Orleans," Sophie said airily. "It's not the safest journey. I wouldn't mind a strong man to get me safely to my grandmother's. And while you're there, you must take in the sights and my grandmother's hospitality, of course. She loves to hear travelers' stories. She doesn't leave the house much anymore, so it's imperative we bring her new and interesting people to talk to. It keeps the madness from settling in. By the way, what is it you do for a living, Mr. Woodroffe?"

He answered without hesitation, "Bounty hunting."

Hettie wasn't sure whether to laugh or groan at the revulsion and intrigue fighting for dominance on Sophie's face, never mind Jemma's. The maid sized them both up as if they were bound to rob her.

"It's a bit busy here," the debutante finally said after a moment's fluster. "Why don't we move to that establishment there and sit for some tea? Perhaps we can discuss an...arrangement."

Walker tipped his hat again. "If you'll wait for me there, Miss Favreau, I'll gather my compatriots, and you can vet them yourself. They're all from Newhaven, too. I think you'll be more comfortable with folks you're familiar with watching your back."

"I trust *you*, Mr. Woodroffe. And I'm a very good judge of character." She gave Walker a smoldering look as they bid farewell.

As soon as Sophie was out of earshot, Hettie said, "You can't be serious. We can't waste our time visiting some rich old shut-in."

"That rich old shut-in is Patrice Favreau, the Soothsayer of the South. Anyhow, Miss Favreau said she'll pay our way to Arizona. We lucked out finding her. The least we can do for her is pay her grandmother a visit." Walker peered into her face, arching a dark eyebrow. "You're not jealous of her, are you?"

"Of course not!" she snorted. "I just can't abide ungrateful, spoiled girls. She didn't even thank me for saving her life."

The bounty hunter smothered his smile behind a gloved hand. He'd better, Hettie thought darkly. He was smiling way too much for her liking.

CHAPTER SIXTEEN

They met up with Ling and Uncle and proceeded to the Gold Rose hotel. The lounge on the main floor had highly polished wood floors and tables covered with brocade tablecloths. Men in clean, fashionable suits with well-starched collars pored over sheaves of paper as they sipped coffee. Sophie sat at a table for two, sipping tea daintily. She waved at them, looking perfectly at home. Though no one spared the travelers a second glance, Hettie felt inadequate in her dirty shirt and trousers. She was grubby and probably stank from the weeks on the road.

Behind Sophie, Jemma scanned the room with a fierce look, brandishing her Bible as if it were a bludgeon and glaring daggers at anyone who so much as glanced at her. She was the most effective chaperone Hettie had ever seen, though clearly Sophie was her own mistress and would readily accept the company of a tall, dark, dangerous stranger against Jemma's better judgment.

Walker introduced Ling and Jeremiah. Sophie acknowledged them with the barest of nods. She and Walker were going to "talk business," she told them pertly—a clear dismissal. Walker eyed them and nodded imperceptibly.

"We can't afford anything they'll be serving for dinner anyhow," Uncle said gruffly as they left the stuffy dining room.

They found a chophouse and for a few pennies got bowls of greasy stew made up of mostly potatoes and carrots. The softhearted cook took pity on Cymon and gave him a large soup bone, which the dog happily gnawed at Hettie's feet.

After dinner, they went back to the hotel, but a peek into the dining room told them Sophie and Walker weren't done talking. Their heads were close together. Sophie's giggles tinkled against the din.

Hettie didn't see what Sophie or Walker had to laugh about. Hadn't he told her about Abby, locked away in some godforsaken dungeon? What was taking them so long?

She barely noticed Jemma stalking toward them. "Miz Sophie invites you to enjoy dessert in the dining room." She pointed at a table far away from the pair.

"Well, that's mighty kind of her," Uncle said with a lopsided smile for Jemma. The maid barely acknowledged him and marched back to her post, watching her mistress unobtrusively from the sideboard.

"I'm full from dinner," Hettie said. The sour taste in her mouth couldn't be tempered with any amount of dessert. "I'm going out for some fresh air."

Beneath the hotel's overhang, she propped herself against the wall, watching the foot traffic and letting the cool evening calm her restless nerves. Cymon lay at her feet and gave an impatient sigh. How was all this sitting around helping Abby? The longer they delayed, the less chance they had of finding her.

She squeezed her eyes shut. This had all been her idea, of course. She just hadn't thought it would take so long. She had to be patient. She was not going to lose hope. She let out a long breath and reached out with her mind. *I'm coming, Abby. Just hang on.*

Cymon raised his head and sat up, staring into the street. Three men in immaculate suits and bowler hats strode purposefully through the intersection, and the crowd parted for them. Their guns showed plainly on their hips. Another group of men joined them. The first group presented them with a thick sheaf of papers, and Hettie caught sight of a familiar silver eye badge glinting from one man's breast pocket.

Pinkertons! Hettie's heart leaped as Cymon growled. She grabbed his collar and hastily pulled him back into the alley next to the hotel. They hurried through a side door that led into the kitchen and ignored the indignant shouts as they pushed through the service corridor and ran into the Gold Rose's dining room.

Sophie was still talking to Walker, one of her dainty hands resting on his forearm. Hettie drew up short, blew out an angry breath, and went to Uncle and Ling's table instead. The two were mulling over cups of rich-smelling coffee. "The Pinks are here," she told them, swallowing down the lump of panic. It tumbled into her gut, and she started trembling.

Uncle sat up. "You're sure?"

"I just saw three men show papers to the local deputies. They let them keep their guns."

"It's possible they're here for someone else," Ling said.

"We can't take any chances." Uncle stood. "Horses are the priority. Then guns. Go get that slack-jawed Romeo."

When Ling didn't immediately come back with Walker, Hettie craned her neck to see what the holdup was. Sophie was standing, one hand clamped tightly on Walker's arm.

"I will not be ignored and deserted, Mr. Woodroffe. I thought our agreement was fair and sealed. Do you not honor your contracts?"

He bent and said something Hettie couldn't hear, but it became clear when Sophie shrieked, "You're sorry? I'm the one who's sorry! Sorry for believing you a gentleman—"

"Your attention!" A man's voice boomed. The noise level dropped abruptly, and Sophie's voice carried clearly through the room.

"—who considered me as more than a strumpet bed warmer!"

All eyes went straight to the strumpet. Bright flags of color flamed on her cheeks. Hettie had to admire the way Sophie drew herself up, blond ringlets bouncing defiantly. "What are you all looking at?" she snapped.

"They're here!" the man shouted, drawing his pistol.

In one swift movement, Walker grabbed Sophie around the waist and hauled her in front of him as more men piled into the room. The other diners scattered or dove for cover. The bounty hunter pressed a serrated steak knife against her throat. "Don't anyone move!"

Sophie held perfectly still, straining against her captor. Outrage quickly morphed to terror. "Let me go," she pleaded hoarsely. "I'll pay whatever you want."

Before Hettie could shout a warning, Jemma launched herself at Walker, the Bible flying aside to reveal a short blade aimed at his face. With uncanny speed, Ling intercepted her. He chopped the blade out of her hand, parried an outthrust leg, and caught her wrist, twisting her around in an awkward angle. She let out a long string of cuss words as they struggled, crashing from one table to the next. The room stood paralyzed by the ferocity of the battle. Finally, he locked an arm around her neck, squeezing and cutting off her air supply, and she went silent, slumping in his arms.

"Jemma!" Sophie screamed.

"She's only unconscious." The menace in Ling's voice suggested that could change as he spun the limp maid to face forward, joining Walker in the hostage-taking.

"Whoa, now, boys, no need to get dramatic. These gentlemen just want to talk to you," the man with the sheriff's badge coaxed. Five men trained their weapons on them. Apart from the silver eye badge, it was easy to tell which of the party were Pinks—they oozed a cold, slick quality, like snakes crawling through pitch. "Drop your weapons and let the ladies go. There's nowhere you can flee to from here."

"I'm afraid I can't oblige, sheriff," Walker said, his voice calm and low. "You're going to let us walk free to the Zoom tunnel, understand? I can't be held accountable for my actions otherwise."

"Give it up, boys. This won't end well for any of you." The sheriff, well-aged but a little paunchy, hitched his thumbs in his gun belt. He hadn't drawn his sidearm, which worried Hettie all the more. The man was far too calm. "You ain't got no weapons 'cept that tiny lil' butter knife. And your magic's no good here. I have a dozen deputies surrounding the joint. All it takes is a nod from me, and you'll be blown to smithereens."

"Are you crazy?" Sophie's eyes bulged. "He has a knife to my throat. Do you have any idea who I am?" She didn't give them a chance to answer. "I am Sophie Favreau, of the Louisiana Favreaus. My father is Atherton Homer Favreau, owner and president of Favreau Industries, and my grandmother is Patrice Favreau, Soothsayer of the South."

The dining room patrons stirred. Uncle nudged Hettie gently.

"Girl," he whispered, eyes focused on the Pinkertons. They hadn't noticed them yet. "You got a handle on your little devil?"

At first she thought he meant Cymon, but the dog was silent at her side. A cold sweat broke on her upper lip when she realized he meant Diablo. Her breath shook, with each heartbeat reverberating through her like hammer falls on an anvil.

In her mind, she pictured the rattlesnake perched atop the pile of stones in the desert. It slithered away as she brushed the rocks off and dug her claws into the sand.

A sensation like a soap bubble popping in her palm, and then the gun was in her grip. She stooped with the weight as it wrenched her wrist down painfully.

Walker, Ling, and their hostages edged toward the door to the kitchen. Sophie cried, "If I get hurt, you'll all have my father to answer to!" Hettie had a feeling she was addressing the sheriff and his cohorts, too.

"Can we shoot *her* first?" one of the Pinkerton agents deadpanned. "It'll shut her up and get her out of the way."

"Too much paperwork," the lead agent replied blandly. "Shoot her legs."

The sheriff started to protest as the man took aim. Hettie saw what would happen in the next breath; it was like a cloud of red swimming through her syrup world on a silvery, ghostly vision. Two big holes exploded in Sophie's legs, and she crumpled to the ground, screaming. A bullet pierced Jemma's heart—she sagged to the ground, dragging Ling with her. The healer rocked back as a bullet hole appeared between his eyes. And Walker, unable to stop it, would get a bellyful of lead before he could say a single word in protest.

She saw it clearly as if it were happening. "No!" Fire raced into her chest. She leveled the gun and squeezed the trigger.

Diablo splintered in her hands as she fixed her sights on the three Pinkerton agents—the men who'd killed her friends. The green flash of light fractured, sliced across the room, and smashed through each of the three men's bodies, sending up a brilliant spray of blood.

Hettie fell to the ground screaming. Agony coiled tight inside her, burned through her muscles, and seared her skin. She begged for death in that instant—wondered if maybe she was already dead and enduring the torments of hell itself. But then the pain let up, the fists around her lungs loosening as her scream faded to a hoarse whimper.

Her breaths came out harsh and hot from her raw throat. She thought smoke would pour out of her mouth. Tears streamed from her eyes, but they didn't hide the dark stains on the walls behind where the Pinkertons had stood. She looked to where Walker and Ling lay…except they were still standing, clutching Jemma and Sophie, staring at Hettie in horror. The other customers made vague moaning sounds, vomited or quietly sobbed.

She stared at the bloodstained weapon in her hand. Her trigger finger dripped blood steadily onto the fine carpet.

The sheriff fumbled for his weapon. "Holy mother of…" His deputies had their guns pointed at Hettie. She stared back at them, seeing not men but targets. Diablo hummed in her grip.

"Don't even think about it," she uttered, her throat tight. The room reeked of fear and the fetid stench of death and rich, regurgitated food. Sweat dripped from her forehead as she shakily pushed to her feet. She addressed the sheriff and raised Diablo. "We're getting out of here, and God help you and this whole damned town if you try to stop us."

With a trembling hand, the sheriff signaled to his men, and they lowered their weapons.

The four of them, plus Cymon, their horses, and their two hostages, proceeded through the eerily quiet road to the Zoom tunnel station. It'd taken nearly half an hour to clear the street of all traffic. The sheriff's men stayed out of sight, but Uncle and the others kept a keen eye on the windows.

For good measure, Hettie aimed Diablo at an abandoned cart and fired. The innocent vehicle exploded in a shower of splinters, glowing briefly with unnatural green fire before settling into more mundane orange-yellow flames that gobbled up the cart and sent thick plumes of smoke into the darkening sky.

"That's what'll happen to anyone who tries anything," she shouted into the empty street, voice quavering. Stubbs and the Pinkertons knew all she wanted was to find Abby and end this: the lives of all those agents she'd killed was on *them*. "If you try to stop me, I'll level the whole town."

"That seems dramatic," Uncle muttered.

"There's no need for any more violence," Sophie pleaded. "I'll come willingly. I swear. At least let Jemma go." Jemma had stirred some and was sluggishly tripping along in front of Ling. She snarled the occasional curse but was otherwise compliant.

Hettie ignored Sophie's request. She had other things to worry about.

They went unchallenged on the short walk to the station. She sensed rather than saw the sheriff and his men following at a distance.

"Will the Pinkertons open a remote Zoom tunnel here?" she asked Uncle.

"No. The null spell keeps that from happening. They'd have to arrive well outside of town limits."

"I don't know that going into a building with only one way in and out is such a good idea," Walker said, knife held limply at Sophie's throat. With Diablo in Hettie's grip, it hardly seemed necessary.

"They won't fire." Uncle kept his eyes trained on their pursuers. He held the leads of the four horses, with Cymon bringing up the rear as if he could corral them like sheep. "They'll risk damaging the Zoom aperture if they have a firefight in the station. All that flying lead ain't good for it, and Barney's Rock can't lose its only source of income."

"Doesn't mean they won't try."

The platform was little more than a wooden stage in a large room, like a railway station except without tracks. The stage faced a stone wall upon which many talismans were tacked, ringed by a series of runes. In the center of the platform sat a squat pyramid-shaped stone that came up to Hettie's knees. Yellow warning lines were drawn around it. Like the streets, the station had been emptied to accommodate the hostage-takers.

As they ascended the platform, the sheriff and three of his men entered the great hall. The conductor was ushered out of his cozy station office, irate at having his supper hour interrupted. At the sight of the fugitives and their hostages, however, he sobered.

"Bring us our weapons, sheriff," Hettie said. "Nice and slow."

"See here, Miss Alabama." She flinched at the use of her name. The Pinks must have told him about her. "There's no need to threaten those ladies. No need for you to be with this band of ruffians, neither. Why don't you let them go and hand over your gun?"

Diablo hummed in her hand, nudging her aim toward the man's midriff. How easy it would be to blow a hole through him to show him who the real ruffian among them was. "I think, sheriff, that you take me for a simpering idiot."

He held up his hands. "At least consider a trade. Miss Favreau for me."

"No deal," she called back before any of the others could answer. "You strike me as the heroic type, sheriff. And I won't let you martyr yourself."

His gaze darkened. "The law won't spare you from the noose on account of your sex, you know. You're going to regret this, young lady."

"Maybe." She didn't. Not a bit. Even those Pinkertons... She thought of the stain on the walls and felt nothing. A picture of Abby's smiling face came to mind. Her sister was all that mattered. And if she had to kill every last man standing between them, she would.

Two deputies brought the metal storage boxes containing their weapons and charms, and they unlocked and dropped them at the edge of the platform. Uncle picked up the gun belts and slung them over his shoulder, then stuffed all the talismans into a sack. Neither Ling nor Walker relinquished their hostages.

"The Zoom tunnel to New Orleans will open in one minute," the conductor informed them nervously. It was an unscheduled Zoom—which meant that the conductor on the other side had been telegraphed and given notice to open the aperture, as well.

"I've shown you a lot of goodwill," the sheriff said. "How about returning the favor? Let the ladies go. They don't need to be involved any longer."

"We have to take them with us," Walker muttered to her, switching his steak knife for a gun. Sophie whimpered. "The law might be waiting on the other side for all we know."

"Thirty seconds," the conductor said shakily, fingering his pocket watch in sweaty hands.

"Don't worry about us, sheriff," Sophie said evenly. She met Hettie's eye then and gave her a smug smile that made Hettie's doubts flood in. "Grandmère knew this would happen."

"Step up, step up!" the conductor boomed, automatically sliding into his role despite the gravity of the situation. He snapped his pocket watch closed and picked up a long staff set with a giant hunk of quartz bound with snakeskins and feathers. "Nine-thirty-five Zoom to New Orleans arriving!" He swung the staff up in a wide arc.

The far wall darkened as a vortex formed at its center. Cold wind blew out from the black hole, and when it was big enough to fit a fist through the stationmaster plunged the staff into the pyramid receptacle, completing the connection.

The black hole burst into a brilliant spectrum of light, forming a prismatic pathway between the aperture and the staff. The Zoom tunnel irised open, blasting them with frigid air that made the hairs in Hettie's nostrils freeze. When her eyes adjusted to the light, she could see straight through to the other side, where another station platform waited.

"Take the horses through," she ordered them. "I'll be right behind you." She kept her gun pointed at the sheriff.

"This ain't over," he said quietly. "You're crossing state lines using a hijacked Zoom tunnel with hostages in tow. That's all on top of the three men you just killed."

"It's up to you to make sure that body count doesn't rise, sheriff," Hettie said.

He frowned deeply. "Does it make you feel good? To know you ended them, left their widows and children without a provider?"

She swallowed drily. "Better make sure it's all worth it then."

"Come on!" Uncle shouted behind her.

Hettie quickly backed away from Barney's Rock, stepping off the platform. She felt a slight suck-pull as she breached the threshold. Her cheeks burned with cold as she emerged on the New Orleans side of the tunnel. Muggy heat enveloped her, closing around her skin and dampening her clothes. The tunnel flickered, the swirling pattern of dark and light shrinking in diameter like water spiraling down a drain, disappearing against the stone wall in the Zoom tunnel station hundreds of miles away from the one they'd just left.

All her muscles turned to jelly. She let out a long breath, and turned...

To face two dozen rifles pointed at her.

CHAPTER SEVENTEEN

Drop your weapons and release your hostages or we'll shoot." The man with the short, neat ginger beard leveled a pair of pistols at her, amber eyes hard.

Hettie licked her lips. She didn't think Diablo could fire in all directions at once, though the quadrupling of its weight told her it was willing to try.

No, she told it firmly. She couldn't risk the others. *Not today, not with these men.*

The weight eased. She slowly lowered the revolver. "All right," she called. "Don't shoot. Walker, Ling."

The men dropped their knives and let go of the women. The moment Sophie and Jemma were out of the line of fire, the ring of soldiers cocked their weapons.

"Hey! We did as you asked!" Hettie said. Diablo was in her hand once more, the barrel pointed at Ginger Beard. He growled.

"I said put the gun down."

"I can't," she said between clenched teeth. "Not while everyone is trying to kill me."

Ginger Beard squinted, then made a noise. "Bloody hell." He held out his pistols in a motion of surrender. "Look at me, girl. I'm putting my guns away, all right? So don't go blowing my head off with your bleedin' mage gun."

Hettie watched as he slowly bent and placed the weapons on the ground. "You have me at a disadvantage now, miss. For your friends' sakes, I suggest you lower your gun."

"Are you going to shoot us the minute I do?"

"My employer has asked me not to, so I won't."

"Doesn't mean you don't *want* to, English," Uncle muttered, his hands raised.

Hettie's heart beat hard. She didn't have much choice. She tossed Diablo to the ground and put her hands up.

The soldiers closed in around them, shackling their wrists behind their backs and divesting them of their belongings. Ling gave a shout, and someone punched him in the ribs, silencing him. Ginger Beard scooped Diablo off the ground. He hastily dropped it in a sack, muttering a spell as he tied a dried vine around it. Then someone put a hood over Hettie's head.

Prodded on by her captors, Hettie and her companions stumbled across the uneven gravel-strewn ground. The hood stank of fish and blocked out all light. Uncle grumbled as his steps shuffled along. Ling's colorful barrage of insults in both English and Cantonese overlapped the cry of a gull, the rumble of a far-off cart, and a clanging too high-pitched to be a church bell. Cymon snarled as the men wrestled with him, and Ginger Beard shouted orders to subdue the dog.

"Cymon, heel," Hettie said. He whined obediently. She didn't want him getting hurt.

They were pushed into an enclosed wagon and driven for some time across a bumpy road. Hettie tried conjuring Diablo, but it wouldn't come. A sense of foreboding filled her.

"Who are these people?" Ling asked, his voice muffled.

"They're not Pinkerton agents, I can tell you that much," Uncle said.

"They aren't local law, either. The uniform suggests a militia of some kind, but who can afford a private army?"

"More people than you think," Jeremiah muttered. "Hettie?"

She knew what he was asking. "I can't conjure Diablo."

"I can't do anything, either," Ling said.

"None of us can. It's the manacles. They're made of iron." Walker banged them against the wall of the wagon with a loud clang. "Big metal box, too."

"Where are they taking us?"

"Guess we're about to find out." The wagon slowed and came to a sudden standstill. They were wrestled to their feet and marched into a building. Their boots echoed loudly across hard tiled floor.

Hettie sensed a door opening before her. The smell of decaying flowers tickled her nostrils, sweet and cloying, but sour too. Someone grabbed her by the shoulder and thrust her forward. Then her backside hit a plush seat. The bag was yanked off her head, and she let her eyes adjust to the dim light. Ginger Beard loomed above her, glaring.

"If you try *anything*," he warned, "I'll be forced to do unpleasant things."

As he exited, he pulled the door shut behind him. She was alone. She gazed around the empty parlor. Silks, velvet, and lace covered every surface, leaving no hard edges or empty spaces anywhere. Bowls and vases overflowed with roses of every color in various stages of decay. One vase had only a few skeletal stems with desiccated buds hanging limply from them. The water in some of the bowls had gone fetid, thick with multicolored sludge, or dried up into dusty white rings flecked with mold. A kind of vivid despondency pressed in all around her. It had soaked into the lavish wallpaper and thick pile rugs like a bad smell.

"I keep it that way because it reminds me that once something has spoiled, it cannot be unspoiled."

The throaty rasp made her jump. A figure draped in a rose-patterned shawl sat hunched in a plush armchair, camouflaged against her surroundings. Fine lines radiated from a benign smile on a round face. Soft white curls streaked with gray flowed down her back from a loose chignon. "Welcome." Her dark, rheumy, violet-rimmed eyes made Hettie uneasy. The woman seemed to be looking straight into her, and it made the back of her neck prickle. She reached out for Diablo again, but it didn't come. The knot in her stomach tightened.

"You're looking for this?" The old woman produced the Devil's Revolver from beneath her shawl. The hands that held the gun were as gnarled as the shriveled roses.

Hettie struggled for composure. "Where are my friends?" she demanded with more bravado than she felt. "Who are you? What do you want?"

"There's no need to work yourself up, Miss Alabama. All those answers will come in time. But first, you must eat." She picked up a tiny silver bell and gave it a tinkle. A moment later, a servant came in bearing a covered silver platter. He set it in front of Hettie and lifted the lid, revealing a piping hot roast beef dinner dripping with gravy, the bright green peas rolling in a sea of butter and the mashed potatoes piled high like fluffy clouds. Despite having eaten earlier, Hettie's stomach groaned.

"Miss?" The servant nodded, his expression inscrutable. "If you'll sit forward, I'll unbind your hands."

She stared. What kind of prisoner was she? She let the man undo her manacles, and she rubbed her wrists as he exited, taking the cuffs with him.

"Eat." The old woman nodded. "Cook will be very upset if you let it get cold."

"Where are my friends?" She might have reached for the knife for her own protection, but the impulse was stifled, like a fire being smothered by a damp cloth. Powerful suppression spells were at work here.

"I promise you, they're all fine," the woman reassured her. "You see, Sophie is my granddaughter."

Granddaughter? She blinked at the woman. "You're Patrice Favreau. You're the Soothsayer of the South."

Her eyes twinkled. "Please, eat. It distresses me to see such a thin girl."

Hettie balked. She reached out for Diablo again, but still it did not respond to her call.

"I wouldn't poison you or hurt you, if that's your fear." Patrice tilted her chin to one side. "There's no reason for you to be afraid of me." She folded her hands over the gun, as if withholding a toy from a child until she cleaned her plate.

Hettie wasn't about to attack an old woman, especially considering Ginger Beard's threat. She picked up the fork and knife and cut into the slab of meat. The first piece melted on her tongue, the juices bursting forth. Memories of her mother's holiday roasts blossomed in her mind. She took another bite and thought of her father, whittling by the fire. A third bite brought Abby's laughter to mind. Hettie ravenously devoured the rest of the dinner, not caring anymore that the woman had Diablo, not caring where her friends were or even where Abby was. Memories as sweet and succulent and real as the roast warmed her through and through, and as she swiped up the last of the potatoes and gravy, tears began streaming down her cheeks. She wiped them away hastily, holding back an inexplicable sob. The plate was so empty. There was nothing left...

"It's all right," the soothsayer said. "It's not a weakness to cry in front of an old woman like me. You can put up a brave face for the others, but here you're safe to show your true feelings."

A hiccup burst from Hettie's mouth, and suddenly she was bawling into the fine linen napkin laid across her lap. Wordless cries poured from her. She didn't even know why she was crying, only that she was so tired, and letting go of this grief was such a relief. She hadn't realized what a weight she'd been carrying.

"There, there. It's all right." A hand brushed against her damp cheeks as the last of her sobs dissipated. Patrice flipped a small lever on her wheelchair armrest down, braking the device. The thing used Mechanik technology, apparently. "I'm sorry to admit I did have to slip you a little something to help ease your emotional block. But I could see you needed the release."

Hettie didn't have the heart to be angry. She did feel better.

She peeked at the revolver in the old woman's lap, swallowing past a lump in her throat.

"It's yours, of course," Patrice said, glancing down. "But I wonder whether you know how or why."

"I didn't mean to bond with it. I didn't mean for any of this to happen." Hettie blew her nose. The fine napkin was utterly ruined. "I wasn't supposed to open the box..."

"But you did. You can't change that." She gathered the gun in her cupped palms and placed it in Hettie's hands. "You belong to it as much as it belongs to you. You are each other's keepers."

"I don't understand. No one else I've met can hold Diablo, so why can you? And why didn't it come back to me when I tried to conjure it?"

"Perhaps it simply knows who to trust."

"You talk about it as if it were a person."

A secretive smile tipped her lips up. "In a way, it is. A mage gun like Diablo is more than simply an enchanted weapon, just as a horse is more than a means of conveyance." Her eyes flickered. "Do you know how soothsaying works?"

Hettie shook her head.

Her eyes closed. "When a soothsayer scries, we delve into the threads of life, see the past, the present, the future, the tangles they make, the knots they tie, and all the loose ends dangling from the great web. Simple objects don't have threads—they just are. But Diablo has a thread of its own. In your gun, I can see history, personality, and beyond that, a yearning for greatness."

Hettie glanced down at the gun, then back at the soothsayer. "You know something about mage guns?"

"Marcus, my head of security, owns a pair." Her eyes canted toward the door. She must've meant Ginger Beard. "I admit I wanted to see the legendary Devil's Revolver for myself, but now that my curiosity has been sated, we can get down to business."

"What are you talking about?" Hettie was immediately on alert.

"I called my granddaughter to come visit because I knew she would run into you and bring you here. It was one of the last visions I had before the darkness came. You see, I have a message to deliver." Her dark eyes with their violet rings widened slightly. "Your sister, Abby, is alive."

Hettie shot to the edge of her chair. "Are you sure? How do you know?"

"I'm not always certain of the things I see, but this was not a customary circumstance. You see, *she* reached out to me."

Hettie pressed a tight fist against her lips as fresh tears stung her eyes. So it was true. Abby could speak to people across long distances. And she'd reached out to the most powerful soothsayer in the country.

"I take it this is a good piece of news to you?" Patrice asked.

Hettie nodded, eyes hot. The skeptical part of her wondered if she was being manipulated, but she couldn't think of any reason why this woman would lie. "I thought I was crazy. She showed me where she was..."

Patrice nodded slowly, a sad smile on her face. "I should mention," she said, "that I do not usually give information away for free, Miss Alabama. This is my livelihood, after all. But I know you must have some questions. I will answer them if I can."

Hettie was too impatient to hear more about Abby to care what the price would be. "Where is she? I've seen her in a dungeon, and we're sure she's somewhere in Arizona—"

"I don't know. I've tried to find her, but..." Patrice shook her head. Hettie sagged in her chair. The old woman ventured, "You've had visions?"

"I think so. I'm not gifted, but these were too real to be dreams." She told her about Walker's theory that Abby had been reaching out to her, and about what they'd discovered about her whereabouts through Ling. Then she remembered how she'd thought she first heard Abby's voice calling to her when she'd gone back to the ranch with Uncle. Patrice listened intently as she told her everything. "I also spoke to the spirit of an Indian woman and met a dream walker while we were traveling through Wyoming. And then, back in Hawksville, I think I had a premonition of some kind. I knew what was going to happen before it happened, and I stopped it. Same thing happened just now, in Barney's Rock." She rubbed her temples. "I'm not going crazy, am I? The elders never found a trace of the gift on me."

Patrice contemplated the matter. "Diablo may be lending you some of its power. But you say you heard your sister talking to you *before* you bonded with the Devil's Revolver?"

"When I was back on my ranch. Uncle said I was grieving..." Her nails bit into the napkin. "I thought she was by the stream, so I went there. I *heard* her. I know I did." She paused. "Abby said she could hear her friends better when she stood in the creek. Walker said some people can talk over great distances. Is it possible...?"

"That she is one of those precious few? I would say most definitely. As for the creek, there are a great many mysteries we've yet to discover about the land and its magical gifts, but we've killed off so many of its custodians, lost its secrets to time and to arrogance..." She shook her head.

"Maybe the Division has the answers," Hettie said, unsure of herself. Patrice scowled.

"The Division doesn't have half the answers it thinks it does. Don't trust them, Hettie. I had all my gifted children and grandchildren privately trained for a reason. The Academy has become nothing more than a mill for government sorcerers."

She tucked that warning away. "So... Abby could be something else?"

"Possibly. Other cultures may have come across children like Abby and the dream walker you met, but I imagine we've lost more knowledge about magic than we've ever been able to learn. One way or another, your sister is obviously a unique potential."

Hettie bit her lip. "She said she's talked to our brother, Paul. Our dead brother, I mean."

Patrice took this in and closed her eyes. "The simple fact that she managed to reach out to both of us tells me she is something no sorcerer in our time has ever encountered before. But it is you I am more interested in right now."

"Me?"

The old soothsayer released the catch on her chair, and it moved on silent wheels, guided by some unseen force. Hettie heard a puff of air and a slight whirring noise as the chair turned to a desk on the opposite side of the salon. "You said you've never had visions before, never been sensitive or gifted. But Diablo has bonded with you in a way few bond with objects of power. I do have a theory about these visions of yours, Miss Alabama."

She raised her chin, lips pressed tight. "Don't think me rude for asking, but... have you, by any chance, made a deal with the devil?"

CHAPTER EIGHTEEN

Hettie stared. "The devil? No. Why would I...? How could I possibly...?" She tripped over the words tumbling through her head, none of them landing on her tongue. Did she even believe in the devil? She supposed she believed in God, for all the times He'd ignored her prayers to help Ma and Abby get better. Or maybe she didn't believe, and the devil was all there was...

"I don't mean to inspire a crisis of faith, Miss Alabama," Patrice said softly. "In magical terms, the forces I speak of are likely more complicated than good and evil, God and Satan. For our purposes, though, I do mean 'the devil' as you see in the good book—horns, tail, and all."

Patrice rolled the chair to a desk where an old leather-bound tome lay. The act of even opening the cover looked laborious. "Before they called themselves the Kukulos, the old practitioners of blood magic used to cut out pieces of their souls so they could be filled with dark power." The thick vellum pages crinkled as she turned them slowly. "Men and women would sometimes bring themselves to the brink of death to pay homage to the Dark One and trade pieces of themselves—or others—for power." She held the book out to Hettie.

A gruesome woodblock print depicted an enormous black gate, cracked open to reveal myriad tentacles grasping for the tiny human figures standing by the entryway, arms raised in supplication, their eyes pure black, like holes in the page. The shadow of some great beast loomed beyond the gate.

Butch Crowe's scarred, demonic face flashed across Hettie's mind. The air was suddenly too close, too hot, and the blackness of the ink seemed to suck her into the pages as a roar filled her ears. A cold sweat broke over her brow, and she snapped the book shut.

"I didn't make any kind of deal." She put the book down onto a table. "I would never do anything like that. I don't even know how to."

Patrice held her gaze. "Perhaps it wasn't you...but a proxy."

"What does that mean?"

"It means that at some point, someone took you to the brink of death and traded a piece of you off without you knowing it."

Her stomach squirmed. The roast beef wasn't sitting so well now. "That's insane." *You're insane.* Hettie spun away from her, went to the window. "There's nothing wrong with me." But even as she spoke the words, she knew it wasn't true. Something had been missing—she'd known since she'd woken up from death that the void in her was unnatural; that thoughts of her parents rendered her numb. She simply hadn't understood why, nor had she wanted to acknowledge it.

"I know it sounds like the ramblings of an old woman, but it makes sense to me. I can't explain how else you might be having these visions if you weren't gifted before. You can't borrow magic unwillingly, so it's not as though someone juiced you without your knowledge. Necromancy, soothsaying, and telepathy aren't like other magics. They're not talents that can be passed on person to person. Which leads me to believe Diablo's powers are leaking into the hole in your soul."

Hettie squeezed the flesh between her eyes where a headache was forming. "It's just a gun. Why would it need the power to see the future? How is that even possible?"

"If the legends about Diablo are true, that mage gun has a demon bound to it. It's an instrument of the devil. Its purpose is to destroy.

What better defense does it have than knowing who its enemies are ahead of time?"

"That still doesn't explain who would want me to have visions, or why."

"Perhaps this was an unanticipated side effect."

"You mean, my soul wasn't traded for power?"

Patrice's eyes gleamed, her expression inscrutable.

But if that were true, then what would her soul be traded for? What was so vital that someone needed her alive to…

The answer smacked her between the eyes. She reeled. Patrice's expression sobered as Hettie shot to her feet and bolted for the exit, flinging the double doors open.

"Where do you think you're going?" Marcus Ginger Beard unstuck himself from his post and followed.

She didn't answer, nor did he try to stop her as she wound her way through the mansion.

She wasn't sure how, but when she saw a pair of doors guarded by two men, she knew she'd found the right room.

She faced them full on and brandished Diablo. "Stop me and you'll regret it."

The men stepped away from the double doors quickly. She flung them open.

The salon sported cheery yellow wallpaper and fancy gilded chairs. Walker, Ling, and Uncle sat rigidly facing each other, arranged around a low rectangular filigreed coffee table, their feet flat on the ground, palms resting on their knees.

"Miss Hettie!" Ling cried as she entered.

"Good gods, we thought you were being tortured." Walker's head tilted back in relief.

She barely heard them. She headed straight toward Jeremiah, her vision hazy as pieces of a great big puzzle started snapping together in her mind. "You did something to me."

"Excuse me?" He remained seated, his expression stony.

"There's a piece of me missing. A piece of my soul. What did you do?"

Uncle paled briefly and looked away. Hettie's hands clenched and unclenched, jaw grinding. *"Tell me."*

"What's going on, Bassett?" Walker asked. "What's she talking about?"

"I'll tell you what's happening. This is the home of the Soothsayer of the South. Patrice Favreau told me part of me is missing. It's why I'm having visions of Abby when I never could before. You left a hole in me. You took a piece of me out and gave it to the devil!" She slammed her hands on the armrests. "What did you take?" Deep down, she knew the answer. But she had to hear it from Uncle.

When he didn't answer, Diablo leaped into her hand. She pointed it at Jeremiah's head, trigger finger twitching. "You've been lying to me since the day I was born." She'd felt as though a hole were expanding in her chest. She'd tried to ignore it, tried to focus on finding Abby and staying alive. But that emptiness had consumed her, slowly but surely. "You took my soul. Now I'm half a woman, and not even that. You think this is what Pa wanted for me?"

"I did this for John," he barked, hurt shining in his eyes. "He made me promise to take care of you, so I did. I pulled you out of death's clutches. But there had to be a trade-off. Life for a piece of you."

Blood rushed through her ears. "What piece?" she asked again, just above a whisper.

Jeremiah's gaze didn't waver. "Love...for your parents."

Her vision blurred. Her arms lost all strength and flopped to her sides, and she dropped the gun.

"You traded love for life?" Ling whispered, horrified.

"A soul's no good to a dead girl." Uncle's coldly detached voice was like a razor-sharp blade slicing through her—it took a moment to feel the bite. "It was the only way. The only piece you could afford. I was doing you a favor. You wouldn't have survived if I didn't cut that piece out anyhow. You'd have died of a broken heart."

"A hole in your soul...So that's what I couldn't heal," Ling murmured.

"It's why Diablo likes her so much, isn't it? The Devil's Revolver doesn't bind itself to just anyone and allow them to conjure it." Walker strained in the chair, his body flexing though he still didn't stand. "Was that your plan all along? Attach her to it like a ball and chain until you knew how to better control it yourself?"

"You don't know anything, you swaggering, juiced-up pretender," the old man snapped. "I've done my best by her and her pa. Always have, always will."

"Which is why you'd shoot her sooner than let Diablo fall into another's hands."

"There are things you don't understand about that gun." Shadows deepened his eyes, and he heaved a long, frustrated sigh. "I didn't think she'd open the damn box. I didn't think she'd be dumb enough to steal the thing from me, much less touch the box with her blood on her hands."

"The box..." Hettie spoke the words distantly. "It could only be opened by my blood."

"Your father's blood. Alabama blood."

"Is that why you kept me alive? So you'd have a way to open the box?" She leaned heavily against a side table.

He stared down at his lap.

Pa had told Uncle to leave with that box. He'd planned to take his family away in the opposite direction. He'd known there would be no way to open that box unless his blood—or his children's— was used. And if Butch had killed them all...

But he hadn't. He'd kept Abby in reserve. And then Uncle had come back and found Hettie, salvaging what he could...

Her wrist strained as she raised the gun once more. "This is all about Diablo. You just wanted the revolver." Her pulse pounded in her throat.

The old man hissed through his teeth. "I don't want or need that blasted—"

"Stop lying. I should be dead. I should be with them." She tried to summon a feeling of warmth for her mother and father, but when she thought of them, she felt...nothing. It was like digging her hands into the sand and expecting to find diamonds. She remembered the life they'd shared, yet none of those moments elicited more than mild apathy, as if all she'd done was read a boring textbook about her parents. The harder she tried to feel something for them, the more alien they seemed. "They killed Ma and Pa and me for this. But you...*you* took my parents away from me." That violation, more than anything, made her cock the gun.

Jeremiah Bassett gazed down the barrel of the Devil's Revolver, his eyes going flat. "You're not going to pull that trigger, Hettie."

"Why shouldn't I?"

"Because you're not the one in control. Diablo's got a mind of its own. It was built to do one thing—kill. And it's not going to let a little girl stop it." His eyes flickered to her tenuous grip. "The longer you keep it from achieving its purpose, the harder it'll be to master. When you pull that trigger, I know it won't be you. It'll never be you."

Her rage flickered like a wildfire in a rainstorm, and yet she was cold. So cold. "I'm the one pointing Diablo at you. I'm the one who's bonded to it. I *am* in control."

"So pull the trigger. I've stared down that muzzle before, and down the barrels of a hundred other guns before that. An angry little girl doesn't scare me as much as the thought of Diablo landing in the wrong hands. If I thought it'd bring me peace to go quietly, I'd draw and make you shoot me now. But it won't. So I'll say my peace now and let you get it over with." His throat bobbed as he swallowed. "For all of your stubborn, ill-conceived impetuousness...I forgive you, Hettie."

She set her teeth. She could pull the trigger. Blow his brains out and remove one more problem from her already messed-up life. What did she have to lose? She'd already killed six men—what was one more Judas?

Seven, a voice in the back of her head prompted. The first man she'd ever killed had been the one she'd shot in Newhaven, back when all this had begun with Ling, with Walker, with her pa killing Shadow Frank. She looked down at the stained ivory grip, blood oozing from her trigger finger stigmata. Her hands would never be clean.

"That's enough, Miss Alabama." Patrice's wheelchair glided to her side. She placed a withered hand over her arm.

The pressure inside her eased, the heat of her anger dissipating. With effort, she stepped away, pocketing the Devil's Revolver. Marcus entered the room and took a post by the door, feet apart, arms folded as he studied her intently. Hettie wheeled away and faced the large bay window, her emotions in a tumult. Her eyes unfocused as she traced the gaps of darkness around the silhouette of city lights in the distance.

"Patrice Favreau, I assume." Walker nodded toward the older woman.

"Precisely, Mr. Woodroffe." She preened. "I see why my granddaughter was so taken with you."

"If you're expecting a gentlemanly bow, you're gonna be waiting awhile," Uncle harrumphed.

"It's for your own good," Marcus said sharply.

"Marcus, Miss Alabama and her friends are our guests. I think we should allow them this courtesy at least." Patrice waved a hand and gave a dismissive word. The three men sagged as their invisible bonds released. "My apologies for the precautions, gentlemen. My head of security can be somewhat... enthusiastic when it comes to neutralizing threats to me and mine."

Hettie sensed Walker at her side. "Are you all right?"

She took a moment to gather her voice. "I keep thinking about my parents." She stared out into nothing, clutching the window frame. "I remember all the things they did for me, but I don't know who they are anymore. They're like strangers I lived with. I don't *feel* for them like I should. And I feel bad because I *don't* feel anything."

"I think it's about as close as you can feel to love for them right now." He settled a warm, strong hand on her shoulder. She closed her eyes, imagining it was her father trying to offer comfort. Nothing.

She shrugged off his hand and took a stiff step back. "How are the rest of you doing?"

"Just a little bruised pride, I think. There's some pretty strong suppression magic here, but it seems to be just on us." He eyed Marcus. "Ling busted a few noses when they took those bags off our heads. He might have taken a few hits to his ribs, but he won't admit he's in pain."

"Please accept my humblest apologies for this treatment," Patrice said. Evidently, she'd overheard them. "I didn't mean you any harm."

"Could've fooled us," Jeremiah muttered. Hettie glowered at him, irked by his rudeness, but also cross with him in general. She wasn't sure she could ever forgive him.

"To be fair, you did hold my daughter and her companion at knifepoint." Patrice smiled tightly. "I'd like you all to stay here as long as you need. I know you'll want to continue your search for Abigail Alabama. I will provide whatever assistance I can."

"Why?" Ling asked, suspicious. "What's in it for you?"

The old woman favored him with a cool look. "There is more going on than we think. For the past several months, my visions have been growing fainter, as if they're being obscured by a thick, deep shadow. Other soothsayers have told me the same thing has been happening to them. It's been difficult for those of us who make a living from telling people's fortunes." The corners of her mouth twitched. "I would ask that you keep this in strictest confidence."

Of course Patrice would want that information kept private. If word got out that the soothsaying community could no longer scry the future, people might turn to alternative fortune tellers, who claimed to see the future through tea leaves and crystals. Soothsayers' rates were absurdly high, after all—no one needed the extra push away from their services.

"From what I know, not even iron or null spells can stop visions from happening. What could obscure soothsaying magic?" Walker asked.

"Old magics. Forbidden magics. But for what purpose they might be used, none of us know."

"But... Hettie's had visions of Abby," Ling pointed out.

"My guess is that Hettie's unique circumstances, and the fact that Abigail Alabama is something of a magical anomaly, allowed for this to happen." She explained her theory about Diablo's magic filling the hole in Hettie's soul. "Abby used her abilities to reach out to her sister and to me. Perhaps a few other soothsayers have heard her but did not realize who she was."

"So someone is deliberately obscuring soothsaying magic, and Abby has been the only person who's broken through this... blackout?"

She tugged at the cuffs of her sleeves. "Blackout...an apt description. Yes, I fear that whoever is responsible may even know Abby has done so."

"What reason would anyone have to black out soothsayers' powers?" Walker asked.

"To hide something they don't want anyone else to see," Marcus chimed in, stepping farther into the room. "And to preserve the element of surprise. A few sorcerers did it during your Civil War to keep the soothsayers on opposing sides from knowing the others' plans."

"Didn't work well for anyone," Uncle muttered, and Marcus nodded.

"But what does Abby have to do with all this?"

"I don't know for sure. But it's no coincidence that Abby is connected somehow. Someone took her from the ranch. They would not have bothered with a remote Zoom tunnel if they didn't mean to get her away quickly." Patrice rubbed her temples and sighed. "My proposal is this: in exchange for your help discovering the cause of this blackout, I will help you find your sister. I will provide transport, weapons, resources, provisions...whatever you need. I have a feeling that wherever Abby is, you'll also find the answers to our mystery." She nodded. "Do we have a deal?"

Her gaze was fixed on Hettie. She wasn't asking Walker, an experienced bounty hunter, or Uncle, a former division man, or Ling. She was asking Hettie. This was her choice to make.

The Favreaus' resources were more than she could ever dream of. But what was the catch? Patrice was wealthy beyond imagination, yet she hadn't employed anyone else to take on this quest. Hettie couldn't help her suspicious nature, so she didn't respond.

"You need time to think about it," the soothsayer reasoned, nodding. "I understand. Sleep on it, and we can discuss things in the morning." Patrice's wheelchair glided toward the door. "Rooms and meals have been prepared for you all. You are free to roam the grounds, but I suggest you not venture beyond the perimeter. There are a great many dangers beyond the gate."

Was that a warning or a threat? Hettie wasn't sure she wanted to know.

CHAPTER NINETEEN

A servant led them to rooms on the second floor of the three-story mansion. Hettie's was located at the end of the long, carpeted hall. It was so finely furnished she was afraid to step in and dirty the floors.

A mostly silent but extremely efficient maid directed her to the bath, hastily taking her soiled clothing away to be laundered. At first Hettie wasn't sure she wanted to bathe—it felt wrong to be luxuriating while Abby was still missing—but she was sore and needed to drown out Uncle's betrayal. The moment she stepped into the clawfoot tub, all her reservations fled, and she sank into the hot, scented bathwater.

She soaked her head and shampooed her oily, matted hair, combing the short length until it felt like silk. The water turned brown-gray with old blood and dirt. She scrubbed every inch and rubbed her skin with scented oils from a basket the maid had left. Hettie had never felt so decadent or spoiled. All her injuries and the aches of weeks of riding leached out of her muscles. She closed her eyes with a sigh, letting her head dip back until her ears were submerged underwater.

Hettie . . . Hettie, please . . .

Her eyes snapped open, and she bolted upright. No one was in the room with her.

She stared at the murky bathwater. Carefully, she lay back, pinching her nose shut as she slid under.

It's dark here, Hettie. There are rats and big bugs I don't like. I miss the sun, and Ma and Pa and you and Uncle and Cymon. I miss the farm. Why won't you come, Hettie?

I'm coming, Hettie called back, practically shouting. *I'm coming and I'm bringing help. Tell me where you are!*

No response. Hettie waited, straining to hear. Her lungs were about to burst when a pair or strong hands hauled her out of the water with a great splash. Hettie gasped as the maid shouted at her. "Miss, are you mad? What could you be thinking, scaring me like that?"

"I...I..." She wiped the water out of her eyes. She wasn't about to get into long explanations. "I'm sorry. I must have fallen asleep."

The woman gave her a pitying look. "Well, it's no wonder, all this excitement. It's not fit for a young woman to be riding all over the place with these rough types. Let's get you out of there and into bed."

As soft as the down mattress was, Hettie couldn't sleep. She knew for certain that Abby was alive and out there somewhere, waiting for her. She got up to look out the window. As she passed the vanity, her reflection startled a gasp from her.

A woman with her father's strong jaw and her mother's dark eyes and high cheekbones stared back at her. Her short hair had grown some so it was a ragged mess around her ears. The plume-shaped scar stretching from her temple along her cheek still showed quite clearly. But her slightly upturned nose had straightened, her puffy cheeks were now more delicate apples. She turned her head this way and that, and then, in a moment of curiosity, went to the cheval mirror and inspected the rest of her body.

Someone knocked on her door. She dropped the hem of her nightgown and quickly slipped into the robe hanging in the armoire before opening the door.

"Sorry to disturb you." Only the gruff voice betrayed the identity of the strange man before her. Walker stood in a clean white shirt and trousers, his square jaw shaven, his wet hair slicked back from his forehead. He smelled like soap and whiskey and leather. Hettie blinked up at him, not realizing until that moment just how dashing a figure he cut. Self-conscious, she clutched the neck of her nightgown closed. He glanced around surreptitiously. "May I speak to you privately?"

Heat flushed through her cheeks. Ma would have had a conniption fit if she knew a man was alone with her in her room at this hour. Not that Hettie suspected he had any designs on her innocence, but whatever the reason, it seemed urgent. "Meet me downstairs in the drawing room in ten minutes. I'll get dressed."

"Let's make it the stables instead. I want to check on Lilith. You should check on Blackie, too. I hear they had a hell— pardon me, hard time getting him into the corral."

Hettie didn't miss his slip of the tongue. She supposed being surrounded by such finery civilized a person. She donned the plain day dress the maid had left her, pulled on her boots, and hurried out.

A few lamps lit the stables, turned down so the horses could sleep. Cymon lay curled up on a pile of hay by the door, an enormous bone sandwiched between his paws. He looked up briefly as Hettie scratched his big head, then settled back in, sighing contentedly as he snuggled the bone.

She found Walker in the second aisle by one of the stalls, stroking Lilith's neck. He turned his head, gaze landing squarely on her. His Adam's apple bobbed. "The grooms gave her a thorough rubdown," he said, and nodded down the aisle. "The others are in good shape, too."

"It's very kind of Mrs. Favreau to host us."

He glanced around. Without warning, he grabbed her hand and dragged her into the shadow, pulling her against his chest.

"What are you—"

"Shh." His lips grazed her neck. "I'm sorry, this is the only way we can speak freely. There are ears all over this house."

She fought against the sensation sizzling through her and tried to pry herself away, but Walker pulled her flush against his hard body. "Stop struggling." His command came as a harsh, hot breath poured over her scarred temple. She stilled despite her pounding heart. Her fingers curled against his shirt. She closed her eyes, ashamed at the thrill coursing through her.

"Hettie, if you want to find your sister, we should leave your uncle and Ling here. They're slowing us down. Between you and me on Lilith and Blackie, we can cover a lot more distance." His fingers tightened around her waist. "Once we find your sister, we're going to need speed to get her somewhere safe."

"We can't just leave. Patrice said she'd help us find Abby."

"What do you even know about her, Hettie? What makes you think you can trust her?"

"I just do." Her instincts told her this was someone she could believe. "She's the only person who's been up-front with me since the moment I met her."

"That's because she has nothing to lose. She has all the power here, don't you see? People like her don't do things for nothing. She wants something from you."

And so did Walker, she reminded herself. She pushed him off. "All she wants is for me to find out what's causing the soothsayers' blackout."

The bounty hunter planted his hands on his hips. "She didn't make her fortune by keeping contract terms simple. Soothsayers always have the advantage, Hettie. They know what's going to happen."

"If this blackout is real, then she doesn't know. Besides," she added, "if we leave, Uncle will just track us down again. I don't think he'll let me out of his sight."

"And Ling?" He took a step closer. "What's he to you?"

She stared. "He wants to pay off his debt." Walker's skeptical look made her fold her arms across her front and take a step back. "He wants to help Abby."

He snorted. "If that's what you think."

Hettie studied him closely. "If I didn't know any better, I'd say you were jealous of him."

He glowered, then kicked the tip of his boot against a stall, dislodging a bit of muck. "You know your uncle doesn't care if your sister is alive or dead, right?"

Having it spelled out for her in such black-and-white terms made her flinch. "He's got his own agenda," Walker continued. "He wants to get you and Diablo away from everything. He'd probably hide you both in a box and bury you in the ground if he had a chance."

A small part of her wished he had. But despite everything, and knowing now her sister was alive, she couldn't let go of such a valuable ally. "I'm not leaving him behind again. He knows things about the Crowe gang and Diablo, and about the Pinkertons. And he's a powerful sorcerer."

"You can't trust him after what you learned tonight. The moment he's decided he's had enough of you chasing after your sister, who knows what he'll do?"

"And what about you? What about when *you've* decided you've had enough?"

His nostrils flared. "We made a deal. I honor my contracts."

"And your word should mean something to me?" She turned away, but he planted a palm on either side of her head, trapping her against the stall. She could see the silver flecks in his narrowed blue eyes as he closed in on her. She glared back, squelching the urge to get closer and breathe his scent.

"You've got to trust someone," he said. "If you want to save your sister, you need an ally. Someone who understands what you're going through."

"I don't see how you could possibly understand my situation."

"I understand more than you'll ever know." She barely heard his words, but something about them struck a chord in her. She brushed away the feeling and ducked out of the circle of his arms, marching out of his reach. Walker might have enough magic to keep them both safe, but right now, with the four of them, they had a posse. They were going up against one of the most ruthless gangs in the West. More men was definitely better than fewer. "You want me to leave the others behind so that you can take Diablo for yourself."

"I won't lie and tell you it hadn't crossed my mind. If I could've taken it from you, I would have. Every time you use it to kill...I hate watching you scream like that." He let out a labored breath, as if it was a trial to admit.

And what was that supposed to mean? She must make quite a racket. "It's hurting less and less. I think it is. I'm getting used to it."

"You're not supposed to get used to something like that." His expression softened, and he searched her face. "Does it still hurt?" He brushed big, blunt fingertips over her scar.

She shivered. "N-no. Not anymore."

"That's good." He glanced at Blackie, who watched them steadily. "We could leave tonight." His voice was low and urgent once more, luring her closer. "We can pack our things, take the horses and go before anyone even knows. Just you and me. Cymon could come along, too. He's good in a scrape."

Hettie's lips moved, but no words came. She tried to shake her head, but her chin only nodded, as if...

"What are you two doing out here?"

They turned together. Ling glared at them, arms folded over his chest. Who knew how long he'd been standing there? Hettie stepped away from Walker quickly, cheeks burning, unable to meet Ling's eye.

The bounty hunter hitched his thumbs in his belt and inserted himself between her and the healer. "I was just making sure Miss Alabama was safe out here. She wanted to check on Blackie."

Ling's fixed expression didn't waver. "Both of you should get some sleep." He eyed Hettie. "You're no good to Miss Abby if you get sick."

She hastened back toward the stable, heartbeat skittering as she tried to even out her breathing. Only when she reached the doorway did she realize the two men were not behind her, and she glanced back.

Ling stood toe to toe with the bounty hunter, radiating menace like an ornery goat facing down a placid bull. They spoke in low tones. Ling said something that made Walker jerk back. The bounty hunter gestured sharply and loomed over the healer, but Ling didn't budge. They stood locked like that for a moment longer, muscles tense, then broke apart and headed toward her.

"Get to bed, Miss Hettie," Ling commanded sharply, sounding for all the world like her father. "You don't need to worry about the horses. They'll all be safe here tonight."

Υ

At the breakfast table the next morning, it was clear no one had slept well despite the amenities. Sophie joined them, looking radiant as ever in a lavender dress, her hair dripping with silk ribbons. A bath and a beard trimming had done little to improve Uncle's haggard, haunted look as he sipped his coffee—apparently, the dirt and grime had been hiding his mottled complexion and sickly air. Ling watched Walker furtively, his gaze flickering speculatively to Hettie and narrowing with disapproval. The bounty hunter ignored them all and conversed with their hosts.

Sophie looked none the worse for wear since her ordeal in Hawksville, and didn't seem to care that her kidnappers now broke bread with her elderly grandmother. She talked animatedly to Walker, and the bounty hunter listened raptly. He didn't have a choice—Sophie didn't let him get a word in edgewise. Marcus stood within earshot, keeping a close eye on the diners, his weathered face crinkled as if he'd smelled something bad. Jemma was nowhere to be seen.

After breakfast, they all gathered in the yellow salon the men had occupied the previous evening. Sophie took Walker's arm, and he escorted her in as if he were some debonair gentleman. Hettie might even believe it, considering how handsome the bounty hunter looked in a freshly pressed vest, crisp white shirt, and trousers.

"I said I'd offer you help in your search." Patrice approached Hettie on silent wheels. "I'd like to try connecting to Abby through you. If I can reach her, you can talk to her directly, and she might be able to tell you where she is."

"You can do that?"

"I spoke with Mr. Tsang about it this morning, and he has a theory." She nodded at the healer.

"If Miss Abby has actually managed to connect with Miss Hettie, she'll have left a dream path. Usually, such trails are too weak to trace back"—Ling nodded toward Walker—"but Mrs. Favreau has also touched Abby's mind. I believe that if Mrs. Favreau plumbs Hettie's memories for more details, the combination of both their experiences will be enough to retrace the dream path all the way back to Abby's exact location."

"Like putting together pieces of a ripped-up map," Sophie murmured. "That is quite ingenious, Grandmère, but are you sure you're up to it?"

"I'll be fine, child. Hettie will be doing most of the work, anyhow. If she agrees to this, of course."

Walker had offered to do something similar—plumb her mind for clues. She hadn't trusted him because he had his own agenda. He still did. But could she trust Patrice not to manipulate her the way Uncle had?

Then again, Patrice could have harmed her anytime since her arrival, but she hadn't. Hettie consented with a nod.

"I warn you," Patrice said, "what you see and feel might seem real, but it's not. It's important you remember that so your mind doesn't get lost on the path."

The soothsayer's wrinkled hands clasped hers. She closed her eyes. The old woman chanted in what sounded like French. It seemed to take a long time, but as she relaxed into her seat, the words blended together. Behind her eyelids, the darkness swirled, then became a rush of light, and suddenly she was flying, straight out of her seat and through the gilded ceiling, into the sky, darting through thick cloud cover straight as an arrow. The horizon stretched to forever, lit by the brilliant globe of the sun, kissing the curve of the world between the earth and the stars.

She didn't see herself or Patrice, but she knew the soothsayer was there with her, still holding her hands, and she clung to that sensation as she was pulled along an invisible line like a fish being reeled in. The ground rushed past beneath her. They soared across the countryside, pointed west. Dark greens changed to fields of gold grass that thinned, giving way to gray and red rock and endless stretches of coarse sand and tough weeds.

"What do you see?" Patrice's calm voice came from a distance. Hettie peered around.

"The sand here is reddish. There's lots of hills. It's rocky, too. Not a lot of green. Little shrubs everywhere, and some cactus, but not much else."

"Do you see the Wall?"

Hettie squinted, but her vision didn't improve. "No. I must be pretty far north... Wait." A dark line appeared due south. "I think I see it now."

She'd known the Wall was big, but she hadn't realized just how intimidating it was. Some of the most powerful sorcerers in Mexico had raised the earth and moved mountains to construct the monument after the Mexican-American War. But there was something about the rapidly approaching perimeter apart from its massive size that frightened Hettie. The Wall was pure black, standing a hundred feet high. It wasn't a straight, flat wall made of a line of bricks, but a steep pile with plateaus and gantries cut into its facade. The monolithic landmark made her cringe inwardly.

She plummeted, and her heart flew into her stomach. She screamed, but before her brains were dashed across the ground her body jerked up so that she soared parallel to the road at shoulder height.

"You can't be hurt here, Hettie," Patrice assured her. "We're starting to see the path that Abby remembers. She traveled this route, and she used this same trail to find you in her mind's eye."

Hettie fought to pull herself higher as the path zoomed sharply to the east. The Wall cast a long, dark shadow as black as the stone itself.

A cluster of ramshackle buildings came into view. It looked like a mining camp, with a few lean-tos and several collapsed and ruined tents. Boxes and crates and broken wagons littered the area, along with the bleached bones of a few horses and cattle. But there were no people around. Or birds or insects. Nothing alive. Was that because this was still just a vision?

She plunged toward a rocky hill where the gaping maw of a cave swallowed her in darkness. Hettie broke into a sweat. She didn't normally have problems with tight, dark spaces, but this place felt... wrong. The cavern narrowed, twisting and turning in near pitch-black. She breathed deep, squeezing Patrice's hands.

The floor leveled out. The walls here were smooth, the corners gently rounded. The whole place had been shaped by human hands. She passed innumerable forks and intersections. Hettie tried to keep track of where she went, but it got darker, more oppressive.

The air in her lungs became close and dank, and she struggled for breath.

"What is it?" Walker's voice reminded her she wasn't really here.

"We're deep underground. It's a maze down here…" Something cool slid over her skin, and she recoiled. "I don't like it."

"Do you see Abby?"

"No."

Her spine jarred as she was yanked roughly into a room. The walls were lined with cages, the stone gray and damp. The door slammed shut with a resounding boom.

Abby stood in the center of the room. She wore a plain brown cotton smock dress, but no shoes. Her bronze-gold hair hung in a soft waterfall around her shoulders. Her expression was dreamy and distant.

And she wasn't alone.

CHAPTER TWENTY

The man standing behind Abby had one slender hand resting on her shoulder. As smooth and flawless as his features were, Hettie sensed he was older than he appeared. His blond curls made a soft halo around an angular face. His skin was so fine and thin she could see the blood pumping through the blue veins standing out on his neck.

His all-black eyes shone with satisfaction, and his red lips curved up. *"Hello, Hettie."*

His mellifluous voice sent shivers along her spine. She ground her teeth together to suppress her trembling. "Who are you?"

"I'm a friend of your sister's. You can call me Zavi. Abigail, won't you say hello?"

Abby lifted a limp hand. Something was terribly wrong. Her eyes were vacant, lifeless. She wasn't looking at Hettie at all.

"This…this isn't real." Hettie squeezed her eyes closed, trying to remember what Patrice had said. "This can't be happening. We're traveling on a memory, retracing Abby's steps…"

"Oh, I'm here. And so are you." In the blink of an eye, he was standing toe-to-toe with her. He brushed his fingertips against her scar. *"You can feel this, can't you?"*

Tendrils like spider web tickled her skin. Distant voices shouted for her from down the corridor. She tried to pull away, but he snatched her hands and gripped them until her fingers ached.

"*No, my sweet, you aren't going anywhere. The only place you're going to be is here, within the week. Otherwise, I'm going to have to do something drastic.*" He glanced over at Abby.

"What do you want?" she demanded, leaning as far away from him as she could. Her feet felt as though they'd been glued to the ground.

"*Diablo, of course.*" His oily smile revealed brilliant white teeth against red gums. "*All you have to do is come to me with the Devil's Revolver, and I will release your sister. That is what you want, isn't it?*"

She balked. "If you want Diablo so bad, why don't you come and get it yourself?"

"*I have more pressing matters to attend to. Besides, I don't think Abby's well enough to travel just now.*"

Something inside of Hettie clawed its way to the surface. She broke out of Zavi's hold and pointed Diablo at him. "What have you done to her?"

He grinned. He had an enormous mouth. When he didn't respond, she waved the gun at his head. "I said, what have you done?"

"Hettie, no!" Patrice swung her around, and Hettie stared at her. "You're straying off the path. You're going to get lost. This isn't real."

"*I see you've made allies.*"

Patrice slowly turned. She wasn't confined to a wheelchair, and she didn't appear as old as she looked in the real world...

The real world. This was just a dream. A vision. But Patrice was here with her...

"*Madame Patrice Favreau, it is an honor to meet you.*" Zavi swept a low bow.

Patrice gave a primal cry and lunged, her hands outstretched as if she'd strangle him. Hettie watched in horror as the unearthly beautiful man slugged the woman in the chest. She flew backward. Her body smashed into the wall and fell to a crumpled heap.

"Patrice!"

Zavi sighed. "*I think you should hurry, Hettie. Abby's dying to see you.*" He stroked her cheek, leaving sticky, clinging threads of sensation. "*Don't dawdle.*"

He waved a hand, and the vision exploded in a shower of light. Hettie reeled back as though she'd been kicked in the head by a horse. When she came to, she was blinking up dazedly at the gilded ceiling of Patrice Favreau's salon.

Walker and Uncle helped her into a sitting position. Black spots danced in her vision. "What happened? You went white as a sheet and…" The bounty hunter grimaced, looked behind him.

Sophie knelt by her grandmother's side, weeping over the old woman's prone body. Marcus shouted orders at the servants, who rushed in and out with blankets, hot water, medicine, and talismans. Two sorcerers swinging censers chanted above her, weaving purging spells and protection spells. When Patrice didn't stir, they carried her out on a stretcher, leaving the room empty except for Hettie and her companions.

Hettie's hands started to shake. She looked to Ling. "Can you…?"

"I already tried. There's nothing wrong with her body—it's her mind. It's not there."

She slumped into a chair. This was all her fault. The soothsayer had only been trying to help her find her sister. She forked her fingers through her short hair, trying to recall everything she'd seen. "There was a man. He said his name was Zavi. He has Abby. He wants Diablo." She gripped her pounding head, unable to shake the afterimage of those black eyes against his white face seemingly burned into her vision.

"He spoke to you? As in, had a conversation?" Uncle asked.

Hettie nodded.

Walker rubbed his jaw. "I've never heard of anyone communicating through a vision like this."

"Maybe he knew Abby could reach out with this ability," Ling said. "Maybe he gave her this memory. He's been waiting for you to reach out to her—perhaps he rehearsed some lines with Abby."

"I don't think so. He wasn't giving a speech. He was talking to me, just like we are now. And then I pulled Diablo on him." She pressed a fist against her mouth. "It was just a vision—how could I do that?"

Walker laid a hand on her shoulder. "What happened to Patrice?"

She described what she'd seen, told them about what Zavi wanted. The men exchanged disturbed looks.

"I think...I think he's going to hurt Abby." She pushed to her feet. "We need to get to Arizona."

"Hang on, Hettie. We shouldn't go rushing into this with this sorcerer in the mix," Walker cautioned.

"He's powerful, no doubt." Uncle tugged on his beard. "What did he look like?"

"Tall, thin, curly blond hair down to here. His eyes were really black." She shuddered, remembering the dark fire burning in his gaze. She'd almost prefer to face Butch Crowe—at least he was human.

"Hmm. Must be a Kukulos warlock. Using blood magic turns their eyes all black. They say it's from staring into the bowels of hell." Uncle scratched his chin. "Fits with the fact that the Crowes are shape-shifting, assuming this Zavi's the one they're with."

Hettie chewed on her lip. "We need to get going."

"Now wait just a minute." Walker stood. "Our agreement was that I'd help you get Abby out of the hands of the Crowe gang, not away from some hell-soaked Kukulos warlock."

"If you're too afraid, then now's the time to back out."

The bounty hunter glowered. "I'm not leaving you to do this alone. But I'm not charging in guns blazing, either."

"Why not? If we know where they are and we know they have Abby, we can gather a posse and have her out of there in minutes."

"I don't like the sound of this fella's plans." Uncle paced. "If he can open remote Zoom tunnels, then why hasn't he sent men after you the way the Pinks have? Why is he holding Abby hostage and making you go to him? If all he wanted was Diablo, there are a hundred ways someone as powerful as he is could get it."

"Mr. Bassett is right," Ling said. "The Crowe gang came for it first. If they're working with this Zavi, then they could have been sent to find you any other time you fired it off."

"That's only assuming he's as powerful or has the resources the Pinks have," Walker pointed out.

Uncle grimaced. "The man hijacked a vision to communicate with Hettie and nearly killed one of the world's most powerful soothsayers. I'd say he's plenty powerful."

"But to what end?" Ling closed his eyes and gripped the back of a chair. "Why does he want Diablo?"

"I don't care why," Hettie said. "He has Abby. My sister is alive, and I intend to bring her home. Come with me or don't, but I'm leaving."

"None of you are going anywhere." Marcus planted himself in front of the doors, pistols drawn. Hettie's arm whipped up, revolver in hand, finger poised on the trigger. She imagined the security man staring down Diablo's lone black eye the same way she stared down those twin mage gun barrels, heart beating hard. The air between them crackled.

"You people take a young girl hostage, take advantage of my lady's hospitality, render her senseless, and now you think you're just going to leave?" His aim didn't waver. His anger was cool— Hettie sensed she'd find a bullet between her eyes before she could do anything to avoid it. Diablo teased her, daring her to test its power against the security man's mage guns.

But she couldn't pull the trigger. For one, Marcus didn't deserve it—he was only trying to protect his charges. Besides, the Pinkertons were still a threat, and if she pulled the trigger and announced to the world where they were, they would be trapped in that house. "Marcus," she said carefully, "I'm sorry about what happened to Patrice. And I'm sorry for what we did to Sophie and Jemma. But we're not the enemy. I didn't mean for any of this to happen."

"Whether your intention was noble or not, it doesn't justify kidnapping and murder."

"It was self-protection," Hettie said. "I have to save my sister."

"Is that what you tell yourself so you can sleep at night? How many more will die for your crusade?"

"Marcus." Sophie appeared at the man's side and placed a hand on his arm, and he startled. No one had seen her come in. "Put the guns down."

"Justice must be done, Miss Sophie. We can't let these criminals escape punishment."

"That's not for us to decide." Sophie's voice was soft, but firm and commanding. "Right now, Grandmère needs us. Blame me if the authorities come, but I will not have any bloodshed in my grandmother's house. Is that clear?"

Hettie was surprised by the steel in Sophie's voice. "I'm lowering my weapon." She eased Diablo back into her pocket. "I have no intention of harming you, Marcus, or anyone else here."

His hands betrayed the slightest tremor before he shoved his weapons back into their holsters. With a scathing look, he marched out.

Y

Later, after the healers had left Patrice's room, Hettie went to the old soothsayer's bedside to see how she was doing. She lay in the ornate four-poster, her floral-patterned bedspread tucked up under her chin, white-gray hair spread around her like a halo. Sweet-smelling incense burned on the nightstand, and bundles of sage and talismans hung above from the canopy. Sophie occupied a chair on the opposite side of the bed, watching her grandmother with red-rimmed eyes.

"They say she's in a coma," she said distantly. "A magically induced one. Whatever happened...her body shut down to protect itself. They can't bring her out of it."

"I'm very sorry, Sophie," Hettie said. "I didn't mean for this to happen." She leaned by the bed and took Patrice's cool, papery hand. The old woman had been kind and thoughtful and had believed her when no one else did. A mix of hope and fury burned in her chest. "I promise, Patrice, I'll get to the bottom of whatever's causing this blackout."

Something rippled through her, a buzz that zipped up her arm and into her chest. Hettie shivered. Sophie stared.

"You...you just made a contract with her."

Hettie let go. "What?"

"She must still be able to hear you somehow. A contract spell doesn't work without consent. Talk to her," Sophie urged.

Hettie licked her dry lips. "Patrice? Can you hear me? It's Hettie Alabama."

There was no response.

"Try again," Sophie said.

"Patrice?" She called her name over and over, shook her, but clearly whatever had allowed the contract spell to take hold no longer applied. After ten minutes of cajoling, Hettie stood back. "It's no use, Sophie. I'm sorry."

The debutante shook her head despondently and sat back. "Perhaps it is not all lost, then. You've given me hope, at least, that she will get through this." She adjusted the bedspread. "Grandmère takes a great many risks when she scries for others. Most people don't know what her power costs her."

They rejoined the others in the salon and gave them an update on Patrice's condition. Sophie lifted her chin and straightened her spine, assuming the mantle of her grandmother's authority as mistress of the household. "I stand in my grandmother's place while she is indisposed. As promised, I will provide whatever you need to find out what is causing her coma."

Technically, Patrice had only asked Hettie to find out the cause of the soothsayers' blackout, not how to wake her from her fugue. But Hettie didn't know what to say except, "I'll do my best."

Sophie shook her head. "I'm not sure that's good enough." She fixed her with a hard gaze. "Grandmère never does anything without a reason. None of this was coincidence. She didn't call me all the way out here without a valid reason. I think I finally understand what my purpose here is." She took a step forward. "I will go to Arizona with you and help you find your sister and the cause of the blackout."

Hettie exchanged wary glances with the others. "Begging your pardon, Miss Favreau," Walker began diplomatically, "but where we're headed, there're no fancy hotels to stay in."

"You think I'm a pampered, spoiled princess," she concluded primly. "I'll have you know my father took me camping plenty. I can rough it just as well as the rest of you."

Hettie suppressed a skeptical snort. She got that Sophie was trying to help, but the girl would only slow them down.

"It's not safe for a lady," Uncle insisted. "If you thought *we* were merciless criminals—"

"Your lot didn't scare me one whit." She planted her fists on her hips. "All that screaming and crying in Barney's Rock was for show. And anyhow, Hettie's with you, isn't she? If she can handle the road, so can I. Besides"—she gave a wave of her hand—"who says we have to camp out under the stars every night? The Favreau name will let you into any establishment, no questions asked."

"I don't think you get it," Hettie said, impatience growing. "We've got the law and the Pinkerton Agency after us, not to mention who or what this sorcerer, Zavi, might throw our way. I've nearly been killed more times than I can count. The men we're going up against won't hesitate to kill you because you bat your eyelashes at them."

"You'd be surprised how far a pretty face and a little charm can get you," Sophie returned smoothly. "But then, I suppose you wouldn't know that firsthand."

If Hettie had been developing any softer feelings for the girl, they were instantly wiped out. Sophie went on airily, "My grandfather, Georges Favreau, was one of the most successful blockade runners who'd ever lived. He always said the best way to hide something was in plain sight." She studied them thoughtfully and snapped her fingers. "I could pass you off as my servants and escorts, and we could take the train to Yuma."

"No." Marcus reentered the room, apparently having overheard Sophie's plans. He planted himself before the young lady. "I won't let you endanger yourself this way, Miss Sophie. Your grandmother would be furious. Think of what your parents would say."

"You don't get to tell me what my own grandmother thinks," she reminded him imperiously. "Besides, if Father knew about Grandmère's condition and found out I could've helped but didn't, he'd string me up by my ears."

The Englishman planted his feet as if he faced a gale-force wind. Sophie barely reached his shoulder, but her status towered over his. Hettie could see that the man had no way to stop or dissuade her. "You won't go alone," he said. "You'll take Jemma."

"That goes without saying."

"And me," he added, eyeing the rest of the group.

"Excuse me, but I haven't said any of you can come," Hettie protested.

"You would deny my help?" Sophie scoffed. "You don't even have a proper saddle for your horse, or a holster for that silly gun of yours."

"We've managed fine."

"And when you find your sister, how will you get Abby back? Who will she ride with? Where will you take her? What if she's injured or sick?"

Hettie hadn't thought that far. She realized she'd only thought of this mission as a one-way trip—not exactly optimistic on her part. "I'll figure it out when it comes up."

Uncle hedged. "Hettie..."

She shook her head. "I can't be responsible for three more," she said, almost to herself. Her gaze clashed with Marcus's then. Understanding lurked in his amber eyes. She was sure he didn't want Sophie along for this escapade any more than she did. But he was willing to follow her to hell to keep her safe.

"I won't be deterred," Sophie declared. "You can accept my help and all it entails, or you can leave the premises right now and ride your poor shoeless mustang to Arizona until you both go lame."

Hettie's jaw worked. This was the best chance she had of getting Abby back safe. She had to accept Sophie's offer—whatever the girl could provide would make things easier. But if she slowed her down, Hettie would have to rethink her plans.

"You said you wanted a posse," Walker said wryly, and added under his breath, "I bet you're wishing now it was just you and me."

He wasn't incorrect.

CHAPTER TWENTY-ONE

They spent the following day preparing for the journey to Yuma. Servants scrambled to pack provisions for the group. The horses were reshod, and Blackie was fitted with a proper saddle from the Favreaus' vast tack room. Sophie commanded Marcus to take Hettie and the men down to the armory and have them properly equipped. He let them have their pick of weapons and supplies, and helped fit Hettie with an appropriate belt and holster for Diablo.

"You want this sitting low so you can draw it easily," the security man said as he adjusted the leather.

"Quick draw's not really as issue." She held her hand up and summoned the gun. It came instantaneously.

Marcus shook his head. "You shouldn't count on magic to get you out of a tight spot."

"He's right, Hettie," Walker said. "You should be practicing."

"As if I could." She shoved the gun in the holster and drew it the way Uncle had shown her. That evening behind the house seemed eons ago.

"The price and privilege of owning a mage gun," Marcus said somberly, "is that as much as it can do for you, it can only do so much."

She glanced at his weapons. "Are you...bonded?"

"Not in the same way you are—not by blood. What I have with Luna and Claire has been built over years of working together. It's a marriage of sorts," he said with a crooked smile. "They aren't jealous like your Diablo. They'll share me with worthy weapons."

"That's what some'd call a Mormon wedding," Jeremiah said as he inspected a bolt-action rifle. Hettie wanted to ask Marcus more about his weapons, but Uncle interrupted. "Mighty generous of Miss Favreau to be giving us all this."

"It's on loan only," the security man clarified, "and you won't be carrying any of this on you. All provisions will stay with Miss Sophie's other baggage. We'll keep the weapons trunk with us aboard the train. You'll be traveling in the passenger cars as her servants, and you'll be expected to act the part."

"Assumin' you mean I should be bowing and scraping, don't worry," Uncle said, "I'll just take my cues from Ling, here."

Ling glared. Hettie gave Jeremiah a quelling look—she didn't understand why he needled the man so much.

Unfazed, Marcus continued, "You'll all be given proper household uniforms. Mr. Tsang will be a footman, while Mr. Bassett will play the role of valet. Miss Alabama will be a lady's maid and will wait on Miss Favreau as needed, taking Jemma's instructions."

"What about me?" Walker asked.

Marcus cleared his throat. "Miss Favreau has insisted that you play the part of her…escort."

Ling snickered, while Uncle grumbled something about young men's luck. Hettie kept her face carefully blank as Walker resumed inspecting his weapons.

They departed for the train station the following morning, riding in a grand carriage, the horses tied to the back. Hettie was forced to sit in the car with Walker, Sophie, and Jemma, while Marcus, Ling, and Uncle rode up front and on top.

Ling and Uncle looked uncomfortably confined in starched black-and-white household uniforms, their hair slicked back with pomade. Hettie's dress belonged on a taller, thinner woman, her collar too high and tight. What hair she had had been tucked under a white cap, exposing her scar. She'd argued that she'd be better off in boy's clothes dressed as a footman, but Sophie had refused.

"They'll be looking for a girl dressed as a boy, and pardon me for saying so, but you're looking more and more like a woman as your hair grows out. Besides, you'll be safer riding inside with me. We're trying to hide in plain sight, remember?"

She wasn't sure that was going to be possible, and she had the sneaking suspicion Sophie enjoyed having her glowing beauty magnified by sitting next to her. Walker certainly didn't look away from her the whole ride.

The train station teemed with travelers. As they piled out of the carriage, Jemma barked orders at Uncle and Ling. The maid—though she was clearly more than that, considering her brawl with Ling—had emerged from the kidnapping quite sore and had protested her mistress's involvement with their abductors, but in the end she'd had no choice but to go along with Sophie's plan. Two station porters helped unload the trunks, and soon they were strolling along the platform, Sophie arm in arm with Walker, Jemma and Hettie a few steps behind. Marcus had forged ahead, sharp eye sweeping the area.

"I don't like this," Hettie heard Walker mutter.

"Does the outfit not suit you, darling? It's the latest from France you know." She lowered her voice. "And the only thing I could get last-minute that would fit."

"There are sheriff's men everywhere," Hettie whispered.

"But they're not looking for you, are they? They'll be looking for a gang of common thugs. And you're not common thugs," Sophie tossed over her shoulder. "Trust me."

Marcus returned to them with the train conductor at his side. The nervous-looking old man dipped his head in greeting, doffing his hat. "Miss Favreau, it's an honor to have you here. Mr. Wellington just apprised me of your request. I'm afraid we weren't prepared to have you aboard. Your private car wasn't scheduled to come in, and—"

"Please, there's no need to panic. All I require are two cabins. If I know my father, one of his private cars should be housed in Houston. We can pick it up there when the train stops."

"But...that would delay the train..." Sophie gave him a beneficent, understanding smile, and the ridges of worry etched into his brow softened. "Of course, we can afford a few minutes' layover. I'll see that your car is ready when we arrive and get you those cabins." He gave another little bow and hurried back toward the train, shouting orders.

"Must be nice to have so much power you can delay a train," Ling murmured.

"You hush your mouth," Jemma snapped. "Footmen don't talk about their masters. Certainly not in public."

Ling shrugged and slouched away. "Never met such an uppity Chinaman," Jemma grumbled, eyeing the healer. "Who does he think he is, putting on those airs?"

"Hettie." Uncle nodded toward a group of men headed straight at them. Two of them carried shotguns. Each of them wore deputy sheriff badges on their breasts.

"Everyone stay close," Sophie hissed through her smile. "Remember what I told you."

Don't speak unless spoken to. Don't make eye contact. And don't panic and run or draw any attention to yourself. Most importantly, Sophie had said, *stay close.*

The leader of the group was a tall, barrel-chested blond man with a handlebar mustache and twinkling eyes. He swaggered ahead and stopped in front of Sophie.

"Miss Favreau," he drawled. He bent over her hand and kissed the air above her gloved fingers. "Mighty fine pleasure to see you hereabouts."

Sophie fluttered. "Marshal Shaw, how lovely to see you again."

"I heard you'd only arrived two days ago." His elongated vowels made him sound drowsy. "I was going to come calling at your grandmother's."

Sophie gave a light laugh. "Ah, well, it is too late for that. You see, I was just passing through."

"Really? Funny, that. I'd heard you'd encountered some rough folks on your journey through Hawksville."

She gave a dismissive wave. "A silly rumor. I was merely given a bit of a scare and had my purse stolen. I took the earlier Zoom as a result, and my grandmother's men overreacted and escorted me to her home. As you can see, I've recovered."

"Hearty and hale as your grandmother in her heyday." His white-toothed grin blinded Hettie. "Where are you heading?"

"Yuma," she said. "We're visiting a friend. You know Grandmère's interest in the asylum there."

"What a coincidence. We're escorting a prisoner to Yuma. Perhaps we can take tea together on the train?"

Walker cleared his throat then, and the man's blue eyes snapped toward him, as if only noticing him for the first time. He blinked rapidly. "I beg your pardon..."

Sophie faltered. "Marshal, this is Mr.——"

"Montcalme," Walker said in an affected French accent. "Monsieur Michael Montcalme. I'm Sophie's fiancé."

That declaration had the whole group falling into a dead silence. Sophie's cheeks turned bright pink. Shaw's mouth opened and closed. "I...I suppose this warrants congratulations." His smile wasn't nearly so bright now as he shook Walker's hand dazedly.

Sophie regained her senses. "Thank you. I...it was a recent development. We haven't had time to tell anyone, and..."

"I'm sorry, marshal," Walker interrupted, "perhaps we can continue this conversation later. The train won't wait forever, and we wouldn't want to keep you from your duties."

"Of course." The marshal gave him a crooked smile. "In fact, why don't we have dinner together to celebrate? Then you can tell me all about how you two met."

"Certainly," Sophie said at the same time Walker said, "No."

"We'd be delighted," she corrected with a bright, vacant smile for her "fiancé."

Shaw's grin widened. He doffed his hat and gestured at his men, and they headed for the train.

"Why did you do that?" Sophie exclaimed once the lawman was out of earshot. "I told you not to say anything. I could have kept you all safe."

"I didn't want him asking any more questions about you and how you got here, or why you're leaving so soon. A man like him would've heard about the situation in Hawksville. Why'd you accept his invitation? We don't need a marshal sniffing around us."

"He's an old family friend—I couldn't brush him off. Why'd you say anything about being engaged?" she moaned. "What if this gets back to my father? I'll be ruined."

While the newly betrothed pair bickered, Hettie watched Shaw and his people board. Two men flanked a dark, lanky prisoner in manacles and helped him up the steps.

The prisoner paused. He turned his head and met her eye. Her blood ran cold.

"Hettie?" Ling prodded her gently. The others had boarded, and she was still standing on the platform. "What's the matter?"

"That man was at the ranch the night my parents were killed," she rasped. "That's Hedley."

Despite their plush surroundings, Hettie couldn't sit still, knowing one of the men responsible for her parents' murder was aboard. When Marcus had left to patrol the corridor, she explained to Uncle what she'd seen.

"Never thought I'd see the day when Isaac Hedley would get caught." He sat back and contemplated his cup of tea with a deep frown. "That two-bit sack of pig shit has raped more women than the law can count. Fancies himself a Casanova, too. He curses his victims after the fact and makes 'em believe they weren't forced so they don't go to the authorities until he's well out of town and the spell's run out."

Hettie didn't point out that Uncle had done something similar to the Gunnersons. "Why do you reckon he's here?"

"You don't think this is coincidence," Ling concluded.

She nodded. "Zavi wants me to bring him Diablo, and the Crowe gang works with him, if not *for* him. Teddy said he'd left the gang, but he didn't mention anything about the rest of them. And when Hedley got on the train…he saw me and smiled." She shuddered.

"A smile don't mean anything from that sick bastard," Uncle said. "He's always thinking the same thing."

"He has to know where the hideout is," Hettie said. "He'll know details—how many men guard it, what's going on in there, where Abby is. I want to know what he knows and find out why Zavi's so interested in Diablo."

Uncle didn't say anything at first. He was studying the tips of his boots. "This ain't right." He rested his fists against his hips. "None of it is. If we were smart, we'd turn right around and get you and that infernal gun away from this warlock."

"Abby's alive. You can't tell me to give up now. What would Pa say if you gave up on his youngest and turned away a chance to help Patrice Favreau?"

He sighed. "You're bent on interviewing Hedley, then."

She nodded. "But I can't do it without your help. Both of you."

Ling folded his hands in front of him. "The prisoner car will be the one farthest from the other passengers, five cars toward the end. Marshal Shaw's men will be there, armed to the teeth."

"We'll need to distract them." Hettie thought hard. "Do you know any sleeping spells?"

"A few. But I can only perform it on one person at a time, and I'll need a nap myself after that."

"Uncle?"

"Not a chance. For one, I'm way too old to do something quite so widespread. Second, I'm a little busy keeping us under cover. Maybe Woodroffe can do it."

"I need him to keep Marshal Shaw occupied during dinner. That'll be the best time for us to strike."

"Maybe you need to go for a more direct approach," Marcus said, startling them all.

"Nothing you have to concern yourself with, English," Uncle said dismissively, giving him the briefest of looks. "Pretend you didn't hear us say anything about assaulting no officers of the law."

Marcus inspected his nails. "I heard no such conspiracy. I'm simply stating the fact that the rapist Isaac Hedley is chained and at the mercy of the law just now. Those men will be sworn to protect him all the way to Yuma. They'll be sore about that. Seems to me they won't need much convincing to let a young lady who might've suffered at his hands have a few words with him."

At dinner Hettie made sure Shaw was firmly seated in the cabin with Sophie and Walker before embarking on her mission to see Hedley. Marcus promised to distract the lawman if he tried to return to the prisoner car too early.

"I should be going with you," Walker said when she'd told them their plan. "That son of a bitch would talk a lot faster if I beat it out of him." Uncle had informed her that the train car would likely be made of iron and would negate any truth spells he tried on him.

"You need to play this thing through. You're the one who came up with the fiancé charade. Make a good show of it, Monsieur Montcalme."

Uncle and Ling trailed her through the cars. The other passengers took little notice—no one ever looked twice at servants, after all. They reached the prisoner car and found a guard by the door, a double-barreled shotgun slung across his chest. "Hold it right there. This car's private."

Hettie drew herself up, going for a brave face on a small, broken girl. It wasn't that hard. "Is the prisoner you hold named Isaac Hedley?"

He gave her a critical once-over. "What if he is?"

"Isaac Hedley raped my sister. She was so ashamed she flung herself and her unborn baby off a cliff." She forced tears to her eyes. "I want to look this bastard in the eye and spit on him, tell him what grief he's caused me and mine."

The lawman's impassive expression didn't change. "No one sees the prisoner."

"I need to do this," Hettie insisted. "I just want five minutes with him."

He gave a shake of his head. "For your own sake, miss, I don't recommend it. He'll be brought to proper justice in due course."

Uncle notched his chin up. "C'mon, deputy. You can't seriously think that. A man like him deserves to be hung by his balls and flayed alive. If we announced to the rest of the train's passengers the crimes this man has committed, I'm sure the mob would agree."

The guard's eyes narrowed. "Don't threaten me, old man."

"Do you have any idea who I am?" Uncle got into the guard's face. "I'm Mr. Montcalme's valet. That's right, Michael Montcalme, who's getting married to Sophie Favreau, the same one your dear Marshal Shaw is supping with tonight. Now, he told us explicitly we could see the man to assuage this poor girl's conscience and free her of her nightmares. I know she'll fare better just seeing that he's locked away and in your capable hands."

The deputy pursed his lips. "Wait here." He ducked into the car and returned a moment later. "You get five minutes. But you have to wear these." He held out large iron bracelets that suppressed magical abilities the same way the manacles had. They grudgingly agreed and let the guard lock them on. He searched both Ling and Uncle but didn't check Hettie, which was just as well since Diablo was in her pocket.

He opened the door for them. Within, two more deputies lounged at a small card table, their sidearms dangling from belts slung on the chair backs. A row of iron cages was bolted to the floor in the center of the car. They were all empty except for the smallest one, barely large enough to hold a stool and the buzzard-thin rapist Isaac Hedley.

He sat hunched, elbows on his wide-set knees, forehead resting against steepled fingers as if in prayer. The outer door shut with a clang, and he peeked up. He sat back as much as the small space allowed and smoothed a hand over his oily hair. "So they sent me a little entertainment after all." He broke into a lascivious grin, red tongue darting out to lick his cracked lips. "Accommodating, this railway is. I'll have to look into investing in it."

Hettie glanced at the lawmen, who were engrossed in their poker game. They didn't seem too concerned with what one maid could do. Maybe the guard outside was the only one who cared. She stepped forward. "You know who I am?" she asked Hedley lowly.

He gave her a long, leisurely look that made her skin crawl. "Not in the biblical sense, but we can correct that. Lots I can do through bars, girlie. Just lift up your skirt and come here. I can show you a good time."

Ling grabbed Hedley by the back of his collar and yanked him hard so his skull cracked against the bars. The lawmen looked up, smirking, and went back to their game. "Your tongue will be civil, or I will cut it out," he hissed in the man's ear.

"Mighty loyal, ain't he?" He leered. "Must be a hell of a ride in the sack. Tell me, how big is he? 'Cuz I guarantee you mine's bigger." Hedley rubbed the front of his pants suggestively. "The ladies all love it."

Hettie trembled with fury and disgust. She'd be doing the world a favor by blowing a hole through his gut. Perhaps it was a good thing the bracelets kept Diablo from jumping straight into her hand. "I want to know where my sister is."

"Thirty miles north-northeast of Yuma, in an abandoned underground Zoom station," he answered without hesitation. "Can't tell you what room exactly—they didn't want me seeing her. Shame, really. She looked awfully lonely, and I never had me a retar—"

Ling bashed the man's forehead against the bars and wrapped his hands around the man's throat. The deputies got up from their game, but weren't too swift about it, and dragged Ling off. Hedley coughed and spat, gave a wheezing laugh. The men let go of Ling after giving him a halfhearted warning, then sat and resumed their card game.

"Tell us about the compound." She knew he wanted to goad her into a reaction. Maybe he was trying to get her to shoot him— alerting the Pinkertons now could be disastrous.

"What's there to tell? Home sweet home." Hedley's teeth were a mess of jagged yellow tombstones arrayed every which way in his mouth. "Got ourselves a whole happy family there. Not much in the way of entertainment, though. Not what we got." He sighed wistfully.

"What about Zavi? Who is he?"

"Zavi?" He scoffed. "Who knows what's in that bastard's head? But he pays us handsome."

"With borrowed magic," Uncle prompted.

"Some people think that's enough. Me, I want more'n just fur and claws every now and then." His eyes trailed over Hettie hungrily. "But then you get guys like Bill . . . why, he had barely enough power to light a matchstick. Him and some of the others get a nice healthy dose of Zavi's juice, and suddenly they're working for him." He snickered. "Butch don't like that much."

"What does Zavi want Diablo for?" Hettie demanded.

"Could want it to scratch his asshole for all I know."

"But . . . doesn't Butch want it?"

Hedley snorted. "Butch has been chasing Diablo since Jack made off with it. Zavi promised him he'd get it after he was done with it, whatever that means. And that's all I know." He smiled slowly and perused her body again. "You know, girlie, I am good in the sack.

242

If you ain't been pricked yet, I could show you how it could be. Seeing as Butch or Zavi'll probably kill you, I'd do you that favor."

Hettie stared through the ratty, oily-haired man. And she thought what a disgusting, pathetic creature he was and how much he deserved death.

Do it, Diablo urged.

The bracelets around her wrists suddenly snapped open and tumbled to the ground. Diablo appeared in her hand, solid and warm.

"Hey— Drop that gun!"

The lawmen drew their sidearms. Hettie was so startled she threw her hands above her head.

The movement made the men panic and fire. Hettie dove for the ground as bullets ricocheted through the steel cabin. The door burst open, and the guard with the shotgun entered, swinging the business end around.

"They're trying to kill me!" Hedley screamed. "They've got a gun!"

"Stop where you are." The guard took aim just as Uncle and Ling scrambled to their feet. Hettie tried to let Diablo fall from her hand, but the thing clung like tar, her fingers convulsing around the grip as she tried to toss it away.

Are you trying to get me killed? she thought, but the revolver would not let go.

She raised her hands. "Stop! I'm not going to shoot!"

"Put the gun down!"

"I can't!"

Another shot rang out. Without meaning to, she squeezed the trigger.

CHAPTER TWENTY-TWO

The air thickened, and she watched the ball of energy soar through the room and explode against the far wall. Shrapnel and fire blew out through the huge rent torn in the metal, as if a giant fiery fist had punched through it like paper. The lawmen were thrown to the ground, and wind whistled into the car as the train sped on, the flat grasslands rushing by in a blur.

The guard with the shotgun lurched to his feet. Hettie rolled behind a crate as he fired. Ling tackled him to the ground and knocked him out cold while Uncle trussed up the other two stunned guards.

"Well, aren't you all a bunch of surprises." Hedley's whoop devolved into a fit of coughing, and he clutched his stomach. Blood poured from a wound in his gut. One of the guard's bullets must have hit him.

"C'mon, we gotta move," Uncle shouted. "The Pinkertons will be on us."

"But...we're on a moving train."

"Ain't gonna stop them."

"Wait," Hedley pleaded. "I could take you to Zavi's camp. Let me out and I'll take you straight there."

"Ain't no one gonna let you outta that cage," Uncle snapped.

"He has power you can't begin to imagine," Hedley said urgently. "He's a Kukulos warlock, but he's more powerful than anyone I've ever known. He has a secret..." He screwed up his eyes as agony took hold. "You gotta take me with you."

Hettie chewed her lip. Assuming he'd told her the truth about where Zavi and Butch and his gang were holed up, she had no need of him. And she couldn't trust a single thing out of his mouth in this desperate hour.

Ling said quietly, "That gutshot's not going to heal. I can't do anything for him."

"What's Zavi's secret?" she demanded.

"Open the cage and I'll tell you."

The man was dying. He had little left to lose. Hettie searched the guards' pockets and produced a large iron key while Uncle and Ling unlocked their iron bracelets.

"You're insane, you know that?" Uncle grumped.

"I have to know." She unlocked Hedley's cage and stepped back as he dragged himself out. Blood flooded his hand, and he moaned.

"Damn," he gritted, then laughed. "This is not the way I was supposed to go."

She stooped down to his level. "Tell me about Zavi and I'll have Ling heal you." She cut the healer a look. He didn't speak.

"Zavi...He's worse than any Kukulos I've known. He had us...bringing him kids. Little ones. Paid Butch handsomely for them. I don't know what happens to them, but they keep them in a room deep down..." He moaned. Sweat sheened his pale face. "Damn, I'm thirsty. You have water?"

"Tell me everything and I'll bring you anything you like. Why does Zavi want the children?"

"Sacrifice. I think he means to use 'em in some ritual. I don't know, he doesn't talk to me. Butch'll know."

"How many children are there?"

Hedley rolled to his side and vomited blood.

"Hell's bells, Hettie." Uncle yanked her back. "We don't got time for this."

"*How many children?*" She grabbed Hedley by the hair and pulled back to look into his face.

But Hedley was in too much pain to respond. The acid in his stomach was boiling out of the bullet wound, eating him alive. He reeked of sick and defecation.

Hettie pushed him back, furious and disgusted.

"Wait—you promised..." he sobbed.

She paused only briefly. Abby's smile flashed in her mind, but so did the look of terror in her mother's eyes. She turned her back on the writhing man.

"For crying out loud." Uncle drew the guard's sidearm from its holster and put a neat hole in between Isaac Hedley's eyes. Jeremiah's murderous glare pierced her cold heart. "You don't leave a man to suffer. Not when he's sure to die. If you're going to kill a man, you do it cleanly, get the job done."

Hettie raised her chin defiantly as her conviction crystallized. "He didn't deserve a quick death."

Their gazes clashed. Uncle looked away first as he shoved the gun in his waistband. "Let's move. The Pinks are coming."

"How'd you get your bracelets off?" Ling asked as they made their way back through the train. People stared as they passed. They must have caused quite a ruckus, but if anyone suspected them of foul play, they weren't getting up to stop them.

"Diablo did it." Hettie couldn't say how she knew, but she did. She'd thought the Devil's Revolver couldn't be summoned within the confines of the metal car, but apparently the rules of magic did not apply to the infernal mage gun. It was as if it had a mind and will of its own.

"It's gaining strength," Uncle murmured. They reached Sophie's cabin. Marcus frowned as he surveyed them. "We need to get off this train. Now."

"We're nowhere close to Houston."

"We don't need to be." Uncle held up a round stone with a small depression on it. "I found this on one of the guards. Judging by the type of magic coming off it, I'm pretty sure it belonged to Hedley."

Hettie took it from him and turned it over in her hand. "This is like one of those stones the Pinkertons sent me."

"It's a remote Zoom beacon. If Hedley had this on him, it meant he expected he'd be returning to wherever he'd come from. Maybe even with you in tow."

She put the stone in her pocket. "So you're saying whoever is opening Zoom tunnels for him is waiting for his signal."

"Exactly."

"How do you even know it's his?"

"The local marshals barely have enough for horse feed. You think they could afford remote Zoom sorcerers?"

"It could belong to the Pinkertons," Marcus said.

Uncle shook his head. "I doubt it. No reason to be giving these out to random sheriff's deputies. The Pinks don't have any interest in Hedley. They work for hire, not for justice."

"Where do you think the tunnel will open?"

"It can only open to one place, and that's wherever the conductor is. Although with the remote Zoom it usually takes a group of twelve or more sorcerers—"

"Or one very powerful Kukulos warlock," Ling finished.

Uncle nodded. "What we have, then, is the key to Zavi's hideout."

Hettie started toward Sophie's cabin. Marcus said, "Shaw's still in there—"

She flung the door open. Walker, Sophie, Shaw, and Jemma all looked up.

"Mr. Shaw! I think something's happened to your men— we heard gunshots!" Hettie sent Sophie a look. She understood instantly.

"Oh, my!" she exclaimed. "Is it bandits? Has there been a jailbreak?"

The marshal shot out of his seat. "All of you stay in your cabins. I'll investigate."

"Oh, do be careful, Mr. Shaw," Sophie added fretfully as he marched out. They didn't scramble until he'd left the car. "Well played, Hettie. You might have a future as an actress."

"Why on earth did you do that?" Uncle exclaimed. "As soon as his men come to, they'll tell him what we did."

"We've just bought ourselves an extra five minutes. It'll take him that long to get to the prison car, rouse his men, and come back for us."

"We shoulda thrown them off the train," Uncle grumbled.

"What happened?" Walker loosened his tie and reached up into the overhead storage for the trunk that carried their weapons.

"Hedley's dead. We need to get off the train. The Pinkertons are coming."

Walker glared at her. "You fired Diablo again?"

"What are we worrying about? We're on a moving train."

"*That's* the worry," Walker said. "They'll track Diablo's energy and try to open the Zoom aperture as close as possible."

"You mean...in the train?"

"Or on the track, if they get it wrong. And if that happens while the train is moving—"

"Half the train and the passengers could end up on the other side of the tunnel where there are no tracks. It'll tear the train apart."

Hettie scrambled to the window and flung it open. She threw Diablo as far as she could. It landed on a grassy slope. "That should buy us some time."

"We have to get off right now," Uncle reiterated. "There's no telling what the Pinks'll do once they realize we're aboard."

"You think they'll try to stop the train?" Sophie said.

He cut her a jaded look. "No, I think they'll blow the whole damn train sky-high if they know we're all on it."

"It's not like we can jump off," Marcus said. "Even if we survived, what then? We can't leave the horses behind."

"We can disconnect the horse car," Hettie said. "It's the last one on the train, right? So we unhitch it and let the rest of the train move on, and get off as it slows."

"That means going through the prison car," Ling said. "I don't think Shaw and his men are going to be too pleased to see us again."

But they were already hurrying back through the cars. Passengers stirred uneasily, wondering what all the rush and panic was about.

"Sophie, you don't have to come with us," Hettie told her earnestly. She knew what Uncle was thinking—they'd use the beacon to open the Zoom tunnel. If the Pinks were after them, he wouldn't care where it led, even if it was straight into the mouth of hell. "Just tell the lawmen we had you under an influence spell or were holding you hostage."

"I've no intention of giving up now. Besides, this is such an exciting adventure." She grinned.

"You're going to be the death of me, Miz Sophie," Jemma muttered, following on quick feet.

Hettie estimated that Shaw would just be getting the story out of his men now. They would be heading back through the train to apprehend them any minute. She forged ahead. One car before the prison car, she stopped. "Shaw will be looking for us," Hettie shouted over the whistling wind. "We have to move across the prison car on the roof and climb back down to the horse car." Everyone hustled up the ladder. If anything should have scared Sophie and her two protectors off, it was climbing a shaky ladder on a moving train, but the debutante plowed on fearlessly, billowing skirts and all.

"Be careful. The train is moving faster than you think, and it's slippery," Walker warned.

The wind bit through Hettie's dress and tossed her skirts about violently. Trails of smoke and steam streaked and billowed at her back from the powerful engine, stinging her eyes. Her cap flew off, and her freed hair lashed her cheeks. Walker led the way across the rooftop, crouched against the rush of air buffeting their backs. At the end of the car, he peeked down at the couplings, then put a finger to his lips and gestured at the group to wait. He hopped across the gap onto the roof of the prison car, lithe as a cat, and kept low as he crouch-walked across. Once he hopped the next gap, he gestured for the rest to follow. Ling went after him, making the trip look easy. Uncle deferred to Sophie and Jemma to go ahead. The train took a gentle curving turn as it climbed a slight rise, which made Hettie's depth perception wobble.

Suddenly, the cars clattered and jolted, and Sophie lost her footing. She fell to her stomach, her chin bouncing hard on the roof, then started sliding over the edge. Jemma cried out and lunged for her hand, but she'd already tipped off the precipice.

Marcus flung himself across the gap and landed next to Jemma, nearly piling on top of her to grab Sophie's other hand. They stopped her fall, but she dangled from the train, screaming, legs kicking.

Below, Hettie heard voices. "What in the blazes——?"

She shouldn't have looked down. Marshal Shaw stared up at her, confusion turning to recognition and understanding in a lightning flash. He drew his handgun and shouted over his shoulder.

"Uncle!" She pulled back from the gap as the first bullets whizzed past her ear. She flattened herself against the roof at the boom of a shotgun. Jeremiah swore and pulled out his sidearm. Diablo appeared in Hettie's grasp, making clinging for her life a little more difficult as the train again shifted on the track snaking around the low hills.

Sophie wailed as Jemma and Marcus tried pulling her back from the edge. Walker and Ling had drawn their sidearms, but they were looking north where an ominous pitch-black iris formed midair.

Uncle rolled to one side as the shotgun peeked up over the roof and sent a blind blast in their direction. Hettie flinched as pellet shot grazed the edge of her bunched-up skirt, fluttering high above her knees. She raised Diablo.

You just have to stop that gun, she thought as the muzzle of the shotgun popped up once more. She squeezed the trigger.

The ball of fire that exploded from Diablo seemed to expand as it neared its target. The shotgun caught the blast full-on, glowing red, then white-hot in the blink of an eye. The shooter yelped and tossed the weapon away.

Hettie glanced back. The remote Zoom tunnel had fully opened, and she felt the flash freeze even from here. It was a big tunnel, and it quickly became apparent why.

She'd only ever seen pictures, but the two automobiles that came barreling out of the aperture were unmistakable, their engines roaring like grizzly bears. Eight fast horses followed. One of the cars had a great machine in the back that looked like a telescope or something on a tripod, and the man behind it was draped in long, wide belts of bullets.

"Gatling gun!" Uncle shouted. "They're going to mow down everything that— Ah!" He cried out as blood blossomed on his chest. Shaw rose from the gap and fired again, aiming to kill.

"No!"

Hettie's heart seized as Diablo exploded in a pulse of light that leaped from the muzzle to the lawman's gophering head. One moment, Shaw's face was there. In the next, it was not. All that was left was shoulders spattered with blood.

The buzz in her bones exploded into an all-out assault as her body ripped itself apart. The anguish of aging another year was only momentarily interrupted as she slid from the roof, hit the gravel by the side of the tracks, and rolled away from the speeding locomotive.

She surfaced long enough to see the caboose whip past, the figures of her friends growing smaller as the train plowed on. Hettie struggled to stand, but she'd bruised her ribs, and every muscle screamed.

The Pinkertons peeled away from their pursuit of the train and circled back toward her. Hettie breathed through her agony and climbed unsteadily to her feet. Diablo hung heavy in her hand.

The Gatling gun swung around as the automobiles neared, spluttering and jouncing across the uneven terrain. The horses reined in, panting hard, nostrils flaring, and their riders trained every gun they owned on her.

Hettie panned the semicircle of men surrounding her, heartbeat slackening. Slowly, she raised her hands in the air.

"Put the gun down!" one man shouted.

Hettie opened her hand, but Diablo stuck fast.

We can get out of this, it urged her, and her fingers curled tightly around the grip once more.

"Hold your fire, everyone." Out of the second car—the one without the Gatling gun—hopped Thomas Stubbs. He leered at her as he straightened his jacket. "Nice to see you again, Miss Alabama. You're looking... well." The way he said it made her feel slimy all over. "You've led us on a merry chase." He strutted toward her.

Hettie didn't say anything. She was busy counting guns and the number of bullets each held. It seemed like thousands.

"We've been here before, so let's cut to the chase. Relinquish Diablo to me and I'll let you live."

The Devil's Revolver gave a plaintive shudder in her mind. Her palm felt as though it had welded itself to the gun's butter-smooth grip. "I don't think that's likely to happen. You'll kill me either way."

"Probably." He shrugged. "But I'd rather we do this the easy way. We've expended a great deal of resources hunting you. I'd rather not have to deal with a gateway to hell opening up on top of that." He pinned her with a sneering look. "If you prefer, though, we could take you back to Chicago. Lock you up in a cell guarded by men who haven't seen a female prisoner as pretty as you in a long time."

Her hand flexed, finger twitching. She decided if she only got one shot off, it would be for him. "I'm not afraid of you."

"You ought to be. I could make it so no one ever found you. I could make it so you never even existed. And I could prolong your misery for a very long time with no one the wiser. You and your friends have killed countless men in this...this desperado quest of yours. No court in the world would let you get away with it. The best you can hope for now is a quick death."

The man really did enjoy his dramatic speeches. He liked the sound of his own voice, she realized. She could use that. She lifted her chin high. "Why do you want Diablo anyhow?"

"*I* don't want Diablo. I simply work for an organization that works to meet our clients' needs. As the resident expert on Diablo, I was assigned to the case."

"So you're not thinking of maybe taking it for yourself?" she asked casually, and took a stab in the dark. "After all these years searching, it must get your goat that you're this close but will never hold it in your own hands." She scoffed, giving him a haughty look. "*Obsession.* That's the word Jeremiah Bassett used. It's why the government fired you, isn't it?"

"No one fired me," he snapped. "*I* left them. They wouldn't give me what I needed for the search."

"You're not the only person after it, you know. And I'm betting some of those folks would be willing to pay you more than what your client's offered. I bet someone's already offered you a chunk of cash to bring Diablo to them rather than your client. If there even is one."

Stubbs pulled his gun and aimed it at her head. "You keep talking and I'll put a hole in your neck you can speak from."

She'd hit the mark, blind as her shots had been. She kept pushing. "How much did they offer you? Using up Pinkerton resources to chase after one girl and a gun can't exactly be good for business. C'mon, Stubbs. The cougars? That was you, right? And the grass trap, too. I don't know a lot about magic, but I know you'd've needed a lot more than a few sorcerers to spread that wide a net."

"I said be quiet."

Hettie was on a roll now. "I wondered how you planned to get away once you had Diablo. Unless, of course, all of your men are in your pocket. He promise you any of the cut?" she asked loudly, casting her gaze around.

The glances among the men were suspicious, furtive. Any of them could be in on the take, but perhaps not all of them. Hettie had banked on their innate paranoia to fertilize the seeds of doubt and distrust she was sowing.

Stubbs's eyes grew cold. He shouted, "Wilson, go for a drive and check on our friends on the train."

The car with the Gatling gun sped off, kicking up a stream of dirt as it cut across the field to intercept the train. Hettie's stomach tied itself into knots. "The thing you don't get, Miss Alabama, is that my men are incorruptible. We have a contract, forged by magic, that ensures our client gets what he wants, and in this case it'll be by any means necessary." Cold calm enveloped him. "I'm giving you to a count of five to hand over Diablo before Wilson opens up on all your friends and every living soul on that train."

"Are you insane? There are women and children aboard. You can't——"

"Of course I can. It'll be a simple matter to make this look like a botched train robbery. We can pin the deaths on the four notorious criminals whose bodies we found nearby. Besides, train accidents happen all the time."

Hettie licked her dry lips, prepared to call his bluff. "You're worse than the Crowe gang. And if your men listen to you, they're no better."

"Wilson, are you in position?" Stubbs asked the air.

"Yes, sir." The reply came back loud and clear.

"Five seconds, Miss Alabama, or I open fire. Five...four..."

The car kept pace with the train. She couldn't see any of her companions on the roof, though—had they slipped back inside? Were they saddling the horses? Did they even know of the danger driving alongside them?

"Three..."

We could take them all out, Diablo whispered. *You can't give me up.*

Eight horsemen. Stubbs, plus three men in the remaining car. Each carried at least one sidearm and one rifle or shotgun. That was a lot of bullets.

"Two..." Stubbs pursed his lips, sweat sheening his brow. "Don't be a fool, Miss Alabama. I *will* kill every last person on that train if you don't give me what I want right now."

Abby, Diablo whispered. *You can't let go of me if you want your sister back.* Her grip tightened.

"Stop toying with me!" Spittle flew from Stubbs's mouth. "I'll do it!"

Hettie stared into his face as it slowly turned dark purple, his eyes bulging. "Wilson. Open it up!"

CHAPTER TWENTY-THREE

W ait!" Hettie screamed. Her heart gave a lurch
as she tried to breathe past the lump in her
throat. "I'll give it up, okay? Leave the train
alone. Don't hurt anyone."

Stubbs exhaled shakily. A smug look slowly eased onto his
sweating face. The other men shifted uneasily. "I knew you'd see
reason. You're not a bad person. Not like me."

She sucked in her lower lip, defeat and defiance warring inside
her. "I'm going to put Diablo on the ground."

"I don't think so. You could conjure it back the minute I reach for
it. So what you're going to do is hand it over to me directly. You're
going to tell that infernal piece I'm the boss, and then, if you're
lucky, I'll take you back to Chicago to stand trial for murdering
my agents." He rolled his shoulders back. "Maybe the judge will be
lenient, seeing as you're obviously just a confused girl. We can tell
him you're grieving, that you don't know what's what anymore.
He'll probably commit you to an asylum instead of sending you to
the gallows." He said it as though he were reciting a lovely fairy tale.

Hettie glanced at the thin stream of smoke drifting up from the
train. "You promise not to hurt anyone?"

"I can't speak for what will happen when Jeremiah Bassett and the rest of that motley crew of yours stops at the next station. But for now..." He lifted a shoulder. "No reason to waste the bullets."

"Call your men back first."

He smiled. "Smart, aren't you?" He lifted his chin. "Wilson, come on back."

"Yes, sir."

Diablo thrashed in her mind as she let her hands drift to her sides and reversed her grip on the revolver in her left hand. Slowly, she walked toward Stubbs, sliding the tips of her fingers into her pocket until she felt the hard edge of the round beacon stone. She fit her bloodied trigger finger into the depression and squeezed hard enough to make tears jump into her eyes.

Stubbs reached out. "Well?"

She stalled, swallowing. She'd hoped something would happen by now but remembered it'd taken a while before the remote Zoom tunnel opened in Newhaven when she'd first contacted the Pinkerton Agency.

Maybe the talisman wasn't a beacon after all. Maybe it was just a stone. Uncle could've been wrong. Or maybe he'd been lying.

The Pinkerton agents were inching closer, guns at the ready. Stubbs took a menacing step forward. "Give it to me."

She extended her hand, the weight of the gun almost feather-light, as if it were threatening to fly away rather than leave her grasp.

"Tell Diablo it belongs to me now," he demanded. "Give it to me."

You can't. If you hand it over, they'll kill you, and Abby will suffer.

At least she'd saved Uncle and the others. They were safe aboard that train, and hopefully they were smart enough to get as far away as possible.

She waited two more heartbeats before lowering her arm. "No."

Stubbs's face paled. His eyes widened, and he stepped back.

Hettie felt a cold prickle of ice over her neck. She turned. A dark, swirling vortex bloomed directly in front of her, faster than any of the Zoom tunnels she'd ever seen. It yawned wide, but instead of a doorway opening she felt a powerful draw on her flesh. Her dress rippled as a gale-force wind clawed at her. Her feet slid forward, even as she leaned back. She slid to her knees and clung to the earth, but she couldn't escape the pull.

Thomas Stubbs dove for her. He grabbed her wrists. "Hang on!"

Hettie grabbed onto his forearms, letting go of Diablo, but the moment she did the Pinkerton agent's eyes gleamed in triumph, and he snatched his arm out of hers and grabbed the revolver. He cried out as his glove evaporated in a puff of ash, and his flesh sizzled and bubbled horribly as if he'd plunged his hand into molten lava.

He let go of Hettie's other hand. She screamed as the vortex dragged her in.

A freezing cold tunnel of darkness engulfed her, and her guts seemed to float freely inside her chest. It felt as though she were plummeting endlessly through a clear, crisp winter night sky.

She smashed shoulder-first into the ground, the dirt gritty and damp against her cheek. Her head spun. She couldn't see much, but she knew she was indoors in a cavernous space. The air was fuggy with the smell of sweat and damp fur, weak whiskey and piss. And she was surrounded by people.

"Hell, where's Hedley?"

Her blood froze. She knew that voice. She tried to lift her head, but then someone grabbed her roughly and yanked her into a sitting position.

"Butch, it's her." A man held a lamp too close. Sour sweat assailed her nostrils, and she nearly gagged as a grimy hand pinched her chin and turned her head to one side. "See the scar? She looks just like Jack, don't she?"

"So it's true." Butch Crowe's voice was close, but she still couldn't see him. Her vision seemed to be dancing in and out of darkness, darting side to side as if her eyeballs spun inside the sockets. "Huh. I thought I killed you that night."

She tasted bile. If she could aim, she would have thrown up on the man's boots, but instead she smiled and said, "You did. But the devil sent me back. I killed Teddy, and Hedley, too. Now I've come for you, Butch Crowe."

Had those words really come out of her mouth? She laughed then, all the while thinking perhaps she'd finally gone mad. Fear and that ride through the void had pushed her to the brink. Now she was a sheep in a den of wolves, bleating for her own comfort.

Someone groaned at Hettie's feet. She glanced over and was surprised to find Thomas Stubbs sprawled out on the floor.

"Who's this?" Butch asked.

Hettie shrugged. "Who knows? Some idiot got too close."

"Really." Butch drew a wicked bowie knife and skinned it up the front of the man's jacket, removing all the buttons from the front placket in one go. He reached into the inner pocket roughly and removed the silver Pinkerton eye badge. "Interesting friends you're keeping here. Pinkerton, eh?"

The men around her muttered and uttered catcalls. Hettie's vision cleared enough for her to see she was in a very large cave. Greasy yellow firelight threw inhuman-looking shadows against the walls. The skitter of claws over stone and low, menacing growls echoed throughout. She shuddered.

"Can't say I'm a fan of the Pinks." Butch spat as Thomas Stubbs was pulled to his feet. "In fact, I can rightly say I *hate* Pinkertons. A Pinkerton shot my daddy, you know. But he died a long, slow death because you fools don't know how to use a gun proper." He drew his sidearm and pointed it between Stubbs's eyes. "How about I give you a lesson?"

"I came here for my sister," Hettie declared loudly, trying to draw the men's attention. "I've brought Diablo. Bring her to me, and you can have it."

Butch paused and holstered his gun. He looked her over. His starburst scar stretched as his lips lifted. "I don't see anything on you. But then, maybe you're hiding it under your skirt."

She held out her hand and called Diablo to her. The gun appeared, muzzle aimed at Butch's cold heart. Her finger twitched as she remembered how this man had destroyed everything that had ever mattered to her, and she fought to keep the gun aloft.

"Well, I'll be damned," someone exclaimed. "Even your pa couldn't conjure Diablo like that."

"Shut up," Butch barked. "My daddy was the best Elias Blackthorn ever. That gun rightly belongs to me, and when I have it, I'll show you all who the real boss is."

"You're not getting anything until I see my sister," Hettie said. The revolver strained her wrist. She could practically sense its giddiness. She was among men she had no feelings for, men she would prefer to see wiped off the face of the earth. And Diablo was eager to please.

"We'll see about that." Butch pointed his gun at Hettie. She met his gimlet eye, strangely calm. She'd come this far to rescue Abby—it seemed absurd to think she'd ever get any farther, and yet everything inside her challenged the Crowe gang's leader to pull that trigger, to test the limits of his courage.

Opening a gate to hell with her death wouldn't be that bad if it meant taking all these outlaws with her.

Do it, Diablo taunted from behind her eyes, and she smiled to herself.

"Butch."

The dulcet voice drifted down from high above, breaking her out of her cool possession. All the men looked up.

Her skin crawled like a swarming anthill as a lean figure glided down a set of roughly hewn steps cut into the rock. His complexion was so fair it glowed. His straw-blond hair fell in gentle waves over his shoulders. He wore a loose-fitting white shirt, black pants, and high boots. He looked more like a swashbuckler from the penny dreadfuls than any gentleman or cowpoke she'd ever seen.

"Hello, Hettie," he said in that deadly soft voice when he reached the bottom stair. "I see you received my invitation."

"Zavi." He seemed more dreamlike in the flesh than he did in her vision. She swallowed thickly. "Where's Abby?"

He inclined his chin toward Butch. "Crowe, put your gun away. It's impolite to threaten our guest."

Coarse, criminal men who'd likely never seen the inside of a Bible removed their hats and bent their heads, avoiding the warlock's uncanny gaze as Zavi passed. Butch, however, stared the warlock dead in the face, unable to soften his sacrilegious glower.

Zavi's wet, bloodred lips stretched into a baleful smile as he assessed her, tar-black eyes shining. "Your sister is in her room, resting. She's quite tired, you know. Opening remote Zoom tunnels takes a lot out of a person."

Hettie stared. "What are you talking about?"

"Of course, you didn't know, did you?" He shook his head. "She was the one who opened the remote Zoom just now. You'll have to forgive her if you had a rough ride—the spells are still a bit new to her, but she's an excellent student. While she's resting, you'll be my guest here."

She raised Diablo, her blood boiling through her veins. "I'll not be your anything. Bring me to Abby right now or I'll blow your head off."

Zavi raised a dark blond eyebrow. "Such dramatics." He tossed his hair imperiously. "If it'll make you feel better, then by all means, go ahead and shoot."

Hettie didn't hesitate. Green light exploded from the muzzle, and her amber cocoon of time closed around her as the world was dipped in syrup. Zavi stood barely ten feet away, but just as Diablo's firepower crept across that narrow space between them, he stepped into the discharge, arms outstretched to receive the blast.

The fire burst soaked into his shirt, suffusing his chest. Energy rippled across his skin. He smiled as his body lit up from the inside, as if he were a walking human lantern. The light subsided slowly. He sent Hettie a mild look. "Feel better now?"

The world around them remained suspended in gold, the men's shock rounding their cracked lips and bleary eyes. "H-how...?"

He turned and beckoned. "Come along. We don't need to discuss things in this drafty hall." He walked ahead, plowing through the amber world unimpeded.

Hettie hesitated. She looked down at the weapon in her hand and pocketed it. It wasn't going to help her now. She considered not following the warlock just to be difficult, but doubted that would achieve anything. She took a hesitant step forward. Surprisingly, her bubble of time moved with her, and she carefully wove around Butch and the other men.

Zavi didn't bother looking back as he made his way up the stairs. She followed him into a wide, twisting passageway. Oil lanterns lit the tunnels. The floor was worn smooth with two parallel ruts at the outer edges—cart tracks, she realized. This passage had been used frequently in the past. It could have been a mine, she supposed, but most mines had rails with cars to bring ore to the surface. These passages were much wider and too clean. As if they had been designed to accommodate people.

Hedley hadn't been lying, then. In school, they'd studied the locations of all the natural Zoom tunnels, but over time a few had destabilized and stopped working altogether. This had to be Sonora station, which had stopped functioning before the war broke out. The enormous cavern she'd appeared in would have been large enough to serve as a Zoom tunnel station. It meant this place was, or at least had once been, a focal node of magic, like the one Blackie had led them to. Maybe that was why Zavi had chosen it for his hideout.

He turned down a branching corridor and opened a large, heavy door. "Come. Your sister's in here."

She expected a dank, putrid dungeon like the one from her vision. But this room, despite being cut from stone, was brightly lit and warm and dry. The ceilings were surprisingly high, and a big brazier hung in the middle. Fragrant smoke vented through a hole in the ceiling. The walls had been whitewashed so that the light seemed even brighter. Against one wall stood a washstand with a pitcher. A privacy screen hid a commode. Thick woven rugs covered the floor. And on the simple bed, sleeping soundly beneath a pile of blankets, lay Abby.

Hettie's eyes welled with tears. She forgot everything—the danger they were in, the man who held her sister hostage here—and rushed to kneel by the bed. As she reached out with a trembling hand, the amber world melted away. Hettie held her breath, waiting for her sister to stir. Her chest rose and fell, but she didn't awaken.

"Things have been difficult for her. She was quite ill when she first arrived." Zavi said it as though he were genuinely regretful and concerned—a doting parent rather than her captor. "It took a lot of nursing her back to health. But she's doing better now, and getting stronger every day with her training."

"Training?" Hettie snapped back to the moment. "What do you mean? What are you doing to her?"

"I'm simply showing her how to use her abilities. You knew she was special, didn't you?"

She set her teeth. "She hasn't been tested yet."

"But you knew," he insisted quietly. "She reached out to me years ago. I heard her pleas, listened to her when everyone around her dismissed her and rejected her. I found out she could see things no one else could, do things few could even dream of achieving. Abigail is going to be one of the most powerful sorcerers of her generation." He raised his chin, his eyes growing flinty. "And you had her on a leash."

Gut-churning heat burned through her chest. She pushed aside her shame as she remembered where she was, who she was dealing with. "Enough of this. What do you want from me?"

He paced to the other side of the room, folding his hands behind him. "Diablo would be a good start."

"Why do you want Diablo?"

"For the same reason you've come all this way for your sister. Diablo is kin to me just as Abby is kin to you. And now it's time for my family to be reunited."

He had to be insane, Hettie thought. But she'd seen how ineffective the weapon had been on him. "Diablo ain't kin. It was forged by Javier Punta."

"Punta." Malice contorted Zavi's face into an ugly gargoyle mask. "That fool should have known better than to tamper—" He cut himself off ruthlessly, taking a moment to compose himself. He turned back to her, frigid serenity replaced. "There are consequences to magic, Hettie Alabama. You've seen them for yourself." He turned away briskly. "I will leave you now to be with your sister."

He didn't close the door behind him.

She turned back to Abby and smoothed a gold lock away from her soft, pale cheeks. Deep shadows hung under her eyes. Hettie wondered if they'd been feeding her right, and regretted for an instant that Zavi wasn't there to tell her.

Her sister's lashes fluttered. Hettie leaned forward. "Abby?"

The little girl's eyes slitted open, just barely, the lids heavy. Her lips moved, but no sound came.

"It's okay. I heard you. I came." She swiped a fresh track of tears from her face. "You have to wake up now. I have to take you out of here. You understand?" Where they would go or how they would get out she had no idea. But she was growing too desperate to think that far ahead.

Abby closed her eyes once more, snugging the blanket under her chin.

"No, Abby, don't go back to sleep." She yanked the blankets off, and the little girl pulled her knees up and gave a plaintive whimper.

All she had on was a thin shift with a smock on top. Hettie took one of the lighter blankets and wrapped it around her sister, then gathered her up in her arms.

She was heavier and lankier than Hettie remembered—had she grown in the weeks she'd been missing? Her bare, callused feet were black with grime. Hettie shifted her around to carry her piggyback style, scanned the corridor, then headed out the door.

She followed the tunnel for a long time. If this was Sonora station, it stood to reason that all of these man-made pathways would lead to either the surface or the Zoom platform. The gentle upward slope suggested she was pointed in the right direction.

Her back and ribs ached, her shoulder smarted awfully, and she felt completely drained, but Abby's whimpers spurred her on. *Soon*, she promised silently, *soon we'll be out of here and on our way back to the ranch. Back home.*

She tripped and landed on her knees, scraping them and tearing the hem of her skirt. What she wouldn't give for trousers. "Abby, you have to wake up. I can't carry you all the way out."

"Don't wanna."

"Abby." She tried to force some of Ma's severity into her tone, but she was so tired it came out a sob. "Get to your feet. We have to get out of here."

"Don't wanna go." Her lids fluttered open, and Hettie gasped.

Her sister's eyes were completely black.

CHAPTER TWENTY-FOUR

Hettie stared, horrified. It was as if Abby's eyes had been replaced by smooth spheres of pure black oil. They gave her a slightly reptilian look, and Hettie fought against the urge to recoil.

"I wanna stay," her sister said petulantly. "I like it here."

Hettie pushed down the sick feeling bunching in her stomach and summoned her courage. "These people are bad, Abby. You can't stay with them."

"Zavi's my friend," she protested, rubbing those liquid black eyes. For a sickening moment, Hettie thought she might shed inky tears. "He helps me hear them all. He teaches me magic, and he takes care of me."

"He's not your friend, Abby." Hettie squeezed her hands. "He made those men kill Ma and Pa, and he hurt me. He's hurting you, too."

"You're lying!" Abby yanked her hands away. "Mr. Butch is just grumpy. He wants his gun back is all."

They couldn't stand there and argue. "Abby, listen to me. We have to leave right now."

"No!" Abby twisted out of her hold and fled down the corridor.

Hettie sprinted after her. Abby was faster than she'd thought, but then, Hettie was banged up badly. Every jouncing step sent jolts of pain singing through her bones.

The path narrowed, twisting and heading down into the bowels of the cave. The lanterns grew farther apart until Hettie was feeling her way through the dark for long intervals. The walls here were wet and sticky. A fetid, stale smell hit her as she sensed the corridor widen, and then the tang of blood and urine burned her eyes.

Hettie pressed her sleeve to her nose and tried not to gag. When her vision adjusted to the darkness, she ventured forward. "Abby?" she called softly. A shuffling noise and a distant whisper echoed around her. She pushed on, her grip on Diablo slick with sweat.

At first she thought the room she'd entered was filled with rows and rows of shelves, none of them much taller than her. Upon closer inspection, she saw they weren't shelves, but narrow beds. And in each bed lay the body of a child.

Hettie covered her mouth to stifle her half scream, half gasp. Nearly a hundred beds filled the room. On the nearest bunk lay two towheaded boys, about eight years old, fast asleep—or possibly dead. The boys were thin and pale; their lips were gray-blue, and their chests barely moved, their breathing shallow and slow.

Hettie crept along the rows, afraid to touch anything or anyone. The oldest children were in their early teens, but she saw no one older than that. They came from all backgrounds—many of them were Indian, though, and she remembered the tribe who'd been massacred in the canyon. These couldn't be their children, though—that had happened a long time ago.

And it's still happening now. Her skin grew cold.

She caught the flutter of something in her peripheral vision and spun just as the hem of Abby's dress slipped around the corner. She raced between the aisles and stopped dead in her tracks at the sight of Abby standing over one prone form, head tilted to one side as she surveyed the boy. Hettie approached cautiously. The youngster on the bed wore stained, tattered pajamas, the sleeves and pant legs of which were about two inches too short. His wide-open eyes stared blankly up.

"This is Jonah," Abby said cheerfully without looking at her. Whatever had driven Abby to flee from her own sister was gone now. "He's been here the longest. He has two sisters who used to be here, but they're not now." She patted his forehead. "Zavi says he's very strong."

"Strong how?" Hettie asked in a whisper, trembling.

"He's lived and lived. Zavi says most of them die very quickly. That's why Mr. Butch has to keep bringing more kids here. They're all my friends."

Hettie swallowed drily. All the pieces were starting to snap together, forming a breathlessly hideous picture.

"You're not as bright as I'd hoped." Zavi's voice slipped down her spine like treacle. She whipped around to find him standing barely ten feet away. He held a small, curved knife, and he reached across to the boy closest to him, nicking his neck and licking the blood off the knife as if he'd just sampled a bit of cheese. "But then, your sister does worship you." His gaze flickered over her shoulder, and he smiled. "Abigail, dear, you should be resting."

"Hettie says you're a bad man." She glanced at her toes, restless hands drifting from the edge of the table to her sides. "She wants to take me away."

Zavi heaved a sigh. "Well, she's your sister, Abigail. Your blood kin. You remember I told you how important blood is, don't you?" Abby gave a hesitant nod, and Zavi went on, "I told her I'd let you go home if she gave me Diablo. I intend to keep that promise." His gaze slid back to Hettie, his smile cold.

"I'm hungry. Can I have something to eat?" Abby asked in a quiet voice.

"Of course. You must be starving after opening that Zoom tunnel. You were so brave and so wonderful!" He clapped and spread his arms.

Abby raced past Hettie, knocking her elbow in her rush. Zavi scooped her up, leaned over the boy, and punctured a hole near the base of his neck with the curved knife. Abby climbed onto the table and lay across the boy's body. Hettie watched in horror as Abby began suckling from the wound, her thin curtain of pale hair concealing the gruesome meal.

"What have you done to her?" Hettie fought her rising gorge, but it was no good. She turned away from the awful sight, trying to shut out the slurping noises Abby made.

"Done *to* her?" Zavi's brow wrinkled in genuine upset. "Done *for* her, you mean. I've fed her, clothed her, educated her. I've provided her succor and protection. I've freed her from society's expectations. I've given her a chance to become more than the burden you all saw her as. I've done what any parent ought to do." He placed a protective hand over Abby's shoulder. Real love shone in his foul eyes. It was a demented sight.

Hettie struggled against the genuine feeling behind his words. This... *monster* couldn't feel love. "You killed my parents. You killed me!"

His voice softened, but his features remained hard and cold as ice. "That was Butch's doing, not mine. I have no personal vendetta against you. I truly am sorry he killed your parents—I didn't order that. Maybe if they were still alive, you wouldn't be here now. You'd all be back on your ranch grieving for your lost sister and moving on with your lives."

"No." Hettie shook her head, tears of rage burning the backs of her eyes. "Never. As long as I have breath, I'll never leave Abby behind."

He sighed. "Well, I promised I'd relinquish your sister to you if you gave me Diablo, and so I will. Abigail"—he squeezed her shoulder—"after you're done eating, we have to pack your things so you can go home."

Abby's head popped up from the boy's neck. Her eyes were even blacker than before, if that were possible. A trail of blood ran from the corner of her mouth, and she wiped it away with the back of her hand. "I don't wanna go!" Her snarl of conviction made Hettie flinch.

"You have to," Zavi said firmly. "Diablo is my family, and Hettie is yours."

"I don't wanna be her family. I wanna stay here with you."

Hettie's chest caved, the space where her heart should have been echoing hollowly. She couldn't believe what she was hearing. This was not her sister. This was not the little girl who'd called to her in dreams, hated the dark, hated the smells and the bugs, was terrified of everything—

"You've put her under some kind of spell." Then it came to her. It was the blood. Drinking it made her stronger... made her bold and terrifying and not Abby. To all outsiders, she was simply behaving like a belligerent ten-year-old, throwing a tantrum because she wasn't getting what she wanted. But this version of Abby was like some macabre marionette. A shell possessed by something more sinister than a demon.

"I can't change Abigail's wishes any more than you can." Zavi sounded so calm and reasonable that Hettie wanted to blow his face off.

She raised Diablo. Maybe he wouldn't be affected by it, but pulling that trigger sure would make her feel better.

"Don't you hurt him!" Abby inserted herself in front of the Kukulos warlock. "If you hurt him, I'll never ever speak to you again. Never!"

Zavi gave another laborious sigh. "Abigail, please. Let me talk with your sister alone."

"If you make me go with her, I'll run away! I'll open a tunnel and find my way back here, you'll see." Abby crossed her arms and stuck her chin out.

Zavi brushed his flaxen hair out of his face and sent Hettie a halfhearted smile. "She's got quite a stubborn streak. Not unlike her sister, I suppose."

Everything inside Hettie recoiled. How could this... this *creature* have any hold over her pure, sweet sister? Her emotions crashed inside her, and panic started to take hold.

"Come here, Abby," she ordered, mouth dry.

"No!"

Hettie ground her teeth, frustration, desperation, and anguish fighting for dominance. "Don't be difficult. You think Ma would take this sass from you?"

"You can't tell me what to do." Abby pleaded with the warlock. "Why do you even need it? You have me now. I can open the portal!"

Instead of replying, Zavi took a step back, folding his hands behind him. He invited Hettie to proceed with the barest nod of his chin. She started toward her sister. She'd drag her out kicking and screaming if she had to. She reached her and grabbed her wrist. Abby flinched and snarled a word.

An invisible force slammed into Hettie, knocking her backward, and she landed on her bottom, dazed.

Abby's black eyes blazed, hands extended in a shoving motion. "Don't touch me. I won't go with you."

The finality of her words struck Hettie harder than the blow had. She sat stunned as her sister marched away, leaving her alone with the Kukulos warlock.

"I can't make her go to you," Zavi said matter-of-factly, and for the first time she detected the note of triumph in his voice.

She got to her feet. "We had a deal."

"Deals change. I can't control the circumstances. Funny thing about... *life*"—the words slid from his tongue wryly—"you think you have control, but then..." He lifted a shoulder and waved his hand airily.

"I don't get Abby, you don't get Diablo."

He tipped his chin to one side, regarding her. "Oh, but you've already given it to me. The moment you arrived and swore to get Abby away from here, Diablo heard it, and so did I. You said you would do whatever it took, including give up the Devil's Revolver. It's been mine all this time."

She stared, even as her stomach bottomed out. "But... why? Why put on the charade if you had everything you wanted?"

"Why, to break you, of course. You'd only keep coming back if I kept her. But now you see. She wants to stay. She loves me."

Something inside her crumbled. "No." She pointed Diablo at his head and pulled the trigger.

Nothing happened.

The faintest of smiles curved Zavi's red lips. "As I said, Diablo is mine now. And I won't have its power wasted on your petty revenge." His eyes canted to the side. Seemingly out of nowhere, three hairy men—Weres who'd partially transformed to embody the most grotesque features of their wolf forms—appeared and tackled her to the ground. Hettie screamed and scratched and bit, but they pinned her arms and kicked the revolver out of her hand. One of the men punched her in the side of the head, and she reeled. The world spun and darkened.

"The only thing I need now," Zavi said as he picked up the gun, "is for you to die."

Υ

When the door to her pitch-black prison slammed shut, the first thing Hettie did was try to summon Diablo. She felt the tug of it in her mind, but it was as if it had snagged on a thorn. She reached and pulled, but it was no use. Somehow, Zavi had a firm handle on the Devil's Revolver. The only comfort she took was the fact that he couldn't seem to conjure it the way she could. If he'd been able to, she reasoned, he would've done so from the start.

Alone with her thoughts, she brooded. He had Diablo. He had Abby. But if obtaining the mage gun was his only goal, why hadn't he locked her up the moment she'd arrived? Why play out this charade with Abby? What was Zavi waiting for?

Hettie felt her way along the wall, slowly adjusting to the light seeping in around the door frame. She heard the scrape of something on the ground and stopped, holding her breath. A foul smell hit her, and someone moaned. "Who's there?"

The moan came again, low and wordless and vaguely familiar. "Mr. Stubbs?"

The man coughed and groaned. Hettie found him with the tip of her boot. The Pinkerton agent lay curled up on the ground, sticky wetness soaking his clothes. He must've taken quite a beating. It was a miracle he was still alive.

"Don't worry, Mr. Stubbs. We'll get out of here." She said it more to comfort herself than to reassure him. She couldn't give two figs about him, considering the hell he'd put her through, but she didn't like that he was hurt, and she had to admit she was glad to have some company in her misery. She sat on the sandy, uneven floor. "I'm sure Uncle and the others will figure out what's happened."

Stubbs gave a raspy gurgle. Of course she didn't know that at all. She did know that Uncle wouldn't give up on finding her and Diablo, though. He'd tracked her across Montana and Wyoming—he'd do it again, she was sure.

But the last glimpse she'd had of him, he'd been shot in the chest...

She pressed a fist against her mouth to stifle a sob. Ling was with him. He could heal Uncle. They would regroup and track her down...

But how long would it be before they discovered this hideout? Hedley had told them where it was, but the place had to be magicked, hidden from curious eyes despite the landmark. By the time her friends got a bead on her, she could already be dead. Or Abby could be.

She closed her eyes. Her sister's transformation…the black eyes and blood hunger…she wished those were just part of the nightmare. Zavi's revelation that Abby was a potential—not just that, but a powerful sorcerer—didn't stun her as much as the fact that Abby had attacked her. She'd always been such a sweet and docile girl. She'd never hurt anyone or anything intentionally. Hettie desperately wanted to believe Zavi's influence had made her this way, but what if it was all Abby? What if Zavi was telling the truth and he'd simply freed her from the confines her family had placed upon her?

And the blood drinking…There hadn't been vampires since the Civil War. Kukulos warlocks used blood in lots of ways in their magic rituals, but drinking it was reserved for the most extreme of warlocks. Blood was sacred and forbidden…what Abby had been doing was monstrous beyond words.

Despite the fears tumbling through her, the cloying darkness closed around her and she succumbed to exhaustion. She fell asleep propped against the wall.

A scraping sound startled her from a fitful, dreamless slumber. Hettie flinched as blinding light stabbed her eyes. The door opened, and a huge, shadowy figure lumbered in and raised a lamp to his face.

"Get up." It was Butch Crowe. She scrambled backward on her bottom, bumping into Stubbs.

"Get up," Butch said again. "You wanna live, you'll come with me."

She traced the starburst scar across his face with her eyes and swallowed tightly. "I'm not going anywhere with you."

He drew his gun. "You can die here on your knees right now or on your feet while we get your sister out of here. Either way, I don't care, but I'd rather you handle that little witch."

Confused, she slowly stood. "What're you talking about?"

"You can ask questions later. The patrol will be here soon. Now git."

Hettie didn't have a choice, not with that gun waving at her face. Butch had missed once; she was sure he wouldn't a second time. She glanced back at Stubbs. "What about him?"

"Leave 'im." He stuck his head back out the corridor and gestured for her to follow.

Stubbs's hand clamped around her ankle. He made a pitiful noise in his throat—something must've been wrong that he couldn't speak. "I'm sorry, Mr. Stubbs. I promise, I'll come back for you. I've got to see what this is all about."

His fingers clawed at her skirt as she shook him off. Only the tiniest sliver of guilt needled her.

Butch holstered his gun and made his way through the corridor, holding the lamp aloft. "Where are you taking me?"

"You want your sister, right?" She didn't respond. "There's a way out the back. You'll have to climb through a vent shaft, but I think you're small enough to fit. You take her out of here and you get her as far away as possible."

"And in exchange?"

"You give me Diablo."

"I don't have it."

"It ain't about who's got it, just who controls it." He snorted in frustration. "That gun belongs to me rightly. Jack stole it from me."

"That's not what I heard. I heard your pa gave it to him."

He whirled on her. "'Cuz the old man didn't know better!" Spittle flew from his mouth. "I was his kin. His blood. I was supposed to be the next Elias, not your coward of a pa. You think any of this would be happening if he'd given it to me?"

Hettie didn't reply.

Butch's nostrils flared as he regained composure, and he stalked on. "C'mon. We don't have much time."

"Why? What's happening?"

"It's a full moon tonight. You know that means stronger powers for thems that use blood magic, right? He'll probably try it tonight."

"Try what? Why are you helping me?"

"I ain't helping no one," he snapped. "I just ain't fixin' to see the end of the world."

"*What?*"

"You stupid or something? Don't you know what happens when Diablo's wielder is killed?"

Her skin erupted in goose bumps. "He's trying to open the gate to hell?"

"Not just that. Your little bloodsucking witch sister is going to help him *keep* it open. With the gate left wide, all manner of demons and power will flood through. He wants to scorch the earth."

"But...why?"

"Who knows?" he growled. "He's mad as a march hare. And the rest of my boys...well, I'd blame the juice, but that Zavi's a silver-tongue Beelzebub. He's got them zealous about a new order or some almighty bullshit. He makes fire-and-brimstone preachers sound like choirboys. It's an influence spell, if you ask me."

"And you're not affected?"

He snorted and set his jaw. "One thing I do owe my pa—he made sure I was charmed against them hexes that fix a man's mind to doing what he don't want to." He pointed at the scar. "This ain't just for show, y'know."

He stopped at a bend, then dragged her down a side tunnel. He shoved her into a small room, barely larger than a storage closet, and threw himself in after her, quietly pulling the door closed.

A low snuffling sound brushed past the door. She could just make out the giant paws of the Weres padding past, their nails clicking against the stone. Hettie held her breath. Could they smell the stink of fear on her? She thought back to the night on the ranch and glanced at Butch. She waited until the Weres had passed, then, just as the outlaw cracked the door open, she grabbed his gun and pointed it at his chest.

"Why should I believe anything you're telling me?" she asked coldly.

He gave her a bland look and waited. The tingle on her palms quickly built to a searing pain, but she refused to let go. She had him—she would finally get her vengeance.

"You're a stubborn one," he said, "or a stupid one, maybe. You think I don't know you can't hold another weapon?"

She kept her grip firm, though her hands felt as though they were on fire. "Bet I can hold it long enough to pull the trigger."

"Then you better get it over with. And you better not miss. Hope you've thought about how you're going to get out of here without my help."

The pain became too much, and she cursed and dropped the gun, squeezing her palms between her thighs. Butch scooped up his gun, then yanked her head back by her hair. "Listen good, you little tomboy. My hide's at stake, just like yours."

She glared at him through tear-filled eyes. "If you knew Zavi was going to end the world, why'd you join up with him in the first place?"

"You think I wanted to?" He let her go abruptly and pointed. "Something you need to understand is that Zavi found *me*. He was looking for Elias Blackthorn—the true Elias Blackthorn who wielded the Devil's Revolver. I was the closest he could find, on account of my daddy. I told him about your pa, how he'd stolen Diablo and run off. He said he could help find Diablo for me, and I believed him. He looked everywhere, but Zavi could never find it or Jack."

His lips curled in self-disgust. "I'll admit I was blinded by his power. Never clued in to his two-faced shenanigans. All I wanted was what belonged to me. So we helped him, brought him children so he could amplify his powers in his search. We did this for months. Wasn't till later that I realized he'd been collecting young 'uns a lot longer than that.

"When he brought in 'new recruits,' I should've known he was fixin' for a coup. Zavi's men got all my boys hooked on the juice. That blasted warlock's magic poisoned them, sure as dope poisons a fiend. They won't live without their Were powers anymore, and soon they were following his orders. I stayed clean, mostly. But the others…" He trailed off, lips pursed in a tight line.

Hedley had been telling the truth. Butch had lost control of his gang. "So you came after Diablo yourself and took my sister as collateral?"

He gave a harsh laugh, quiet in the tiny room. "Other way around. Zavi sent us to collect your sister. It was pure coincidence she was Jack's kin. Fate, you might say. The day I found out Jack was alive—the day he shot Shadow Frank—I knew I had an opportunity to reclaim what was mine, and I didn't need Zavi to do it. So we traced your pa back to your ranch. You know the rest."

Zavi sent us to collect your sister. The warlock's interest had been in Abby all along. Hettie felt a sick twist in her gut. She'd dismissed her sister's ramblings about the "friends" she spoke with, hadn't once thought there might be something behind them.

"So the deal's this." Butch got in close. His breath reeked. "I get you to your sister, I take you to the shaft, you give up Diablo to me, and we never see each other again."

"And then what? You shoot me in the back? Finish the job?"

"I don't give a damn what you do once you're out of my sight. I wouldn't even have bothered with you and yours if your pa had just given me Diablo like I asked. If you wanna blame someone for all this, you blame *him*."

The sting of his words was as effective as ice water. She knew he was right in the darkest corner of her mind. This was her father's fault. And yet she felt no grief—just a cold, numbing anger.

Butch glanced through the crack in the door and checked his gun. "You wanna live? You want your sister back? Then do as I say. I'm just as happy killing you where you stand. Either way, I'm gonna get back what's mine. Now are you in, or do I shoot you and leave you to die in a broom closet?"

CHAPTER TWENTY-FIVE

The scarred outlaw led her through the maze of corridors, ducking out of sight of several Weres patrolling the warren. Hettie had only heard about shape-shifting in school, had heard rumors of men who enjoyed taking animal forms for carnal pleasures, but since it was forbidden, she knew of no sorcerers who practiced it. It was said a powerful sorcerer could temporarily change a man, but this seemed to be a permanent ability. Men in several states of transformation inhabited the hideout. Some were regular men walking upright and armed, though they remained barefoot. Some preferred the lurching half-transformed versions of themselves, though what advantage their stooped, hairy bodies afforded them, she couldn't guess at. Others walked on all fours, fully in wolf form. She glanced at Butch, who was one of only a handful of men who remained fully human and fully clothed.

The closer they got to the main Zoom chamber, the more patrols they saw. They managed to slip past the guards, but when they arrived at Abby's room, she wasn't there. Butch swore. "They must be preparing her for the ceremony." He checked his pocket watch. The starburst scar bunched as his eyes narrowed. "It wasn't supposed to happen until midnight."

He glanced at her, then grabbed her wrists and began to tie them together with the rope from his belt. Hettie struggled. "What are you doing?"

"Soon as they realize you're missing, they're gonna know something's wrong. They spot me with you and the jig is up." He bound the rope tight and pushed her ahead of him. "Keep moving."

Hettie wondered if this had all been a ruse to get her to trust Butch. She couldn't see any reason for such an elaborate game, though.

They made their way to the old Zoom tunnel platform. A great bonfire had been built near the dais, illuminating the chamber. The more humanlike Weres were repainting the archaic symbols on the wall with fresh, dripping blood. Hettie had the sick feeling she knew where the blood had come from, too. Other Weres were simply carrying loads of boxes and barrels out to clear the room. They barked and growled at each other in thick, almost unrecognizable guttural English, their wolf lips slurring relayed orders.

Butch pointed to a doorway on the far wall. "That tunnel there dead-ends in a room, but there's a small opening you should be able to squeeze through that climbs right up to the surface. The shaft will lead you out on the north side of the hill. If you walk northwest for five miles, you'll hit a small town. Understand?"

"Wait, what about Abby?"

"It's too late for her. She'll be with Zavi. There's no chance of getting her away now."

"I'm not leaving—"

"What're you doing, Butch?"

Hettie spun to find three men standing behind them. Butch grabbed Hettie by her collar and flung her out into the open. "Bringing the little chit to Zavi."

Hettie recognized the man between the two hirsute hulks. The blond sorcerer was Shadow Frank's brother, Bill. He looked bigger and older somehow, not quite as pale and sickly as he had that night on the ranch. His muscles bunched as if ready to leap, and his nostrils flared wide. She saw he wasn't wearing any shoes; he must be in some in-between state of Weredom. He assessed the two of them with steady eyes. "She ain't been prepared yet."

"What's to prepare? I'm just doing what Zavi says." He spat at Bill's feet. The young man didn't move, but his eyes flickered, and his gaze cooled ten degrees further.

"Well then, what're you waiting for?"

Butch gave him a dirty look before pushing Hettie ahead of him. "Stinking no-good Judas," Butch grumbled as they descended the steps. "That son of a two-bit whore was barely a parlor magician when he signed on with our crew. He gets a little taste of power and now he thinks he runs the place."

On the Zoom platform level, some of the more fully transformed Weres stopped to stare, eyes blazing, ears flattened back. Butch shoved her toward the dais.

"You've got one shot at this," Butch said as he pushed her into a chair. He tied a rope around her and bent over her ear. "When I give the signal, all you have to do is tell Diablo it belongs to me, and you'll be free of it."

She closed her eyes and reached out again for the Devil's Revolver. The tenuous filaments that kept them connected stretched, but still it would not come to her. How Butch intended to get his hands on it even if she did relinquish her hold, she had no idea, but she couldn't contemplate that now.

The warlock Zavi appeared on the stairway above. Behind him, Abby floated down serenely, wearing a long white dress. She looked like something between a baby about to be baptized and a ghostly child bride. Her face held that faraway look Hettie knew too well. Gone was the belligerent, willful girl from before. Gone was the innocent smiling child. This creature with the tar-black eyes was something else.

No. She refused to believe Abby was gone. Her sister was in there somewhere. Hettie wouldn't leave her behind.

"How industrious of you, Mr. Crowe," Zavi remarked, black gaze touching Hettie. "I was just about to send the men up to retrieve Miss Alabama."

"Just doing my part for the cause." He stepped back, with only the slightest hint of irony affecting his obsequious bow.

Zavi's red lips parted on his smile. "And for that, you will be greatly rewarded. As will all of those loyal to me."

"Thank you, sir." He backed off, cutting Hettie a sharp look before walking away.

The Kukulos warlock approached her and crooked one finger beneath her chin. His white teeth stood out brilliantly against his dark pink gums. "You've been trying to take Diablo back."

She kept her face a mask, but wondered if it would do anything. If he could feel her fighting for possession of the Devil's Revolver, what else could he sense?

He gestured toward Abby. "What do you think? Doesn't she look beautiful?"

Hettie studied her sister's vacant look. "What have you done to her?"

"Why do you keep insisting *I'm* the one who's done anything to her? This is simply the state she chooses to be in when she's performing magic. I envy her." He sighed wistfully. "Being able to shut out the world completely, even ignoring her body's basic needs. She is singular in her purpose."

"And what would that be?"

"She has a great task ahead. Perhaps the greatest she will ever know." He beckoned to someone behind her. "Bill, will you please?"

The blond sorcerer grabbed Hettie's hair and yanked her head back, wrenching a surprised cry from her. He muttered a short incantation as he lifted a dagger and lay the cold blade upon her forehead. A flick of his wrist, and the blade bit into her flesh. Hettie screamed. She'd heard about scalping, and she struggled—

Blood poured from the wound and soaked into her temples. Some of it ran in her eyes, and she squeezed them shut.

Suddenly, the blond sorcerer let go and brought the knife to Zavi. Hettie lifted her chin, dazed and confused. The warlock held the blade to Abby's lips, and she ran her tongue along the edge and grinned as if she'd just popped a taffy drop into her mouth. Hettie's stomach turned.

Butch caught her eye with the jerky movement of one hand. He angled his body toward her one means of escape, then tilted his chin up. Above the dais was a hook the size of a horse attached to a heavy chain and strung up by a series of pulleys and wheels on a rail system high above. The apparatus had probably once been used to haul heavy cargo up to the tunnel level from the Zoom aperture.

Butch leaned casually against a pillar sporting the release lever and yawned.

Hettie focused on counting the number of steps between Abby and the way out. She could do it. She had to. She couldn't leave Abby behind. Butch scowled and gave an imperceptible shake of his head.

"Abigail, darling, are you ready?" Zavi asked. Her sister nodded dreamily.

The sorcerer drew Diablo and aimed it at Hettie's heart. He looked almost apologetic. "Rest in peace," he said.

"Butch, Diablo's yours!" Hettie shouted, and rolled the chair to the side just as the giant iron hook swung down, smashing into Zavi and flinging him off the dais as if he were a rag doll. His body arched across the room and landed in a crumpled heap in a corner. Hettie slipped the rope off the chair and dove away, rolling to a crouch. Bill shouted as the Weres rushed toward their fallen leader. Abby remained standing in place, unfazed as the hook swung back, crashing into several more bodies.

Bill whipped toward her, his face contorted with rage. He held out a hand and began chanting. Hettie tackled him, smashing into his middle and rolling on top of his back. In a flash, she had the rope looped around his neck. She pulled upward, planting her knees against his shoulder blades. If he completed his incantation and cast his spell, she'd be a goner. His spine bowed upward, and he jerked and twisted beneath her, clawing at the rope.

She focused on her hands, which burned from gripping the rough hemp. Her entire body sang with its aches. Finally, he gave a shudder and stopped moving.

She let go with a gasp and lurched to her feet, shaking. The Weres were regrouping as they got control of the wildly swinging hook. She ran toward Abby, who was slowly standing from a crouch, and halted.

Abby cradled Diablo in her hands. Thin trails of smoke drifted up from her sister's burning palms, but Abby didn't seem to notice. The blank look in her face was gone, replaced by one of smoldering anger. She wrapped her fingers around the grip and pointed the muzzle at Hettie.

"Abby…put that thing down. It's hurting you."

"Zavi says you're a bad person." Her tiny voice had a ragged edge to it. "You hurt him. You hurt my friend."

"Abby—"

In her peripheral vision, Butch raised his sidearm.

"No!"

It happened too quickly. His gun cracked. Abby spun and pulled the trigger simultaneously. The explosion of green fire plowed through Butch, and he lit up like a greasy green-flamed candle. His screams cut off abruptly as his flesh melted away.

Diablo tumbled to the ground with a thud.

"Abby, are you—"

The words evaporated on her breath. Abby's hands, held out as if in supplication, were charred and oozing, as if they were pieces of fatty pork stuck into a blacksmith's oven. Blood blossomed against Abby's snow-white breast.

She crumpled to her knees.

Hettie's mind blanked. She dove and caught her sister. Abby's lips moved, but no words accompanied the wet, hissing breaths. Hettie pawed at the gushing bullet hole. She could stanch it...stop the bleeding. She could bring her to the doctor and...

The blood soaked through her gown, cooling quickly.

Abby pawed at the air blindly. "S-shh...it's going to be okay..." Hettie's meaningless words stuttered out on a sob. She clung and clung as Abby turned her black eyes up to the dark ceiling and went still.

Hettie didn't feel her sister die. She didn't feel her heart break. She didn't feel anything.

All that was left inside was the great, empty void. One that mirrored the window of blackness opening where the charred remains of Butch Crowe once stood.

Hettie suppressed a scream. The gate to hell was open. And it was reaching for her sister.

A dark, slimy tentacle slithered out and wrapped around Abby's ankle. Hettie kicked at it, but two more grasped her sister by the wrist and waist and dragged her out of Hettie's arms.

The gates widened, and more inky black appendages snaked out, hungrily seeking prey. Two Weres yelped as the tentacles snared their legs and dragged them into the unfathomably dark maw with alarming speed. The other Crowe gang members skittered back, or turned their guns toward the hellmouth. Bullets were nothing to the void.

Hettie stomped on the tentacles wrapped around Abby, but they evaporated like smoke, yet still grasped her as a jealous child would a favorite toy. They reeled her toward the black orifice almost languidly. Hettie panicked. She looked around—Diablo lay only a few feet away. Still holding Abby's hand, she stretched out and snagged it.

She swung around and fired blindly into the void, but even the power of the Devil's Revolver was swallowed up by that pitch-black portal.

"Let go, varmint!" she shrieked at the hell gate, and impaled her finger on the thorn.

A pure green blast of power poured from the barrel, briefly illuminating the interior. Hettie thought she saw...she didn't know what. She didn't want to think what. It would drive a person mad...

A bone-deep rumble crept through the cavern. The tentacles shuddered and retreated into the mouth of the vortex. Hettie gathered Abby close, but as she reached her sister the gate exploded in ribbons of darkness that saturated the room and swallowed Hettie and Abby whole.

For a heartbeat, the void was all there was, the black nothingness a cocoon of undoing. Fear filled her like ice-cold water in a deep well. She thought of those long-ago sermons that had turned Pa away from his faith, and the descriptions of that fiery eternity she didn't want to contemplate.

And hell heard her deepest fears.

She felt it first as a flaming fist exploding from the silo, then the barn. The squeals of the pigs and chickens trying desperately to escape the blaze. The cries of her mother and father and Abby as her world went up in smoke tore at her. And then the fire reached her.

The heat of a furnace, the sun, the hottest fires of hell boiled off her clothes, her hair, her skin. Hettie screamed, though she heard nothing from her lips. Her head felt as though it would explode as her memories were torn from her, every moment of her life relived in the space of a heartbeat and shredded. Her muscles wrenched and pulled, as if her body were a piece of rope some child would practice knots on. Every piece of her was invaded, turned inside out, ripped apart and set aflame. But still she clung to Abby's hand.

Let hell do its worst. She would not let go of her sister. She would take her home.

"I came back from death for her!" she shouted, the edges of her mind fraying. Because being trapped in hell could only bring on insanity, she reasoned in that little space left for rational thought, and she laughed out loud. "You won't get her. She's mine!"

That only seemed to make her formless tormentor angrier. The searing lashes of a thousand whips flayed her raw flesh. Needles plunged through her. She thought distantly how much this felt like the unnatural side effects of killing someone with Diablo. It was almost bearable in comparison.

"Is *that* the worst you can do?" She laughed maniacally.

She could almost feel the rage of hell itself. The darkness flexed around her, squeezing her, crushing her, wringing her out, blasting her with fire, then cold. She weathered it all, clutching Abby's hand tight, even though she couldn't see her. She knew she was there. Abby was her anchor. Her reminder of who and what she was and the task still ahead of her.

Save Abby. That was all she'd set out to do the moment she'd opened her eyes and realized she was as good as dead.

You gotta take care of Abby now, Hettie.

She brandished Diablo, wondering how she'd managed to keep a hold on it all this time when it was burning away layer after layer of flesh from her palm. Taking a deep breath, she pulled the trigger and fired into the dark.

The blackness recoiled sharply, and the pain stopped. Hettie gasped and stumbled to her knees. She found herself in a field of long, tall green grass. It was summertime. A warm breeze laden with the scent of ripe peaches and plums tickled her nose. She turned to see the silo shining in the sun, the pigs lazing in the mud, the chickens strutting and scratching. The vegetable patch was laden with fruit. Laundry hung on the line in the yard.

She was back on the ranch.

Hettie looked around frantically. Abby! Where was Abby? She started toward the house. She hadn't let go, not for a moment—

"Don't be afraid." A deep, familiar voice filled her with longing, with pure love.

She stopped and turned slowly.

John Alabama stood with his hands in his pockets, his thick black mustache twitching with amusement, eyes sparkling. He tipped up his black hat and opened his arms. "Hey, Hettie."

"Pa?" The grief that had been absent at his death suddenly swamped her, and she staggered under its weight. "Pa!" She ran into her father's arms and held him tight, smelling the leather, horses, and tobacco on his skin. Tears poured from her eyes as she sobbed against his deep, warm chest. Memories of all the good times flooded her, filled every crevice in her heart with joy. She sank to the grass, and Pa went with her, cradling her in his arms as if she were a baby again. Tears of joy and sorrow soaked her collar as she blubbered, "I missed you, Pa."

"I missed you, too." He stroked her hair and kissed her forehead.

Another set of arms curled around her, followed by the scent of cloves, fresh-baked bread, and clean linens. Hettie turned into Grace Alabama's embrace. Grief, so sweet and bitter and achingly, wonderfully terrible, had finally found her.

"My brave, strong girl." Her mother cupped her chin. "You've come such a long way."

"Why is this happening?" She looked between them. "Where am I?"

"Does it matter?" John chucked her under the chin. "You're here with us now."

"But...I was with Abby—"

"Abby doesn't matter anymore."

Everything inside Hettie froze. The sun dimmed as it took refuge behind a cloud, and her skin chilled instantly. "Where's Abby?"

Her mother's eyes went soft. "She's not yours to worry about anymore. She's gone."

"No. She's not gone."

"Hettie, it's time to let go."

"No!" She threw their arms off and struggled to her feet. Diablo appeared in her hand, and she pointed it at her parents. "Where's my sister? Give her back."

John and Grace watched her placidly, their warmth and humanity gone. "It was her time. You can't undo what's happened."

"Yes, I can. Someone gave up a piece of me so that I could live." She raised her chin. "What would it cost to bring her back?"

The man who looked like her father assessed her. "You would bargain for her?"

"She's my sister. My blood. I'm not letting her go. Not to you, and not like this."

"The price will be high," the mother-woman said.

"Then take it, whatever it is. Let Abby live. Send her back and make sure she's safe and whole, and I will give you whatever you want."

"Anything?" the father-man grinned. The sky darkened to the color of a bruise.

Hettie raised her chin. After all her sins, all the lives she'd taken and the lies she'd told, she knew she was probably going to end up here anyhow after a long trip on a short rope. She might as well pay for the penny tour. "Save Abby. Take me instead."

Father-man and mother-woman smiled.

CHAPTER TWENTY-SIX

Hettie opened her eyes and found herself on the cold, hard floor of the underground cavern. She sat up dizzily, just in time to see the black hell gate close like a pair of doors shutting on night.

Diablo rested in one whole, unmolested hand. Abby's tiny palm was clutched in the other.

Her sister's eyes fluttered open. The irises were violet once more. "Hettie?" she croaked.

"Abby." Hettie's heart filled with relief, with joy, and almost immediately with doubt. She'd made a bargain, but she was still alive—why hadn't they collected their debt?

Her sister pushed up to her knees and crawled to Hettie's side, hugging her tight. "I'm sorry..."

The rallying bay of the Weres had her bolting upright. "We have to get out of here." She pulled Abby to her feet and half carried her to the stairs. She couldn't trust Butch's exit, if it even existed.

Three Weres in full wolf form lunged for them. She whipped Abby ahead of her and fired blindly over her shoulder, hoping to scare the creatures—she couldn't afford to be incapacitated. The green glow from the demonic mage gun splashed against the wall, churning it into white-hot liquid rock that slid down into the Weres' big canine paws. They yelped and danced back, their fur alight, but it was too late—panicked, they thrashed and collapsed as their legs were eaten up by the molten rock. Their blood-curdling howls pierced her ears.

She barely had time to give the revolver's new power a thought. "Hang on!" She slung Abby onto her back, then ran full tilt up the stairs, legs pumping, firing behind her and melting the steps to keep anyone from following. Above, a man emerged from the tunnel, gun raised. Hettie swung her arm around lightning quick, and Diablo's cannon blast punched through a column of rock. The wall tumbled down over his head. He fell wordlessly into the molten chaos below as Hettie ducked into the tunnel.

Abby climbed off her back, and they ran hand in hand through the corridors, scanning each intersection for pursuers. "Do you know the way out?" she asked Abby.

"Mr. Butch brought me here on a little train car. It's that way." She pointed down a tunnel.

Hettie's conscience pricked her as she remembered the hundreds of children in the warlock's thrall. "Abby, this is important. Can you get away from here on your own?"

"I'm not leaving you behind. Zavi's going to be mad, and…" Her eyes clouded.

Hettie gave her a shake, panic swamping her. "Stay with me, Abby. We have to get out of here."

She shook her head slowly. "He's mad…"

Hettie hauled her sister forward. She hated the thought of abandoning those other children, but she didn't have a choice. She had to get to the surface and get away from Zavi. She headed in the direction her sister had pointed, her own shaky memories of the place becoming clearer with each turn. She used Diablo's rock-melting firepower to close off each passage. She wasn't even sure she knew how she was doing it.

Soon she found the tracks and the cars that would presumably take them to the surface.

She put Abby in one of the four-person passenger cars. With no idea how to work the great Mechanikal motors that ran the contraption, she threw several levers and spun up the knobs and wheels randomly until the machine revved its engine and she heard a series of distant clanks and a bell.

Abby's car shot off. Hettie cried out and started to chase her up the track, but the vehicle traveled faster than she could run.

She hopped into the next car, kicking the brake release. The car jerked and flew up the rail through the gently curving tunnel. She could hear Abby's car clattering and chugging its way ahead, and caught glimpses at each wide turn. Farther along, the lanterns in the tunnel were spaced quite far apart so that her vision strobed between light and dark, the only things to be seen the pillars and lintels, the rock walls and the track. But from what she could see, the path was getting wider.

Behind her, she heard voices and low growls. Zavi must have mustered his forces, and they were gaining. She could hear their snarls and shouts growing louder. She knew she didn't have a choice—they wouldn't get far out in the desert. Zavi would eventually find her and Abby again and drag her back to this place. Hettie had to end this now.

At a turn where the ground was mostly even, she pulled the brake so the cart juddered to a halt and hopped out, then used Diablo to melt the tracks behind her. She hardly felt the bite of the thorn as she held the trigger down, unleashing a torrent of green firepower. It was too risky to try closing the tunnel off here—there was no telling if it would start a cave-in on top of Abby. So she yanked a lantern from the wall and tossed it into the car, setting the spilled oil ablaze. That should buy Abby enough time to get to the surface.

She ran. The tracks sloped gently upward, and she could hear a whirr that matched the Mechanikal engine at the other end. She couldn't be too far from the surface now.

A great crash behind her and she knew their pursuers had arrived. She told herself not to panic as she kept climbing. Her lungs burned, and her legs felt like soft noodles. But as long as Abby was in danger, she couldn't stop.

Ahead, she saw a light, but it wasn't the exit to the surface. For a moment, she thought Abby had left her car and come back down the tunnel, but it wasn't her sister. Crying Sparrow, the little girl who'd guided her to the in-between, beckoned to her, pointing at a small side tunnel. Hettie hesitated only briefly, then slipped through the narrow fissure and felt her way through the dark until she entered a large space lit by a shaft of glorious gold sunlight that nearly blinded her.

Relief rushed into her as she estimated the height of the ceiling. Thirty feet, at most. Abby must be outside by now, waiting for her. All she had to do was climb out of this hole...

"And so we come to the site of your grave." The liquid voice was slightly choked, the words tripping from a tongue that sounded as if it had been bitten in half. Hettie spun, raising Diablo, but froze at the gruesome figure who met her.

Zavi lurched into the room, stepping in a stiff hobble, as if his joints could swing in any direction. His jaw moved in strange circular motions as he spoke, the clicking of his bones and teeth amplified by a cavernous red mouth that couldn't quite close. The odd angle of his neck and the distended jut of his shoulder blades reminded her of a pile of fallen timbers. His once-pristine clothes were torn, burned, and bloody, and his flaxen hair and porcelain complexion were matted and stained with blood. His black eyes gleamed like pools of oil. Any trace of ethereal serenity was gone.

"You've led a merry chase, Miss Alabama." He sounded like he was speaking through a metal grate, his voice strangely gravelly.

She backed farther into the room, groping behind her. Cold sweat soaked her neck.

Zavi's mouth stretched wide. She heard his jaw crack as it straightened out. He jammed the heel of his palm against the side of his head and popped his neck straight, then slammed a dislocated shoulder against a boulder with a sickening *thwap!* It didn't take him long to rearrange his bones until he stood tall and straight again.

Hettie stuffed down her scream. What on earth was he? "You'll pardon the acrobatics," he said. "I don't like to kill someone when I'm not at my best. Now where's Abby?"

"She opened a Zoom tunnel. She's gone."

He smirked. "You'd never let her go off on her own. Abigail, dear, if you're here, come out. I won't hurt you. I'm not mad. I'll even spare your sister."

A beat, and he sighed. "I suppose you might have been telling the truth. That makes this easier." He opened his glowing palms. Hettie leaped behind a boulder as lightning burst from his hands. Dust and gravel rained down on her, and she crawled on her stomach to cover.

"I hated the thought of killing you in front of Abby. She's so sensitive. She had such terrible nightmares when she first arrived. That was Butch's fault." Zavi fired off another sizzling bolt that shattered a stalagmite. Dust filled the air, wafting around in swirling eddies. "But she's strong. She'll get used to death. She just doesn't understand yet what a privilege it is. That's what I'm offering you now, you know. Though I'm sorry to say I can't promise you a quick death. You've caused me too much trouble, and I've acquired a taste for vengeance."

She got up and fired twice in his direction, then ducked back down as lightning enveloped her hiding spot. Her skin buzzed, and the hairs on her body stood on end. She smelled something burning—the hem of her dress was on fire! She beat it out with her hands and dove from the lightning-engulfed pocket of rocks as it exploded in a cloud of dust.

"Don't worry," Zavi called. "Once you're gone, I won't punish Abby for disobeying me. She's too precious to me. Besides, she was led astray by *your* bad influence. You're the snake in my Garden of Eden, and you corrupted my little Eve." He tilted his head. "She'll mourn you for a time, but she'll get over it. I plan on displaying your bones in her room. That way, you'll never have to leave her." He threw another bolt of lightning at the far wall. Sharp stone chips and sparks sprayed her back. "I really am getting tired of this. Come out and die like a good little girl."

She couldn't keep dodging and hiding. Eventually he'd blast every last rock to smithereens.

She caught a gleam in the corner. The spirit of Crying Sparrow stood just outside of a shaft of light shining down from a crumbling hole in the ceiling where lightning had struck. The girl notched her chin up. Hettie understood.

She grabbed a rock and lobbed it at Zavi's head. He roared when it struck him right between the eyes, and she almost laughed as she ran for the next bit of cover. Finding her target, she stood, Diablo poised, praying Abby was smart enough to get away if this didn't work.

Zavi's hands glowed bright white, lighting up his hell-dark eyes. "It ends now."

"Yup." She pointed Diablo up and squeezed the trigger.

Green fire splashed against the ceiling, and Hettie let the amber moment envelop her. She strained through the syrup and dragged Diablo's flame up behind her. Zavi caught on a fraction of a second too late. He lunged toward her a beat behind, his movements only half as fast as hers. His lightning didn't make it, though. It stayed tethered to his hands as the power arced toward the spot she'd just vacated. The blue-white jags tangled as he turned, dancing up his arms and wrapping around his torso. Hettie leaped for the crevice just as the molten slag spilled down on Zavi and brought with it tons of rock, burying the screaming warlock. Normal time resumed, and she scrambled into the shelter of the opening as the cave tumbled down around her.

Memories of her life, of her family and the ranch, swirled through her. She clasped her hands around Diablo, knowing she'd soon be headed back to that dark place, and made the only request she could of her maker. *Please take care of Abby.*

Sunlight knifed into the chamber as the ceiling crumbled. Hettie closed her eyes and said her final prayers as clouds of dust filled the air. But the crush of darkness never came.

Suddenly, the world stopped falling apart, and the whole bowl of the cavern was open to a cloudless, brilliantly blue morning sky.

CHAPTER TWENTY-SEVEN

Hettie wiped the grit from her watering eyes as she stared up, dazed.

"Hettie!" Abby's voice was a sweet, clear warble, followed by a second rough shout.

"Hettie!"

She stared up in amazement. "Walker?" The bounty hunter stood next to her sister, a broad, dark shadow with a rope coiled over his shoulders, a shotgun in one hand. The other hand clamped over Abby's shoulder to keep her away from the gaping hole.

"You all right?" he called down.

She looked back to the pile of rocks. Zavi was under there somewhere. "I'm fine."

"Hold tight." The bounty hunter disappeared with Abby, and a moment later the rope dropped over the edge. Walker swung down, rappelling with ease. His big boots landed on the shifting rock pile. He drew his sidearm and scanned the area.

"We should get out of here," Hettie urged, dropping Diablo into her pocket. "There are hundreds of Weres below—the whole Crowe gang. Butch is dead, and I found the missing children, and—"

"It's all right, Hettie." The look on his face didn't say everything would be fine, though. He gestured above. "Let's move before the rest of this hole crumbles away."

"How did you find me? Where are Uncle and Ling and—"

"It's a long story." His face was hard as he looped the rope around the two of them. "Climb onto my back and hold tight." He braced himself, muttered a short spell, then planted his boot against the wall and climbed up fast, scaling the rock with the ease of a spider.

He swung them both over the grassy lip of the hole and dismissed the spell with a word, exhaling hard and shaking out his hands. Hettie clambered off him and sat up. Her eyes widened.

Not a hundred feet away, a posse—no, an *army*—was gathered around the cave entrance. Mounted and armed, the uniformed men numbered in the hundreds and were in the process of gunning down the Weres trying to escape through various shafts and exits all around what she recognized as the compound from her vision— Sonora Station. The wolf-men bounded from the holes like scared jackrabbits and were put down easily and bloodily by men with Gatling guns spitting out wavering ribbons of bullets. Others hounded the strays from horseback, shooting them as they ran, or in a few cases, cutting them down with sabers. There would be no trials for the Weres—they were abominations, after all, and went against the laws of natural magic. As they crumpled to the ground, the magic left their bodies, and the wolf forms sloughed off. Fur filled the air, taken away by the hot, dry wind. Blood watered the red earth.

"Hettie." Abby threw her arms around Hettie's waist, sobbing.

"Abby." She slid to her knees, hugging her sister tight. She cupped her face in her hands, smearing blood on her cheeks, and looked into her violet eyes. "Are you all right?" She nodded, and Hettie thought her sister seemed more...present. Older. She smiled through burning eyes. "You were so brave."

"Because Paul was there. He told me you would come for me. He told me you wouldn't leave me alone."

She would have to thank Paul whenever she saw him next.

Cymon barreled into her, whining and wagging his whole body as he bathed her face with his slobbery tongue. Abby squealed and wrapped her arms around the mutt's thick neck. He barked and wrestled her to the ground, half sitting, half lying on top of her like a mother hen on a wayward chick. Abby giggled and let him lick the dirt and blood from her face.

"C'mon," Walker said, "we have to go."

"Go? But—" She gestured at the army.

"Hettie, *now*."

"Where's Uncle? Is he all right? And what about Sophie and Jemma and Marcus?"

Walker's eyes kept darting around. "Please, Hettie, just listen to me. We have to get away from here. These men will come after you next."

It took a second too long to register what he was saying. She heard the distinct sound of a Winchester lever, followed by the action of several other rifles. She turned slowly.

Grim-faced, Ling pointed a pistol at Walker's head. A man with straw-colored hair and a big mustache stood next to him. "Hettie Alabama," he declared, cocking his sidearm, "you are under arrest for the murders of Marshal Phineas Shaw, the criminal Isaac Hedley, and three Pinkerton agents, obstruction of justice, theft, kidnapping…" He wiped his brow. "Well, I can read you the list of charges when we get out of this sun, but it'd be a good idea to come with us, miss."

Cymon's hackles went up, and he growled, snarling as the men surrounded them. Diablo leaped into Hettie's hand. She whipped her arm out automatically.

"Captain, this isn't fair. Hettie wasn't in control—" Walker stepped in front of her, and Ling intercepted him.

"Step away, Woodroffe," the healer said quietly. "You don't need to be involved in this. Just take the dog and get out of the way."

"You son of a bitch." Walker glowered and took a step toward him. "You know none of this is her fault. She had no choice."

Ling's face was a mask of calm, but conflict flickered in his dark eyes. Abby gave a frightened wail. She clung to Hettie's side, directly in the line of fire. Cymon snarled, foam gathering around his mouth. His low barks grew louder and more insistent, as if to defend Hettie.

"Should we shoot the dog, captain?"

"He's just a dumb animal, private. You wanna shoot some dogs, go after them Weres."

Cymon continued barking.

"For lands' sake, shyaddap!" The captain fired his pistol in the air with a loud crack. Abby screamed and grabbed Cymon around the neck. He whimpered, chastened.

"Stop, everyone!" Hettie raised her hands. Diablo stuck fast to her palm. "I'm not going to hurt anyone. I'm going to put the gun on the ground." She did just that, and the men closed around her.

"No one touch that infernal thing," the mustachioed captain ordered. "Put a stasis ward on it. I want it guarded at all times until the Division retrieval team arrives."

The men rushed her. Heavy iron manacles were clamped onto Hettie's wrists. Abby cried out. She struggled against the soldiers who dragged her away, and she began to wail.

"Don't hurt her!" Hettie shouted, but saw that her alarm only made her sister more agitated. She said quickly, "Abby—it's going to be okay. Everything's going to be fine. Just go with these men for now. They'll take care of you."

Abby quieted some, though she was still bawling. Ling and the mustachioed leader approached Hettie and her two guards. The older man watched as Abby was led away. "I can't believe a little girl gave you such trouble, Agent Tsang," he muttered.

"*Agent* Tsang?"

He glanced at her, but before he could open his mouth the men gave a surprised cry. Hettie only just caught them flying ten feet away from Abby as she continued to scream.

"Dammit, someone put a collar on that girl!" The captain drew a smaller sidearm from a holster at his back.

"What are you doing?"

"It's just a sedative," Ling said firmly. "It's to calm her down."

She turned a hateful glare on him. "What are you talking about? *Who are you?*"

Abby ran toward Hettie, and Cymon kept the men who tried to stop her at bay.

"Don't let them take me, Hettie! They want to hurt me!"

The captain took aim. Abby flinched as a small dart appeared in her throat. Her eyes rolled up, and she plowed face-first into the dust.

"She'll be fine when she wakes, besides a bit of a headache." The man holstered his dart weapon. "Get that collar and some bracelets

298

on her. We don't need her punching folks clear across the county."
He nodded at Ling. "Guess you were right about her."

Two men carried the unconscious Abby to a tent flanked by two
more men. The soldiers swatted at Cymon, who lunged for their
heels. When one made to draw his weapon, Walker swooped in and
grabbed his wrist, pinning him with a narrow look. He bent to
one knee and murmured something to Cymon, who immediately
settled down.

"I don't recall any mention in the reports that her powers had
manifested." The captain addressed Ling, rubbing his bristly jaw.

"This is new," Ling replied grimly.

"What is going on here?" Hettie demanded. "Who are you?"

"We're the folks who saved your hide, far as I can tell." He hitched
his chin toward the Were massacre. The gunfire was trailing off.
"But if you're going to be formal about thanking me, I'm Captain
William Bradley with the Division of Sorcery Enforcement."

She ignored him and directed her attention on Ling. "Where's
Uncle Jeremiah? And Sophie and the others?"

"They're all fine. We left Sophie and her people in Yuma. Your
uncle was shot on the train, but I got the bullet out and healed
him before there was too much damage. He's resting." Ling looked
toward a series of tents. "Mr. Bassett used up a lot of power tracking
you down."

"Wily old bastard." Captain Bradley lit a cigarette. "Say what you
will about his methods, but he did find you." He smirked. "You
wanna see him?"

Captain Bradley led the way to what was apparently a command
tent. As Ling entered, the officers saluted him smartly before
turning back to their maps and plans.

She stared. Officers did not salute civilians, and certainly not
Celestials. Not unless...

"Try not to disturb him." He pointed.

Her eyes went directly to the far corner, where Jeremiah Bassett
lay on a narrow cot. The air stopped in her lungs. He looked pale
and waxy, his cheeks sunken, with dark circles under his eyes. A
man with a medic's badge stooped over him, checking his pulse.

"Is he going to be all right?" she asked breathlessly.

"He hasn't slept for three days. He's been burning his reserves and boosting his powers with some godforsaken Eastern potions." The medic cut a suspicious look at Ling. "Could be poison for all I know."

Hettie turned slowly, gathering her fractured thoughts and focusing on the impassive Ling. "Okay. Tell me what's going on, *Agent* Tsang."

"I'm a Paladin-class healer with the Division of Sorcery," he said without preamble. "The government recruited me when I arrived in California almost twelve years ago."

Paladin-class. Even Hettie knew that meant he had about the same rank as a mundane nongifted military captain. "Recruited? For what?"

He rubbed the back of his head. "That's a very long story."

"Well, then, get to the part where you're a government agent. You've been lying to me all this time. Why were you on our farm?" She was getting angrier by the second. Was anyone in her life what they seemed? Next they'd be telling her Cymon was a prince in disguise.

Ling clasped his hands in front of him and took a breath. "The Division of Sorcery has been keeping tabs on Abby since the moment she was born. You see, your sister is what's known as an indigo child. These are special individuals who can use a wide range of powers without incantations, spells, or talismans. That in itself isn't unusual—you've seen me use ether magic. But in Abby's case, we believe she has been gifted with extraordinary powers that aren't linked to magic as we know it. A few of these indigo children have been found over the years, but many of them don't live past their early teens." He rubbed his chin. "I was assigned to watch her and report any manifestations of her abilities."

She blinked rapidly. If they'd known…If they'd warned them before the Crowe gang had come, they could have stopped all this from happening. They could have protected her from Zavi. Hettie straightened. "So if she did…*manifest* her gift, then what?"

He gazed at her impassively. "For her protection—and yours— we would have taken her to a facility where she could develop her skills and learn to control her powers."

"A facility." She gasped. "You mean the Academy."

"No. Not the Academy." Ling's gaze was hard. "She is unique, her powers unstable and unfathomable. They won't jeopardize the other potentials. They'll take her somewhere they can...study her." His lips firmed, and he looked away.

Hettie's skin prickled all over. Sending Abby off to the Academy would've been bad enough—she'd heard the stories about how the students were treated. But a new kind of hell awaited Abby. Even Ling didn't seem keen on sending her there.

Was that why it'd taken so long for him to recognize her gift? Had Ling known about the way Abby talked with her "friends"? Had he reported that or dismissed it as childish rambling? One thing was certain—he didn't know she'd opened the remote Zoom tunnel by herself. He didn't know about anything that had happened with Zavi, and she wasn't about to tell him.

He shuffled his feet. "I'm sorry to have deceived you for so long, but I had to keep my mission a secret. I grew lax in my duties and thought only of myself when I left town. It was the act of a coward." He lowered his chin. "I never anticipated that any of this would happen."

Hettie twisted her skirt in a knot, digging her nails into her thighs. This man whom she'd trusted most among her companions—a man her father had vouched for—had turned out to be a liar too. She wanted to lash out at him, but she was too weary, too filled with grief and anger and exhaustion. And she couldn't blame him for anything. He hadn't known about Pa or Diablo. He couldn't have known the men who'd attacked him in town were Butch Crowe's men. And the government wouldn't have had any soothsayers who could tell them this would happen because of the blackout.

None of these facts soothed the sting of betrayal though. "So, *Agent Tsang*, how'd you get all *this*?" She waved around, indicating the military might surrounding them.

"That was mainly your uncle's doing. And Miss Favreau's. I only revealed myself when things got desperate. I suppose I shouldn't have been surprised that Jeremiah Bassett already knew what I was."

Yet another secret the old man had kept from her. She ought to smother him in his sleep.

"Shoulda said something right off the bat, Tsang." Captain Bradley blew out a cloud of blue smoke. "If you'd reported in like

301

you were supposed to, we coulda had her bundled up safe weeks ago and saved you lot the trouble." He said it as if they would have known exactly where to find her. As if they could have swooped in and saved the day. Considering Zavi's seemingly limitless power, she doubted his claim.

"So what happens now?" Hettie asked.

The captain shrugged. "You'll be taken to Chicago to stand trial for the murders of the Pinkerton agents. Seeing as you're only a woman, I suspect they'll spare you the noose and instead give you enough lifetime sentences to keep you in jail till you're dust. Bassett there will stand trial in Newhaven, seeing as he killed a Pink there. We ain't got anything on that Woodroffe. Nothing that'll stick, anyhow. As for that infernal revolver"—he spat on the floor—"it'll be taken somewhere safe."

"Nowhere's safe," Hettie said. "Too many people are after it. It needs to be destroyed."

"I just follow orders, miss. You'd be better off if you piped down and accepted your lot now."

"And Abby?"

Ling said, "She'll come with me back to the Division of Sorcery's headquarters. She'll be well taken care of, Miss Hettie. She'll get magical training by the greatest master sorcerers alive." He didn't exactly sound excited by the prospect—resigned, more like.

She squeezed her eyes shut. No, it couldn't end like this. Not after everything she'd been through to find her sister. "Ling, please. Abby's too young to go to the Academy, much less whatever facility you're taking her to. You know what she's like. She's not ready. Abby needs me."

Ling's eyes remained steady on her. "You're going to jail, Hettie. You're going to be punished for the crimes you've committed." His lips pressed tight. "I'm sorry."

She clenched her fists, and the manacles felt as if they were tightening around her wrists. Her whole body shook. "I haven't done anything any man wouldn't have done in my situation. And I wouldn't even be here if I hadn't rescued you...*twice*. Is *this* what your honor is worth?"

He stared at her, unflinching. She hoped her eyes bored holes through his skull. She hoped he never got another night's rest for this betrayal.

A soldier ran in, snapping the tension. "Sir, we found a room near the old station chamber full of children. Some of them are in real bad shape."

"God's beard, the old man was telling the truth." The captain stubbed out his cigarette hastily. "We're going to need stretchers and wagons and all the healers we can round up." The men at the command table rallied as Captain Bradley barked out orders. He left two guards at the tent flap and told them to keep an eye on the prisoners. Ling followed them out, regret plain on his face.

Exhausted, Hettie dropped into a chair next to Uncle's cot. So this was it. She was headed for jail.

Maybe her sister would be better off. What kind of life could she have offered after this? They had the house, but in the back of her mind hadn't she only saved it so that she and Abby could be buried there? Had she really believed this quest would end with the two of them going home? She laughed to herself, her chuckles bubbling up into near-hysterical laughter.

"Madness finally settling in?" Walker entered the tent. It was with a little suspicion and envy that she noticed he wasn't wearing manacles or bracelets, and walked around freely. He fidgeted with his belt. "I was...concerned," he began slowly. "When we saw you fall from the train and the Pinks surrounding you...And then that remote Zoom tunnel opened." He turned a tortured look on her. "We thought they were taking you back to the headquarters in Chicago."

She suddenly remembered. "Thomas Stubbs is in a cell down in the caverns. He got dragged into the Zoom with me. He'll need a healer. The Crowe gang worked him over pretty hard."

"So Butch and his boys were definitely working for Zavi?"

Hettie opened her mouth to speak but was suddenly swamped with the memory of Bill struggling beneath her. The final trembling and slackening of his muscles as she throttled him with nothing more than rough rope. She glanced down at her rope-burned hands to hide the cold elation trembling through her. "Yeah. He was lending them shape-shifting magic in exchange for their services.

Butch lost control of most of his gang. He said it was because they were hooked on juice."

Walker's features flickered. "You seem mighty calm for someone who faced down a Kukulos warlock and a gang of outlaw Weres."

She stared at him, detached as she cataloged the horrors she'd witnessed, the hell she'd literally been dragged through. She could see he wanted to hear her story. She shuddered. There would be time to tell the tale later. "I've had worse days."

He didn't push her for more.

"Tell me what happened after I fell off the train. Where are Sophie and Jemma and Marcus?"

"Sophie went on to Yuma so she could petition for more troops in case we needed them. We stopped in the next town and went to the local marshal, who sent a message by Zoom to the Division of Sorcery. At first the man wouldn't listen, thought we were crazy. Then Sophie waved her name under his nose, added a touch of glamor magic, and it changed his mind."

Her head popped up. "Sophie uses glamor?"

"You didn't know?" He smiled lopsidedly. "It's plain as the rouge on her cheeks. But I can see through the layers of frosting to the cake underneath. Mind you, she doesn't need it."

She tried to stay focused. "So you got the marshal's support…"

"He contacted the DOS. We got a telephone call, can you imagine, and *that* was when Ling pulled out his badge. Things moved fast after that. It took half a day to gather everyone by remote Zoom to a location close to where we tracked you. Bassett didn't eat or sleep. I've never seen anyone sweat blood before, but he did. At one point late last night, he cried out and had a fit. When he recovered he started laughing like a madman. It was right around when we infiltrated the compound that he plum passed out." He peeked over at the old man, grimacing. "He'd better live through this. I want to see his face when he lays eyes on you."

She glanced over at Jeremiah, emotions swelling inside her chest. She rubbed at her wet eyes and gave a short laugh. "He'll probably call me an idiot and slap me with his hat."

"I'd call you a clumsy dolt who doesn't know any better first," Uncle muttered, eyes still closed.

Hettie shot up in her chair and stood over his cot. "You been awake all this time?"

"The dead couldn't sleep with you two lovebirds cooing over me." He cracked his eyes open. The whites were bloody and yellowing. "You look terrible."

Something inside her eased, and she blinked her tears away. She knelt down and placed a hand over his and squeezed. "You don't look too good yourself, old man."

The cold metal of her manacles clinked against his. He glanced down and muttered an oath. "Shoulda known better than to trust that two-faced son of a lizard."

She had so many questions. So much she needed to hear, including an apology. But he looked thoroughly worn-out. "Did you know about Abby's potential gift? Ling says she's an indigo child, whatever that means."

"She was a little too canny sometimes to be just simple, but I didn't have a clue. Ling, on the other hand, I knew right off wasn't just some coolie looking for ranch work. But once I figured out he wasn't after Diablo, I thought an extra pair of eyes around the ranch couldn't hurt. He wasn't doing anything I couldn't have stopped him from doing."

"You keep telling yourself that. He says he's Paladin class."

"Paladin-class *healer*. Not good for much unless you need fixing up." He tried to sit up but sank back into his pillow with a moan. "Did you find out what was blocking the soothsayers' visions?"

"I can't say for sure. Zavi had a lot of things going on down there, but at least I know what he was hiding." She told him everything she'd learned about the operation, the kidnapped children who'd fed Zavi's powers, and how the warlock had wanted to open the gate to hell.

"Good thing you put a stop to all that." Uncle's lips pressed into a firm line, and he exhaled slowly. "I'm sorry I didn't believe in you. If I'd done what I wanted and hidden you and Diablo away, things would've turned out much differently."

"Not that we're in great shape now." She held up her manacled wrists with a frown.

Jeremiah squinted. He took her hands gently and inspected her palms. To her shock, they were glowing, as if covered in gold dust and bathed in sunlight. "Where's Diablo?"

"Outside. Why?"

"Summon it."

"I can't." She jangled the short chain linking her bracelets.

"Try."

Hettie concentrated. She could see the revolver on the ground exactly where she'd dropped it. The land dripped with gold in her vision as she stooped to pick it up, snapping out the wheel and spinning it to find it loaded. Always loaded. It hadn't spent a single cartridge since she'd put her bullets in it.

She opened her eyes. Uncle stared at her. The manacles lay in a pile of molten metal on the ground. And Diablo was in her hand.

"Hell's bells, what did you do?" He turned her wrist to expose the revolver's solid black grip. The ivory had taken on an ebony matte finish as if it had been charred in a fire. She didn't know when it had changed—deep down, it almost felt as though it had always been like this, its true self revealed after the ivory was scraped away.

She heard noises outside. Men rushing back and forth, shouts of "Fire!"

Cymon barked steadily.

Jeremiah pushed out of the cot and stumbled. Hettie slung his arm around her shoulders, and they made their way to the tent flap. The guards didn't notice them. They were too preoccupied by the sight of the tents going up in flames.

Heatless flames. She looked around—where had Walker gotten to?

Horses screamed and scattered. Most of the soldiers were in the cave underground helping the children out, but those who remained beat uselessly at the fire and started forming bucket lines. Where they expected to get water out in the Arizona desert, Hettie had no idea.

The four men who'd carried Abby into a tent rushed out. She thrashed wildly in their midst. Three of the men were suddenly snatched out of the air, as if by invisible birds, and tossed aside. The remaining man who carried her gave a yelp as he ran with all speed toward Hettie.

It was then that the guards realized their captives were out and about. Jeremiah extended a hand and shouted a word, and a flash of light blinded them. He groaned and doubled over. Hettie reversed her grip on Diablo, coldcocked one guard, then kicked the other in the stomach and relieved him of his rifle, smashing it over his shoulder.

Burning needles stabbed through her palms, and she dropped the weapon. As the second guard turned over onto his back, she pointed the revolver at his head.

"Hettie, what are you doing?" Uncle rasped.

Her finger hovered over the trigger. It would be easier this way. One less man to track her down. One less man to shoot at her.

The soldier's eyes widened and rolled up into his head as he slumped. He'd fainted. Slowly, she lowered the gun, disappointment and fear tumbling through her.

"Hettie!" The man carrying Abby practically flew toward them, legs pumping. The young girl hopped out of his arms as if he were simply a cart rumbling down the road, but he kept running, his lungs heaving, the whites of his eyes clear. He ran through the tent flap, crashing into the furniture, straight to the back of the tent, where he dove headfirst through the canvas and landed on his side. His legs continued kicking wildly, even as the fabric gathered around him. He groaned as the tent collapsed on top of him.

Abby had done that to him somehow. A little thrill of fear and awe zipped along Hettie's spine. If it hadn't been for the tent, the soldier might've run straight into the desert and kept on going. Hexed to run, just like a horse.

Abby threw her arms around Hettie's waist. "Don't let them take me. *Please.*"

"I won't. Ever." She clasped her sister in her arms. She would protect Abby and vowed to stay with her, no matter what it took. Her sister needed her. "We gotta get out of here." Hettie helped Uncle to his feet. They needed horses. They needed a way out. They needed—

A pair of distinct whinnies, the thunder of horse hooves, and Blackie and Jezebel streaked toward them, led by Walker riding Lilith. Smoke curled around them, as if they'd emerged from the fires of Hades.

"Let's git!" Walker shouted, reining in sharply.

Hettie boosted Abby into Blackie's saddle while Uncle pulled himself onto Jezebel. As Hettie mounted, she spotted Ling through the smoke, watching them with an expression that bordered on roguish. He gave a slight bow, then turned away.

She flicked the reins, and Blackie whirled with a snort. "Where do we go?"

"South. To the Wall." Walker flashed his wolfish grin. "We made a bargain, Hettie Alabama. And I intend to make sure you keep your end of it."

They spurred the horses into a gallop, leaving Arizona behind in a trail of dust and fire.

AUTHOR'S ACKNOWLEDGMENTS

I would like to thank and acknowledge Dr. Angela Jaime, associate professor and chair of American Indian Studies at the University of Wyoming, who helped me understand the appropriate context for the use of certain terms with respect to Native culture, and ultimately started me on the path to decolonizing my writing. Her insights were invaluable to building the magical world of *The Devil's Revolver*. All mistakes and misunderstandings are my own.

The Devil's Revolver would not be here without the steadfast support of my agent, Courtney Miller-Callihan of Handspun Literary, who believed in this story when I first brought it to her over four years ago. She persisted.

I also want to give my humblest appreciation and thanks to my editor and publishers, Mary Ann Hudson, and to Ruthie Knox of Brain Mill Press, who put their full faith into my series. I am so grateful to you for welcoming me and Hettie into your lives.

I would like to acknowledge funding support from the Ontario Arts Council, an agency of the Government of Ontario, for giving me a grant to continue working on the series.

My love and appreciation to John for all the love and support he's given to me and my writing career over the years. Thanks also to my parents, who gave me everything, my sisters, and the friends who've bought my books and rooted me on.

This story is dedicated to Mara.

ABOUT THE AUTHOR

Vicki So, writing as V. S. McGrath, is a published romance author (as Vicki Essex) and has six books with Harlequin Superromance: *Her Son's Hero* (July 2011); *Back to the Good Fortune Diner* (January 2013), which was picked for the Smart Bitches Trashy Books Sizzling Book Club; *In Her Corner* (March 2014); *A Recipe for Reunion* (March 2015); *Red Carpet Arrangement* (January 2016); and *Matinees with Miriam* (November 2016). She lives in Toronto, Canada.

CPSIA information can be obtained
at www.ICGtesting.com
Printed in the USA
LVHW082317121219
640357LV00011B/190/P